About the Author

Growing up in Northern Minnesota around lakes and exploring woods with my dog, I wanted to become a fish and game officer, vowing I'd never be confined to an office. After graduate school, I moved to New York and sat in a cubicle writing advertising copy. For twenty years, I wrote for others, including corporate speeches, early literacy materials and video memoirs for hospice patients. Finally, I was able to write what I was passionate about: mountain lions, dogs and dolphins, and protecting the environment we all live in. If we cannot save our wildlife, we cannot save ourselves.

DD Berquist

Dedication

I became motivated to write this book because, despite world opinion, international agreements, and Herculean efforts by individuals and organizations, juvenile dolphins continue to be kidnapped from their pod families and used for human entertainment.

That inspired me to imagine a better world and posit two questions in my novel: (1) What if there appeared, out of the blue, two passionate characters from opposite sides of the Pacific who alter the course of human events and upend history by reaching across the divide and persuading governments to ban the capturing of dolphins? And (2) What if we could decode dolphin language and communicate with them?

This book is dedicated to all those who have worked tirelessly, in and out of the water, to protect the world's wildlife and their habitats. I can only borrow from their work and write fictional accounts that speak to the need to respect the rights of fellow species to live free. I hope, in turn, I might inspire readers to care and become activists on their behalf.

DD Berquist

SOMEWHERE BEYOND THE SEA

Two Hearts Bound and Torn
by the Forces of Nature

AUSTIN MACAULEY PUBLISHERS®

LONDON * CAMBRIDGE * NEW YORK * SHARJAH

Ordering Information
Quantity sales: Special discounts are available on quantity purchases by corporations, associations, and others. For details, contact the publisher at the address below.

Publisher's Cataloging-in-Publication data
Berquist, DD
Somewhere Beyond the Sea

ISBN 9781649799432 (Paperback)
ISBN 9781649799449 (ePub e-book)

Library of Congress Control Number: 2024905286

www.austinmacauley.com/us

First Published 2024
Austin Macauley Publishers LLC
40 Wall Street, 33rd Floor, Suite 3302
New York, NY 10005
USA

mail-usa@austinmacauley.com
+1 (646) 5125767

Acknowledgement

Please give your support to these and many other organizations that support wildlife:

World Wildlife Fund. Sea Shepherd Conservation Society. Save the Whales. Oceanic Preservation Society. American Cetacean Society. Ocean Conservancy. Ric O' Barry's Dolphin Project, Pacific Whale Foundation. Whale and Dolphin Conservation Society. The Nature Conservancy.

Table of Contents

Introduction

As an American who often travelled to Japan with my close Japanese colleague and worked with many locals, I became fascinated with how our attitudes and approaches differ. As you will note when you read, most of the story takes place forty-plus years ago when cultural stereotyping was more common.

After years of researching Japanese history and cultural traditions, I focused on this one issue that harbored a vast divide. In the process, I developed a great respect for the Japanese people and found shared humanity. I hope that exploring our respective cultural beliefs in this fictional work might serve to build awareness and understanding of our mutual need to protect our planet's wildlife.

"Any attempt to understand the Japanese must begin with their version of what it means to 'take one's proper station'. Their reliance upon order and hierarchy and our (American) faith in freedom and equality are poles apart..."—Ruth Benedict in *The Chrysanthemum and the Sword: Patterns of Japanese Culture*, 1946.

Part One

Glossary of Japanese terms used in this book:

Shudan ishiki: The Japanese cultural emphasis on harmony and group consciousness. *"The Japanese Mind"* by Roger Davies and Osamu Ikeno, 2002.

Deru kui wa utareru: 'The nail that sticks out will be hammered down'.

Honne, tatemae: A Japanese virtue to keep separate genuinely held personal feelings (*honne*) from publicly expressed opinions (*tatemae*) in order to get along well with others.

Kenkyo: In Japanese society, individuals are expected to be modest and self-assertive displays of personal abilities are frowned upon.

Sempai: Elders or leaders that younger and subordinate individuals (*Kohai*) must always show respect to.

ie: The old, now waning tradition, where the head of household, typically the father, had total control over the family.

Yo no naka ni osoroshii mono ga yottsu ari: Jishin, kaminari, kaji, oyaji: old saying meaning, 'in the world there are four fearsome things: earthquakes, lightning, fire and father.' *"Looking back historically, with the Second World War as a turning point, the father's role has begun to be devalued."* Kohsuke

Yamazaki M.D. Department of Child Psychiatry, Sapporo City General Hospital.

Iitiko-Dori: Long established Japanese tradition of adopting practical elements of foreign culture.

Pan pan girls: Young, brightly dressed female sex workers often seen on the streets of Japanese cities with American GI's. *"Love, Sex and Democracy in Japan During the American Occupation"* by Mark McLelland, 2012.

Renai kekkon: Marriage of love. Arranged marriages (*Omiai*) are still popular in modern Japan.

Zengakuren: the radical university student movement that protested against war, American influence and flagrant capitalism that became violent in the 1960's.

Ryoshi: Small, rural fishermen, often looked down upon as being dirty and carefree. *"Takashima A Japanese Fishing Community"* by Edward Norbek, 1954

Yama ga li: In traditional Japanese fishermen language, it meant having a good internal compass to navigate the sea and recognize critical turning points. Utsumi Nobukichi in *"Traditional Ecological Knowledge in the beliefs of Japanese Fishing Villages"* by Jahannes Wilhelm, 1990.

Ebisu: The patron deity of fishing often depicted carrying a fishing rod and a red sea bream. *"The Forgotten Japanese"* by Miyamoto Tsuneichi, 2010. According to the Japanese view, whales and dolphins are seen as the manifestation of this god and the interdependence of supernatural, human and animal worlds.

Chapter One
1975 Miami, Florida

The looming Miami skyline and its promise of a fresh start excited Elizabeth as she gazed out the taxi window. The tropical colors reflecting off the buildings reminded her briefly of Malibu. The pain she'd hoped to leave behind threatened her rising excitement, but she shook the thought away.

"I'm Lorenzo," the cabbie said, pointing to his Cuba Libre shirt. "What brings you to Miami?"

"Work." She couldn't help but smile and sit up a bit taller. "I'm a reporter."

"Ay, Caray." The driver looked at her in the rear-view mirror as he spoke. "I thought for sure you were a student."

"Yeah," Elizabeth acknowledged with a sheepish grin. "Just graduated. My first job."

"Congratulations," he said like a doting father, bouncing his Groucho Marx eyebrows.

"Thank you." This was her dream job. Catherine, her boss, took a big gamble on her. Even with her messed up life at the time, Elizabeth had beat out seasoned reporters. "It's yours," Cath had said, "You've got the passion and dedication."

I only hope I can justify her faith in me.

"Where're you from?" the driver asked.

"Los Angeles."

"Oy Mi! Is it really as crazy out there as they say?"

"Worse, especially in Malibu." Elizabeth feigned a laugh. The cabbie was sweet and usually she enjoyed small talk, but today her nerves were getting the best of her.

Jammed in an intersection, the driver took his hands off the wheel. "Sorry, Miss. Once we get on Collins Avenue, it'll only be a few minutes."

"No problem," she said. She took a compact out of her purse and checked herself in the mirror. *Do I really look that young?* She tucked her shoulder-length, auburn hair behind her left ear. Maybe the rosy satin choker that enhanced her long neck was too mod. Although her friends had told her she looks like that older actress Maureen O'Hara.

Elizabeth added a coat of nude lip-gloss before running her fingers over the small birth mark on top of her right cheek. Familiar insecurities rushed to her thoughts. Her ex, Greg, hated the mark. He always said it looked like a tear and asked her to cover it up with concealer. She swallowed down the hurt of his hypocritical words, and how he had hurt her.

"Here we are," Lorenzo announced as they pulled up in front of the hotel.

She paid the driver with a handsome tip and took in a big breath of the humid air as she stepped out of the cab. *How am I ever going to pull this off?* She let out a deep sigh, entered the lobby, and headed to the ballroom and got behind the line.

With sweaty palms, Elizabeth handed over her press credentials. She was on a mission to expose the conference for what it was—a ruthless organization bent on enslaving defenseless beings.

"Sure you're at the right place, Miss Worthington?" the official asked, sneering at her, then at her papers and back at her again. "We're about marine parks, not marine life."

Elizabeth fidgeted with the ends of her long hair and forced a smile. "Yes. Elizabeth Worthington, *Mother Ocean magazine*." As he glanced down at his attendance list, she worried if she'd be accepted, but asked, "Is there a problem?"

The man huffed, made a checkmark, and handed her a badge. "Okay, you're clear," he said and nodded toward the cavernous hall.

Wearing her favorite white linen pantsuit and heels to match, she strode into the dimly lit ballroom of the Miami Fontainebleau Hotel. The stares of the men in the audience proved her choice of fashion for the conference as they would notice her, maybe even come to like her.

She found a seat next to a man wearing a Seaquarium Miami sweatshirt. "Is this seat taken?"

"It's yours," the fifty-ish-year-old man said with a wink. "Where are you from?"

"Los Angeles." Liz smiled and shuffled through some papers in her briefcase.

"Yeah, you don't look like a marine park exec. Why are you...?"

She pointed to herself. "Me? Oh, kind of a personal interest. I write about marine animals. How about you?"

"Do I look like an executive?" He pinched his sweatshirt. "They required all department heads to attend. They say the guest speaker is something of a messiah."

"Maybe an oppressor," she mumbled, thinking the only thing she knew about him was that he was an internationally famous dolphin trainer.

"What?" The man cocked his head.

She waved it off. "Don't mind me. Uh, so what department do you run?"

"Park maintenance."

She smiled broadly. "That's a big job."

"It is. I've got thirty-eight good men and women who keep the place spotless for the tourists."

Elizabeth knew the support staff well. At SeaWorld San Diego, most were good, hard-working people, but unwitting accomplices to the charade. A picture of Greg manhandling the river dolphins popped into her mind and made her shudder. She asked, "Do you ever get to interact with the dolphins?"

"Ah." The man leaned back in his chair and crossed his arms over his chest. "You're interested in *those* animals. How come?"

"Well," Elizabeth began, "When I was swimming as a kid, a dolphin saved me from a shark attack."

He shook his head. "Huh, no wonder you care about them."

"A lot," she said. "Do you have any interaction with them?"

"Nah. We only clean their overnight holding tanks."

She pulled a pen and notebook out of her briefcase. "How does that work?"

"They move the dolphins to another pen. We drain it and scrub all the gunk off the walls and floor. I have to pressure the night crew to work fast."

"How come?" she asked as she scribbled down his response to the previous question.

"The dolphins sometimes fight with each other, bloody the water up and all. If that happens, we call the animal handlers to take care of it and have the vet patch up the wounds."

She gasped, tension forming in her neck. "Do...do you ever see the dolphins fight?"

"Well. I...I'm not supposed to talk about..." He paused and turned his body toward her, eyes narrowing at the pen in her hand. "Why are you asking?"

"I just need to know," she blurted out, taking her trembling fingers off the ends of her hair. "Sorry," she added, pressing her lips together. *Control your fury, Lizzie. Why are you badgering this guy? He's not involved in the exploitation.*

"Are you alright?" the man asked.

"Sorry..." Her voice cracked. "I'm just a little on edge. Didn't sleep a wink last night." *Shit, Lizzie. Remember, the pen not the sword. Not yet.*

"No problem." He pointed toward the podium and checked his watch. "They're gathering on stage for the presentation. Should only be another ten or fifteen minutes."

"Great," she acknowledged and looked over her list of questions. Were they too soft? Too harsh? She took the mini tape recorder out of her briefcase and put it within easy reach. She needed to focus her energies on interviewing the presenter, or should she say, the monster?

Elizabeth exhaled deeply and sat back. *Relax girl. You've got this. Talk to the staff. Conversational, not confrontational. Get the facts. Then write one kick-butt story. You are worthy.*

You. Are. Worthy.

Chapter Two

"Yes, Sir. I realize that," Kaito Yamamoto answered, talking into the phone. Pacing back and forth in the dressing room behind the Fontainebleau's ballroom stage, he was obligated to listen to his boss, OceanWorld's CEO, Sato Yamaguchi.

"Yes, Sir. I know it means a lot to you. Of course, Sir. Will do my best." Kaito glanced at his watch, knowing the CEO called him first thing in the morning, Tokyo time. "Sir, I've only got fifteen minutes before I go on. When I return, can we discuss adding some educational programming?"

Kaito stopped walking and stiffened as Yamaguchi began a familiar tirade about what really mattered to him: the bottom dollar. Kaito buried the receiver into his gut and muttered, "The bakayarou! The shows and ticket revenues, that's all he cares about." He could picture the CEO shaking his finger as his muffled voice came through the speaker.

"You should be grateful I hired you over ten years ago as a nineteen-year-old, university flunky," Yamaguchi said. "Remember, I was the one who enabled you to become a dolphin trainer and celebrity showman at thirty."

That line always hit Kaito the hardest. How his lifelong dream to decode dolphin language was taken away from him.

"Stay focused on the job, Yamamoto." He slammed down the phone before Kaito could say, "Yes, sir."

Kaito rushed to the door when someone knocked. He smiled as Aaron Stickle, President of the American Association of Marine Parks, entered.

"I hope this dressing room gave you a chance to relax before your presentation, Mr. Yamamoto." Patting Kaito on the back, he gestured toward a semi-circular couch. "Please, sit. Let's have a drink."

"It's fine. Thank you, sir," Kaito answered as he took a seat, a distance away from the loud man. "Water will be good."

The president opened a bottle of Perrier for Kaito and poured a scotch for himself. "We are so honored to have such a celebrity speaker for our conference. Your CEO has told me much about your dolphin shows, the number one-selling attraction at Tokyo's OceanWorld."

Kaito nodded to the outlandish praise. "Mr. Yamaguchi is too kind. He is the businessman; I am only the showman."

"Ha!" The president slapped his knee. "The showman brings in the dough. I hear all of Tokyo goes crazy for your acts. And your superbly trained dolphin."

Kaito nodded. "Yes, Manami is a real star."

Stickle glanced at his watch. "We've got a few more minutes before show time. I'm curious, how did you come to be a dolphin whisperer?"

Kaito's shoulders slumped, and he cleared his throat. "When I was about ten years old, I was swimming in a harbor when I saw a pod of dolphins chasing little mullets into a trap. They made a net of swirling bubbles…" he twirled his hand in the air, "And gobbled them up. When I listened, they seemed to talk among themselves. I remember turning to my *okaasan…*" he looked away. "My mother and saying that dolphins must be the smartest fishermen in the sea. From then on, I wanted to learn everything I could about them. That was it. Not to *whisper* to them but communicate *with* them."

"That's really something," Stickle said, glancing at his watch again. "I can hardly wait to see those film clips of your shows." He stood up. "I've got to double-check the equipment. Why don't you relax for another five minutes, and then I'll come and get you for the introduction?"

"Thank you, Mr. Stickle." Kaito nodded, waiting for him to exit.

Rushing to the bathroom, he plopped himself down on the toilet, stomach twisting and gurgling. He could hear the voice of his CEO ringing in his ears. *"Kaito, I don't really give a kuso for the big-headed, round eyes in America, but we'll show them that our dolphin shows are entertainment products as good as Hollywood's."*

Kaito stood and examined his appearance in front of the mirror. He splashed a bit of water on his face, and brushed his spikey, black hair over his large ears as best he could. Having never been to America, he thought his dark almond-shaped eyes and pale complexion would make them wonder what kind of Asian he was. "I really don't want to be here," he said to his reflection, straightening his tie. "I am more than the showman everyone sees. Demonstrating tricks I taught the dolphins is not enough. Someday, I will discover a language between our species."

He checked his watch for the fourth time. The acid in his stomach rose to his throat and he unwrapped a lozenge. Then, quietly clapping his hands together three times, he bowed his head and closed his eyes. Slowly, a feeling of rejuvenation washed over him. He opened his eyes. *Time to go. I will do my best and the presentation will be over in an hour. Tomorrow, I'll be out of here. Away from these beguiling yet overbearing people—ones that used to intrigue me as a child.*

Chapter Three
An Hour Later

At the podium, Kaito advanced to the last slide. A close-up photo of a dolphin kissing him faded to black and applause filled the room. Kaito bowed and said to himself, *Arigatai,* it's over.

President Stickle stepped up on the stage. "On behalf of our members, Mr. Yamamoto, let me thank you for your impressive work. Would you take a few questions?"

Kaito smiled. "Of course."

A young woman dressed in white quickly raised her hand. "Thank you, Mr. Yamamoto. Your show and relationship with your dolphin, Manami, seems quite remarkable, but can you tell me if she's happy?"

Kaito's heart raced. *Happy? Not the kind of question I expected.*

A murmur ran through the crowd. President Stickle chuckled. "Well, we are very fortunate, aren't we, that bottlenose dolphins have perpetual smiles on their faces. Makes our audiences just love them."

He handed the mic back to Kaito, who searched for the proper words in English, "Ahh…thank you, miss, for your question. I am so sorry. I am not sure what you mean, but I can say that Manami loves to please and perform for the crowd."

The woman restated her question. The lighting was dim, but he could tell that the American woman was attractive. And irritated. Her lips had pursed for a moment before she restated her question. "What I mean, sir, is do you think it's in this animal's nature to want to please humans?"

A nervous itch rose in Kaito's scalp, but he resisted the urge to scratch it away. The president took the mic and pointed at a man in the front row. "Moving on. Let's take this gentleman's question."

The man in the audience stood up, but the woman interrupted. "Excuse me! May I please get an answer to my question?"

Kaito glanced back and forth between the two.

The president extended his hand toward Kaito. "Please, Mr. Yamamoto, address the man's question." Glaring at the woman, Stickle added, "This is a *business* meeting, miss."

"Thank you," the man in the audience said. "What is your production schedule and audience capacity at OceanWorld?"

Kaito watched as the woman shoved her way through the assembly, the ballroom lights highlighting her reddish hair as she departed.

He clenched his jaw and tried to smile. "Ma...Manami gives three show a day, six days a week. The stadium hold twelve-hundred-fifty people. Ninety-four percent capacity." The audience gasped.

"What is your monthly gross?" the man asked.

"Gross would be over million American dollars a month. More for guest dolphin-feeding program."

The man shook his head. "That swamps what we get at SeaWorld." The audience chuckled.

President Stickle pointed toward the back. "One more question."

A tall man with gray hair stood. "Thanks for all your insights, Mr. Yamamoto. I wonder what you see for the future of marine mammal amusement parks?"

"I see generations of families worldwide coming to not just adore these animals, but to learn about them and respect how intelligent and social these fellow mammals are."

"Thank you so much, Mr. Yamamoto," President Stickle said, patting Kaito on the back. "The session is now closed."

The audience rose and clapped. Kaito let out a deep breath.

Out in the hallway, a few of the association board members flocked to Kaito, attempting to woo him to enjoy the Miami nightlife.

"Blaze Starr is at the Centro Espanol Gentlemen's club," said Stickle, nudging Kaito with his elbow.

"What is a gentlemen's club?" Kaito asked.

"You know, where girls dance. You must have them in Tokyo," one of the association men explained.

"Oh, I understand," Kaito said, his face warming as he turned away. "Not my cup of tea, I'm afraid."

"They have a bikini bar too, if you're not into dancing."

He squinted his eyes. "No, thank you, Mr. Stickle and gentlemen, but I am very tired from the trip, and I will be heading back to Tokyo tomorrow."

"Understood," he said. "But perhaps you'll return and teach our dolphins how to accomplish those amazing tricks."

"Ah, perhaps, and thank you." Kaito made a deep bow and headed to the lobby elevators. He spotted the young woman in the white pantsuit coming toward him. He couldn't help but notice the way her beautiful hair bounced around her shoulders. He had been right—it was more red than brown. A beautiful shade he had never seen in person. She was an American beauty. Just like the ones he saw in the movie magazine the GI had given him when he was a young boy. He averted his eyes and pushed the elevator button.

She smiled and extended her hand. "Honored to meet you, Mr. Yamamoto. I'm Elizabeth Worthington, from *Mother Ocean magazine*. Your presentation was great."

Kaito's face warmed and he waved his palm in front of him. "Thank you," he said and shook her hand.

"Might I ask you some questions?" Elizabeth's eyes pleaded. "I'm doing an article on how dolphinariums can teach the public about the animal's intelligence."

Her boldness flustered him. Because of her earlier questions from the floor, he was hesitant, but she seemed sincere. He had a hard enough time talking to women in his native language, but since this was a topic of personal interest to him, he relented. "I guess so, Miss Washington. Do you mean right now?"

She smiled. "Could you? That would be super. But please, call me Elizabeth."

Kaito's stomach fluttered when she pointed toward the lobby chairs. Her body was shapely and full. Curvy, they called it in the American movies he enjoyed. He sat, deftly balanced on the edge of his chair, and waited for her to start asking questions.

She opened her notebook. "I was impressed by your dolphin acts as well as your vast knowledge of dolphin behavior."

"Thank you," he said, straightening his back. "I studied marine biology at University of Tokyo. Also, English since high school, but first time speak much."

"Your English is quite good," she offered. "What do you think of America? Americans?"

"Thank you." He grinned, wondering if she was being gratuitous. "Only been in the hotel and airport. Very nice. People here are very…uh, friendly."

"Well," She smiled openly. "I hope you get a chance to spend more time here."

Catching a glimmer of the emotive color in her eyes, he sighed. "I was thinking of maybe seeing a U.S. dolphin show tomorrow, then back to Tokyo. But don't have much time and besides, my dolphin, Manami, will not perform without me."

Elizabeth made a note, then leaned forward. "The bond and communication you have with Manami is extraordinary. You know, I was planning on attending a show tomorrow as well. I could meet you there, show you around."

He smiled through tightened lips. "Well, m…maybe."

"We can talk," she said, hesitating. "Maybe I can share with you the exciting studies being done in the U.S. on intra-species communication."

"I'd like that," he replied, eyes widening with interest. "There is great potential in that subject. May I ask please, what your magazine article is about?"

"The mission of our magazine is to protect wild sea life, and we want our readers to know how dolphins in captivity can help."

"I strongly believe we need to protect our ocean." He remained poised, avoiding eye contact. "Japanese people have a great love of nature. What is it you want to know?"

"My magazine focuses on all marine life, but since you're a dolphin expert and trainer, can I ask what your audience learns from watching the dolphins in your shows?"

"Our dolphins are ambassadors for their species." He glanced sideways at her. "Our audience learns what intelligent animals they are. They learn to love and care about them."

"For sure," she agreed, "But is that dolphin behavior natural? In the wild, they spend eighty percent of their time underwater, diving down hundreds of feet. In the pool, they're mostly on the surface."

Crossing his arms, Kaito replied, "Yes, I am aware. I know very well how dolphins behave in the wild. But these are show dolphins."

"Fair enough," she said, writing in her notebook. "Knowing that wild dolphins use echolocation for sensing and survival, I wonder…" She put a finger to her chin. "Have you ever thought it might be a problem in a small pool?"

Kaito narrowed his eyes. "Excuse me, please, I am not understanding what you ask me?"

She cleared her throat. "I mean, have you seen any ill effects from echoes bouncing off a pool's concrete walls?"

Kaito sensed the top of his head itch again, but he stayed straight and steady in his chair and shook his head.

She continued, "I'm sorry if my questions are difficult, but anything that hurts dolphins, I take personally…" she placed a hand on her heart…"and it hurts me as well. For example, in the States, they've found problems of constant pacing in the pool, ulcers, and even self-mutilation."

Even though Kaito understood and shared her passion for dolphins, he answered, "No, miss, we have not." He looked away and added, "We closely monitor the health of our dolphins."

Elizabeth nodded while writing down his response. When she looked up, he abruptly stood and bowed. "I am sorry, miss. I don't think I can be any more help to your story."

She rubbed the back of her neck. "I'm sorry, Mr. Yamamoto. I apologize for being so direct. It's…it's only that I care about these animals, whether in the wild or in captivity." She seemed to study him, then added, "And I sense you care for them as well, so if you could bear with me."

Kaito now saw how her eyes shifted from green to gray—they seemed to change with her emotions. They reminded him of how the water turns as one sails out of the harbor into the open ocean. Despite his reservations, he was struck by her whole-heartedness. He pulled at his necktie and sat back down.

She returned to her notebook. "Thank you so much, Mr. Yamamoto. Are you familiar with our recent U.S. Marine Mammal Protection Act?"

"Yes, I know of it."

"And? May I ask your opinion of it?"

He let out a breath. "Your country prohibits the taking of whales and dolphins." To gather his thoughts, he looked to the ceiling. "Let me say, I agree that when dolphins are caught in purse seins, it is very bad. Thousands of dolphins have drowned this way." Straining to find a hopeful note, he added, "But the species are a long way from being endangered."

Elizabeth raised her eyebrows. "Do you think this act should apply on a worldwide basis? The United Nations and the International Whaling Commission have asked the Japanese government to sign on for years."

Kaito's jaw tightened. "It is not our way to argue such things with those who might not agree with us." He looked to the side. "Even my opinion doesn't matter. Japan's Interior Minister Nakayama has the authority for government policy."

"Do you know him?" she asked.

"Yes, I went to university with him, but you'd have to speak to him directly."

Still scribbling in her notepad, she continued, "Yes, but please Mr. Yamamoto. I want to know how you feel…"

Kaito didn't speak for several moments then put his hands together. "Please, do not take my answer as disrespect for your views, but no. I do not think it should apply." He raised his chin. "Whaling has been part of the Japanese culture for centuries."

Elizabeth looked down. "I'm sorry. I don't mean to insult you or your country."

He went on. "And remember, up until a few years ago, your own fishermen were taking many, many whales."

Elizabeth pushed hard on her pencil, snapping the lead.

"Maybe you did not know," he continued, "But after the war, Japan had no fishing industry left. The American occupiers retrofitted huge tankers for us. Those ships were start of Japanese factory whaling industry. It was the fastest way to feed a starving nation." Kaito bowed his head and lowered his voice. "But then, in 1954, U.S. nuclear bomb testing in the Pacific killed our fishing industry. My father, *otosan* in Japanese, was aboard the Lucky Dragon and the radiation almost killed him."

Elizabeth winced and drew back. The notebook slipped from her hand onto the floor. She didn't move for it, seemingly paralyzed by what he said.

He picked up her notebook and handed it to her, accidentally brushing the tips of her long fingers. Their eyes locked. His heart raced. "Did I say something wrong, miss? Should I continue?"

"No…I mean yes, please. I'm struck by your sincere answer. Please continue."

He leaned forward. "You are very kind. Thank you. But I am curious. If you do not mind, what is your personal interest in dolphins?"

She tilted her head toward him. "Well, like you, I've been fascinated…" she hesitated…"maybe obsessed with them since childhood. Swam with them in California most of my life. I've dedicated my life to writing about them—protecting them." She paused and leaned back in her seat. "All my friends say I care more about dolphins than people."

"People say same thing about me." He smiled, and she shot a matching one at him.

He puckered his full lips. "Some say I even look like dolphin."

"Hah, a pretty handsome dolphin no less." She fixed her eyes on him. "You must have thousands of adoring fans."

Face flushing, he said, "I do have fans but am too busy for socializing." Changing the subject, he asked, "Do you have a full-time job as reporter for the magazine?"

"Yes," she nodded. "I proposed this series to speak for the dolphins."

Kaito was curious at her choice of words. "Could I ask how you speak for dolphins?"

"Well, I can't presume to read their minds, but I try to get into their flippers, so to speak. That's how I got my job at *Mother Ocean* right out of college. I sent them an essay about how a dolphin might think and maybe even feel."

"Please go on."

"They wanted someone who was passionate about marine mammals. I was looking from the dolphin's point of view."

"Interesting. I talk with Manami. Someday, I will develop a language between species."

"Wow! That's an incredible goal, even revolutionary. I can only imagine what they feel. Would you like to read my essay? I always keep a copy with me for inspiration."

"Certainly," he said politely as she frantically dug into her case. "With their brains and vocalizations, I always wondered what they are saying."

"Yeah!" She nodded. "But that's hard we can barely know what another human being is thinking or feeling, unless they tell you." She tucked a wisp of long hair behind her ear. "Even then, you don't know if they're telling you the truth." She pulled a paper out of her briefcase. "Please, understand I was fresh out of college when I wrote this." Hesitating to hand it to him, she said, "I know more now."

Kaito took the paper. "I would be honored to read it." He slipped it into his jacket pocket and stood. "Thank you. It was a pleasure meeting you, Miss Washington."

"Pleasure's all mine," she said, then added, "But before I let you go…"

Kaito stiffened. *Let me go? What does she mean by that?*

"The Protection Act also prohibits the capturing of wild dolphins. You know how social these animals are and how a mother stays with her offspring for life. What are your thoughts on this?"

He froze. Her words about young dolphins being separated from their mothers struck his heart like a dragon sneaking up to a character in a Kabuki play. *She must have suspected that I stole Manami from her mother.* He stared across the room, unflinching.

"Mr. Yamamoto, what's wrong?" she asked.

He stood up and bowed sharply. "Nothing. I must go now."

"I'm sorry for my probing questions, Mr. Yamamoto. I can be too zealous for my own good." She looked to the ground for a moment, then asked, "Could I at least give you, my card?"

"Yes, of course." They exchanged cards.

He bowed and headed toward the elevators.

She followed and called from behind him. "Can we meet again? Like maybe at the Seaquarium?"

He did not turn around.

"By speaking from your heart, you are giving me a much more balanced story."

He pushed the elevator button. *Why do I listen to this woman?*

"Thank you, then, Mr. Yamamoto."

He turned around, finally, and said, "I care about *all* dolphins."

As the doors were closing, he thought he heard her say, "I know."

Chapter Four

Elizabeth watched as Mr. Yamamoto entered the elevator and the doors closed. Had the doors just shut on her exclusive story? She searched the lobby for conference attendees to interview, approaching a dozen men, with most telling her—or lying—that they weren't from one of the marine parks or in attendance.

At the hotel bar, Elizabeth sat slumped and depressed sipping a coke when her ears perked up to the shouts and laughter at a distant table. A group of men were rapt, listening to a stocky, mop-haired guy hold forth. He had the commanding presence of Peter Wilson, the anti-whaling activist she had seen a photo of in a recent article in The Guardian, the U.K.-based independent newspaper. How the Russian factory ships sailed off the northern coast of California hunting sperm whales for their oil. Not to use for light as in the colonial days, but for building intercontinental ballistic missiles. Cath told her he might be at the conference. "Try and get his take on things," she had requested.

At this point, she was fed up with men. The sleezy guy at the bar. And before that, the too nice but still culpable Japanese guy she offended with her fanatical ways to the detriment of her story. But she was intrigued by Wilson's bravery and commitment to protecting marine mammals. She wanted to find out what motivated him to put himself in between fleeing pods of whales and the menacing harpoon guns. Meet and get to know the hero she wanted to be, or at least emulate.

She wandered over in their direction to make sure it was Wilson and catch his eye.

Only feet away, Peter halted his oration, ran his hand through that incredible hair and gave her the roaming eye.

She moved closer and he stood and waved. "Might you be the woman in white these guys been tellin' me about?"

"It seems so. I'm Elizabeth Worthington from Mother Ocean magazine. Are you Peter Wilson?"

"I am," he crowed, expanding his already muscular chest. "Your editor told me you'd be here to interview me."

She nodded. "Yes, would this be a good time?"

Wilson turned to his adoring crew. "Okay guys, no more bullshit. I've got this dynamite…" he paused…"reporter, who wants to know the real me." A round of dilatory handshakes and backslaps later, the boys left, and Peter winked at Elizabeth and opened his arms wide.

"Elizabeth. So good to see a fearless *woman* warrior for a change. The boys tell me you really laid into that Jap guy."

Clutching her briefcase in front of her with both hands, she accepted Peter's welcoming bear hug. His strength was apparent, and his arms gave her a mix of feelings. A sense of security, like she once needed her father to give her. At the same time, she was surprised to feel a sexual charge. Feel the touch and body of a man. It had been almost two years since she left Greg.

"Come sit," he said, guiding her elbow to a settee and plopping down beside her. "I heard you're quite a reporter and writer, dedicated like me to saving cetaceans."

"For sure the latter," she said, wondering if he'd put the make on her. "But I've yet to prove myself."

She got out her pencil and notebook and began. "I'd like to hear more about your encounter in June with the Russian whalers. Our readers would be curious to know what motivates you to put yourself in danger for these animals."

On cue, he began retelling the incident with bravado, energetically acting out the moves as though he was right there. Elizabeth saw how he relished the action and danger, a trait that didn't quite reside within herself.

"So, Peter. You told The Guardian a close call with a sperm whale changed the trajectory of your life. Tell me about that."

"Yes. I was in a Zodiac inflatable when a harpoon flew past me and hit a large male in the head. He screamed in pain struggling with death. He kept diving then rising up with pink bubbles of blood oozing out the gash."

Peter quit his animated delivery and took on a meditative posture as though he was receiving a message from a higher authority. Elizabeth suspended her notetaking.

He lowered his voice, and, like a western Gandhi, he recalled, "On the next dive, he rose up right alongside my Zodiac and his dark eye looked right into mine." He turned to Elizabeth to be sure she was empathizing with his telling of the encounter. "I even saw my reflection in his eye. Then, he collapsed on the surface and died in front of me."

Elizabeth pleaded with her flooded eyes for him to continue.

"At that moment, I wondered if he saw me as someone who was trying to save him from the hunters, or was I one of the predators? I dedicated my life to protecting these creatures. I still ask, how are we humans going to be able to survive if we let our oceans die?" He fixed his eyes on Elizabeth and said, "We die."

Elizabeth grabbed a tissue from her briefcase to wipe her mascara-streaked cheeks, then reached over to console Peter, laying a hand on his arm. He really was the swash-buckling modern man who used the sword to affect change. His passion relit the flame within her. But she would not allow it be the physical kind. They were spiritual crusaders. She would join his journey with her pen.

Turning to him, she was surprised to find his steely blue eyes piercing the air past her, fixed in a determined but detached stare. *Was this the kind of passion she would need in direct battle with evildoers?*

Without a word, he snapped out of his trance. "So, what else do you want to know?"

She sat back and away then asked, "What did you think of the presentation?"

"I'm afraid I missed it. Came here to meet with Dick O'Meery to plot out some new strategies to defend our finny friends. Do you know Dick?"

"Never met him," Elizabeth replied, "But I'm aware of his background. Is he here?"

"No. He left this morning for the Antilles. Trying to release some caged dolphins. He's another man after your heart, eh?"

She wrinkled her brow. "What do you mean?"

"I mean us dedicated soulmates are a rare breed and we've got to stick together. You know, keep our mojo going."

"Mojo?"

"You know, the stuff between a man and a woman. How about if we continue the interview up in my room?"

"How about a no go. I'm here on business."

"Sorry," he said with a chuckle. "I was under the impression you were a woman of passion."

"It depends on the passion."

"Fair enough then," he said. "Maybe you'll join us on the *Sea Savior* to go after the Japs next. Show them where they can shoot their harpoons." He stood up and extended his hand.

"I've got to run," he said and began to open his arms.

She reached out her hand and gave him a limp shake. "Thanks for your time, Peter."

As he strutted out of the bar, Elizabeth stood there, shaking her head. Feeling flush from the experience, she asked herself, *what was that?* She placed her notebook into the briefcase and sat back down. Elizabeth was both drawn to and distracted by Peter and that other man she had come to know. Both had connections with dolphins but couldn't be more different. Peter had the allure and energy of a stallion in heat, but of dubious character. Then, there's Yamamoto, a gracious and noble man of uncertain passion, one that I insulted with my insensitive nature. *Why am I even thinking about men? I've got a career to start and a job to do.*

Feeling unhappy with herself, Elizabeth decided to walk the several blocks to the hotel and cool off in the evening air. She whipped her hair into a bun, stuffed her jacket under her arm, and cursed with every step. Back into reality. There was no way she could tell, Cath, her editor, who had bought into the story potential and travel expenses, that she'd blown the interview with Yamamoto. She could hear her editor now: *you promised an exposé about the cruel-hearted Japanese dolphin hunters and trainers, Liz, but you only exposed your failings.*

She picked up the scent of salty sea air and lifted her face into the breeze, turning down Ocean Drive and toward her hotel. On the sidewalk, she began ticking off what went wrong. First, Yamamoto simply didn't fit her expectations of an animal abuser. His seemingly modest, respectful demeanor caught her off-balance—surely the trick of a showman. She had to admit, though, he did make her aware of her country's hypocrisy when it came to whaling. And, to a degree, made her aware of her own personal and sometimes ridged views.

Strangely, she couldn't figure out why his demeanor changed so much during the interview. How they strangely seemed to relate to each other. A different kind of man.

Forget that, Liz. Remember what that bastard did: he delivered a convincing presentation that will end up greatly increasing the number of wild dolphins captured, enslaved, and tortured for human entertainment. Were her expectations off base, her interview approach too rough, or was she doubting her editor, her mission?

Just as the noise from the traffic started to disrupt her thoughts, she spotted a palm-tree-lined public beach and entered Lummus Park. She hoped being close to the ocean and the creatures within would rekindle her devotion to protecting the species.

Liz took off her heels and straddled the shoreline. The lapping of the waves reminded her of her ocean home on the other coast, and she wondered if the Atlantic dolphins had the same temperaments as her Pacific ones.

Up ahead and near the sand, she came upon a sign marking Muscle Beach. And, sure enough, there was an afternoon gathering of athletic men, sweating and grunting on benches and bars. The sight of these hunks in bathing suits and Peter Wilson's lingering hug reminded her of Greg and what had set her on her career path. Her mind played back the time she overheard her boyfriend talking to his new assistant, Steve. How they had to discipline the dolphins by withdrawing food if they did not complete the tricks, often isolating them, and sometimes even poking and punching them if they misbehaved.

Elizabeth kicked at the little ridges of sand, recalling how she had confronted Greg, and how he denied doing those things. "I was just BS-ing, Liz. None of it was true. Come on, honey," he'd said, grabbing her arm.

"How can I trust you?" she remembered telling him as she swatted his hand away. "Tony and Alexi saw you punch the river dolphins many times."

That prompted her to investigate even further, and her trust in Greg was shattered. It was then she made the proposal to Roy Paulsin at *The Freep* to do a story on SeaWorld's abuse of show animals. Although she never mentioned Greg by name in the article, he got fired. Things spiraled from there.

"Hey, lady!" a young girl wearing a Miami Dolphins jersey yelled out. A nerf football bounced in the sand past Elizabeth. The girl's happiness seemed so free and natural. Elizabeth caught the ball on the water's edge before it floated into the surf. Standing ankle deep in the warm, gray Atlantic waters, she handed it to the girl.

She took it and smiled brightly. "Thanks for catching it," she said.

"You're welcome," Elizabeth replied, looking back at the caring faces of her watchful her parents. "You are a lovely, lucky girl."

Arriving at her hotel, she checked in with the desk clerk to see if she had any messages. The clerk told her she had two which were transferred to her room phone where she could push number nine to listen.

She listened to the first recording. "*Lizzy,* her mother pleaded, choking back a sob. *You've got to call me right away; our group leader said some horrible things to me. You've got to come right away and get me out of this place. Or...or I'll kill myself.*"

Her stomach dropped, and she clenched her fists at her side. "Shit, Mom!" That guilt trip wouldn't work on her anymore. Her demands only drained what she had left in her. She needed to get on with her life. Get back to her home, her job. Dr. Schmitz had reminded her repeatedly that patients often try to avoid therapy by enlisting family members as enablers to quit the program. It's probably another false alarm. *But what if?*

She rang her mother. After multiple rings, she finally answered, though incoherently.

"Crissy? Is that you?"

Jesus Christ, Elizabeth thought, Crissy hadn't been in her mom's life for years. Mother abandoned both of them years ago. "No, Mom, it's Lizzy. Are you alright?"

"Oh, I had a horrible day, but I'm better now. That group leader, Harley, apologized and they finally gave me a sedative. Can you believe that asshole asked me if I was denying that I needed a drink to forget about my fights with your father?"

Elizabeth could imagine those fights. She's been there, after all. She'd often hid in her room or locked herself in the bathroom until Dad left and Mom blacked out.

"Lizzy, please come in the morning and get me released from this damned prison."

"Mom, I'm at work now in Florida. Don't you remember me telling you about my assignment? I can't come until the day after tomorrow."

"Why can't you just take the time now to call Dr. Schmitz?"

"Mom! When I get back. I've got things in my life too."

"Don't forget."

"Yes, Mom. I must go now. Goodbye."

She hung up the phone, but a heaviness settled across her chest. Elizabeth knew from experience her demands wouldn't end. *She's so damned selfish. My father, sister too. That's how I thought people were. How I had to be.*

Sighing, she hit play on the second message. Catherine's voice met her ears. *"Hi Liz, it's Cath. Hope your coverage and interview went well. It's still early here, so call me when you get in. I'm so excited for you and Mother Ocean."*

Elizabeth's heart raced as she dialed Cath back, hoping she'd be able to skim over what she didn't get. Try and convince her there was enough potential to allow her to stay with the story.

"Hey, Liz. Glad you called. How's that sunny, southeast coast treating you?"

"Humid, Cath, and I'm hot on the story."

"Tell me."

"I had a long interview with that guru of Japanese dolphin shows, Yamamoto. He's an interesting guy and, honestly, a bit of a surprise."

"How so?"

"He just didn't seem like the evil dolphin abuser I pictured these guys to be. Of course, he had all the arguments in defense of the shows, you know, educating people about sea life, getting them to love them."

Catherine scoffed. "Sounds about right. Did he say anything about dolphin capturing, conditions and so forth?"

"Kind of. He's clearly an enemy of our cause, but he actually made good points in defending his culture."

"So, what you're saying is, he didn't give you any meat to hang your story on, expose his moral corruption and bad practices?"

"Well, not...not yet actually."

"Not yet?" Her voice raised an octave. "How about the interviews with the conference attendees? Did you get anything from them?"

Elizabeth rubbed the phone receiver against her midriff and quietly growled to come up with a good answer. "You know, Cath, I didn't have to speak face-to-face with any of them to know how they ate up every word and image he presented. They have this one, star show dolphin, Manami, who is basically a movie star to the audience over there. Everyone wanted to learn his techniques, learn how he taught Manami all of her tricks. Believe me, they hung on Yamamoto's every word. I got it all on tape."

"Okay, but without a first-hand account of abuse, this sounds mostly like a short opinion piece."

"I did get one off the record comment from an employee of the nearby Seaquarium. He confirmed their dolphins sometimes fight and bloody the waters."

"That's something, but are you coming home tomorrow?"

Stick to your guns, Lizzy girl. "With further investigation, I believe I can develop more than another 'bad guy' story. I just need a little more time for a more revealing, complete story."

No response on the other end.

Elizabeth could almost see Catherine shaking her head. "Trust me. I have a gut feeling this guy is key to a much bigger story. I hope to catch him at Seaquarium tomorrow," she added with little confidence. "Please let me stay another day?"

"I'm sorry. It's just hard to believe someone who trains dolphins would open up to you about how they produce their acts."

"I know, but he already gave me some clues and he's so transparent. He actually loves his dolphins, even if it may seem like a cruel sort of love."

After a long, loud exhale, she relented. "Okay, Lizzy, I'm banking on you, but don't let this guy or your zeal for saving every dolphin in the ocean get in the way of a good story. Stay in touch, okay?"

"You got it, boss. Thanks. See you soon. Bye."

As soon as Elizabeth hung up, she realized she'd put herself in a precarious position. Who knew if she'd even find Yamamoto at whatever dolphin show he planned to attend tomorrow. If he would even attend a show at all. And if he did, would it be in Miami, or maybe Orlando? And if she did find him, would he even speak to her after he'd read her essay? She'd attacked the foundation of his career, his fame.

Hell, I could lose my job trusting my gut about this guy.

Chapter Five

After walking up and down the halls to stretch his legs, Kaito went to his hotel room. As soon as he entered, he released a huge sigh of relief. He plopped down on the king-sized bed, arms spread out, hoping the soft mattress would absorb some of his fatigue. Snatching up the chocolate sitting on the bed's pillow, he was grateful for the energy boost the candy gave him. Talking to the ceiling, he recapped his day.

Everything went well, until that pushy reporter cornered me. Are all Americans, including their women, like that? Or just the ones with an agenda, with such strong opinions? At least she didn't seem superficial. Self-righteous? Yes, but sincere too.

He had to admit his interest was captured when she mentioned the American research on intra-species communication. Intrigued by the possibility of decoding dolphin language, he considered whether someday he could make a scientific breakthrough.

When he reached to switch off the night lamp, he spotted Elizabeth's business card on the table. *Elizabeth Worthington, Reporter at Large, Mother Ocean magazine.* Shit! How embarrassing. He had called her Miss Washington. *She wants to meet again, but do I?* He didn't think the interview would help his career. Would she quote him, or maybe misquote him, in her article? It would hurt if the wrong article reached his boss or offended his countrymen or government. Could he trust her?

Then, he remembered the essay Elizabeth had given him. He got up and flicked on the television, putting the sound on mute. Emotionally tired, but physically awake, he pulled her essay out of his briefcase. "Wouldn't hurt to read it," he said to the silent newscaster on the TV. Laying back down on the bed, he began reading.

Dying to Make Us Happy
By Elizabeth Worthington

Where am I? Alone in a strange water place, the unchanging blue liquid stings my throat. Where are the shifting currents of my home? When I dive, I cannot find the sand, the kelp beds, the shellfish that I know. Where are the waves I used to glide over? I have been abandoned, locked in a shallow tidal pool, smooth white rock surrounding me.

I call to my mother. I call to my family. I listen. Even when they were far away, I would always hear them. But all I can hear is my own voice bouncing off the rock. Above the surface, I see the land creatures. They make noises I cannot understand. I am hungry. I want to nudge the folds of my mother's belly to drink her warm milk.

The land creature tosses a strange object onto the surface. I am curious. After touching the floating thing, they throw me a dead fish. I do not want to eat something I cannot catch, but I grow hungrier. The creatures rub my head. I miss my own kind.

Above the big pool there are many land creatures. Their loud noise attacks my senses. They jump and roar when we play their games. The air thunders with steady booms that electrify the water and explode in my skull. You have deprived me of my family, my talent, and my own way of being. You took me from my home in the sea and froze my life in this tiny place. If I could look now and find sand at a shore, I would beach myself. Then you would have me completely.

Throwing the essay on the floor, Kaito rubbed his throbbing head. He remembered how Manami had clung to her mother while she thrashed in the shallow waters of Taiji Harbor. He could hear her mother almost scream as he pushed her away. He could still feel the heft of Manami's slippery, struggling body as he took her.

Kaito felt his throat begin to close. His pulse kicked up and he could hear the thrum from inside his ears. It always started this way. The panic. The guilt. Questioning what he had done and for what.

Within seconds, sweat drenched his body as he fought to gulp back air. His guilt weighed even heavier. He rushed into the shower. The water pelting his head could not wash away what had happened after he brought Manami to her pool at OceanWorld.

He had watched as she circled endlessly, calling and looking for her mother and the rest of her pod. *Sure, it was his job to acquire new animals for the*

43

shows. But at what cost? Cost to his own sense of what was right. Right for the poor creature?

Staring at the blue-tiled wall of the shower and shielding the water from his eyes, he wondered, *did the American woman suspect he had personally captured Manami?*

The shower water turned cool against his skin. He shuddered, got out, and wrapped himself in a towel.

Climbing naked into the bed for warmth, he remembered how Manami had let him pet her head, how he felt her loneliness. "I will play with you, teach you," he recalled trying to tell her. She clicked and chirped in return. Manami had no one else, so she had followed him like a duckling. She knew what he had wanted her to do. Took to everything he showed her. Higher. Faster. She was being challenged; he was sure. But she used her intelligence and skills to please him and ultimately made the crowds laugh. He whispered, "How we've come to love you."

Kaito got up and went into the bathroom. He had a plane to catch in the afternoon, so he needed to get to sleep. Digging through his shaving kit, he found the sleeping pills. He took two and got back into bed. His pulse and thoughts slowed, but images of Elizabeth and her essay still floated through his mind. How could a human understand what another species was feeling? But. Elizabeth did seem to feel, maybe know, we could.

He wasn't sure about the feeling part but believed we could talk with them. Learn their feelings this way. Despite his empirical mind, a corner of Kaito's heart wanted to connect with hers. Finally, he dropped off to sleep.

Chapter Six
The Next Day

Seaquarium, Miami, Florida

Kaito went to watch an American dolphin show, hoping his boss at OceanWorld would like to start building a relationship with U.S. marine parks. Besides, he was curious to see how they trained and showed their dolphins. Maybe he could learn something. Maybe Elizabeth would be there.

Taking his seat in the bleachers, the moist, fishy smell comforted him as he watched the crowds of young families enter. The joy on the faces of the children, their sunburned cheeks and excited laughter, tickled him. Thinking momentarily of his troubled youth, he could not imagine wanting children of his own. He searched for other Japanese faces, but finding none, he concluded most of his countrymen immigrated to California.

He saw a young couple, honeymooners he expected, holding hands and kissing often—something he'd rarely seen, even in Tokyo. He found the stadium's Tiki village harbor backdrop rather enchanting and was more at ease here than he had at any point yesterday. Just thinking of yesterday's speech and the complicated meeting with Elizabeth blanketed him with anxiety.

Still, his thoughts stayed with Elizabeth. He tried to dismiss his attraction to her, calling it only physical and pointless—a fantasy from the pages of the Hollywood movie magazine he kept under his bed. But her beautiful reddish hair, full body and captivating eyes made him keep thinking about her.

As the crowds settled into their seats, Kaito pulled the complimentary plastic poncho out from under his seat and slid his small suitcase in its place.

"Oh, hi," a woman's familiar voice called out over the crowd.

Elizabeth waved and walked toward him.

He spun around in his seat. She looked stunning in a white t-shirt and short pleated skirt that showed off her long, toned legs. A tennis outfit, like the ones he saw in the tennis courts from his apartment window. He stood up and bowed slightly. "Good morning, Miss Worthington."

"Good morning to you, Mr. Yamamoto. Glad to see you here. Could I join you?"

"Oh…oh, sure." He cleared his throat and scooted over nervously.

"You look good in a sport shirt," she commented. "I bet you feel quite at home in a stadium."

He fingered the collar of his blue OceanWorld polo shirt. "Yes, I do and it's good for the humid weather."

"I want to apologize for yesterday," she said. "I was probably out of bounds with my questions. My…my activism sometimes gets in the way."

"No, I must apologize. I was rude. I called you Miss Washington." He blushed.

She laughed. "I've been called worse. Elizabeth is best."

Music filled the stadium. A male trainer, wearing a sailor cap and red, white and blue swim trunks, entered the stage singing. The crowd erupted in applause. He was joined, stage right, by a woman with a red flower in her blonde hair, wearing a two-piece swimsuit.

Elizabeth raised her eyebrows and chuckled. "Cute. That's really Bobby Darin singing on a recording—he was so cool."

A trio of dolphins shot out of the water like missiles. The audience stood and cheered as they circled the pool at top speed. The trio stopped in front of the crowd, powered up on their tails, and waved with their flippers, clicking and squealing to say hello.

"Good morning, land lubbers. Welcome to our tropical dolphin show. I'm Amy and this is my fellow trainer, Rodney."

Rodney waved. "Thanks Amy. Let me introduce our stars." He pointed to one dolphin. "Here's Pokey." The biggest of the three turned and bowed to the crowd.

"And Sparky." The smallest shot straight in the air, his way of saying *hello*.

"And here's Cookie." The last dolphin flipped on her back, swam in a circle, and yipped.

"Pokey is our lazy dolphin," Amy said. "She doesn't always want to do her chores. Pokey, show us that you can be a good girl. Go and get the ball." Amy signaled and the dolphin nodded, then flipped onto her back and slowly floated around the pool. She whistled a song and squirted jets of water into the air, ignoring the ball.

The audience broke out in laughter. Elizabeth chuckled. Kaito nodded.

Rodney pointed to Sparky. "Sparky is a rascal. She sometimes does the opposite of what she's been told."

"Go get the hoop, Sparky." The dolphin shook her head. "Okay then, go and do a back flip." Instead, Sparky got the hoop, and the audience relished the joke.

Elizabeth leaned over to Kaito. "How does this compare to your shows in Japan?"

Keeping his eyes focused on the performance, he answered, "It's a fine show, but yours are more…basic?"

"What do you mean?" Elizabeth asked.

"They treat their dolphins like small children. They are not children, but highly intelligent, social, and emotional animals like you described in your essay. My shows in Japan are more acrobatic; they reveal their amazing intelligence and natural connection to humans."

Her mouth dropped, forming a perfect o. "Wow, you read my essay?"

"Yes. It was very strong. Your feelings certainly came through in your words."

"How so?" she asked. The dolphins performed a simultaneous hoop-jump to the delight of the noisy crowd.

"I found it intriguing. How you empathized with how dolphins might react being in a pool. Personally, it was hard for me to consider, but your writing was quite remarkable."

She placed her hand on her heart. "Thank you so much, Mr. Yamamoto. That means a lot to me."

Kaito remembered the faint floral scent of her perfume from yesterday along with her sincere acceptance of his well-meant praise.

A loud drumroll filled the stadium as Rodney threw a hula hoop high into the air. "There she goes to the bottom," he announced. The dolphin dove. "Come on, Sparky! Show 'em your stuff. How high can you go?"

Amy started clapping to a 'go-go' beat as the audience picked up the chant, egging the dolphin on.

Sparky exploded out of the water some twenty feet in the air. She dove and through the hoop before it began to descend.

"Pretty amazing," Elizabeth said loudly to Kaito among the crowd's roar.

Kaito nodded. "Yes, good height and accuracy. Nothing like the style my Manami would display." He paused. "She'd do a double twist before she entered the hoop." He smiled at Elizabeth, looking for her reaction. "But it's not all about physical abilities. You would see the amazing connection between her and me."

"You miss her, don't you?"

He nodded, conceding.

"I can tell you really love your dolphin," she said, dropping her voice as their eyes met.

Kaito couldn't help but think about when he first started training Manami. "I would not where I am in my career, if I didn't have her."

Elizabeth listened intently, her eyes never wavering from his.

"I'd probably be a fisherman in Kushimoto like my *otosan*. In a way, Manami saved me. It was she who took my early interest in dolphins to a much higher level. Ever since I was a child, I was fascinated with the dolphin, always knew they were special. When Manami and I began working together, I got to know the animal close-up I…I guess you could say…" he glanced at Elizabeth. "We bonded."

"Please, go on," Elizabeth encouraged him.

Kaito noticed she had more interest in talking than watching the show. "Well, Manami's probably very lonely right now. She's stuck in her holding tank and refusing to perform with any other trainer. Wondering where I am and when we can perform again together."

Kaito saw Elizabeth's eyes beginning to tear up with emotion, seemingly changing color. "That's so beautiful, but so sad," she offered. "You'll be seeing her soon, though." Taking a deep breath, she added, "Funny, I was saved by a dolphin too, but never knew its name."

"Really? Tell me about it," he said, focusing on her, ignoring the dolphins.

"I get embarrassed sometimes telling the full story because most people don't believe it. But my connection with dolphins was also in my childhood. Five years old, actually. One day, when I was floating on an inflated ring in Santa Monica Bay, a shark circled me in shallow waters. I can only remember being scared by people screaming. My mom and dad rushed out to get me."

"After they yelled at me and argued about who was at fault, my mother said I was saved by a dolphin who scared away a shark. I didn't actually see the dolphin, but I felt it in the swirl of water under me."

"I remember my mother telling me I had a guardian angel, one with fins instead of wings. From that day on, dolphins have watched over me, keeping me out of trouble. I owe my life to them. I felt it is my responsibility to protect them in return." She looked at Kaito. "Sorry if I sound sort of corny."

Kaito was blown away by her story. So similar to his experience and belief in the dolphin's extraordinary intelligence. Maybe his dolphin was more motivational, her's more spiritual, but definitely the mainspring in both of our lives.

"I do believe every word of it," he said, eyes sparkling. "Especially what it meant to you. History is ripe with dolphins rescuing humans since the time of ancient Greeks. You're a living example of their friendship for another species."

Following their interchange, the pair sat quietly watching the dolphins perform their routine. Pokey, Sparky, and Cookie perfectly executed their somersaults, spins, and jumps, always ending with a token herring thrown from a bucket.

Elizabeth broke the silence. "Thank you, Kaito…I mean Mr. Yamamoto. I am touched that you would listen and understand. I did not expect…" She paused. "I really like hearing you speak openly. I hope my essay didn't offend you."

He looked away from the stadium action and met her eyes. "I don't think you meant harm. I admire your sincerity. I know you have a deep respect and love for them." He looked to the floor, embarrassed that he spoke so freely. *What changed?* He shrugged. *Why am I…I don't know. Guess I'm not as reserved as most Japanese men. At least when I'm not in Japan.*

"Well, I'm glad you're here and sharing with me. Makes me wonder. Could I ask how you honestly feel about dolphins being captured for human entertainment?"

The crowd roared as Pokey flipped Amy off her back, propelling her high in the air.

Kaito was thrown off-balance, torn between the push of her questions and the pull of her passion for dolphins. He looked at her, then at the audience. "Are you asking that as a reporter? I'm here representing OceanWorld management, but they don't necessarily represent me."

"Good question. I'm not sure myself. I guess I'm seeing a different person than I originally met. How about if we keep your own beliefs separate from OceanWorld's? Kind of, off the record?"

"Fair enough. Miss Worthington."

"Elizabeth, please."

He smiled. "Miss Elizabeth. Please, I have different views from management, and I want more education in the acts, but they keep resisting." He narrowed his eyes. "You know, in Japan, authority must always be respected."

"I gathered that. I suppose they feel that by describing the animal's true nature and abilities in the wild would make customers think they should not be confined to a pool. All of which could affect attendance."

"Exactly."

She leaned in. "You know you could leverage your value to them."

"Leverage? I don't understand the term."

"It means you add a lot to their bottom line. Probably have more influence than you know. If you'd let me, I could help you with that. You know I worked summers on the 'Snorkel with Dolphins' boat tours out of Dana Point and learned how to teach customers about dolphins in the wild. I have many ideas on that. I also have a minor in education along with my journalism degree. I could help you."

"That's very kind of you. Maybe someday, some way I could take you up on that, but I should explain something."

"Please do."

Cheers rang out from the crowd. Rodney stood on the backs of two dolphins, holding reins and whooping like a cowboy as they swam. "Ooooh!" The audience cried as he slipped and fell into the water.

"Look at that," Elizabeth said. "Maybe the dolphins didn't like being treated like horses."

"You know, Elizabeth, I am not who you think I am. I sort of fell into the job as a dolphin trainer. Before I was a trainer, I studied at university specializing in cetacean behavior while I played water polo." He lowered his voice. "When I had to leave the university, OceanWorld was just starting up and they found me. I couldn't go back to my home in Kushimoto, so I took the job." He scratched his head. "Not what I planned."

"What had you planned?" she asked.

"I wanted to become a scientist to understand dolphins as equal species," he answered, even though he knew he didn't have the credentials. "Make research breakthroughs."

"What kind of breakthroughs?"

"Decoding their language. Finding ways to communicate with them."

"Is that still your dream?"

He sighed. "That's what's funny about coming to America. Up until yesterday, I had forgotten that. Caught up in my job. I lost focus, lost my dream. Now, I'm serious about it again."

"Maybe you *can* follow it."

"Yes. I just need more time and space to pursue it."

"Ladies and gentlemen and all lovers of dolphins," Rodney announced. "Are you ready for our grand finale? Please put on your ponchos."

Those in the front rows dug out their ponchos. Children squealed. Elizabeth struggled to get her poncho on. Reaching behind her back, he helped her arm into the sleeve noticing her full, shapely body compared to the mostly trim Japanese women. He quickly looked away before she could see him redden from embarrassment.

"There they go!" Amy yelled as the dolphins circled the pool at top speed. Carly Simon's hit record blared over the speakers and the audience stood and swayed back and forth singing, "Anticipation…Anticipation…is driving me crazy."

The dolphins leaped before the turn and landed, one at a time, in front of the stands, splashing the first four rows of fans, much to their delight.

Laughing while they took off their ponchos, Elizabeth's bangs dripping, Kaito's spiked hair flattened, Elizabeth spoke, "That was fun. Do you do that at your show?"

"Yes, we do, and I have the dolphins come back and laugh and wave goodbye to the crowd."

"I'd love someday to see you and Manami work together and educate your audience at the same time," she said. "In the States, we call it edutainment. Also, I'd like to know more about what your plans were for research."

"Only just started," he said. "You mentioned yesterday U.S. research on dolphin communications."

"Yeah, well, here's an example of how research can run amuck. Science can abuse animals even more than entertainment does."

Drawing back, Kaito asked, "How so?"

"There was this one major study conducted by the U.S. government in secret for many years, the details of which are now just trickling out."

Kaito raised an eyebrow.

51

"It was run by a Dr. John Lilly, and it involved a young woman volunteer, Margaret, who agreed to live twenty-four hours a day in a tank with a juvenile dolphin named Peter. She slept, ate and lived with Peter in the water. Her goal was to become like a mother to the juvenile male and begin to form a language between them."

"Incredible," Kaito interjected.

"Yeah. Amazingly, the dolphin started mimicking the sounds and cadence of her voice, at least as much as a dolphin's voice box could. The woman loved all animals and through the months became very close to Peter to the point of forming a bond. As Peter matured, he rubbed his body up against hers for comfort and attention and she would pet him."

Elizabeth abruptly stopped talking and fixed her eyes on Kaito's. "You sure you want to hear the rest?"

"Yes," he said, his brows narrowing.

"But it got out of hand as the lonely dolphin tried to mate with Margaret." Elizabeth took a deep breath and blew it out. "Innocently, she relieved his urges."

"Oh, no!" Kaito cried out. "And they let that continue? Horrible."

"I knew you'd be repulsed by it, but it didn't end there. At the same time, in the sixties, there were other studies being done on psychedelic drugs. They fed Peter LSD and the dolphin repeatedly rammed himself into the walls of the tank. He eventually died."

Kaito seethed. "That is immoral, shameful work."

"Yes, and that gives you an idea why I have come to hate any form of abuse, especially misguided use of animals as tools. I might add, I am relieved that you would never conduct such an experiment."

A rotund, uniformed man, carrying a mop and bucket, stood in front of them and barked, "The show is over, folks and we need to close the gate. Can you…"

"Of course," Elizabeth said, and they stood to leave. "Want to get a coke or something? I'd love to talk more with you." She looked into his face. "Maybe a brighter subject, okay?"

"Yes, that would be good. I do have some time before I head to the airport."

They walked through the park until they saw the huge open jaws and triangular shaped teeth of the Shark Snack Shack. They sat down at a manta ray shaped table and Elizabeth offered to get their drinks.

Pulling out a straw from her tall glass, she asked, "So, Mr. Yamamoto, besides your shows, what do you do for fun?"

"My shows run seven days a week. Working with the dolphins is my fun. I do not have time to play." He stirred his drink thinking about his single-focus life. "How about you, Miss Worthington?"

"Similar in a way; since my job requires a lot of secondhand research on marine life, I'm currently focusing on interviewing experts on whales and dolphins. Other than that, I'm dealing with my family back home in California. How about your family?"

"My *otosan* lives in Kushimoto, a tiny fishing village, and my mom lives in Osaka."

"Hmm, brothers or sisters?"

Not wanting to talk about his sister, Etsuko, he answered, "One sister, Etsuko. How about your family?"

"Huh," she scoffed. "What's left of it is a bit messy. My mom is in an alcoholic rehab facility, divorced from my emotionally absent father. And my sister, Crissy, continues to abuse drugs after she tried to commit suicide."

Kaito offered a sad smile, thinking how open Americans are to sharing their family secrets. His family problems seemed minor compared to hers. "Sorry to hear that. You do not have to tell me these things."

"No. It helps to talk it out. Crissy tried to drown herself off the Malibu Pier. She was only sixteen and was really messed up." Elizabeth spoke slowly as if to calm herself. "It was about drugs, boys, and our parents—they were going through a divorce at the time. Crissy and I were very close."

A mother and child skipped by in front of them. A blow-up dolphin bobbled in the breeze behind the little girl. Elizabeth gave a slight smile. "Do you mind, Mr. Yamamoto, me going on like this?"

Kaito had never experienced such an open outpouring of emotions by anyone, let alone a stranger. Americans seemed to speak the way they felt, unlike himself who resisted talking about how his own sister had both suffered and caused great pain. He wanted to reach his hand out and comfort Elizabeth but felt it improper. He swirled the almost-melted ice cubes in his drink. "Please go on—if you feel you need to."

She took a drink.

"I was lost for a while," she swiped her cheeks, "But I was always clean."

Kaito stared at her in confusion.

"Oh, I mean I never took drugs. And don't drink alcohol. The consequences are too real and scary for me." She chuckled and held her drink toward Kaito. "But you know, we've got our dolphins, don't we?"

Kaito lifted his glass, thinking that's all he had. "Kampai!" He clinked her glass. "You are right, we do."

They drank and Kaito asked, "So, Elizabeth, you told me about that childhood incident with your guardian angel dolphin, what else interested you about them?"

Elizabeth's eyes brightened. "Our dolphins are easier to talk about, thanks for changing the subject." She twirled her straw between her fingers. "Well, like a lot of kids my age, I got hooked on the Flipper TV series, read everything I could about dolphins."

"Ah, yes," Kaito interjected, "That TV show did much to promote live dolphin shows around the world."

Elizabeth continued, "Later, I won a writing contest about them. In high school, I mentioned I worked summers on that dolphin and whale watching tour boat, where I snorkeled eye-to-eye with many bottlenose dolphins. But most of my learning about them came from later hanging out at SeaWorld San Diego, where I met Greg, a guy who worked at the dolphin show. That's why I was initially attracted to him. We went out for over a year."

"Could I ask where you went?"

Elizabeth gave him a strange look. "Ah! We went out, I mean, we dated for over a year. Sorry, American expression."

"I see." Kaito narrowed his brow. "Are you…?"

"No longer. He was a fake. I found out he abused the dolphins. I confronted him. Learned first-hand he was also a brute."

"A mean man?" Kaito asked.

She hesitated for a moment, then answered, "Yes, and he hurt me. My guardian angel, who first led me to him, now told me to let him go."

Kaito's jaw lowered. "I am sorry for you." He waited for her to regain her composure. "Could I ask if…?"

"They fired him?" She nodded. "Yes, and not long after that I learned of Dick O'Meery's change of heart and his fight against capturing dolphins. He became my hero."

"Who was he?" Kaito asked.

"He was a top dolphin trainer right here at Miami Seaquarium." She waved her hand over the park. "And for the Flipper shows. One of the dolphins he trained was Kathy, who after years of show and TV work, they retired her, isolated in a small pool where she committed suicide in Dick's arms." Elizabeth closed her eyes and turned her head away.

"Are you alright?"

She swiped her face of tears and said, "Kathy's heart was shattered, and she lost the will to live and let go of her breathing."

Kaito swallowed hard and coughed. "We...we do know dolphins have to consciously decide when to breathe, but how can we know it is suicide?"

She glared at him. "I just know."

"Okay," he said, shuffling in his seat. "But you should know, we do not abuse our animals at OceanWorld."

"I believe you believe that." She shook her head. "Only thing is, there are different kinds and levels of abuse."

Kaito's hands turned clammy. Did she suspect that he had captured Manami to make her into a show dolphin?

Elizabeth pushed away from the table, scraping her chair noisily on the floor. "I am sorry. Best we do not get into that again." She picked up her cup. "I'm going to get a refill. Can I get you one?"

"No, thank you," he said stiffly and stood with her. He wanted to explain his feelings about Manami. *What was I supposed to do? The fishermen kill and slaughter for meat all those not captured for shows. She lives now. She gives joy to thousands.*

He lowered his head in shame, thinking of the irony in his choice to give his dolphin the name Manami, meaning 'for the love of the sea'.

Elizabeth returned and sat. "Please, Kaito, I didn't mean to suggest that you were an abuser." She reached across the table. "I understand where you were in your life, back then..." She placed her hand over his.

He jerked back his hand and stiffened.

She brought her hands to her face. "I'm sorry, I didn't mean to..."

His head began to itch but he caught himself before digging his fingers into his scalp. *Why did I show such a physical reaction to her concern? What must she think? I'm emotionally underdeveloped? A cold, unfeeling man? Maybe homosexual?*

She bit her lip and continued to stare into his face. "I didn't know—"

Kaito could not find the words to explain.

"Sorry for getting carried away," she said. "Maybe it's something like Japanese reticence. Jousting with my American arrogance." She smiled and let out a small chuckle. "Maybe just a clash of cultures."

"Yes, some of that, but with me…I have difficulty expressing my personal beliefs."

"And I express mine too emotionally."

The Tiki harbor foghorn moaned in the distance and they both looked at their watches.

"I only have fifteen minutes or so before I must get a taxi. I need to make my flight to San Francisco, then to Tokyo."

"Sure, I understand, but before you go, I have a confession to make." She sucked down a breath. "I lied."

He narrowed his eyes.

"I didn't just happen to meet you at the show. I came to find you to ask for your help."

"Oh." He breathed a sigh of relief that she hadn't lied about something more sinister. "Go ahead, ask. You were helpful to me."

"I wonder if I might see you in Japan in a few months?"

"You're going to Japan? What would you be doing there?"

"Researching a new feature series on dolphin and whale hunting in your country."

He glared at her, thinking she would stir up controversy for him and his countrymen.

"You gave me a glimpse and some appreciation of your different cultural traditions. Many Americans feel your dolphin harvesting trade and 'research whaling' are wrong. So, I want to learn more. Write a broader and more balanced story."

Skeptical, he replied, "Your goal is good, but that would be a real challenge."

She straightened her shoulders. "Maybe I can meet it. Look at your success. With my American will, there's a way."

"I like your optimism, but there are cultural barriers."

"I know, but you can help me get around them. Open doors."

"To where?"

"Taiji gulf, for example." She held her pencil in the air. "You know it well, where most of the dolphins today are…"

He interrupted her. "Yes, and I know these dolphin fishermen. They are my friends, my people. Fishing is their way of life. Their livelihoods. They would not look favorably upon an American who pokes her nose into their business."

"I know, but as an insider, you can get me leads, interviews."

"You should understand big picture, Elizabeth. Japan is an island nation, surrounded by water. No vast prairies for cattle. We've gotten most of our protein from the seas for centuries and…"

Elizabeth interrupted him. "Yes, that's what makes the story interesting. However, they've only been recently harvesting dolphins for shows. Maybe they could harvest something else for food."

Frustrated with her brashness, he scoffed and said, "There's a history too. My *otosan* would say, 'They beat us at war, but can't beat our traditions out of us.' And your Greenpeace movement has already tried to shame Japan and other countries for doing what they have for centuries."

"I'm sorry, Kaito, but isn't there room for enlightenment and policy change at the highest levels? You could help with that."

"How so?"

"Look, you're famous and very influential in your country, and you told me you knew fisheries deputy minister, Nakayama."

Kaito winced, then shook his head. The memory of Nakayama's treachery still pained him. "That's the problem, I know him too well. He's a bad guy. A corrupt politician and a scientist."

"Okay, but you can help me find a way to get around him. You're a scientist. Maybe we'd all like to learn the facts surrounding Japanese whaling?"

"I am not a scientist. Only a showman," he raised his voice. "Maybe I once was. Dreamed to be. But I am just a showman." He waved his hand in the air. "Owing all my success to a dolphin."

Elizabeth drew back. "You won't help me, then?"

"Maybe…maybe I would if I could." He furiously rubbed his head. "But it is a foolish errand. I can't believe your editor would give you this assignment in Japan."

Elizabeth stared at him, her silence somehow louder than the stadium when it was filled with families and honeymooners.

"Even if you got interviews, no respectable journal would cover or translate your stories for publication." *How might it hurt my fishing friends, my father, my country? And my career?*

Elizabeth lowered her head, still not speaking.

"Miss Worthington, I do respect what you are trying to do, and I don't disagree with many of your motivations and beliefs." He gave her a half-smile, worried how his quotes could hurt him.

She looked up.

"Please, Elizabeth, it's not personal, but I think you need to write stories somewhere beyond our seas."

Her eyes welled up. Finally, she spoke, "The seas connect all of us, including those who call it home."

His voice wasn't so harsh. "Listen, I've got my shows seven days a week and Manami."

"So, there's no place in your heart…" she caught herself. "No place in your schedule to help me?"

He glanced at his watch, "No." He stood at the table. "Thank you, Elizabeth, but excuse me, I need to get taxi."

She stood and extended her hand. "Thank you, Mr. Yamamoto. Goodbye and have a good flight."

He didn't look back.

#

Kaito watched a young American couple holding hands and kissing on the lips as he sat waiting for the announcement to board the plane. Something one would rarely see in Japan, even Tokyo. He wondered what Elizabeth thought of him when he pulled his hand away from hers.

They were so different. So far apart in their cultures. He had opened up to this woman in only two days, more than he ever had to another person. And it wasn't just because he thought he'd never see her again. Her honest sharing inspired him to do the same. Sure, he was physically attracted to her full body, her mysterious eyes and glowing hair. He liked her independent character. Unlike most submissive Japanese women, she was more like his mother.

That's what really appealed to him. Not that it mattered. He'd never see her again. Besides, how could anyone ever understand someone so daring, so dripping with emotion…so American?

Chapter Seven
Malibu, California

A day later

After a long flight and thus, a sleepless night, Liz was in no mood to tax herself with meetings, but that's what her job and her family required. *Shit, girl, get off your ass and get it done.* The top priority, of course, was to meet with her editor to present plans for the feature series she dubbed: "Oceans of Abuse: Japan at the Vortex." Catherine wasn't available until four that afternoon, so she first needed to clear her head before she could pitch her way to Tokyo. She'd never be able to make the deal and make that trip until she dealt with what would be left behind in Malibu.

Liz twirled the pencil between her fingers, jotting down her agenda as she spoke. "Okay, I'll go first to Malibu to see Mom at ten, sneak in a jog at the beach before meeting Dad in Santa Monica for lunch. Later, I'll catch up with Rhonda in Malibu before heading up the canyon road to Thousand Oaks and the *Mother Ocean* offices." She closed her date book, drank her third cup of coffee for breakfast and headed out the door.

When she pulled her baby-blue VW Beetle up to the ocean view and columned façade of the Changing Times Treatment Center, she hesitated. The sight of it made the acid in her stomach rise and burn the back of her throat. Entering her mother's lavish stateroom, she knew what to expect from Maggie O'Leary, the red-headed Irish American scrapper from South Side Chicago. In a moment, she would soon bound out of her corner of the patio and start, 'Swinging'. No hellos, no hugs, only her rapid-fire jabs and parries from a bitter and beaten woman.

"Where've you been?" she snarled, wiping her mouth. "It's about time you visited your mother."

"I'm here Mom, been away on assignment. How've you been?"

"Stuck in this hellhole your father put me in. How do you think I've been?" Her angry voice turned pleading. "You gotta get me out of here, Lizzie. I'm not an alcoholic."

Elizabeth stood, looking into her mother's now tragic green eyes—the same color she inherited, but without that pain. She backed up to the patio rail and withstood her mother's pummeling anger and desperation until Maggie was spent and broke down, exhausted.

Holding her and sobbing together on the couch, Elizabeth became deadened by a burden of hopelessness. This being the fourth rehab center in over three years, Elizabeth was also exhausted. She was the only one carrying this emotional load on her shoulders. Her sister, Crissy, had walked away from her, from Mom, to soak in her own vices. She relapsed twice as often as their mother. Elizabeth could count on her as much as she could count on their father, who was only good for paying the bills.

Over the years, it became increasingly difficult to sympathize with the treatment her mother received from her negligent father. Elizabeth wondered how much longer she could continue caring for her mother.

Afterwards, Elizabeth had a meeting with Dr. Schmitz who reminded her that until her mom takes the first step of the twelve and admits she has a problem, therapy won't really help. He also suggested she may have a much deeper problem.

Elizabeth sought clarification. "Like what, doctor?"

"She might have suffered abuse as a child and that causes her to drown out the emotional hurt."

"Really?" Elizabeth asked. "Something back in her childhood is still affecting her?"

"Could well be," he said, taking on a professorial demeanor. "Those early childhood years—how a child attaches to their mother and father—plays a critical role in social and emotional development. And, because it often gets repressed, can affect future generations."

Elizabeth shrugged her shoulders. "Don't we all just have to grow up?"

"In part, but with sensitive kids...take your sister, for example. I've watched her over the years, and I think her risky behavior may have been caused by the lack of attention and love in her childhood."

"Well, that could be for her. I don't drink alcohol or take drugs. I don't believe in that Freudian gobbledygook."

"It's more than therapy-speak Elizabeth, and I'm not suggesting anything, but drug abuse or sexual promiscuity are only some of the ways adults deal with it. One can become obsessed with anything and repress it, putting up walls to keep from getting hurt again."

"Yeah, well, it's too complicated for me. Maybe you'll get there with Mom someday." She glanced at her watch. "I can only do so much, Doctor Schmitz. I need to look out for myself too."

"Please do that, Elizabeth. These things can erupt in many ways, sometimes much later in life."

Averting his eyes, Elizabeth gave him a polite smile. "Thanks for helping and we'll stay in touch, okay?"

By the time Elizabeth got back in her car, she was wasted and drove home under a dense layer of sea fog.

She sped to her place in the Tahitian Terrace mobile home park and changed into her jogging clothes. As her feet pounded into the wet sand along the shore, she vowed to figure out a way to move beyond all the pollution suffocating her life in LA and breathe freely.

It was noon when she returned home. No time for a shower. She grabbed a nylon windbreaker and drove with equal dread to Santa Monica to meet her dad. When she got to the iconic 1921 Pacific Dining Car restaurant and opened the door, the vested, bow-tied host grimaced at her athletic attire.

"Are you in the right place, sweetheart?"

"I'm joining my father, Leland Worthington."

"Oh, excuse me, Miss Worthington, I'll direct you to him."

There, in the middle of a green velvet-tufted banquette, sat her celebrity divorce attorney father. Dressed as usual in his ivy-league, three-piece linen suit, club tie tight to his starched shirt collar, he looked up from his half-rimmed glasses. An awkward smile erupted off his handsome jawline—one that Elizabeth and her sister inherited.

He glared at her outfit. "You knew we were dining here, right?"

She looked down at her sweats. "Sure. I was out for a jog. Do I smell?"

"That's my Lizzy," he grunted.

"Hardly," she said and plopped down, thinking he seemed his usual, condescending self—but perhaps a bit lonely? She changed her tone. "How have you been, Father?"

"Oh, all right, I guess," he answered, fiddling with the menu on the table.

"How's Vyma?" she asked, picturing the blonde Swedish bimbo that he callously brought to the hospital the day Crissy tried committing suicide.

"Gone," he said, staring out the window. Then, he added, "She took off with her hairy Latin co-star from *Creature of the Fjord.*"

"That's too bad," Elizabeth said, wanting to tell him he'd find another girlfriend. His clients were always trading them in for a newer model.

Fidgeting a bit, he asked, "How're things with that guy you were hot to trot with? Greg, was it?"

She scoffed, realizing it'd been over a year since she last saw her father at Grandmother's funeral. "Dad, I left that asshole long ago. He was more the *physical* abuser type." She watched for his reaction.

"Oh," he grunted sheepishly. "So, what are you doing with your life these days? Still trying to be a writer?"

"I am a writer," she said, narrowing her eyes. Her hands clutched the side of the table as she braced to leave.

"I remember," he chuckled. "You won that little contest about Dauphine the dolphin. I always thought you had more going for you than your boy-crazy sister. Even if it was writing about..." he curled his lip. "Those daffy dolphins."

"Yes, and I still am, Father," she answered, holding back her bitterness. "Better than writing about double-dealing humans." She glared at him. "Look. I'm proud of it. I've turned my talent and love for cetaceans it into a full-time job." She waited. *Would he say anything more?*

"Oh," he said. "Whales too."

"Yeah. Investigative reporter for *Mother Ocean* magazine and I'm onto a big story to put public pressure on the Japanese government to stop dolphin and whale hunting."

"Well, that's certainly a step above the trash your mother wrote."

"Thanks, Dad. You could be more supportive, you know." She huffed and stood up. "I'm going to the restroom."

After splashing her face and refocusing, Elizabeth dried off and marched back to the table. The waiter had just set down a drink.

Leland was lifting his glass, checking out the clarity. "They have some pretty good twenty-year old single malt scotch here. Want a drink?"

"Nope. I don't drink, remember?" She said, thinking how she learned *not* to drink.

"Right. So why did you call this meeting?"

"Mom."

"I figured that. Suppose she wants a better rehab facility, one with her own wet bar."

"Not funny, Dad. She's real sick."

"Yeah, her own doing."

Elizabeth's jaw clenched and she wanted to scream that he had everything to do with it, including Crissy's drug addiction. Instead, she said, "Dad, let's not relive the past."

He took another sip.

She leaned in. "Dr. Schmitz says your continued support could provide a breakthrough in her treatment."

"Look, Lizzy. I'm tired of paying an arm and a leg for her treatments." He shrugged. "And for what?"

"A breakthrough, Dad. Dr. Schmitz explained that booze might not be her only problem. There may be something underlying it. He said she may have suffered abuse as a child. Do you know anything about that?"

"Sure, but that's water under the bridge. Her father was a drunk too. Beat her on occasion."

Elizabeth lowered her eyes to the table.

"I sort of rescued Maggie. Got her out of town. What's the difference? She's a drunk now."

"Dad. That's not showing much compassion. Dr. Schmitz thinks an approach borrowed from the Minnesota Hazelden treatment program combined with acupuncture and more talk therapy might work. Can you just stay with the program a while longer?"

He slammed his glass on the table. "A while longer? Pay for her to get sober so she can continue writing her nasty gossip column about my clients? Have her slobber all over me to take her back? No fucking way in hell!"

Elizabeth drew back and shook her head at him. "Thanks, Dad, for all your support." She stood. "I've got a meeting with my editor, then I'll be off to Tokyo."

"That's it? You sound bitter like your mother."

Stunned, she glared at him, then said, "Goodbye, Father." And left.

Peeling out of the parking lot, Elizabeth tried to let go of her father's continued neglect, and worried that without his funding, Mom would never get well. But she had things to do, so she headed back to her trailer park home. After changing into a business suit, she was back on the Pacific Coast

Highway. The afternoon sun sparkled on the ocean and lifted her spirits. She was excited to share the launch of her new career with her old friend, Rhonda.

Passing the Malibu Pier, she down shifted to catch the entrance to what was once the Malibu Movie Colony. There, hidden behind a bank of tall Italian cypress trees—planted to muffle traffic noise from the highway—was her mostly unhappy, childhood home. She pulled the Beetle into the porte couchere, as her mother insisted, she call the carport, and found the pool covered and the once-trimmed topiaries overgrown.

She stepped out of the car and stood motionless in front of the heavily carved, Spanish Colonial door. She had closed that door for the last time two years ago, only a few days after her mom lit her bedspread on fire with a cigarette and went into detox at her first rehab center. *I don't live here anymore,* she reminded herself.

Rhonda wouldn't arrive for another twenty minutes, so she entered the vacant house alone, knowing more of its ghosts could haunt her. But with the promise of a new career ahead of her, she felt confident she could leave the past behind.

Entering the hallway, she froze. As clear as the day it had happened, she pictured her mother lying crumbled on the tile floor, telephone in hand and sobbing. Elizabeth stood shuddering as she recalled the moment they'd heard Crissy had attempted suicide.

Flicking on the lights, she shook off that memory, and scooted past the Waterford sconces into the high-ceiling great room. She leaned against the staircase banister, feeling the spider webs laced between the wrought iron rails. She drew back when she saw a black bug lurking, waiting to capture its prey. *Could she, once again, be trapped in Malibu? Or were the webs in her own mind trapping her?*

On the second floor, she peeked into the hall bath and remembered how it had become her sanctuary when the fighting became too much. She stood next to the clawfoot tub, running her fingers along the rim. She considered all the times she laid there, soaking while her mom and dad screamed at each other, how she'd practice holding her breath and keeping her eyes open underwater. Surfacing only to gulp air, she'd look up at the stained-glass window of the dolphin with his black jewel eye. She'd smile at the image of him, leaping from a sea of blues against a fiery sunset, escaping to cavort along with the other sea creatures: a green turtle, purple starfish, and an opalescent seagull.

A knock echoed around the deserted room, and she scrambled down the stairs to open the door.

"Rhonda," Elizabeth squealed, opening the door. "I'm so glad you came."

They hugged and swayed in place, the same way they had ever since middle school. Elizabeth could feel her friend's protruding belly, and she pulled back. "Looks like the happy mother all over again."

"Yeah," she patted her stomach. "A brother for little Arnie. My life's all about the kids these days." She ogled Liz. "But look at you. Haven't seen you since graduation. Now you're the perfect professional in your business suit, and I see a sparkle in your eyes."

"You do?"

"Yeah. Like you found a man or something. Maybe on your Miami trip?"

"Not really. It must be my new job and excitement about following a big story lead in Tokyo."

"Japan? Are you talking about our Little Tokyo in DTLA?"

"No, I mean Tokyo as in *Japan.*"

"Why would you go there when you've got it all here in Malibu?"

"Hah," she scoffed. "Except for you, mostly headaches."

"Story potential, then," Rhonda offered. "You always were a single-minded writer."

"Yes, come sit."

They sat at the long mahogany dinner table, in the same seats she and Crissy used to sit at and caught up on their lives. Rhonda was living with her husband, Jimmy, in his parents' guest house; she, caring for two-year-old Arnie and taking art classes while Jimmy worked construction when he wasn't surfing.

"I know it's not an exciting life," said Rhonda. "But Jimmy's a good husband and father, and you know, not too many worries. Tell me what you've been doing since you graduated. USC?"

"Well. As you know, I'd been freelancing with *Freep* and *Advocate* tabloids and did some occasional on-air reporting with *KTLA*. But the full-time job at *Mother Ocean* magazine has been my dream."

"Environmental, right? Protecting dolphins and whales?"

Elizabeth laughed. "That's it. You know me so well."

"I wanna hear all about it, okay?" Rhonda asked. "But first, how's your mom?"

"Still in rehab," Elizabeth answered flatly. "Demanding as ever."

Rhonda shook her head. "I know, it's always been hard. How's Crissy? She find a man yet?"

Elizabeth's palms started to sweat. She removed her jacket. "I don't know."

"You don't know?" Rhonda asked, her eyebrow arched.

"Not really. She's been up in San Francisco. I saw her a couple of months ago…" Liz didn't want to say she went to bail her out of jail. "When we last spoke, she said she was working in a coffee shop. I've been trying to reach her."

"Is she doing okay though? You know, after her…" Rhonda hesitated and glanced at Elizabeth.

Baffled by the questions about her sister, Elizabeth replied, "You mean her latest bout with drugs, the attempted suicide or the botched abortion?" Lizzy's voice raised and cracked. "Crissy's all fucked up, Rhon."

Rhonda grabbed hold of both of Lizzy's trembling hands. "Geez, Liz, I didn't know about the abortion. You mean she can't have kids?"

"No, I don't think so," Liz said, getting more frustrated by the never-ending attention on her popular older sister.

"It's really sad about her, isn't it? When we were in middle school and she was in high school, Crissy was every girl's idol, the coolest role model ever. All the boys loved her. She was so fun and beautiful." She focused her eyes on Lizzy, offering a sad smile. "Like you."

Lizzy scoffed and feigned a smile, thinking of her early experiences with boys.

"But you," Rhonda continued. "You never stayed with any of the boys you went out with."

Why was it always about Crissy? Elizabeth asked herself, sick of living in her shadow. "No, I didn't, and I can thank Crissy for that."

Rhonda scrunched her eyebrows. "What do you mean?"

"Jesus H. Christ, Rhonda!" she growled. "Crissy was a fucking whore. Wanted to get laid by every boy she dated. That's why she was so popular."

Rhonda bolted; eyes fixed wide. "Geez, Liz, I didn't think you—"

Elizabeth pressed her palms into her forehead, throbbing with guilt and anger. "Rhon." She paused. "I love my sister. At least we had each other. But look. We dealt with boys differently."

"You sure did," said Rhonda. "You never really dated much."

"I did at first," Liz said, biting her lip. "When boys started asking me out, they assumed I would be like Crissy and good for an easy fuck. Including that prick, Frank Carlini, who tried to rape me."

"Really?" Rhonda said. "You never told me."

Liz closed her eyes for a moment, then said, "I was numb. Stayed numb until—"

"Until." Rhonda nodded and looked at Liz. "We went to SeaWorld San Diego, and you got hooked on dolphins and that hunk Gregorio."

Elizabeth winced, hoping she wouldn't bring up Greg.

"Sorry, Lizzy. I know it hurts. You fell hard for him. Seemed like you two were the perfect pair. Falling deeply in love. You know, because of your mutual interest and—"

"You got that right, Rhon. My guardian angel with fins brought me right to him." She nodded. "Then failed me." Elizabeth put her fingers to her throat, still able to feel the hurt. How he put his massive hands around her neck and shook her until she went limp and almost blacked out. *Let it go, Lizzy.*

Rhonda looked at Liz as she tried to stifle the quiver in her chin, then spoke up. "I can see you're still bitter about that man."

Liz nodded. "About all men, I'm afraid."

Rhonda reached over the table and patted Liz's hand. "I'm sorry, Liz."

Liz patted her hand. "And I'm sorry for dumping my anger on you, but I'm having a hard letting it go."

"That's okay," Rhonda said. "But your goal-oriented, smart and successful, I don't want you to become a one-dimensional writer that never finds a partner."

Liz frantically twisted the ends of her hair, thinking she'll never find what's wrong with herself, either. She blurted out, "Not every woman can find, or has to have a faithful husband, or a family, Rhonda."

Rhonda averted her eyes.

Liz sighed. *There you go again, Lizzie. Showing your lack of feelings.* "Sorry, Rhon. I guess I'm just envious of what you have. That's all."

"I understand," she responded. "Jimmy and me may not have much, or even ambition or potential, but having each other is everything."

Liz let out a breath. "Please don't misunderstand me. I think I say these things when I feel envious and closed out. I'm just thankful you're always there to listen to my troubles. But please know I am so happy for you being lucky in love like that."

Rhonda looked caringly at her old best friend. "You can be cynical at times, but you'll find someone again. I just hate to see you build a shell around the hurt in your heart to keep you from finding a man. I saw how happy and in love you once were with Greg, even though it didn't work out."

Liz lowered her head, thinking she could only give back to a man what she didn't have.

Rhonda reached over and patted her hand. "Look, it doesn't mean you can't find it with the right guy. I don't think I was crazy when I saw that glint in your eyes again."

"Hah," Liz laughed. "Must be too many Hollywood romance flicks."

"Maybe you'll find someone in Tokyo. Someone you can be vulnerable with again. No holding back. Love and be loved. That's what I believe, and I want that for you, Lizzy."

Elizabeth reached over and hugged her. "Thank you, Rhon. You've got such a big heart and maybe some of it will rub off on me." She caught a glimpse of her watch. "Oh shit, I'm already late. I gotta go."

At the door, she had to give Rhonda a quick goodbye hug. "Good luck with the baby, and thanks." She cried out and waved.

After she left, Elizabeth ran upstairs to pee. Sitting on the toilet across from the tub, feeling badly about how she treated her old friend, she considered how much she needed to get out of Malibu. Looking into the bathtub, she recalled how Crissy's suicide had affected her:

She remembered what happened that day after they had left the hospital and returned home. She kept wondering how long Crissy held her breath for as the tide took her. Was it possible to drown on purpose?

Tears merged with the bathwater that evening as she vowed to find out.

She opened her mouth. Forced herself to draw water into her throat and nostrils.

One heartbeat. Then another.

Her body convulsed.

She draped herself over the curved side of the tub. She retched on the terrazzo floor; her sinuses and esophagus burned; eyes teared anew.

Distraught from her experiment, she yowled, sobbing until the water chilled.

Elizabeth buried her head in her hands but refused to cry. *God, I'm so tired of all this.* She looked up at the stained-glass dolphin wondering where her guardian angel was now, and whispered, "Let me find the strength."

#

Pulling into the parking lot designated for *Mother Ocean* staff, Elizabeth took a few minutes to close her eyes, clear her head of worries, and psych herself up for a productive meeting with her editor.

She ran up the stairs to her editor's office. Elizabeth took a big breath and knocked. Catherine Dawson, one of the original 'Greenies' from the Seattle protests to save the Orcas, rushed to hug Elizabeth. She said, "You look tired, my dear." She squinted her eyes and wrinkled her nose at Elizabeth. "A bit of jet lag? Traffic? No. More than that. Troubles with your mom?"

"No, she's fine, Cath. Thanks for asking. Your first guess was spot on. I didn't sleep well last night."

"Yah, big story and all. Glad you're back. Let me make you a cup of chamomile tea. Sit." Pouring hot water from an electric pot behind her desk, she asked, "Were you able to corner that Yamamoto guy at Seaquarium?"

Elizabeth squeezed her teabag around a spoon. "Yes, I spent over an hour with him after we watched a dolphin show."

"Did you get what you wanted from him?"

"I did," she answered, "But what I learned is only the start of a much bigger story—a series, actually."

"You said that when we talked on the phone."

"Yes, and I believe *Mother Ocean* would be limiting itself if we just kept writing about how these growing amusement parks use and abuse dolphins and whales. We need to uncover the source of the problem. That source is Japan, Inc. We need to infiltrate the government, a sort of cabal, I believe, that allows and promotes the hunting and capture of cetaceans." Elizabeth hesitated for a moment to see if Catherine was still engaged.

"Go ahead," Catherine waved her on. "I can see you're on a roll."

"Right. Most of the dolphins being harvested for shows worldwide come from one harbor in Japan—Taiji. The bulk of whale hunting today is done by the Japanese under the guise of *research*." She drew quote marks in the air. "We need to dig deeply into a culture that influences the government policies and makes them hide the truth. Exposes them to the world." She looked to Catherine for support. "The kind of expose that gets a segment on Sixty Minutes. Maybe even puts pressure on Washington to try and force Japan to stop the whaling."

"Okay, I get your thrust..." she sat back..."but we're just a small environmental publication, not a television news program."

"Start small, think big." She smiled. "Make a name for yourself."

"Maybe, but how would you go about getting that?"

Elizabeth raised her tone of voice. "By going to Japan."

"Wow. How would you gain access to these people and places?"

"By having an insider."

"You mean, Yamamoto?"

"Yes. This guy is a huge celebrity in Japan, like a rockstar. He has the power and influence to grease the skids for me and expose them all. He even went to college with the interior minister in charge of fisheries, Nakayama. And I believe Yamamoto can get me an interview with him."

"You're kidding me, commune with the devil?"

"Not at all. I don't see him as the enemy. I really think I can schmooze him to get on the inside."

"You can trust him?"

"I wouldn't call it trust." Elizabeth fiddled with her notes. "Kaito...I mean, Yamamoto is a very..." she hesitated. "He's a very thoughtful man. He had a humble upbringing as a fisherman. And believe it or not, he loves the ocean and its creatures as much as you and I do. We understand each other, and I believe I can leverage that."

"Whoa," Catherine jumped in, "You sound like you kind of *like* this guy?"

"You mean as in attracted to him?" she asked, admitting to herself she did admire his character.

"It was just your tone of voice," Catherine said. "It made me think you had a thing for him."

Elizabeth chuckled, avoiding eye contact. "No way. You know me better than that."

"Sorry, for a while there you didn't sound like the woman who had sworn off men."

Elizabeth turned pale. "Don't worry, Cath." She dropped her voice to almost a whisper. "I think he's gay."

"Why would you say that?"

"Oh, I don't know," she said as her mind swirled around words to describe the tugs on her heart. "Never really knew anybody gay, but he was so timid and empathetic. Certainly not like any man I know."

"Ah, being a homosexual might account for why you feel so comfortable around him."

Elizabeth stayed deep in thought, having no good explanation for his neutral sexuality nor his soft demeanor that somehow faintly touched her heart. "Maybe," she murmured, thinking she could trust him.

Catherine tapped her pencil on the desk. "So, practically speaking, has he actually agreed to help?"

"Well...not exactly, but my gut tells me he would."

Catherine twirled her pencil in the air. "Well, even if he would help, and to me, that's still a big if, how long would you stay?"

"I'd need a month."

"That would be an expensive investment for our small travel and living budget, and we can't even be sure of the payoff. Besides, we'd be losing you for the period and not covering all the future stories we promised our U.S. readers, remember?" She looked at Liz for understanding. "There's the growing climate-change influence on sea levels, DDT dumping in coastal waters, wastewater spills, plastic litter consumption by fish and mammals, container ship propeller kills of whales, U.S. Navy sonic testing injuring cetacean echolocation abilities...the list goes on."

"I know, but Cath, isn't *Mother Ocean* about all our oceans, especially the big Pacific, shared by half of our world? Don't we state that in our magazine's mission statement?"

She nodded. "It is. You're right, but we just don't have the resources or staff with you missing to accomplish that mission now. I'm afraid unless that lottery ticket I bought this morning at Seven Eleven wins the jackpot, I'm going to have to say no."

Elizabeth held back her tears. What she was asking was unrealistic, but she couldn't let it go. With her voice cracking, she asked, "If...if we could get the money, would it be possible?"

"Maybe, but I don't have a way right now and the risk is high." She looked at Liz. "Lizzy, I don't want to give you false hope, so unless you're able to find a way, let's get cracking on next month's issue with a small piece on Florida's dolphin shows, okay?"

Elizabeth didn't trust herself to speak, and instead only stared at the seascape watercolor hanging on the wall behind Catherine's desk, thinking of the ocean she yearned to cross.

Her editor finally spoke again. "Hey, Liz. You need to get home and rest this weekend. We'll pick this up on Monday, okay?"

#

As the shower water washed away Elizabeth's tears, she wondered what had happened to her guardian angel. Wasn't he supposed to not just protect her from others, but protect her from herself?

She shut off the water. *It's best that my shitty trailer home doesn't have a bathtub. I'd probably drown myself.*

She dried her hair, put on pajamas, and sat down in front of the tv. She muted the sound on the African wildlife program and opened up a paper container of Chinese food she'd picked up on the way home. Unable to enjoy the cold Chow Mein, she grabbed a pad and pencil and began to ideate.

At the top of the page, she wrote four W's and an H, the journalist's standard acrostic for writing a story. She didn't bother with filling in the Who, Where and When, but under the What, she wrote: Find the money and the way to write stories from Tokyo. Under the How, she wrote down savings, borrow, and Dad.

She came back to the why and stumbled on it. Was the why only going for the story? Or was it the who? Was it Yamamoto? Maybe she mistook his Japanese humility as homosexuality. Or was he only masking his masculinity? He didn't show an interest in me except for what I had to say about dolphins.

Though he did seem to dwell upon my eyes. Was I truly getting at the why? Did I really hope he wasn't gay?

Tapping her pencil on the pad, she remembered a favorite college reading assignment, Mark Twain's *Letters from the Sandwich Islands*, his breakthrough publishing success. *Why not letters from Japan?* A tinge of hope told her that there may be a way to make it happen. She did have the whole weekend to work it out.

After much doodling and scratching, she focused on the people of her day: Mom, Dad, Rhonda, Cath. Then, Crissy popped up.

"Shit!" she yelled out. *I need to go to San Francisco tomorrow. I need to find her. Can't put it off any longer. No one else is going to help her.*

The phone rang. "Miss Worthington. Doctor Schmitz here, sorry to bother you."

"Yes," she answered in a faint voice.

"It's your mom. She's left the facility three to four hours ago, and we can't find her. The sheriff's department is searching the roads, checking the local bars in case she's looking for a drink. Last time she escaped, it set her back badly. Maybe you could come out and be there for her, calm her when we find her."

She let out a long breath. "Yes, thank you, doctor. I'll be there right away. Goodbye."

Out the door, Elizabeth swore, "God dammit Mom! You told me I had a guardian angel, not that I had to be yours. How am I ever going to be able to follow my dreams?"

Chapter Eight
OceanWorld Dolphin Amphitheater

Tokyo, Japan

Though he was exhausted from his trip and the long overnight flight from America, Kaito rushed to reunite with his favorite dolphin. Walking past the holding tanks, hours before the park opened, he was thrilled to hear Manami's distinctive *heeaakk-yip* call, followed by her lively head splashing. *Heeaakk* was her name for him, the *yip* part and splashing at the end meant she was looking for him to come to her.

When he heard her, his heart burst with joy, drowning out the sadness he felt for having left her. "I'm here, my sea-princess," he called back, and she immediately responded with the *heeaakk,* adding a guttural, *gll...gll...gll.* She slapped her tail, telling him she knew he was back—and she was happy.

Quickly changing into his bathing suit, Kaito grabbed a bucket from the refrigerator and opened the gate of her tank. Manami shot into the stadium pool, eyed Kaito standing at the edge and dove deep. In seconds, she soared high into the air, executing her famous quadruple somersault—Kaito's favorite.

Tossing a handful of herring into the pool, Kaito jumped in feet first. Manami ignored the fish and floundered to him, nudging his hand for a nose rub. "Good girl." Kaito hugged her head.

Manami let out a chain of clicks, grunts, giggles and chirps, ending in a slow, deep-in-the-belly moan. What was she saying? Feeling? It was unusual for her to hold this still for a hug. *For me to want to.*

Was she expressing her comfort, safety, belonging? Maybe something like the feelings he had when his *okaasan* held him as a child. Embracing her cool wet head, nothing soft and warm, he experienced a deep connection. What did she need? *What was I needing?*

He shuddered and let go of her head. He remembered Elizabeth's telling of that woman sleeping with the dolphin in a tank in that scandalous U.S. research.

At that same moment, Manami shook her powerful front quarters back and forth, sending Kaito's body thrashing into the water.

Manami steadied herself and fixed her lively blue eyes on his dark, now sullen, eyes and waited for a command. He gestured toward the sinking fish. "Go eat."

Within seconds, the dolphin echolocated the fish scattered at the bottom and gobbled them up on the way back up. *"Cho...cho,"* Manami uttered.

"No, no," Kaito responded, pointing to the empty bleachers above the pool. Laughing, he shook his finger at her bobbling snout. "Too early for a show. What does Manami want?"

She raised her tail and head into the air. *"Kay...kay...kay,"* she chattered.

"Ah, you want to play," he answered, clapping his hands. "Let's race." He flipped over into a fast backstroke.

Manami chirped up a storm and dove directly underneath him. She rose again, did a backflip over him, hit the water, rotated, and continued to jump over Kaito as he swam. Each time she was airborne, she babbled an incoherent series of clicks, whistles, and squeaks as if to laugh at her master's slow progress in the water.

Kaito chuckled, thinking of his discussions with Elizabeth about the potential of one day developing a language between the species. Treading water and looking eye-to-eye with Manami, he told her, "I met someone in America."

Manami nodded and stayed at this side.

"Her name is Elizabeth, and she loves dolphins too. But in a different way. Thinks we could someday talk to each other." He put his hand under her chin. "Maybe you could meet her, and we could swim together. Would you like that, Princess?"

Not getting a response, he cursed to himself. *Kuso! You dumb ass, Elizabeth's on the other side of the Pacific Ocean!*

Manami dove, then surfaced and nudged his feet. She wanted to push him. He held his feet together and she notched her snout in-between his heels and propelled him like a jet ski over the surface. They rocketed across the pool, sending a wake in every direction.

Feeling the exhilarating ride, Kaito became distracted with his thoughts of Elizabeth. She was right. He was not Manami's mother and only provided a bit of what she needed in order to live a full life. And by taking her away from who and what she needed, he received the reward of money and feeling less lonely. *I have to change. Do something more.*

Kaito raised both hands in the air and yelled, "Stop! Let's play *ke ke.*" He gave the signal for "catch and fetch." Playing fetch gave her more exercise, and him a chance to relax.

Manami swam to the ramp at the edge of the pool, tail-swatted a ball into the water and dribbled it to Kaito. Tossing the ball across the pool, Kaito recalled his days playing water polo at the university. He could almost feel the blow to his groin inflicted by Katsu Nakayama.

The amphitheater flood lights flashed on.

"Good morning, Mr. Yamamoto," a voice called in Japanese from the stage. OceanWorld CEO, Yamaguchi, dressed in a suit for an early day in the office, waved for Kaito to come in.

Kaito whistled for Manami to return to her holding tank. On her way, Manami high-jumped and landed in front of the stage, splashing Yamaguchi from head to loafers.

"Damned animal," the CEO cursed.

"So sorry, sir," Kaito said, climbing out of the pool. "She's pretty rambunctious this morning."

"Get her under control, Yamamoto," he said, shaking water off his jacket. "She needs discipline for our shows." He turned to leave. "Meet me in my office ASAP."

"Yes, sir," Kaito bowed, holding back from laughing at the CEO's drooping trousers. Manami didn't like him either.

After changing back into a suit and tie in his private office bathroom, Kaito noticed a voice message blinking on his answering machine and played it.

"Hello, Kaito. It's Mrs. Madori. I have not seen your *otosan* for three days now. I tried to give him your message that you would be out of the country for three days, but he didn't answer the door. His lights are on, but I cannot see him from the windows. Let me know what you want me to do."

His father had done this before. Went into a state of depression. Kaito stood with his hands on his hips, breathing deeply to calm himself.

He quickly called her back. "Thank you, Mrs. Midori. Yes, I know. Father is only threatening *seppuku* again. No, Mrs. Midori, he won't do it. But I will come as soon as I can get away. Thank you for calling."

Yet, the threat could be real. He almost took his life over his daughter and wife leaving him but held onto the honor Kaito bestowed on the family. He would have to make another trip to Kushimoto.

Kaito pushed the play button again. "Hello Mr. Yamamoto, this is Michael Stickle from the American Association of Marine Parks, calling to thank you again for your inspiring presentation in Miami and inviting you to come back soon. We are very keen on you helping SeaWorld in a more direct way on-site. You'll be hearing from us soon."

As soon as Kaito hung up the phone, the intercom light blinked. "Yes, Mr. Yamaguchi," Kaito answered, tightening his necktie, "I'm on my way."

Entering the penthouse floor of the OceanWorld administration building, Kaito girded himself in preparation for another rejection.

"Enter!" Yamaguchi shouted behind his office door. Kaito saw his secretary's desk was empty.

Yamaguchi had the power office—two-hundred eighty degrees of glass giving him a view of the entire park.

Kaito bowed from the waist. "So sorry about Manami's splashing, sir," Kaito said, rising up to face the man's stern military demeanor, complete with an almost shaved head.

The CEO waved it off, "We've got bigger issues. Sit."

Kaito sat, worrying about how he was going to broach the need for time off to develop a new educational program.

"Congratulations, Yamamoto, on a superior job in America."

Surprised, Kaito smiled. "The association president called me yesterday thanking us for a new partnership between our two countries. There's more. After the *Miami Herald* did a story on the conference, the *Wall Street Journal* interviewed Minister Nakayama and the newspaper is writing a feature story on pan-Pacific business opportunities. Nakayama called me last night to thank me."

Kaito grimaced. "So, Yamamoto, how are we going to leverage this opportunity?"

Leverage, the same word Elizabeth used to encourage him to utilize his success to broaden his dolphin show offerings. "Sir, that is all very good, and I am proud to do my part. What I was hoping for is your support to develop a new feature of our shows. One that we can share with the Americans."

78

"Perfect!" the CEO intoned. "I was thinking we could create a cowboy and Indian rodeo act. You know, riding the dolphins around the ring." The CEO leaned forward. "What do you think?"

Kaito scratched his head. "I don't know about that, sir."

"Well, I pay you to know. Do I also have to remind you to get back to Taiji and pick up some new babies and devise some new acts?"

Although the CEO's words cut deeper than his father's bamboo rod, Kaito's trip to America had changed him. He braced himself. "I need some weeks off from shows to design and perfect a student-centered dolphin education program."

Yamaguchi scowled. "That's not what I mean. We've been over this before."

Kaito tightened his jaw. "I will deliver for you and our audiences. I will create shows that make more money."

The CEO stood straight and rigid, like the marine major he was during the war. "Don't be impudent, Yamamoto."

Kaito needed time to devise a new program, to train, rehearse and produce it. How could he move his boss to bend? "Sir, to remain here at OceanWorld, I respectfully ask for the opportunity to show you what we can do with educational programs."

The CEO pounded his fist on the table. "No! Absolutely not. We're not an educational organization, we're in the entertainment business."

"Sir, per our contract, I am granted time off for serious family matters. I need to take care of my ill and aging *otosan*."

Yamaguchi sighed and sat down. "Not again?"

"Yes, sir. You remember he was a victim of the nuclear fallout and suffers from radiation sickness. It is my duty to help him. I need to leave for Kushimoto in the morning."

Yamaguchi nodded, sighing. "Leave then to honor your father. You have one week."

Kushimoto, Wakayama Prefecture, Japan

Walking up the bamboo-lined lane to his childhood home, Kaito managed a smile when he saw his *otosan's* red fishing boots standing alongside the front door. He recalled flopping around in them, wanting to be like Ichiro

Yamamoto, chairman of the village fishing cooperative. How his little heart used to grow big with pride knowing his father's *yama ga li*—his legendary ability to know where to find fish and share that knowledge—made him so beloved and respected.

Kaito unlocked the door of their wood framed cottage with the key still found under the blue cloisonne flowerpot. His *okaasan's* always warming miso soup was no longer on the stove, and jazz on Etsuko's radio no longer filled the air. Entering the dark, musty-smelling house, Kaito rushed into his father's bedroom. There, under the familiar rope of glass fish net floats, was his father on the futon. He approached hesitantly—was he dead? Kaito held his breath, fearing that his father had committed *seppuku*.

A soft snore rose from under the arm that almost covered his face, the other arm dangled to the floor. The scar from the radiation burns to his father's head still haunted Kaito. He exhaled, when realizing he had been holding his breath. He regretted returning to Kushimoto. He feared the net of his father's (*ie*) authority—as traditional Japanese head of household—would capture and drag him under again.

Now that he had seen for himself that his father was alive, Kaito used the time to explore the house. A visit to his *okaasan* would come later.

The center room, where the family ate their meals and watched TV, looked exactly how it used to; the kitchen was neat and clean with everything put away except for one unwashed teacup in the sink. As he peeked into his sister's former room from the doorway, he imagined Etsuko sobbing on her bed.

"Why are you crying, Sister?"

"It's Father again. He cares more about his family's honor than he does about his family."

"What did he do?"

"He can't understand how I want to have a *renai kekkon* with Horito."

Kaito recalled seeing Etsuko meeting with Horito in secret, how he held her in his arms, and they gazed into each other's eyes.

She'd dropped her head. "A marriage for love," she'd said with a sob.

"Father won't let you marry Horito?"

She'd dabbed her eyes with her sleeve. "No. He says that's the evil American way. I must marry a boy he chooses."

"Why?"

"That's all he knows. His *giri* feelings of duty are more important than my *ninjo* feelings of love. His marriage was arranged."

"You mean, he doesn't love Mother?"

"Maybe," she said. "As long as she doesn't dishonor him."

It bothered him a lot, but he shook it off as a distant memory. Stepping into his room, he found the poster of Albert Einstein still hanging on the wall. He appreciated that his mom had bought it to give her son inspiration to become a great scientist, but Einstein's hair and mustache mostly made him laugh.

Looking down at his empty futon, Kaito pictured himself at ten years old, sitting there and crying. Etsuko, hair in an American style flip came in, chomping on *chuingamu*. She'd entered his room and rubbed his shoulders.

"Did Father beat you again?" she'd asked.

"Not that. It's the girls poking fun at me." He choked back a sob.

"They don't want to play with me. The girls call me *ebi kiddo*. I hate them."

"They call you little shrimp? They're teasing. Maybe they are jealous of you because you are so much smarter—a little shrimp with a big brain." She'd giggle, trying to make him laugh.

"They put their hands behind their ears, like this—" He demonstrated. "And they flap them and tell me to go jump in the ocean."

They both began to laugh.

"Your ears aren't so big, Kaito," she'd said, giving him a hug. "When you're older, you'll grow up to be a handsome, world-renowned scientist and all the girls will love you."

"Huh," Kaito had scoffed at the comment.

Shaking off the memory, Kaito went to see if his *otosan* was awake. Finding Ichiro still asleep, he sighed and opened the door to the wardrobe that stood next to the bed. He was drawn to what used to be his *okaasan's* side and slowly pulled the top drawer open, its emptiness reminding him of her stark departure. He tried the second drawer, which creaked as he pulled, but Father didn't wake. Finding a folded winter blanket, he lifted it. Underneath, a riot of red hibiscus flowers burst out of the green palms of a fabric remnant, and he smiled.

He touched it, recalling the joy on his mother's face when she sewed. How proud she was to have won productivity awards during the war for sewing uniforms. During the occupation, she made floral Hawaiian shirts for the GIs in the country. She not only loved doing it, but it provided extra income for when Father couldn't fish, and it paid for the English tutor and science textbooks she bought for Kaito. Her husband never knew. She was good at sewing and even better at keeping secrets.

He knelt and gently rubbed his father's shoulder. "Father, it's me, Kaito. Wake up."

Ichiro twitched and mumbled, "There's the yardarm. Grab the rope, Kaito."

"Father, Father. We're not on the boat, we're home now. Wake up."

His *otosan* sat up, rubbed his eyes. "We made it. Good boy, Kaito." He put his calloused hands on his son's shoulders. When he held him, Kaito no longer felt his power, only his need.

"Oh, you're on break from the university."

"No Father, I'm with OceanWorld now, running the dolphin shows, remember?"

"Of course," his father acknowledged, rapidly shaking his head. "You never did tell me why you left the university."

"It doesn't matter," Kaito lied. "I'm happy at OceanWorld. But tell me, Father, why didn't you answer the door when Mrs. Midori knocked, and what's this talk about ending your life?"

"She's a nosy body," he growled.

"Maybe, but she's a good neighbor. Took in poor Juro when he contracted that horrible Minimata disease."

"That is true," his father acknowledged. "But none of this is about ending my life, it's about ending the dishonor. First Etsuko left me, then your *okaasan* deserted. If you leave me, there's nothing left. Nothing to live for."

"*Otosan*," Kaito said, reaching over and patting his arm. "I care about you."

Ichiro looked off into the distance, then lowered his head.

It was sad for Kaito to see a person bury the truth of his past, but he still wanted to forgive his father. "I'm sorry for disappointing you, Father, but you lost your boat and your health. I had to move on. It was not meant to be."

Tears fell down Ichiro's scarred, weather-beaten face without even a sigh.

"Look at me, Father. You taught me everything I know and love about the ocean and its creatures. I couldn't be where I am without you."

Ichiro almost smiled. "Yes, you were a loyal first mate as a young lad. Remember when *Yoshi Maru* was being tossed about like a cork in ten-meter swells? You swam under the boat to cut free a net that had snarled the propeller. You showed great courage then."

Kaito said, "I like to think I inherited your *yamma ga li*, which guided me on when and where to go after university."

"Your success has given me honor. The neighbors talk of you. See you on TV." He became more animated. "Mrs. Midori told me you went to America. I heard her shout through the door. What did you do there?"

"I shared my expertise of dolphin shows in Miami and they were inspired by my work. Met some intelligent and sincere people."

"Don't ever trust them!" Ichiro scolded. "You were there after they radiated me, destroyed our fishing fleet, and we never got one word of apology."

"Father, it's been thirty years since the war and occupation. Times and people are different."

"Don't believe anything they tell you." Anger burst from the veins in his neck.

Kaito wanted to tell him how he met this one woman with good qualities but knew that it would only enrage him. "Don't worry, I am always cautious." He stood and extended his hand. "Let's go and have some tea."

Drinking chamomile to calm Ichiro's nerves and green to bolster his own, Kaito sat cross-legged on the low table next to his father. "Let me tell you of my new plans for OceanWorld."

"Of course," said Ichiro, "Maybe someday I would see your show."

"I want education built into the entertainment, so the audience can learn more about our dolphins. I want the audience to see films explaining their natural intelligence in the wild. You know how they fish for food, raise their young." Kaito paused, waiting for his father's reaction.

Ichiro set down his cup. "You've always loved dolphins, and are a smart boy, but I hope it's not crazy talking dolphin stuff."

Kaito poured more tea. Now was not the time to speak to his father about Manami.

Ichiro added, "Do the owners of OceanWorld want to add education?"

Hearing his father's truth about Yamaguchi's reaction, Kaito's teacup fell out of his hands, clattering and spilling on the table. Wiping it up, he muttered, "Not exactly."

"You mean you're wishing it so, and they're not in favor of it?"

"I'm working on it."

"Are you disrespecting their authority? Remember what I told you? *Deru kui wa utareru*—the nail that sticks out gets hammered down."

Kaito cursed under his breath as he went to the sink. Here we go again, the lecture about *ie,* the absolute rule of the father. How his duty was to care for his family as he chose, and his honor allowed.

"If they told you no," Ichiro continued. "You must honor that."

Kaito squeezed the wet towel with all his strength. He did the same thing when under the rule of his *otosan*'s bamboo rod. Familiar words that kept beating Kaito down, creating scars that healed on the surface, but never stopped hurting.

"Son, you must always listen to me. Do what I tell you. Always respect me and your elders."

Kaito spun around and shouted, "Father, the only thing I respected was the rod. You're the one who had no respect, no love for your family." Kaito stood, looking down at him. "You traded Etsuko's life like a basket of fish. You snuffed out our *okaasan's* spirit with your stubborn pride. I won't be part of your *ie* world any longer!"

Without looking for his *otosan's* reaction, Kaito walked toward the door and picked up his overnight bag. "I'm catching the late train to Osaka. Goodbye, Father."

On the train to Osaka

As the train swayed and clacked from Kushimoto to Osaka, Kaito considered, *could a son both love and hate his father?* Passing the black pines of Wakayama, he recalled the first time he took this train to Tokyo University, following a dream of his own, not his father's. Sure, back then, he was nervous about his abilities, but now his confidence was broken. He hadn't achieved any progress on devising an educational component to OceanWorld's dolphin shows, let alone research on dolphin language, and it all seemed hopeless now.

He realized his father's harsh, doubting words were due to holding onto his past, but that didn't make things any better. Father was against him pursuing a formal education until he realized his voice no longer mattered, which added to his bitterness.

After a brief nap, Kaito woke to the train slowing into the Osaka station. It was already past midnight.

The taxi dropped him off at building 82D. This was the home of Sakura Silk Design Studios, GK. He punched in the door combination his *okaasan* had given him. The door swung open. Noriko's arms reached out with her familiar radiant smile. How bright it shone from her light crème complexion, framed by her long, gray-streaked black hair.

"My Kaito," she said as they embraced.

She seemed smaller than Kaito remembered, but still, he could feel the same support she gave him as a child. He was now supposed to be the caregiver of his elderly parents—a mother who didn't need much care, a father who threw caring back in his face. Noriko was a strong, independent woman that he deeply admired and wanted so to be like.

"So good to see you again, Son, but you look tired." She tugged his arm. "Come, let me make us some tea."

"It's not too late for you, Mother?"

"Huh. Look," she waved her hand over dozens of busy night-shift workers at their humming sewing-machines.

Kaito gave the workers a shy wave. "What happened to the design studio?"

"Come," she answered, laughing proudly. "That's on the second floor next to my apartment."

Surrounded by fabric wall hangings of dancing cats, geometric fans, Koi ponds, and massive chrysanthemum blossoms, they drank Shincha tea. "The best, this time of year," she said. "Are you hungry?"

"No," he nodded and sipped.

"So, you visited your father." She frowned, "I can see the hurt in your eyes."

"That bad, huh?" He shook his head. "Better to see the joy in *yours*. The business must be doing well."

"Incredibly well, Kaito. We're about to ship a big order of floral prairie dresses to Gunne Sax in New York."

She put a finger to her delicate chin. Kaito admired how his mother had struck out on her own and had great success—a path he wanted to follow.

She put her hand on his knee and looked hard into his eyes. "How about you?"

When she touched him, he not only felt hope he could follow in her footsteps, but that she knew what was holding him back. She was always one to go directly to the crux of his issues. "Talk to me, Son. What's going on?"

"Same sort of crap with Father. Telling Mrs. Midori he wanted to commit *seppuku* and all. I can't help the man anymore."

"I know all about it," she responded. "You need to let go of trying. Get some space and get on with your own life. How are things at OceanWorld? And how was your trip to America?"

Kaito took a long breath and sighed. "Big picture. I need to convince the boss to introduce education into the programs, but he's against it."

"Is that part of your big dream?"

"Yes."

"What's holding you back?"

Kaito thought for a long time. "That I can't do it."

"You mean it's impossible? Hard? Or maybe you shouldn't or won't let yourself?"

Kaito rubbed his head, hoping his mother would show him the way. "I don't know," he said. "I'm confused. I'm alone. Unsure of myself."

"Did you ask yourself what I used to tell you?"

"Yeah, *use your mind, but follow your heart*. Problem is that my heart's all messed up. Doesn't know what it needs."

"Go on," she prodded.

"Well. I met this woman in Florida, she made me doubt what I was doing with my life and at the same time inspired me to do what I always wanted to."

"Hmm," his mother muttered. "Are you attracted to her?"

"You mean do I like her?" He looked into her eyes. "You know I've always been afraid of girls, never dated in college, never had an interest in marriage."

She nodded. "But this girl?"

"I...I guess I was, but what difference would that make? Not like I could, you know...she's an American after all. An ocean away."

"No matter, Kaito. I've been working with Americans for thirty years. At their core, they are the same as us. That shouldn't—"

"Maybe, but I...I can't trust..." he hesitated, searching for the words. He couldn't help but think how much his mother's independence was like Elizabeth's.

Noriko asked, "Her or yourself?"

Hoping she would provide the answer, he said, "I'm trying, Mother, but I don't have the strength that you have. Or even Etsuko had—she acted out of her true feelings." His mother slumped.

Seeing her sadness at the mention of her daughter's name, he asked, "Have you heard anything?"

His mother shook her head for several moments before speaking. "Not since she went to Okinawa. But the agency I hired to find her; said she was never there."

"Sorry, Mother," he said as her sadness filled his heart.

"But you know, it's not just about physically leaving your *otosan* like we did, you have to distance him from your heart."

"Let me get some more tea," Kaito said, heading into the kitchen.

Returning with the teapot, he said, "You know, Mother, I've never met a girl that had strength like you. At OceanWorld, despite how girls scream over me, it's all about work and the dolphins and this silly dream of mine. I could never see myself with…"

Noriko watched as he opened up. "Look, Son, you may not know the strength you have within you right now, but I know you have the courage to find it."

A sigh of relief came over Kaito. He recalled his father's recent words about the courage he had to cut the net from the propeller. *Yama Ga Li? Maybe he did inherit something from his father—a sense of when and where to cast the net.*

"It could be," his mother added, "That you could use some help in finding your way. Maybe you need an ally."

A knock came to the glass door.

Noriko waved the woman in. "Yes, Tomiko."

A tall, thin woman wearing an apron entered and spoke, "We've got the three dozen dresses finished and we're boxing them up now."

"Great, tell the girls to take the rest of the night and tomorrow off for a job well done."

"Sorry, Mother. It's two-thirty a.m. and you're trying to run a business."

"No problem. You're trying to run a life. But I do have to catch an early flight for Paris, we have a booth at the annual textile show. I'm glad you came when you did so I didn't miss you. How about we both catch a little sleep, yes? I've got a bed made up for you in a spare bedroom."

"Sure."

Noriko put her hands on his cheeks and said, "I probably won't see you in the morning, but remember, I know you can succeed." She kissed his forehead and showed him to his room.

Lying in bed, unable to sleep, Kaito wondered if he could follow his own heart.

Chapter Nine
Five Months Later, 1976

OceanWorld East, Kakogawa, Japan

"We can do this, girl," Kaito said to himself and Manami before the drumroll started, and the announcer presented him. "Once we've hooked the audience on the action, we'll educate them."

"Ladies and gentlemen, boys and girls," blared the loudspeaker. "Get ready for a spectacular show of skill and brains between human and animal. Please welcome our first Acqua-bat, Kaiaaaa-to Yamamowww-to!" The spotlight traveled across the crowded amphitheater and shone on Kaiito.

"Kaito! Kaito!" the audience chanted.

Kaito whispered, "Come on, Manami. This is our chance to make something great."

The high stage curtain unfurled. Kaito stepped out onto the diving board, wearing a red cape and a high headdress of yellow mina bird feathers. Squeals and cheers rung out from the audience. Kaito raised his hands high in the air and a huge neon billboard lit up in Japanese and English:

Presenting the Amazing Aqua-bats! Kaito and Manami!

On the edge of the board, Kaito removed his headdress and cape and threw them into the pool. He stretched back his arms, jumped and sprang off the board, rotated into a somersault and slipped silently into the water. Manami, lurking below the surface of the pool, blasted out of the water wearing the headdress and cape tied to her body. The crowd gasped. Mid-air, she spun into a double somersault as the spotlight sparkled on her wet skin.

Kaito emerged below with open arms. All at once, the crowd inhaled. Manami landed with a huge splash in between his arms, and they hugged. The audience went wild.

He untied Manami's costume and jumped on her back, holding onto her dorsal fin. They rocketed across the surface of the pool. The galloping theme music from *The Lone Ranger* blared over the loudspeaker. At the other end, Kaito got off and waited as Manami dove. Under the water, Manami locked her snout beneath Kaito's closed feet and lifted him high in the air as he stood, balanced on her nose.

The crowd cheered as her powerful fluke pushed Kaito across the pool. The dolphin turned and flipped Kaito high in the air. He backflipped before hitting the water. Manami dove, then soared twenty feet in the air, twisting her body before she landed at Kaito's side.

Kaito and Manami faced each other and 'talked' through dolphin clicks, squeaks, and nods. "Remember, the new routine," Kaito told her. "Our futures depend on it."

Kaito pointed to the far end of the pool, then at Manami, then at himself, challenging her to a race across the pool.

The announcer asked the crowd, "Do you want to see a race?"

The regulars in the stands began chanting: *"Resu! Resu! Resu!"*

The spectators began counting: *"Ichi! Ni! San!"*

Man, and dolphin each pushed off, arms and legs, fins and flukes, propelling through the water.

Manami slashed through the water in a streak of silver and reached the other side in four seconds. She turned, watching and waiting for Kaito. The audience held up their dolphin dolls and chanted, *Ma-nami! Ma-nami!* The dolphin circled behind Kaito and goosed him with her nose. The crowd laughed. Feigning surprise, Kaito stopped swimming and turned to look at her. She sprayed jets of water in his face and cackled. The spectators roared.

Manami flapped her pectoral fins together and bowed.

"Do you think they want to play ball?" the announcer asked.

Both nodded as Kaito's stage assistant, Hokata, tossed a basketball into the water. Kaito lobbed it across the pool. Manami surfaced under, grabbed it between her jaws and flipped it back to Kaito. They played catch until Kaito pointed to a basketball hoop descending from the ceiling. He took a shot and missed. Manami recovered the ball and made a perfect basket to the delight of the crowd.

"Great skill, acqua-bats," the announcer said. "How about it, everyone? Do you want to see them dance?"

"Dansu! Dansu! Dansu!" the audience chanted.

Kaito and Manami faced each other and Kaito grabbed hold of both flippers. A Strauss waltz accompanied them as they glide and twirl up to the stadium stage. Kaito climbed up and was given a microphone. "Go ahead, Manami," he said. "Be a showoff."

The music picked up a beat with Abba's "Dancing Queen," and Manami sliced the water's surface like a blade, making an incredible series of leaps, dives, and backflips, and twisted and power-tailed across the pool. The audience oohed and aahed.

Manami returned to the stage, yipping and clicking. Kaito threw her a fish and asked, "Oh, you saw a bit of litter at the bottom, did you?"

Manami nodded.

"Manami has been a big help collecting trash dropped or blown into the pool," Kaito announced. "That's a reminder to all of us to not let plastic bags and straws find their way into the ocean. Sadly, they can be digested by fish and mammals which can kill them. Let's all join Manami in keeping our planet clean and green."

Hearing only polite clapping worried Kaito.

"How does Manami collect the trash?" Kaito asked the audience. "Through something called echolocation. Like a bat, she emits a sound wave and when it bounces back, she will be able to hear and see what it is. A school of fish for supper or a shark wanting to make her into a supper. Would Manami's friends like to see how she does it?"

Applause and cheering filled the stands.

"Great," Kaito said. "I'm going to send my assistant Hokata around the pool with a white bag full of seashells. I want you to show him where to drop the bag in the pool." He pointed to Hokata. "Go ahead, find a good spot while I blindfold Manami."

The crowd pointed and yelled, "There, there. Drop it there."

Kaito commanded, "Go get the litter, Manami."

She circled the pool, dove, and held up the bag in her mouth.

Applause broke out and Kaito gave her a fish reward.

Manami chattered wildly and Kaito bent down to understand. "What's that? Say again? Oh, you'd like to meet some kids from the audience." Kaito looked into the stands. "Okay, let's see if we can get some volunteers. Who would like to come up to the stage and get to know Manami up close and personal?"

Raised hands and screams filled the stadium.

"Okay, good. Hokata will go through the audience and pick two and check with their parents." As Kaito scanned the crowd, he saw a tall woman with reddish hair in the front row, reminding him of Elizabeth. *Can't be. Just another tourist.*

Two children rushed to the stage. "Hello, kids," Kaito said with a handshake. "What are your names and how old are each of you?"

"Daiko. I'm twelve," said the boy.

"Hi. I'm Gimka and I'm ten."

"Good to meet you. Manami is thirteen and many dolphins can live to be as old as fifty. Gimka, would you like to shake Manami's flipper?"

Hesitating for a moment, she extended her hand, and they shook. The crowd clapped.

"Your turn, Daiko." More applause.

"Good job, kids. Now, would you like to feed Manami?"

Manami yelped loudly, opening and closing her mouth.

"Here's a fish," Kaito said, handing them to each. "Great. Now, looking into her mouth, how many teeth do you think she has?"

"One hundred?" Daiko guessed.

"You're very close, Daiko. She actually has one hundred and eighteen teeth. Did you know that dolphins don't use their teeth to chew food?" Kaito caught a glance of the now silent audience and swallowed hard with worry. "Well, they only use their teeth to catch food, which they swallow whole." Was the quiet crowd interested or bored? "Ready, Gimka? You give it to her first."

Manami gulped it down and squeaked. The crowd cheered.

"Your turn, Daiko."

"Great job, kids. Now you know Manami loves you." *So far so good*, Kaito considered, wondering if CEO Yamaguchi would think so. He was convinced Elizabeth would be. "Who would like to give her a belly rub now?"

They both nodded.

Kaito gestured and Manami thrust herself up the ramp and turned over, squealing.

"You want to go first, Gimka?"

They both straddled the dolphin.

"Go ahead," Kaito said.

Manami giggled at their touch, and the crowd laughed.

"How does her skin feel?" Kaito asked, holding the mic toward them.

"Umm," Daiko contemplated. "A wet soccer ball, maybe?"

"Good. How about you, Gimka? You can rub harder."

Manami let out a whooping laugh-like sound.

"It's kind of spongy," the girl said.

"Yes, Gimka. That's a thick layer of blubber that keeps our warm-blooded fellow mammals comfortable in cold ocean waters. So, who wants to give Manami a goodbye hug?"

"I do," they said at the same time.

They hugged, and both Manami and the children giggled. Gimka finished with a kiss.

"Awww!" The audience clapped as the kids exited the stage.

"Thank you, kids." Kaito shook their hands. "Before our grand finale, can I ask everyone to please fill out the form you got with your tickets? Your family can sign up for a 'Close-up with a Dolphin' program held daily during the week. With a trainer at your side, you can have a great personal encounter with our aquatic friends." *I need sign-ups badly. Come on, dolphin lovers.*

"Now, is everybody ready for Manami's grand finale?"

"Iku! Iku!" The audience chanted.

"Great. Here's where everyone in the audience gets to play 'trainer'. Here are the steps: When I say, 'Manami, circle the pool', I need everybody to place their left hand near their waist and make a circle with your right hand like this." Kaito waved his arm.

"Can everybody do that now? That's great. Then, when I say 'jump', I want everybody to throw both hands in the air like this and jump. Are you ready?"

"Okay, Manami, are you ready to say goodbye to these wonderful guests?" She nodded and yipped.

He whispered to her, "Make it work, Princess." Then, he commanded, "Manami, circle the pool."

Manami dove and circled at full speed.

Just as she was about to round a corner, Kaito yelled, "Jump," and the crowd shouted back and jumped.

Manami flew high, landing right in front of the stands, splashing halfway up the bleachers. Everyone screamed with joy.

"Again," Kaito instructed. "Circle, circle. Ready, jump."

With impeccable timing, Manami splashed water over the Plexiglass panels.

"One more time. Circle and…jump."

The crowd went wild. "Thanks for coming," Kaito said, clapping and waving. The spectators waved goodbye and began to exit the stadium. Kaito nodded to Hokata. "Please gather up all the forms and bring them to me with a count."

Kaito remained on the stage, bowing as the customers left.

Walking toward the stage gate, the long-haired Caucasian woman from the stands gave an animated wave that could only be American.

Of course, it was Elizabeth.

There she was, standing at the gate, wearing a white turtleneck sweater and jeans, her hair in a ponytail.

Fumbling the lock, Kaito finally opened it and stood stiffly in his swimsuit.

"Well, look at you, Mr. Yamamoto," said Elizabeth, giving him the same coy smile from the first time they met.

"Miss Worthington. I can't imagine you'd ever just show up…" He stopped talking when he saw her eyes surveying his wet body from head to toe, her eyes stopping on his chest. His heart jumped and he took a deep breath.

She looked down at his narrow waist, at his torso covered by tight blue spandex.

When her eyes reached his bulging swimmer's thighs, Kaito looked down at himself. *She's staring at my body.* He flushed and said, "Hold on."

"No problem," she said. "Take your time."

"Hokata, throw me a towel, please." Kaito caught it and dried himself. Losing his balance while wiping his feet, he turned to mop his wet head.

She smiled. "Never saw your ears before, behind all that hair."

Kaito covered his blushing face with the towel, thinking she was even more bold than he remembered. *Probably trying to distract me before she questions the merits of dolphin shows.*

She extended her hand. "Good to see you again, Mr. Yamamoto."

He gave her hand one fast shake. "Yes, Elizabeth, you caught me at a bad time."

"Sorry if I'm intruding, but I wonder if we could catch up?"

"If you mean talk, I only have fifteen minutes before my next show." *Why didn't she make an appointment?* "We can go into my office."

He wrapped the towel around his waist.

"That's fine," she said. "Show me the way."

He guided her toward his office, then turned. "Can I get you a drink?"

"Sure."

"Hokata, make the lady an Arnold Palmer."

"You drink those here too? Thanks, but make it virgin."

"What?"

"No alcohol, remember?"

"Okay. Have a seat. Pardon me a moment. I'll be right back." He headed into the locker room.

Returning in a knee-length terrycloth robe, he sat across from her and asked, "So, how have you been?"

"Just fine. I can tell you've been fine too. Only need to watch your mastery in the show."

"Thank you. Can I ask what brings you to Tokyo?"

"You. Your show. Business."

Feeling increasingly uncomfortable, he started to cross his legs, but stopped, realizing he had on a bathrobe. "Ah…what did you think of the show?"

"Well, you already know I'm not in favor of any dolphin shows anywhere, but that Polynesian outfit was pretty wild. And your athleticism was amazing. I gotta say, you held that audience in your hands."

Kaito flushed with pride, but only smiled and nodded. "Our audience likes exotic themes. Likes to cheer in harmony." Sweeping his hand over his body, he added, "Management had that silly costume designed."

"I understand. It's entertainment. And, for what it's worth, the show was like you told me—more acrobatic. And a bit more intelligent than American dolphin shows."

"What did you think of Manami?" he asked eagerly.

"Like I expected her to be, incredible."

"How so?"

"Her skill and sense of people is far beyond anything I've ever seen."

Kaito smiled. "Thank you," he said, taking in a big breath.

"Yeah. You were so kind and respectful to your dolphin. You didn't treat her like a child, but more like an equal."

He smiled, feeling the pride Japanese men are not supposed to exhibit. "Manami is really the star of the show."

Her eyes sparkled. "You're too modest, Mr. Yamamoto. You looked so strong and in control out there—in your element. Not stuffed in a suit and tie. Not a macho man, either. Just…sort of…cool."

Kaito didn't know how to respond.

"There I go again," she said. "I'm sorry."

"So, Elizabeth, what I really want to know is, what did you think about the educational aspects of the show?"

"Well, it's a start. You sprinkled in a few facts here and there. From a marketing perspective, and judging by audience engagement and satisfaction, it was successful."

Kaito's insides churned. He glared at her. *Is that all she can say?*

"The kids were cute," she added.

Baka! He cursed to himself. How could this woman be beguiling, yet insensitive? She was the one who prodded me to use leverage to introduce education into my act.

"Yamamoto-san?" A knock at the door. "It's Hokata, sir. You've got five minutes to change for the next show and I've got bunch of sign-ups for the new dolphin close-up programs. I'll give you a count later."

"Thanks, Hokata." *I sure hope we have enough to satisfy Yamaguchi.*

"Sorry, Elizabeth, but I'll have to leave you shortly. You never did tell me what your business is here in Japan."

"You know, what I was working on before. Research on Japanese whale and dolphin hunting."

Kaito furrowed his brow. "You will get nowhere with that here. Did your editor actually give you this assignment?"

"Yes. She's given me a limited time for background and gauging its potential." She opened her eyes wide. "I was hoping you'd be willing to help me get a meeting with Environment Minister Nakayama and the fisheries management people."

Kaito grimaced.

"What's wrong?"

"I cannot do that, Miss Worthington, and even if I could, Nakayama will just feed you government propaganda."

"How can you be so sure?"

"You simply don't understand the psyche of Japanese men in positions of authority. You, especially, would rub them the wrong way."

"That bad, huh?"

"Sorry, but I think so. You would first need to learn a lot about the Japanese culture and the way we do things. Until then, you'd never get to first base, as they say in America. It's way too much to ask."

She slumped. "What do you suggest I do, then? I was hoping you'd at least give me some ideas."

"I have no ideas," he said, shaking his head, but feeling bad that he was letting her down. He paused and reconsidered. "You could start by meeting with small fishermen in villages to learn about their needs and traditions. Understand the Japanese people."

Hokata appeared, pointing to his watch. "Yamamoto-san, you need to change into costume. Now."

Kaito headed backstage. "Sorry, Miss. I have to go," he said, wishing that weren't the case.

She stood up and pleaded with a smile. "I'm staying at the Kamogowa Hotel. Maybe we could meet some evening?"

Chapter Ten
Two Days Later

Minamiboso, Chiba Prefecture

Why do I allow myself to keep helping this woman? Kaito asked himself as he and Elizabeth rounded a cliffside bend in the road. Sure, he wanted to show her his culture, but he had to admit he experienced feelings he never had before. He pointed to the little village sitting on a tongue of land jutting into the harbor. "That's Minamiboso. One of the few towns that permits a finite amount of whaling."

Elizabeth asked, "Do you mean a *fine* amount of whaling?"

"No. Did I use the wrong word?" He asked, feeling his face warm. "I meant only limited amounts. Is finite not proper?"

"It is, but I was surprised at your use of the word." She smiled sheepishly. "Your English is even better than I remember."

"Ah, well," he said, slowing on a curve to let a tour bus pass. "In Miami, my English was not so good, so I've been taking a nightly refresher course at AEON, the top English language school in Japan." He handily downshifted gears, slid to a stop in a parking lot and smiled. "And re-reading John Steinbeck's novels."

"Wow. I'm' impressed. Why Steinbeck?"

"I've loved his humanism ever since I read 'The Angry Raisins' in high school."

She stared momentarily, wrinkling her brow.

He chuckled. "That's what all his Japanese fans called the Grapes of Wrath."

She let out a hardy laugh. "That's funny."

"I learn a lot about your home state too, but not Malibu."

She nodded then gazed out at the harbor. "This place reminds me of the rocky shores of La Jolla, California."

"Yes, we have nice coasts here, too. I'm glad you've come to learn of fishing from villagers." *But would she, I wonder?* He pointed down the road toward the harbor. "My friend lives in this neighborhood. We'll walk from here, Okay?"

"Sure," she said and unfastened her seatbelt. "Oh, by the way, you were right about Minister Nakayama. His assistant to the deputy wouldn't even meet with me. Only gave me a two-year-old public policy statement."

"Not surprised. He is at best..." Kaito scowled, "A difficult man. Besides, government in Japan very secretive."

"And me, a typical stubborn American. I can't go back without a story."

"Yes, you are persistent, but need patience," he added, worrying her blunt ways might offend the villagers. He got out of the car and opened her door. Elizabeth held the bottom of her plaid, knee-length skirt as Kaito helped her out of the low-riding Nissan. He glanced at her legs, then looked up. She'd caught him looking.

They walked toward the old center of the village. The rows of single-story wood houses—stained dark by the sea—were nestled close together, protected from the harsh winds that swept between them.

"Some of these homes date back to the *Edo* period," Kaito said, then realized that Elizabeth was staring at a woman shifting dangling blobs along a wooden rack in front of her house. "That's squid they're drying." He bowed hello to the woman. "Hot sun will bake them to leather brown."

Elizabeth wrinkled her nose, but Kaito was pleased to see her awkwardly imitate his bow. He pointed. "My old friend Umi lives a few doors down. That is whaling memorial in front of his house. He is very wise. He speaks only Japanese. I will translate for him."

Kaito knocked on the door as Elizabeth drew her fingers along the carved relief of the wooden memorial, standing as a reminder of all the fishermen lost at sea.

An elderly man, tall for the Japanese, opened the door. With a shaking hand, he pulled the wire-rimmed glasses from their place on his forehead and ran a hand over his shiny bald head.

"Good morning, dear Shimizu-san," Kaito said in Japanese.

Umi squinted, then smiled. "*Nantekotta,* Yamamoto-san. I am happy and honored to see you."

Kaito's head almost touched that of his friend's as they met each other's bow. "It is my honor to see you again, young man."

"Hah! I'm eighty years now, Kaito." He patted his friend's back. Umi quickly nudged Kaito aside, bowed and welcomed Elizabeth. "*Irasshai, irasshai.*"

She smiled and bowed.

Umi whispered to Kaito, then gently opened both of his calloused hands toward Elizabeth. She looked at Kaito.

Kaito stammered as he translated, "Umi said he is honored that I brought my new bride to meet him."

Elizabeth smiled. "I told him you are writer from America and came to learn about fishing culture."

Umi spoke again. "Umi says you must be an intelligent woman. He welcomes you to his home."

Kaito removed his shoes and nodded toward an alcove containing straw slippers for guests. "They are called *zori.* The straw weave makes them a little scratchy."

They followed Umi, who walked with a stiff limp, his shortened leg making a thump on the floorboards. He took them to the center of a sunken living room. Large square cushions surrounded a low table lacquered black with intricate inlays of abalone shell.

Kaito dropped easily onto his knees and sat comfortably on the back of his feet. He watched Elizabeth struggle, pulling at her tight skirt and sitting in an awkward position with her legs to one side.

"Sorry, I hope not too difficult for you."

She smiled as she used a cushion to settle into a more comfortable position, then gazed at the wood ceiling with posts and beams tied crisscross with rope. The walls shone with a soft glow of light.

"I think you are noticing the *shoji,*" Kaito told her, pointing to the surrounding wood-lattice panels covered by translucent paper. "They keep interiors airy and bright."

Umi returned with a tiny woman, no more than four feet tall. Kaito and Elizabeth stood and bowed.

Kaito introduced her. "Elizabeth, this is Michiko, Umi's wife. She is the fastest and deepest *ama* free diver in all of Chiba." Michiko smiled, then slowly placed each chrysanthemum-patterned cup before them in perfect symmetry.

Kaito added, "She holds the record of eight abalone in one dive."

Umi said something and laughed.

Kaito explained, "Umi says that he married her for her strength. He said his wife's large diving lung shouts him down whenever he's disrespectful."

Michiko poked Umi on the shoulder and they all laughed.

Kaito leaned toward Elizabeth. "Umi added that her love kept him strong for fifty-five years. Do I need to translate how they adore each other?"

"No. It's visible and real charming."

Michiko whispered something to Umi, then left the room. Umi laughed and spoke to Kaito.

Kaito smiled. "Michiko, say you look like Rita Hayworth."

Elizabeth blushed and they sipped their tea.

"Shimizu-san," Kaito began in Japanese, "Would you be willing to answer some questions for Elizabeth? She is most interested in protecting and preserving our oceans."

Kaito listened to Umi's response, then told Elizabeth, "Mr. Shimizu honored to answer your questions. He too believes we need to protect the ocean he loves, and all its creatures. Please go ahead. He will be honest."

Elizabeth nodded. "*Arigatou*, I appreciate your help." She opened her notebook, remembering she had to get to the crux on the Japanese cultural slant. "Can you explain how hunting and eating whale and dolphin meat preserves the oceans?"

Kaito cringed at her directness. He hoped Umi would not see the question as offensive. He translated and his tensed shoulders relaxed when he heard Umi's answer.

"Umi said he was happy to explain. He himself has not fished for whale thirty year now. When he got injured, Michiko told him he had to quit. He explained village allowed to hunt one local beaked whale a year by small boat."

Elizabeth took notes.

Umi continued as Kaito translated.

"Umi believes whale is resource. It sustains itself, as village has been catching those whales many hundred years. And, today, we still have plenty of whale. So, he believes in..." Kaito struggled to find the word..."interdependence with our whales."

Elizabeth seemed puzzled, so Umi continued, "Perhaps hard for *gaijin* to understand, but all forms of life are precious. Whales, like us, have souls. Umi says they have own society. He believes they give up part of their society to

101

us. So, they are renewed through hunting. Most fishermen in Japan believe this."

"What is a *gaijin*?" she asked, shifting uneasily on her cushion.

"*Gaijin* is just a word for foreigner, no bad meaning."

Umi added something, placing his hands together in prayer.

"As good Buddhists, when we kill a whale, we say a *kuya*, a prayer to appease soul of the dead whale. If you look closely on that wood memorial outside, you will see images of both whale and human souls ascending to the top and into heaven."

"Tell Umi for me that this *gaijin* thinks that is beautiful symbolism."

Kaito looked at Elizabeth, surprised at what he hoped was a growing sensitivity. He put his hand on Umi's shoulder and told him of Elizabeth's reaction.

"Umi said you are a good woman and wants to tell you they never take juvenile whales or cows with calves. Also, when they cut up a whale and find a dead fetus, they have a funeral for it and release it to the sea."

Elizabeth put her hand to her throat and swallowed.

Kaito watched her struggle to change her position on the cushion. She banged her knee on the low table.

"Ouch," she cried out, then looked embarrassed.

"Are you okay, Elizabeth?"

"Trying to be," she said with a sheepish smile. Taking a sip of what was now cold tea, she returned to her notebook. She glanced first at Umi, then at Kaito, and said, "What Umi said was poignant from his perspective, but let me turn to the three industrial whaling ships whose homeport lies just a few kilometers from here. These factory ships take hundreds of Minkes and Blue and Gray whales under the guise of what the government calls research."

Kaito leaned toward her and whispered harshly, "Is not fair to ask old, small-time fisherman about modern methods, and people he is not associated with."

She shrugged. "Umi said he'd give honest answers."

Kaito was torn between Elizabeth's need to know and not wanting to insult his friend. After several moments, he spoke to Umi, "Please, excuse my friend, Shimizu-san, but she wants to ask you a very sensitive question."

Umi nodded agreeably.

Elizabeth put her pencil to paper. She was on assignment and had to get his perspective. "Would you ask him his opinion about his government's claim that the factory whale hunting is research?"

Kaito swallowed hard and let out a deep breath. Then, he asked Umi the question in a very deliberate manner.

Umi rocked back and forth and laughed. He pulled up his *monpe* trouser leg and exposed the wooden post that was most of his leg.

Elizabeth gasped.

With his knuckles, Umi knocked on his leg, grinned and spoke at length.

Elizabeth gave Kaito a puzzled look.

Kaito ran his fingers through his hair, looked to Umi, then to Elizabeth and said, "Mr. Shimizu basically said, *shoganai, shoganai.* In English it means there is nothing one can do." He paused, then added, "Like his wooden leg, you have to live with what you cannot control."

Elizabeth straightened her back. "Hmm. You mean like he accepted the government's position?"

Hesitating, Kaito answered, "N…no. He said it was bogus."

Elizabeth squinted at Kaito. "He said *bogus*?"

"Well, not exactly that word."

Elizabeth looked confused, then she frowned.

Kaito looked to the floor, then gestured toward Umi. "Elizabeth, look at Mr. Shimizu. You can see he is frustrated by our talk and looks very tired. We should get ready to go now, okay?"

She nodded and closed her notebook.

Kaito explained to Umi that they had to leave. Umi looked surprised and shook his head many times. He called for his wife.

"Umi says that you are honored guest and a welcomed guest of the community. He wants to share *tare* with you."

"Tell him thanks so much, but what is *tare*?"

"Tare is prepared dried whale meat for special guests and celebrations. When the catch is good, the fishermen always share the bounty with neighbors, firemen, and children's charities. This is the way relationships are cemented and the community becomes bound together by the whale."

Elizabeth shifted on her cushion. He could see she was uncomfortable at the thought of eating whale meat but didn't want to say so.

Kaito turned to Umi and explained that despite Elizabeth's heartfelt gratitude for such an honor, she was a vegetarian and could not partake.

Umi listened, gave them a knowing look, and spoke.

"Umi tells me that he is sad, but he understands the vegetarian tradition. He hopes that you have learned much today."

Umi put his arms around both of them and guided them to the door. Kaito translated, "Umi wants the two of us to visit him again before he dies."

"Tell him I am honored," she said and bowed politely.

Umi hugged Kaito, followed by deep, long bows of goodbye.

"That was quite a visit," Elizabeth said as they walked back along the lane to the car.

"I hope you learned some things."

"Yeah, I did. About you."

"And what was that?" Kaito averted his eyes.

"I now know more about your true feelings. I heard your voice in between Umi's."

"What do you mean?"

"I noticed the change in your tone of voice and the look on your face. Did Umi really answer that the whale research was bogus?"

He cleared his throat, trying to gauge her thinking. "Words are hard...hard to translate. Maybe a better way to say it is—" He rubbed his chin. "Government does not speak for all people."

Elizabeth fixed her eyes on him. "Were those his words or yours?"

He took a deep breath. "Maybe I could explain something. In Japan we have *honne*—personal opinions—but we can also express *tatemae,* public opinions, so we don't offend others."

"Hmm." She stared at him and took some mental notes. "Americans would think that's hypocritical."

"No, so," Kaito said, "It is being respectful. Ways you have to learn in dealing with us Japanese."

"I'm starting to." She tapped her chin. "Would you tell me your *honne* opinion?"

Kaito knew how perceptive she was, and felt he had to be straightforward. "You know, Elizabeth, I do not agree with everything my people, or my government does."

She stopped walking. "I sensed that." She stretched out her hand. "So, when Umi showed his wooden leg after I asked him about industrial whaling." She poked Kaito in the arm. "You must have asked him a different question then?"

Kaito averted his eyes. "I did. I asked him why he likes Americans. He explained he was only sixteen years old when lost his leg at Guadalcanal, but American GIs saved his life. They took him to a field hospital for prisoners."

"That's really something to learn. I liked him too." She sighed, "And I also learned that some Japanese husbands regard their wives as equals." She shrugged her shoulders. "I guess I'll have to get my other question answered by another source."

"That would be wise, Elizabeth."

She touched his elbow. "Oh, yeah, and I have to say I liked seeing your love for Umi and Michiko, almost like they were your parents."

Thinking of his mother and father, Kaito felt his face redden and lowered his head.

Elizabeth spread her hands out. "And thank you. Vegetarian? That was a great save, but how did you know?"

"I assumed. With respect, I would not think you agree with how people raise animals, feed, and care for them, then kill them and eat them."

Elizabeth walked a few paces, then stopped to face him. "You are right, I don't agree. And I am a vegetarian. But today I learned a lot today about cultural differences. It's also great to hear you being upfront with me."

"Good. I'm hungry. There is an excellent seafood restaurant overlooking the water." He smiled and bowed. "Plenty of vegetables, too."

Chapter Eleven
Minamiboso Restaurant, Chiba
Prefecture, Japan

Kaito became nervous as soon as they entered the restaurant. He had forgotten there was only side-by-side seating at a long counter. And diners were already staring at them. At least Elizabeth didn't seem to notice. He had never taken a woman to dinner before, except for his mother, but he relaxed when they were seated with a glorious view of an almost too blue ocean. Elizabeth looked beautiful in the light of the large white lanterns that swayed softly in the breeze.

Elizabeth stared blankly at the menu. "You order what's best, okay?"

"Ooo," he licked his lips. "They have great..." He set down the menu. "Things you will like."

The waitress appeared, carrying a tray of tall, earthenware bottles.

Pointing at the tray, he asked, "Would you like to try some sake? Virgin variety, of course."

Elizabeth nodded.

Kaito ordered confidently, laughing with the waitress as he gestured to himself.

Elizabeth took small sips of her sake. She frowned after swallowing the warm drink.

"Do you not enjoy the sake?"

"Not really," she said, then glanced over her shoulder. "Am I crazy or are people staring at us?"

"Sorry, they are curious. Tourists seldom find this place, and the locals are not used to seeing a *gaijin* woman with a Japanese man."

The waitress sat two small plates in front of them.

Kaito smiled and picked up his chopsticks. "Here's the *Nama*."

Elizabeth took a moment to adjust the wooden utensils in her hand and jabbed at the dusted white mound of tofu.

"That's grated ginger on top," he offered. "You like?"

Struggling to grasp a slippery portion, she finally brought it to her mouth. "Hmm," she uttered, "Very fresh." When she went to snatch another lump, it promptly fell on her lap. "Sorry, I'm such a klutz."

"Could I get you a fork?"

"Thanks, but I'd like to learn."

"Good," he said, admiring her spunk. "Would you try some *kitsune udon*? It may be better."

"Sure."

He signaled the waitress, then watched Elizabeth finish her *nama*. "Try the sake now."

She sipped it and gave a smile of pleasure.

"Harmony important in our culture."

Elizabeth set her glass down. "Michiko and Umi had great harmony."

"Yes," he agreed, appreciating her tender observation. "They understand each other's needs without asking."

After a few uncomfortable moments, Elizabeth looked up at the hanging lamps. "Does the lettering on the lamps mean something?"

"They are haiku. Most of these are about nature. Written by the master Basho in the sixteen hundreds."

"What does the one above us read?"

Kaito tilted his head back to read the words. He shook his head. "This one's not about nature. It is by a poet named Tobuno."

"Will you translate?"

Kaito coughed. "I…I think it would be:

Love is not…not…complex
it demands an…absent mind
and a present heart."

"True. I suppose," she said, leaning forward.

"I suppose," he offered.

"What do you think about the absent-minded part?" she asked. "I'd love to hear your interpretation."

He picked up the sake decanter and nervously refilled her cup He was not used to discussing matters of the heart with anyone, let alone a woman, an American woman that he was attracted to.

She took a sip. "Sorry, if that's getting a personal." She batted her eyelashes and added, "If you'd like you could give me only your *tatemae* opinion.*"

He gazed into her coaxing eyes, thinking of the differences in their cultures, their beliefs, their personalities and all his personal—what had she called them?—hang-ups. *But I really like how she wants to learn.*

"A man with an absent mind…that would be hard," he said, averted his eyes, glad to see the approaching waitress save him from elaborating. "Here comes the *Umi-bodo*. Wait until you experience this."

Elizabeth wrinkled her nose at the bowl of strange, translucent seaweed. Clusters of bubbles shimmered on the leaves like tiny emeralds.

"Some people call it green caviar." Kaito spooned a clump on her plate. "Go ahead."

She picked it up and held it to her open mouth. For a moment, Kaito imagined a haiku about the dangling green morsel on the red curve of her lip, waiting to be savored by the pearls of her teeth.

Elizabeth's eyes brightened with surprise as she chewed.

Kaito thought she was feeling the bubbles crunch and burst. "They are releasing the ocean in your mouth."

She smiled. "I didn't think food could be so sensuo…" She took another bite.

Kaito leaned forward. "What was the word you started to say?"

"Sensuous. I meant that that the salty taste stimulated all the senses. It tingled." Their eyes met. "You have made my first trip to Japan very enjoyable. Better, I think, than your trip to the States."

Catching her warm tone, Kaito wiggled in his seat. Leaning closer, he asked, "Good, but can you explain?"

"Maybe you are comfortable here in your own culture has a lot to do with it. In Miami, you seemed well, stiff and shy maybe. Here I see another…another side of you."

Kaito smiled, then twisted his body in his chair. Pointing at the mock grimace on his face, he said, "You mean you did not like this other side?"

Elizabeth nudged him on the shoulder and laughed. "I like when you're funny. Did you ever write haiku?"

Kaito shook his head and wiggled his hand toward her.

She tapped it and he inhaled sharply at her touch.

"Oh, come on," she said. "I bet you did. You're more sensitive than you let on."

Delighted with her interest, Kaito took a deep breath. "As a boy, fishing with my *otosan*, there was a lot of time *not* fishing."

"Great, I knew it. Tell me."

He closed his eyes, softening even more to her interest. He remembered.

"Dolphins…Dolphins ride our wake
Where is your home, your mother?
Here. Come play with us."

"I suppose you were lonesome for home at the time."

Kaito gazed out at the ocean. At the time, his mother must have already made up her mind to leave the family. "No." He shook his head. "The dolphins were not trying to guide me home. They were showing me how free they were in *their* home." He looked at Elizabeth for understanding.

She placed her hand over his. "Unlike most men, you express yourself so nicely."

Kaito smiled and let her hand remain over his until she removed it. He had flinched the first time she touched him that way. But now, the feel of her hand produced deeper feelings. He wasn't sure if it had to do with Elizabeth openly immersing herself in his culture, or if it was his surprise at being touched by a woman this way. He imagined it was likely both. Catching himself staring at her, he stammered, "Sorry, I was looking at…"

"Please, go ahead."

"Your eyes, actually, they are so different from Japanese eyes."

"As are yours to me."

"Do American women like slender eyes?"

"I do, but to me it's more about what's behind them."

He sat, speechless. He could not understand how she was so freely expressing herself. He had no idea how to put his current feelings into words, he just knew there was something arresting about Elizabeth, and it was growing in more intense within him.

"So." She held a finger in the air. "The dolphins wanted you to join them, right?"

"Exactly."

The waitress stood above them. Embarrassed, Kaito deftly pulled his hand away.

"Here comes the *kitsune udon*. You must like noodles?"

"I do. What's the broth?"

Leaning closer to his bowl and waving his hand up to his nose, he said, "It is only *miso* base, you know, soybean. Not *dashi*, which is fish broth. I asked the waitress to be sure."

"Thank you," she said, poking the floating brown dumpling. Her eyes seemed to ask what it was.

"That is *aburage*. Thin slice fried tofu. Easy to pick up."

"Hmm, it's really tasty."

He smiled broadly. "It's the favorite food of fox."

"Foxes?"

"Yes, Japanese love those animals. Always smile. Smart and has magical powers."

"Interesting. What does it do?"

Kaito picked up his bowl, took a sip of broth, and wiped his chin. "They say fox can take shape of beautiful woman and appear in man's mind."

"Ha!" She laughed. "Pretty cool power."

He swished his noodles around in his bowl, thinking her interest in his culture was story-based, yet she seemed to also have an interest in him. He could only manage to say, "Maybe it's a silly legend."

The waitress came back with another dish on two plates.

"Ah!" Kaito looked up. "Here is the *naruke*. It is sea urchin."

"Kaito? Can I ask you something?"

He waited.

"Before we came to this restaurant, you said it had great seafood. Yet you ordered only vegetarian."

"I want to be good host, but not completely. I confess, I could not pass up my favorite dish." He let out a sigh. "I ordered it in honor of Michiko."

Elizabeth wrinkled her brow as she looked at the gelatinous yellow blobs set in cradles of *nori*.

"It is not vegetable. From insides of the spiny black creatures that crawl along the ocean floor." He ran his fingers along the table. "Much prized by *ama* divers."

Elizabeth, stiffened and stared at the food.

Rubbing his hands together, realizing he had made a mistake ordering, he said, "I'm sorry, Elizabeth. The chef must have assumed we were sharing. Do you mind if I indulge myself in this one special treat?"

She smiled and relaxed back into her chair. "No problem. Please enjoy it."

For the first time, Kaito noticed how her long eyelashes fluttered over the gray-green of her eyes. He speared the *naruke* and relished it. As soon as he finished, he resisted staring at the sea urchin on her plate. She grinned and slid her dish across the table for him.

"Thank you," he said, devouring his favorite seafood. He looked up to catch her enjoying watching him eat, and added, "Sorry for being, how do you say, insatiable?"

"Good word, Kaito," she said tapping the table. "You've got a lot of passion for food *and* dolphins."

Kaito glanced over his shoulder as an older woman walked by the table and glared at him.

"Someone you know, Kaito?"

"No, that woman resembled my *okaasan*, but she glared at me."

"How come?"

"Oh, Japanese couple not supposed to show a…admiration in public, let alone Japanese with Caucasian woman." He scanned the other tables. "But my mother would never have stared like that. She is open-minded and independent, like you."

"Thanks. I would like to hear more about her."

Kaito checked his watch.

"You look like you have to go somewhere."

"Sorry, yes. I always take time, just me and Manami at end of day. Before she spends the night alone in pen."

"I know how important she is to you." She looked at him then added, "Someday, I'd like to meet your dolphin."

Kaito gazed out at the horizon and considered Elizabeth's words. "She is important, but you know, I look beyond OceanWorld—something bigger."

She nodded. "I know that. And I've been thinking about your valiant efforts to teach the public about dolphins in the wild."

"You have? Did I tell you we got a lot of sign-ups for our kid's classes, and management is surprisingly happy?"

"Yeah, an accomplishment considering how they were dead set against it." She took a deep breath. "You know, I believe you could do much more; if only there was a way to move both of you out of the daily grind of the shows—a way to start researching your bigger dream."

Kaito reached out and tapped her hand. "Yes. Get the time and space to seriously study dolphin language. That's exactly what I've been trying to figure out."

She smiled and waved her hand between them. "Well then, we're on the same wave…" She sighed. "Just oceans apart."

Kaito didn't know how to respond, so he chuckled. "Hah, but Japan and California share same ocean."

She laughed.

"So, Elizabeth, how long you stay in Japan?"

"Depends how my research goes. So far, I haven't gotten anywhere."

He wrinkled his brow and tried to read her. "Not surprised. Maybe something develops."

She drummed her fingers on the table. "The magazine is paying for my travel and living expenses for two weeks. So, I need to get my act together by then."

"I suppose," Kaito acknowledged. "Maybe we should be heading back then."

Kaito paid the bill, and they readied to leave. A jocular man dressed in a three-piece suit approached them.

"There is Mr. Ado, the owner. He will want to know how the meal was."

"Ah, Yamamoto-san," Ado said, bowing before adjusting his bowtie. Without looking at Elizabeth, he chatted with Kaito in Japanese.

Kaito thanked him and introduced Elizabeth.

Ado gave her a cursory nod and ogled her from head to toe. Elizabeth shuffled her feet. Ado pulled Kaito to the side and whispered in his ear, finishing with a belly laugh.

Kaito did not laugh. He jerked back, his eyes burning with resentment. His words to Ado were sharp. Without bowing, he took Elizabeth's elbow and they left.

"What was that about?" she asked as he opened the door.

"Nothing, he was just being rude and insular."

"It was more than that, wasn't it? I have never seen you so angry."

"Sometimes people think celebrities from Tokyo lead a different lifestyle, that's all."

Getting into the car, Elizabeth said, "You saw the way he looked at me. He thought I was some sort of exotic eye candy, didn't he?"

Kaito turned the ignition. "Even worse, I'm afraid. I told him I won't be coming back. Sorry, for the outburst."

She looked into his eyes, silent for several moments. Touching his shoulder, she said, "Thank you, Kaito. You are quite the gentleman."

On the drive back up the hilly road, Kaito pondered her words: a gentle man. *Where am I going with this? A relationship I could never imagine—one that enthralls me as much as scares me? She wants to meet Manami, but I should drop her off at her hotel?*

Chapter Twelve
Two Hours Later

OceanWorld East Dolphinarium, Japan

It was past dark and OceanWorld was closed by the time they arrived. Elizabeth's first thought was, what was she doing here alone with this man? But she really wanted to get to meet Manami. Kaito carefully pointed the way and guided her along a row of dim security lights until they reached the dolphin show pool. He flipped a large lever, and the entire stadium flooded with fluorescent white. Elizabeth shaded her eyes.

"Sorry," he said and flipped another lever. She smiled as the underwater pool lights turned the dark gray oblong tank into a luminous and alluring cove. Breathing in the hot night air, together with the cool, rising vapors from the pool, Elizabeth became invigorated.

Heakk-yip! a dolphin called from behind them. "That's Manami, she's heard me. I can't seem to sneak up on her."

Elizabeth spotted a security guard above the stands. He waved at Kaito and bowed deeply before walking away, leaving Kaito and Elizabeth to themselves. A security guard shouted and waved from the stands. Kaito waved back. The guard bowed deeply and continued walking.

"You know, Manami might just circle the pool," Kaito told Elizabeth. "She's never seen strangers with me on our evening swims."

"Understood. I appreciate you letting me see her. I'll just watch you two."

Kaito gestured for Elizabeth to sit on a Polynesian canoe-shaped bench. "She will be coming through the gate on this side. I'll be right back."

Elizabeth wondered why he didn't have her come with, but the blue of the pool enticed her. She took her shoes off, sat at the edge of the pool and dangled her bare legs in the water. A *clunk* and a *splash* sounded at her side and Manami shot into the pool. The dolphin slowed as she swam in front of the stranger, lifting her head ever so slightly out of the water. Elizabeth gave her a friendly wave as she swam back and forth. Both Elizabeth and Manami were oblivious to Kaito's return.

"Oh my god, Kaito. She is soooo beautiful," Elizabeth said as Manami ripped through the water like a silver torpedo, creating a concentric wake in the middle of the pool. "She's like the dolphin that once saved me, you know, the guardian angel I told you about. It's so exciting, I have goosebumps." She rubbed her arms up and down.

Kaito smiled and nodded. "I know, she is very special. Now watch this."

He knelt at the head of a tiled ramp leading into the pool. Placing his hand palm up, he motioned toward his chest.

Manami kept circling the pool.

"Sorry," Elizabeth said. "I must be distracting her."

Kaito repeated the command. "Come, Manami. Come in for a belly rub."

Manami circled slowly in front of the stage, then popped her head up a half-meter in front of Elizabeth and let out a *pfhoo* of air from her blowhole.

"Don't be afraid," Kaito said.

Elizabeth laughed and splashed her feet. "I'm not. I feel like she's a childhood friend coming back to visit me." Thinking of the rhythm in the dolphin's name she began singing in a soulful melody, "Manami, Manami, Manami."

"Did you just make that up?" Kaito asked, sitting close to her. "You have a beautiful voice."

"Thanks. I changed the lyrics of an old jazz standard, 'Emily.'" She began singing again. "And the laughter of children at play."

Kaito's eyes fixed on her. "Your face looks radiant."

She quickly shifted her attention to Kaito. "That is a very nice thing to say. Yours looks pretty proud."

"I am pleased you like Manami."

She patted his knee. "I like you too," she said, surprised by her outburst. She hadn't planned to say this aloud, but the admittance caused her to relax around Kaito. The usual tension in her shoulders eased and it made her curious.

He blushed.

Elizabeth noticed his eyes continued to study her. "Kaito," she called to catch his attention. "What are you thinking?"

"Ah…about how I enjoy watching you."

"Oh," she said as Manami squeaked and clicked. She wondered what Kaito meant by that but didn't voice her question aloud. Instead, she said, "I've been wondering…how come Manami has that half-moon notch on her dorsal fin?"

"A long-ago shark-biting, I assume. She's had that since she was very young."

Elizabeth hummed while dragging her hand on the surface of the water. "You know, as a kid I used to pretend I was swimming with dolphins in my bathtub."

"You did?"

"Yeah. For me, it was a way to…" she caught herself as she remembered her parents fighting. "To escape into a silly fantasy, I guess."

"Funny," he said. "When I was a child, my favorite storybook was Rin Gin. When I swam with dolphins in the harbor, I imagined diving to find the mermaid princess from the book. Hear her enchanting voice calling me to come and join the ocean circus."

"That's so sweet," Elizabeth said.

Manami made a low, long whistling sound. They turned their heads.

"I think she's telling us she's feeling curious," Kaito explained. "Come on. She wants to meet you." He pointed to the ramp and held out his hand.

She took it. "Really? I'd love to."

"Maybe she will let you pet her."

Kneeling together at the ramp, Kaito gave Manami a hand signal.

The dolphin ignored it and returned to swimming in small circles.

"Let me try," Elizabeth said, copying Kaito's signal.

Instantly, Manami made a few powerful strokes of her fluke, slid up the ramp and rolled over.

Elizabeth cheered and clapped. Kaito laughed and pointed at a spot on Manami's belly between her pectoral fins. Manami nodded as if to say, *I'm waiting*.

Taking Elizabeth's hand, he guided it gently over Manami's white belly. A smile lit Elizabeth's face as the dolphin giggled. She turned her gaze to Kaito, almost forgetting their closeness. "Her skin feels like a wetsuit."

"Watch." Rubbing hand-in-hand, the dolphin's flippers flattened against her body. "That means she is becoming relaxed." He paused. "While being out of water, that is."

"Yeah. And I'm being soothed at the same time." Feeling enchanted, Elizabeth closed her eyes and continued stroking her softly.

Kaito was leaning back on his feet and watching.

"It's like there is a feeling between us," Elizabeth remarked.

"There is." He nodded. "Connecting with another species is the most special thing on this planet." Kaito patted Manami and whistled. She flapped her fluke and splashed back into the pool.

Elizabeth wiped the water from her face and smiled. "You sure have a way with her."

Kaito searched Elizabeth's eyes.

"Seems like you do too. There must be something…" He searched for the word…"Metaphysical? Between you."

"Metaphysical." Elizabeth smiled and nodded. "I like that." For a moment, she wondered if he really meant something more between her and him. No, she decided, as her invisible wall went up.

Manami made a high aerial jump and dove in front of them. Elizabeth asked, "So, you'd normally go for a swim with her?"

"Normally, but not tonight," he answered. "We've both got busy mornings."

Manami let out a long string of squeaky, creaky sounds and bobbed her head up and down.

Elizabeth nodded toward Kaito. "Seems to me like she wants your attention."

He nodded back.

"Why don't you go ahead and swim, then?" She shrugged. "I'd love to watch the two of you."

Elizabeth looked at Kaito as he appeared to think it over. His brows knitted together, but then the muscles in his face relaxed and he nodded.

"Okay, just a short one," he said. "I'll go and change."

Returning with a bathrobe over his swimsuit, Kaito bounded to the edge of the pool. As he removed his bathrobe, they caught each other's eyes. "Here we go," he said and dove in, entering the water with hardly a splash.

Elizabeth watched spellbound as man and dolphin effortlessly twirled their bodies in unison. Heads, feet and tail intertwined, creating a steady ripple of waves against the side of the pool. When Kaito surfaced, Manami was at his side, warbling what sounded like a little song.

"Aww." Elizabeth sighed. "So sweet."

He swiped the wet mop of hair from his forehead. "That means she's happy."

"Manami loves to outswim me," Kaito said as he powered into a crawl stroke, shooting across the pool like an Olympic star. Manami lazily dove under and gingerly jumped over him as he swam—chirping each time as though she was goading him.

"It looks like such fun," she said, wanting so much to join them. Despite her belief against using dolphins for show, she found his physical intimacy with Manami captivating.

"It is," he said, lifting his muscular body onto the edge of the pool and looking at Elizabeth. "Maybe someday you could join us."

"I'd love that," she said, feeling it was like an invitation. "Do you ever use this time to practice show tricks with her?"

"No, I try to be more like a pod-mate during these times. Let her take the lead. She usually likes to play hide and seek."

Manami squealed.

Elizabeth put her hands together in her chest and said, "She is so darn cute."

Almost on cue, Manami dove deep and Kaito flipped over into a leisurely back stroke. Elizabeth stood, reached behind her back, unzipped her skirt, and let it drop. Kaito stopped swimming and took in a gulp of water.

Elizabeth was drawn to join in the beauty of it all. All her deeply held beliefs about dolphins being confined, were washed away by seeing how joyful Manami played. She pulled off her blouse, tied it around her hips and stepped to the edge of the pool.

Kaito held his hand up and shouted, "No, Elizabeth! Don't jump in the water. Manami hasn't trained with you."

His voice reflected genuine concern and she felt guilty about ignoring his warning as well as her own thoughts about captive dolphins. But her need to feel a part of this beauty took hold of her. She raised her arms above her head and dove in.

Surfacing, she waved to him. "Sorry, I couldn't resist. I used to snorkel among wild dolphins back in California. Don't worry, I know them," she said and swam toward him.

"Yes, I remember you told me." He swam to her.

Before reaching her, Manami shot up in between them.

"Elizabeth! Watch out."

Manami cozied up to Elizabeth like she was encouraging a pod-mate to play.

"Yay!" Elizabeth cried out.

Manami darted beneath her, rose up to the surface, faced her and warbled the happy song.

"Ha! She's accepted you." Kaito shook his head. "Never seen that before."

"Let's swim," Elizabeth said and dove deep, taking to the water like she was born to it, moving in it like a real-life mermaid. She felt her hair waft and swirl around her neck as she pushed through the water. She loved how the shimmering pool lights bounced over her body. How the ripples formed around her hips as she rhythmically thrusted forward. She caught Kaito's eye; he smiled as he watched. For the first time, a tiny alarm went off in her head. It drained quickly away with Manami's close comfort.

Dancing in a liquid *pas de deux,* the dolphin spun under her, releasing a string of bubbles. The bubbles surrounded every part of Elizabeth's body like silver jewels and lifted her out of a dream.

"Kaito, this is glorious!" She said, surfacing for a breath.

He met her and they treaded and bobbed together in the water. "A bit cold for a pool, but thank you so much," she blurted. "I hope you don't think I'm too crazy."

"You are crazy," he said. "I wish I could be as free-spirited."

She laughed like a school kid, splashed water into his face, and swam off.

Kaito chased alongside her until Manami surfaced between them and Elizabeth slowed. Manami stopped and nudged her arm with her nose, then looked at her.

"She looked right at me, Kaito," Elizabeth exclaimed. "It was hypnotic."

"How so?"

"Our eyes connected. Like I could see her soul and she could see mine."

"I know, I know," he said. "It's a remarkable thing to relate to an animal like you would a person."

Treading water face-to-face, she instinctively said, "You're pretty remarkable yourself, Mr. Yamamoto." As soon as the words slipped out her mouth, she regretted them. Yet, that was how she *felt.*

Kaito dog-paddled closer and smiled broadly. She averted his gaze. A cascade of bubbles rose from below, tickling their legs.

"What was that?" Elizabeth gasped.

"Ha. That was Manami making an updraft with her fluke. She wants us to play." Kaito swam away. "Let me get a toy."

Swimming back with a rubber squid, he tossed it across the pool, and it began sinking. Manami grabbed it in her mouth, circled them, then dropped the toy in front of Elizabeth.

"Grab it and throw it," Kaito encouraged.

She plucked it from the water and hid it behind her back. The dolphin quickly faced her, clicked and chirped up a storm as if to say, *give it back.* Elizabeth threw it high and Manami caught it mid-air.

It seemed like hours had passed as they swam and played in the fluid divide between land and sea creatures. But Elizabeth tired and her chin began to hover on the surface. Kaito reached under her arms and used a powerful polo kick to lift her, then treaded for both.

"Are you ready to go in?" he asked.

"Yeah. I'm cold and my fingers are all gnarly."

They climbed out, caught their breaths, and looked at each other's dripping bodies. She thought of how masculine and strong he was in body and mind, but not at all macho. She caught herself thinking of a man again. *What are you doing girl?*

She closed her hands in front of her, shivering in the cool air. "Thank you, Kaito. That was unforgettable. How about a towel?"

"Ah, yes. Sorry. I'll get some bathrobes." He sprinted behind the stage.

"You don't have to apologize so much you know," she yelled.

Returning wearing a robe, he found Elizabeth huddled on the dugout canoe with her arms wrapped around her knees. "I'm sorry," he said and handed her a robe.

"And the towel?" Elizabeth asked, "I need to dry my hair."

Manami clicked and whistled in front of them.

"She still wants to play," Kaito said, handing her the towel.

"That was so much fun, I felt like a kid again," Elizabeth added, gazing in silence at Manami. "You know, I needed this. It's almost like my guardian angel has come alive for me and was trying to tell me something."

"Probably telling you you're a good swimmer."

"Maybe, but not as strong as you were out there."

Manami made a vertical leap near the edge, sending them a big splash.

Elizabeth laughed. "You know, I feel changed by this experience."

"How so?" he asked, eyes widening.

"I feel free again, more alive than I've felt in years." She studied him. "Like I just had a world open up for me. Thank you so much for a special time, Kaito."

"It felt pretty special to me, too," he said and reached behind her neck and gently pulled her toward him.

She stiffened. Rupturing from the inside. *What was she doing with this man? Done to him?*

"I can't," she said, wanting to explain her shock. "Something's not right."

He frowned and dropped his arm.

"I am sorry, Elizabeth. I thought you were interested in me. I...I should have asked. I...I don't know about these things."

"No, no," she said, holding her hand up between them. "If I...I led you on. I am sorry. I didn't mean to."

Kaito slumped. "What you said...I thought you had feelings for me?"

Her eyes welled up. "Kaito, I am so sorry. I do have feelings for you, but there's a problem." She pointed to herself. "With me. I'm just not ready for..." she put her hand to her throat and winced. "It's hard to explain."

Kaito gazed into her now tear-filled face. He remembered what she had told him in Miami. "It's about that Greg guy, isn't it? Look, Elizabeth, I would never hurt you."

"I know you wouldn't." She swiped away her tears. "I'm a little mixed up right now. I...I need some time."

Straining to find the words, Kaito sighed and said, "I understand, I think. How about if I take you home now?"

Bright spotlights flashed and a loud voice echoed from above, "Yamamoto-san!"

They looked up to the top of the stands. Elizabeth shuddered.

Kaito responded politely and waved the guard off.

"What did he say?" she asked, feeling flustered.

"He announced that the main security gate will be locked for the night in fifteen minutes. Sorry, but we need to get the car. It's after midnight. I have school groups coming in the morning and three performances."

She groaned. "And I've got to educate myself for morning meetings with your Tokyo Greenpeace chapter. Point me to the bathroom? I need to at least fix my hair." She picked up her clothes, shoes, and bag.

He showed her to the staff dressing room. "See you in a few minutes. I'll put Manami into her pen. We've got to hurry."

Elizabeth returned, hair tied on top of her head, wearing the robe over her skirt and blouse.

"What do you think?" she said trying to smile as she glanced at the bottom of her skirt still showing. "Will they let me back into the hotel?"

"Sure, you are a crazy *gaijin.* Ready to go?"

She nodded.

When they arrived at the hotel, Kaito parked the car outside the entrance. He looked at her for several moments, struggling to find the words. Elizabeth worried about what he was going to say.

"H...how many m...more days do you have in Tokyo?"

"Nine," she said.

"Not much time."

"No, but can I call you later?"

"If you really want to."

"I do," she said, feeling the pull of him, despite how she pushed him away. "Maybe I can get things figured out in my head so they make sense to you."

"That would be good."

"I have a dinner meeting with the Greenpeace team tomorrow night, but I will call you after that, okay? We can talk."

"Okay. Goodnight, Elizabeth," he answered.

She exited the car and dashed into the lobby, leaving him alone with his thoughts and the confusion of her feelings.

Chapter Thirteen
Next Morning

After a restless night of tossing and turning in the whirlpool of feelings surrounding Elizabeth, Kaito was late getting to OceanWorld. The shame from his awkward advances and her response confused him. These new feelings for a woman were very real for him, but he was terribly unsure about *her* feelings.

Would she be able to get her head and heart clear? Make sense of things? Could he take what she said afterwards, offer a bit of hope? Would she call? She'd be leaving in eight days. He knew he didn't want her to leave. *Could I ask her to stay?*

He hurried to the stadium pool, but glancing at his watch, it was too late for their usual warmups, and he needed to rework a routine. Energized to perform, Manami let out a cacophony of chirps, blips and whistles together with wild tail-slapping which Kaito understood as her "let's go."

He rubbed her snout. "I'm sorry I was late, princess. We swam with that wonderful woman last night, but I blew it. Should have talked to her first. Now we're both mixed up about it." He patted her head. "Maybe we'll work it out, and she'll be good for me. For us."

Kaito wanted to extend the litter echolocation routine by teaching her to find a second dropped bag at a different spot in the pool. Several practice trials failed to do the trick as Manami kept bringing back one bag at a time. Frustrated at the lack of time, Kaito gave up and told her, "That's okay, girl."

Kaito's assistant, Hokata, shouted, "Fifteen minutes to showtime, Yamamoto-san."

Kaito waved, then turned to Manami. "Are you ready?"

She yipped, 'yes'.

She wasn't.

For the first time, the dolphin botched her dramatic entrance. Coming from the depths of the pool under the diving board, Manami performed a weak somersault. At basketball, she dribbled and shot poorly. "Oh, come on, Manami. You can do better," Kaito chided over the loudspeakers.

Kaito became particularly anxious during the audience interaction section of the show. When volunteers came to pet her, she barely feigned a tickle or sounded a giggle. It seemed as though something was distracting her. But was *he* distracted? His corrective finger-waving only made things worse. Embarrassed, Kaito couldn't wait to bring the show to an end. At the grand finale, he summed up his enthusiasm and prepped the audience for Manami's spectacular circling, jumping and splashing finish. He signaled.

Manami dove. Kaito sensed trouble as she blasted into the turn at an astonishing speed and sharp angle. Kaito blew the 'go-slow' whistle, hoping she would respond by slowing her momentum.

Manami soared out of the water early and high; her splash sent a huge wave of water over the top of the Plexiglass panels, soaking customers several rows up in the stands. Kaito cut the show short and nervously apologized to the crowd. "Sorry folks. Apparently, just like the rest of us, Manami can have a bad day. My sincerest apologies. Thanks for coming." He directed Manami to her holding pen.

Within five minutes of being backstage, Mr. Tanaka, the stadium manager, confronted Kaito. He wasn't smiling.

"What is going on, Yamamoto? Dozens of customers want their money back for not seeing the full show. CEO Yamaguchi sent me down to investigate. What happened?"

Disappointed with the performance and wanting to protect her, he said, "I honestly don't know. I must have given Manami a mixed signal for the finale. I may have confused her. It won't happen again."

"We need your assurances, Yamamoto, or else Yamaguchi will have both our backs." Tanaka marched out.

The threat made Kaito shudder. He recalled the scolding and beatings by his father. How it always made Kaito feel disappointed in himself for dishonoring his father. *You'll bounce back*, his mother was always there to say, *you're a strong and resilient boy*. With her encouragement in his heart, he returned to Manami's pen. He was determined not to let his childhood submissiveness, prevent him from finding the courage and the creativity to solve whatever life throws at him. And that included getting over his fears of women and believing there might still be a chance with Elizabeth.

Bringing Manami a fresh squid, her favorite treat, he sat on the edge of her holding pool. "Here you go, girl," he said, dropping the squid into her eager jaws.

She swallowed and listened quietly.

"I'm sorry for not being the best partner now, but we've got to keep the crowds and management happy. Okay? Let's do some run-throughs before the next show. Can you manage that?"

When Manami didn't respond to the usual higher pitch at the end of his question, Kaito grew worried. Despite his concern and Manami's detached behavior, the two and four o'clock shows went off without a tidal wave into the stands. But when they went for their evening free swim together, his fears mounted. She swam mostly by herself with none of the usual, playful teasing and bumping they always enjoyed.

Manami kept watching the stage as if she was expecting someone. Could it be Elizabeth? Kaito wondered. Perhaps his conflicting emotions were distracting Manami. She had always been good at reading him. Or was she somehow jealous? Kaito could not be sure, and he wished more than ever now that he could speak to his dolphin.

He was sure she'd want to come in for a belly rub. He signaled. Manami powered onto the ramp alright, but to his surprise, she didn't rollover to expose her belly. When he managed to stroke her back, his mind drifted to holding Elizabeth's hand the night before. He was caught in a riptide. Pushed away by his dolphin, while being pulled toward a beautiful but baffling woman.

He was disappointed to not find a phone message from Elizabeth when he came home. Exhausted and worried about Manami and that Elizabeth may never call him, he went to bed, anticipating another restless night.

#

Kamagawa Hotel

It was almost midnight when Elizabeth bolted from the elevator to her hotel room. She had to use the bathroom badly, but when she saw the phone message light blinking, she hoped Kaito might possibly have tried to call her. *Ready for a guy again? Kaito had reached over the wall I put up to protect myself from distrustful men and he touched my heart. I rebuffed him. What's the matter with me?* She played the message:

"Darling, It's Mom. Please call me back right away. I met someone. *"*

"Damn!" Elizabeth cursed. "I never should have told her where I was staying."

Her heart told her to call Kaito. To apologize. *Where did I get that stupid belief that he might be gay? Did I have feelings for him? Feelings I didn't think existed? Jesus, I gotta go to the bathroom.*

The phone rang again. She picked up.

"Lizzy-bell, it's Mom."

"Christ, Mom, it's past midnight."

"Seven in the morning here, dear. You won't believe it. I'm in love."

"That's nice Mom but hold on a bit." She peed.

Mom continued, "His name is Patrick Donnelly; he goes by Paddy. He joined our therapy group last week. A second-generation Mick, just like me. As a matter of fact, he reminds me of my first crush in high school, Francis Sullivan. We hit if off immediately. We're going to stay together after we're both released. What do you think?"

Right away, Elizabeth began to think her thoughts about Kaito were silly and risky, but her mom's feelings seemed sincere. "I'm happy for you, Mother. Where's this guy from, and what does he do?"

"He's a plumbing contractor from the Valley."

"Whoa," she said, thinking about the differences between her and Kaito. "That doesn't sound like a match."

"This one's for real, Lizzy. Not like your wretched father. Paddy said he'd take me to Ireland. Your father never would, said it was beneath us. Leland was all about show."

"What do you mean?" Elizabeth asked.

"He only wanted, needed a glamour-puss on his arm. Eye candy. He never loved me."

Her words hit Elizabeth hard, wondering what she wanted and the elusiveness of love. "Are you saying you never loved him, even at first?"

"Not really. I only created that in my mind. I thought he was better, classier, and it would rub off. Take me out of the Southside. A nice home. Security." She sighed. "Biggest mistake of my life."

Finding herself twisting the ends of her hair, she stopped and asked, "How do you know that this Paddy guy is the one?"

Mother went silent for a moment. "You worry too much. I feel it, sweetie. I feel it in my heart."

Elizabeth asked herself if feelings are enough when things get tough? She asked her mother, "Are you going to stay sober with him?"

"Yeah. That's the pact we made. Giving that to each other."

"Wow," she said, admitting that was something, but could you trust? "That's great, Mom, but maybe you ought to give it some more time." As soon as she said that she realized she was actually contemplating staying longer in Japan. It was like a swim and the attention of a good and trusting man, made all her fears wash away.

"Yes, and…here he is. We're going to breakfast now. Hope you enjoy Japan. Goodbye."

"Jesus," Elizabeth cried out, as she hung up the phone. *More power to her. Maybe there's hope for me. Could I ever give back what I don't even have?*

#

At four-thirty a.m. the next morning, Kaito's phone woke him. He wanted it to be Elizabeth.

"Yamamoto-san, it's Nikira from night security. Sorry to bother you at home, but your dolphin, Manami, she's been making these horrible noises for the last half-hour. Almost a screaming sound. I thought you'd…"

"Thanks, Nikira. I'll be right over."

Maybe she's sick. Something she ate. An infection? I've been so distracted by Elizabeth; I could have missed possible symptoms.

When he arrived at Manami's holding pool, she seemed excited to see him. Relieved, he opened her gate and joined her in the stadium pool to see if anything was wrong with her. Thankfully, she seemed normal and performed well at the first show. Her routines during the second show went smoothly as well.

Considerably relieved, Kaito spent extra time with her between shows, talking to her while he examined her body to see if there were any signs of illness. Despite her return to normalcy, something wasn't right.

His instincts began to prove true when Manami seemed tired during the four o'clock show. As the grand finale approached, he noticed that her nod at the end of the pool was weak. When their eyes met, fear turned to bile rising in his stomach.

"Jump! Splash!" The audience yelled. Reaching the turn for the splash, Manami dove instead, circling the pool again. The audience let out a long *ohh!*

Manami came around, picking up speed. Kaito gave a sharp whistle, and shouted, "Stop!" Instead, Manami blazed into the turn, her body and fluke thrusting at maximum speed.

She shot up through the surface and leaped directly at the two-meter-high Plexiglass panels separating her from the audience. A deep, deadening thump sounded when her entire body hit the panels, bending one over, and almost hitting customers in the first row. The crowd screamed. Manami slid back into the pool.

The staff rushed in to guide the panicked audience to the exits.

Kaito announced, "So sorry, ladies and gentlemen. Please accept our apologies. Manami must be feeling ill."

He could say no more and signaled Manami to return to her pen.

Rushing to see her, a sense of dread came over him as he watched her flapping her fluke with a panic he hadn't seen since first capturing her. Unable to calm her, he went into his office to call the vet, Dr. Endo, only to find she wouldn't be back in town until the morning. He wanted to call Elizabeth to let her know of the problem but dismissed the idea.

Tanaka and Yamaguchi came barging into his office. "You fucking fool, Yamamoto!" Tanaka screamed, "Do you realize what your dolphin could have done?"

Kaito stood but did not respond.

Tanaka pushed his face into Kaito's, shouting, "One hundred kilograms of muscle hurling into the stands? We'd have a lawsuit."

"Do you think I don't know that? She seems to be ailing from something. I'll have Dr. Endo check her out in the morning."

Yamaguchi joined in. "Your show is canceled until you straighten her out or get another dolphin."

Kaito cringed and bowed. Kaito went back to Manami's pen. She circled aimlessly for hours, refusing his calls to come in for a belly rub. Over the years, some of the new dolphins developed medical conditions like ulcers, infections of the liver and even lung disease. His heart sunk for not catching an earlier sign of illness. He dragged a folding cot into her pen to spend the night and be ready first thing in the morning to bring her to the vet clinic where they had the proper equipment to evaluate her. Kaito watched Manami sleep peacefully, as she kept one eye on him and rested half of her brain. Finally, Kaito dozed off.

Late in the quiet of the morning, he awoke to the sound of his phone ringing in the office. Manami was still resting. He rushed to see if there was a message from Elizabeth.

"Where have you been, Yamamoto?" It was CEO Yamaguchi. "You need to call me immediately."

Kaito dialed his number. "Sorry sir, I'm staying at the office tonight, making sure Manami is okay. Just picked up your call."

"You watch Asahi TV, Yamamoto. See the damage your dolphin has done."

"Yes, sir. What…?"

"Do you realize the liabilities we could face, let alone the long-term loss of gate receipts?"

"Sir?"

"You have brought dishonor to our OceanWorld family."

Kaito winced, hearing his father's voice in his mind—feeling the rod sting his backside. As then, the shame he felt now hurt even more.

"Watch the damned TV news, and you'll know what I mean. The public trusts us and if this happens again, we'd have to close the dolphin shows altogether. You retire that beast and train another dolphin."

Kaito could not answer. His heart was being torn from his chest and pulled into his throat. He could barely breathe.

The line went dead. Kaito turned on Channel Five News. Video images, shot by a vacationer with a home movie camera, showed Manami crashing into the pool barrier. Then, the panic of the crowd. He shuddered at the closing comment by the news anchor. "An investigation is underway."

He wondered if Elizabeth might have seen the newscast, but he doubted it. If she had, he couldn't bear the shame. He wanted to believe she cared about

Manami and even him, but a dark part of his heart told him that he was a failure—a nobody without an act. She never called, so he figured he had already lost her. Too wounded to open her heart to someone so lame, so different. What was he thinking, anyway? Elizabeth was only a fiery dream—a fantasy that would never be. He was too distraught to think about her now. He only had it in his heart to worry about Manami.

Kamagowa Hotel

By late afternoon of the second day after her eventful swim with Kaito and his dolphin, Elizabeth had grown depressed. She had to admit she was attracted to this strange man, too quickly and too impulsively. She but she was supposed to swear off all men as untrusting. Yet, somehow, she trusted him and sought an explanation that might make a relationship work. She badly wanted to call him, maybe see him and make amends. Swim with him again.

Liz looked at her watch. A world away, Catherine would be arriving at the California office and expecting Elizabeth's call updating her on progress. What would she tell her if Kaito had backed off? She would no longer able to look to him as a source or gatekeeper to the Japanese authorities.

That was the practical matter at hand, but the possibility she may have already lost the chance of a personal relationship tore at her heart. For now, she needed more time. She could only string Catherine along so far. What could she say about her mixed feelings surrounding Kaito?

She girded herself and dialed the phone. "Good morning, Catherine."

"Ah, Lizzy, right on time as usual. How are things in Tokyo?"

"Hustle and bustle, much noisier and congested than even New York City."

"I've heard that. How are the accommodations?" Cath asked.

"Great. The hotel service people bow to you with every step like a sultan. They come in and out of your room to make sure you have enough soap, your bed is turned down, and you have a candy on your pillow."

"Ha. Sounds decadent. How's the story progressing?"

"Hmm, some progress, I'd say. Met with the Tokyo chapter of Greenpeace yesterday. A fledgling group of environmentally dedicated people, very nice. They were politely sympathetic with sea mammal conservation, but they don't think of it as a priority. They don't have much of a power base in the Diet, what they called the Japanese parliament, and have nobody in the ruling Liberal Democratic party with any clout."

"Too bad," Catherine offered. "How did it go with Yamamoto?"

Elizabeth quietly drew a deep breath. "Well, pretty good," she said.

"Is he receptive?"

"I think so," she answered, recalling how she had pushed him away.

"What have you learned?"

She wanted to say that he was unlike any other man but held back. Instead, she said, "Mostly that he's not lock-step with the government on whale and dolphin hunting. He took me to visit an old whaler friend who explained how village whalers have a spiritual connection with the animal. Get this, Cath. If they find a fetus in a cow they've killed, they give it a ceremonial burial at sea."

"That's weird, huh?" Catherine commented.

"It is by our standards, but they have deeply held generational convictions and are very gracious people."

"Sounds like you're softening toward the Japanese?"

"I am getting good perspective and background," she replied, realizing she had loosened her hard-nosed biases.

"That includes Yamamoto?"

Elizabeth hesitated. She realized she had opened up a jagged crack in her heart for him. "Sort of," she said. "He took me out to dinner, and I found out how much the Japanese love their seafood."

"So," her editor questioned, "You're getting to know him?"

"Yeah. He's the sharing type, writes Haiku. A real gentleman." She caught herself. "Considering his misguided views on show dolphins, of course."

"Only misguided?"

"I believe so. He took me swimming with his dolphin, Manami."

A static silence hung between the lines.

Catherine asked, "You actually went swimming? With one of the dolphins that we dedicate our mission to freeing?"

She hesitated to answer as her mind and heart reimagined the time in the pool. "Yes. I know how it sounds, Catherine. But you always said I needed to get close to and know the problem in order to cover it well. And, besides, you know I have this deeply personal, almost spiritual relationship with the dolphin that saved me as a child. You know the guardian angel I told you about."

"Okay, but that might keep you from being rational, you know writing about the facts. I'm worried about you and this assignment, Liz. What about Yamamoto?"

"That's the part I'm trying to figure out," she said, carefully avoiding the truth. "I believe he actually respects and really loves that dolphin, but in different ways than you…" she hesitated…"*we* do."

"Geez, Liz. You sound like you actually like this guy."

"I do," she said, surprised at how quickly she did. Then added, "In an odd sort of way."

"I thought you told me he was gay?"

"I thought he was." She chewed on her lip. "But I could still like him if he were gay, couldn't I?"

"Well, I suppose! But only if you're absolutely sure you can trust him to realistically help you with the story."

"I believe I can trust him, Catherine," she said. She trusted him more than any man, even after she learned he wasn't gay. She could hear Catherine tapping her pencil on the desk, contemplating.

Elizabeth realized she was perpetuating her stupid falsehood about him. She wanted to be upfront and tell Catherine he wasn't gay, but that would be a bigger problem. If Catherine thought she was romantically interested in this guy, she would never be able to write a truthful story. Despite her gut reaction to his advance, she was interested in him. Maybe give it a chance. Just not sure of herself.

She asked, "Can you give me the few more days, then?"

After some silence, Catherine said, "Yes, as long as it doesn't compromise your ability to get and write a story. I'm depending on you. Be careful, Lizzy."

"I will, don't worry," she said. *I better call Kaito soon or I'll risk losing him for good.* "I hope to see him again tomorrow."

"Good luck. Call me in a couple. Same time, okay?"

"Will do. Thanks, Cath."

The tension in her neck from holding the phone did not go away after she hung up. But by talking to Catherine, she got perspective on her feelings about Kaito. Light was shining at the end of the dark tunnel in her mind.

Strange as it seemed, Elizabeth *was* drawn to Kaito, despite all their differences. In the pool, she felt free again. The attraction was to his kindness, his deep respect for his dolphin. His respect for her. Then he had touched her.

It was not his desire to kiss her. It was the hand on her neck. But she had to remind herself it was *not* Greg's hand. Elizabeth thought she could trust Kaito, despite only days ago feeling she couldn't trust any man.

Looking out her window, she noticed the riverside park across from the hotel. A walk might do her good. Soon, she was gazing down at the bucolic Sumida River, wondering if the water was ever inhabited by river dolphins. That thought led back to Greg and his mistreatment of the animals at SeaWorld.

Deep down, she had an icy fear, a nagging distrust of men. It started with her father, continued with the boys that only wanted sex, and ended with Greg. The man who stole her heart, then beat it to a pulp.

Knowing the problem was only half of it. *Could she, should she, allow another man into her life? Is this the man? Could she really trust a man she barely knows?*

She made a list of the pros and cons in her head about a possible relationship with Kaito. She easily came up with a big number of cons for all their differences. The only pro was the pull of him, which she couldn't explain, only feel. When she swam with him and Manami, it was like her guardian angel was speaking to her, telling her to let go of the past. Showing her, she could trust him.

Had Kaito broken through that high wall of distrust I built around myself? Come on, Manami, my real-life guardian angel with flippers. Mother said you'd always be with me.

Hoping for a sign, the last conversation she had with her mother popped into her mind. Was this Paddy guy just a thing, or the real thing? Making a pact between themselves to get out of rehab together was remarkable. Giving each other the gift of sobriety.

"That's it!" she cried out loud.

Families nearby startled and stared.

We've got things we can give each other, she said to herself. She jogged back to the hotel.

Catching her breath as she held the phone, she frantically dialed Kaito's apartment. When the ring went to his voice asking to leave a message, she hung up and slumped. *Why won't he answer?*

133

Mindlessly, she turned on the TV. Was that OceanWorld? The dolphin show pool? She upped the volume and leaned forward. She couldn't understand the newscaster, but the jumpy video of a dolphin hitting the panels in front of the stands and the crowds rushing out in panic. She gasped. There was Kaito, speaking into the microphone, dread distorting his face. She held her breath. It had to have been Manami.

Her heart sank. The poor guy. *That explains why he didn't call and couldn't make the date.*

She dialed his number. He did not pick up. Shaking her head while she waited for the beep, one part of her thought, *he simply doesn't want me in his troubled life right now.* It just wasn't meant to be. The other part told her: *Despite my fears, I have to give him, and me, a chance.*

"Kaito. I just saw what happened on TV with Manami and I feel so bad." She twisted the phone cord around her wrist. "Can I come and see you? I'm also calling to let you know I've finally worked things out and I want to make things right. Please hear me out, okay?"

She had to tell him so he would understand. She choked up for a moment, then said, "When you reached for me, you were not Greg. But unfairly, it brought up those feelings. I just want you to understand, it was not your fault. I'm sorry. Can we talk?" She ended her message saying, "Please call me."

Then, she had a good cry and went to bed.

Chapter Fourteen

"It's going to be all right, Princess," Kaito told Manami as he and Hokata tied her shaking fluke and got her into a sling. Utilizing a forklift for a gurney, they moved her into the exam room. As Manami lay on a rubberized platform, Dr. Endo's assistant injected her with a sedative, and she quickly relaxed.

The doctor took her vital signs. Her respiration and heartbeat were steady. While she drew blood and took x-rays, Kaito misted Manami's body, stroking and talking to her. A muscle memory of stroking her with Elizabeth flashed through him.

"I can't find anything immediately concerning," she concluded. "I'll have the x-rays later this afternoon. We'll keep her secured in the clinic pool until then."

Kaito left, thanked her and dragged himself past the empty stadium. A signpost read: ALL ACQUA-BATS SHOWS CANCELLED. Humiliated, he wanted to hide in his office.

Soon, Tanaka was on the phone. "I want to meet this afternoon, Yamamoto, to go over plans for the show."

Kaito tried to delay the meeting. "It would be best, sir, if we meet after I hear from Dr. Endo."

"As long as you're not trying to put me off."

"No, sir," Kaito said, cursing him under his breath and hanging up.

Hokata knocked on his door. "Yamamoto-san, someone's waiting for you outside the gate. It's the American woman."

Kaito put his head in his hands.

"Should I tell her you're unavailable?"

Kaito froze. He couldn't possibly face her. *She never called. She's only here to say goodbye before she heads back to America.* He ran his fingers though his hair. *She's probably still mixed up, but he should at least say goodbye.* "No, let her in."

He sat behind his desk, not wanting her to see the jittery tension in his legs.

Elizabeth entered his office and stood only a few feet from the door.

Kaito's heart ached when he saw her beautiful face and the compassion and concern in her eyes. Yet, she did not speak.

"How are you, Elizabeth?"

"Sad. Worried about you and Manami. How is she?"

"I'm not sure," he answered, "But the vet seems to think she's not sick. We won't have x-rays until later today." He lowered his head. "I sense it might be behavioral, but I still worry she might not perform again, at least not safely."

Elizabeth let out a whimper and stepped closer.

He leaned toward her, "How have you been?"

"Not so good, but so glad to see you. Did you listen to the message I left you last night?"

"What message, where?"

"On your phone."

"At my apartment? I spent the night in the office. What did the message say?"

She took a deep breath. "I asked you to forgive me, and that I wanted to make things right between us."

The knots in Kaito's body began to loosen. He stood.

She stepped closer. "I've come to explain why I acted so badly and hurt your feelings."

Kaito moved from around the desk. "You're not here to say goodbye?"

"No," she said and edged her way toward him. "It's complicated and hard to explain, but the feelings we shared in the pool were...*are* very real."

Kaito stepped to within a few feet of her.

She took his hands in hers. "Our swim together changed me, it let me be free again. I've learned how genuine and good you are. I feel I can trust you. Despite our differences, we share a lot." She looked into his eyes.

He pulled her closer.

She whispered. "Maybe get to know each other even better?"

"You don't need to explain further." Despite her emotional ways, but maybe because of them, she was reaching into his heart. Forgetting the practicalities of it all, there was a remote possibility that there could ever be a relationship. He had never had a girlfriend, had never been with a woman, but he wanted to be with her. He stretched out his arms, thinking of how they their bodies first touched in the pool. "Will you go swimming with me again?"

"Yes. Oh please, yes."

They embraced and gently swayed together for several moments.

Hokata appeared at his office door, waving.

"Hold on, Elizabeth."

Kaito spoke quietly to Hokata, then turned back to her. "A couple of guys from the sea lion exhibit have come by to give me their support. Let's get out of here."

"Yes. How about if we take a walk?" Elizabeth suggested. "Is there a place that's quiet? I think it'll do you good."

"Good idea. There is some yet to be developed corporate parkland along the bay." He pointed the way. "It has a beautiful shoreline trail."

As the pair passed through an 'employees only' door, the chatter of the crowds evaporated, and the smell of the park's curry popcorn and pork buns gave way to salty sea air.

The horseshoe-shaped bay spread over several square kilometers. At the mouth, rock outcroppings on both sides cradled its calm and sparkling waters. Walking along swaying reed grasses, Elizabeth brushed her hand over the tops, and they slowed to a stroll.

At the shoreline, a troupe of long-legged plovers danced to the rhythm of the waves and directed their own chirping chorus. Kaito and Elizabeth watched the birds skitter behind the receding waves, spearing snacks from the sand. At the same moment, they turned to smile at each other.

"Thank you for coming." Kaito put his hand on her shoulder. "I felt like the world was closing in on me back there."

"I can only imagine," she said, "Let's sit." She pointed to a large rock made flat by centuries of tidal erosion.

Kaito reached for her hand. She took it, interlocked their fingers, and sighed.

"What do you think happened to Manami yesterday?"

"I do not know." He gazed at the water. "She was so full of joy the other night in the pool with you. Right after that, she changed."

He knelt to pick up a small branch with his free hand, twirling the sea-weathered stick in the air as he his thoughts remained with Manami.

"It was not training," he said. "Maybe she's angry with me. I feel like I failed her somehow." He poked the stick in the sand. "My life is so tied to hers. It is like she is no longer bonded with me. Without her, I will fail my audience—my employer. I feel like that nail that keeps sticking up and needs to be pounded down."

He began striking the branch into the sand, thinking of his father's wrath. '*Thwack!*' The branch cracked and splintered.

Elizabeth jumped, pulling her hand away.

"Are you okay, Elizabeth? I am sorry, I do not know who I am sometimes." He bowed his head. "You're not the only one working through issues. I am not the success you might think I am."

"Don't be so hard on yourself. You're not failing with me."

She put her arm across his shoulder and ran her hand through his hair. He gazed into her eyes for several moments, asking with his heart if it were true.

She touched the side of his face. "You are a kind and passionate man." She brought a finger to his chin. "A man I want to be with."

He closed his eyes. He was glad he was now following his heart, and finally let go of the thinking that kept him hung up for so long. Just because his mother's and sister's relationships turned sour, it didn't mean his had to. He believed that Elizabeth would be different. Maybe they could make a true relationship. Stay together. She could make him a better man.

He took her hand and exhaled deeply.

She squeezed his hand. "Good. Just relax. We'll work out things together."

They both sat in silence, taking in the gentle breeze from the sea. He was feeling both vulnerable but comforted by her warmth—soaking in the scent of her. He wanted to kiss her, but not just out of passion. He needed to try and kiss her again. But he couldn't find the courage, so he turned back to her and said, "I'm struggling to figure out what's wrong with Manami."

"Mm. You know, maybe it's about needs."

Kaito pulled back. Was he being insensitive? "What do you mean?"

"I mean. What does Manami want? Maybe you're missing *her* needs."

Kaito narrowed his brow. "Like maybe missing her natural, in-born needs." She ran her finger up and down on his arm. "Like when she leaped, it might have been her need to be free."

Not letting go of her hand, he said, "We're not getting into the issue of captive show dolphins, are we?"

She shook her head. "No, I didn't mean that at all. Just a wild thought."

His body stiffened. "I wish it were that easy. I'm worried what the vet will find, then I have to go and meet with my boss, Tanaka."

"Don't worry so much. You told me the vet said she seemed to be alright. And you felt it was behavioral."

"But what if Manami can't perform?" He sighed. "If she hurt herself or a customer, she will probably be confined to her holding pen until they decide to euthanize her."

"Kaito, if she's physically okay, you'll work it out. You're bonded with her and with that uncanny ability to communicate, she'll do anything for you."

He was silent. They watched a pair of pelicans fly low and slow. On the rocks at the end of the bay, a family held hands while they climbed along, laughing and yelling. Beyond, a wooden fishing boat about the size of his father's beloved *Yoshi Maru* was moored. It made him think of how wrong his father was about women. Maybe a woman can help a man be stronger.

"How deep is the water in the bay?" Elizabeth asked out of the blue.

"It drops off to twenty to thirty meters."

"Is the water clean?"

Kaito looked puzzled. "There are two ten-meter tides twice a day. I have swum here. It stays very clean. Why are you asking?"

"Oh, I don't know. Sometimes crazy things just come to me. I can imagine Manami swimming free here in this bay but sheltered from the open sea."

"What?"

"Just picture dolphins out there, no longer confined to pools. Would she thrive in this habitat?"

Kaito listened.

"She could dive, catch fish, and have a family and still perform on occasion. They have sanctuaries for elephants and chimpanzees. Why not for dolphins?" She tugged on his arm. "She could be free, Kaito, almost. And customers could visit her."

He jumped up, put his arms around her, and lifted her up in the air. "You are crazy. Crazy and beautiful." He kissed her forehead.

"What's that about?" She asked, laughing.

"It means you're a genius."

"You mean about Manami actually living in the bay?"

"Yes. Although there are a lot of things that would have to be worked out. Like getting clearances from the prefecture. We'd need to build sophisticated porous barriers to prevent her from escaping and prevent sharks from entering. We'd have to add secure spaces for storms. Manami needs to relearn how to catch live fish. Staff would have to constantly monitor the condition and temperature of the water. It could be no less than ten degrees centigrade or more than twenty-eight."

"Yes, yes," Elizabeth said with a nod and a smile.

Kaito went on. "You know, it wouldn't be a fully natural habitat for their wide-ranging, social behavior. But we could bring in young dolphins for her pod. We could add marine plants and make it a dynamic environment so they could express themselves."

"We'd have to draw up preliminary plans for the lagoon. I know this talented construction engineer, Naoki Makuri, who I roomed with at the university. He designed and built many exhibits at OceanWorld. He's no longer under contract. He owes me for helping his daughter get a job." He slow-danced again, then added, "He's quite a character, a bigwig in the Communist party."

Suddenly, Kaito stopped thinking aloud and shook his head.

He kicked at the sand. "Management will never buy it. Spend billions of yen just to give Manami a decent home? I do not think so. OceanWorld is all about growing an audience and making money."

"Maybe they could see the investment would have a big audience payoff," Elizabeth offered. "Maybe another venue beyond shows."

"Yes. Maybe."

"It could lead to doing more than helping Manami. With education, it could help protect all dolphins." She raised a finger in the air. "And you'd have a place and time to start your intra-species communication research."

Her words ebbed and flowed throughout Kaito's body, and he gazed out over the lagoon. He watched the ripple of the waves, kissed by the afternoon sun, drift toward him. Elizabeth had reignited his dream. There was harmony in this. Both a vision and a feeling. *From her to me.*

Turning to look into her eyes, he saw more than enchanting colors. They now reflected oceans—a journeys of discovery. *With Elizabeth?*

She pulled him closer.

Did she want me this time? Trust me? Kaito's lips trembled ever so slightly as he drew near, watching her face for another sign.

Her lips parted.

The sweetness of her breath mixed with the salty sea air.

To be sure, he kissed her lightly.

She closed her eyes and nodded, yes.

They embraced and took each other in. Kissed for a long time.

Kaito's trembling was different now. It danced throughout his body. He was sure he could feel it in hers.

When they parted, he put his hand to the side of her face. "Did that feel okay?"

"Yes. Yes." She ran her finger over his lips. "It felt really good." She smiled shyly. "What possessed you to kiss me now, Mr. Yamamoto?"

"Well. Your...your eyes. The inspiration you gave me." He opened his palms toward her to explain. "You know, about the lagoon and my research. A way to re-dedicate my life to my dream."

"Okay. Okay. I get that." She entreated him, "Anything else?"

"And...and I felt like you could be part of it. Swim with me." He shrugged his shoulders. "But...but I don't know what I could give you in return?"

She placed her hand on his. "Maybe I could be part of this..." she waved her other hand across the lagoon, "...part of Manami's life and yours."

He squeezed her hand. "You'd consider that?"

She nodded. "I have."

"Really?" His voice raised an octave. "Like maybe you could pursue your writing career here in Japan?" he asked then nodded. "You know, I could help you."

She beamed. "We could make it work," and stuck out her hand.

They shook and laughed together. He reached across the small space that lay between them and kissed again. Their oneness disappeared into each other.

A seagull screeched overhead. Elizabeth pulled back and put her finger on his nose. "Now you need to get to work, Yamamoto-san. Get management to believe in you and your idea."

He touched her nose. "Our idea." He clasped his hands together. "But I'm afraid a sanctuary would be so radical."

"It is, but we both know it is right. You could tell them you'd quit if they didn't build it."

"Give up my career?"

"Or give up on your dolphin."

Taken aback by her candor, he shook his head. "Will you help me have the courage?"

She smiled. "You got it."

Chapter Fifteen
OceanWorld Veterinary Clinic

Walking down the hall to the clinic, Kaito's nerves were on edge, but he had a newfound courage while holding Elizabeth's hand. They passed the nursery window where Dr. Endo was bottle-feeding a baby sea lion. From behind the window, she mouthed, 'I'll be right there.'

Kaito and Elizabeth's few minutes in the conference room felt like hours, until Dr. Endo entered at last.

"Dr. Endo, may I introduce Elizabeth Worthington, a journalist from America. She has great interest in dolphin behavior. We're hoping you've got Manami's test results."

"Fortunately, the contusions are only superficial. No indications of any internal damage. She's ready to go back into the water, but she may be lethargic for a few hours."

Under the table, Kaito squeezed Elizabeth's hand. "Thanks. Do you have any idea what could have caused her to leap out of the pool like that?"

"Well, considering her age and general health," Dr. Endo began, "Maybe it was normal."

"Possibly hormonal?" Elizabeth asked.

"Exactly." The doctor nodded. "Her estrogen levels were very high but not unexpected for a ten-year-old bottlenose. The hormonal surge can be overpowering to the animal. Was she floating like a log on her side at all, Kaito?"

"Yes, as a matter of fact, she was. Just thought she was tired."

"Too bad we don't have a mate for her. If we inject altrenogest, it will suppress the progesterone."

Kaito looked puzzled.

Endo added, "She might settle down as a result."

"That would be good. I'll get back to you. Is the sling ready?"

The vet nodded.

"Thanks. I'll call Hokata. May I use your phone?"

Elizabeth watched as Kaito and Hokata lowered the sleepy dolphin into her holding pool. Manami took to the water slowly at first, but when she saw Kaito and Elizabeth sitting poolside, she circled in front for a passing stroke from their hands.

"You were right about her condition," Kaito said. "I had noticed a few weeks ago some...I guess it would have been...foreplay with a young male."

Elizabeth reached over and joined their wet hands. "It was a guess."

"A smart one. I feel stupid not mentioning those behaviors to Dr. Endo as well."

"You shouldn't," she remarked. "It can be hard to interpret the drive to find a mate."

"You've got incredible instincts, Elizabeth, and you deserve a huge thanks for thinking of the dolphin sanctuary. A place where Manami could enjoy more freedom."

"You're welcome, but I want to thank you for..." She gazed into his eyes. "For letting me into your life."

"It was my pleasure," he responded, thinking how glad he was she'd come into his. "Is that what you call it?"

"Uh-huh. What do you think we did?"

Kaito searched for the words. "Umm, found a connection with someone."

She chuckled. "You're such a brainiac."

"What's that?"

"Someone who talks from his mind, not so easily from his heart."

"I am sorry. I just have a hard time getting out of my head."

"I know, but I can help you with that."

"Good," he said, pausing, then asking, "What does *your* heart say, Elizabeth?"

She gazed into his eyes. "To feel again what we felt in the pool that evening." She paused. "That's assuming you would feel comfortable leaving Manami now."

"I would be. Then what?" A nervous excitement came over him and he grinned.

She returned a knowing smile.

Kaito pulled her closer. Their lips met and his sense of self melted away. The sweet taste of her, the closeness of one another, set him free. It was beyond their synergy. She was becoming more of a kindred spirit. His heart felt as though it leaped out of his chest.

Manami let out a *pfhoo* of air and yipped a 'yes'.

They laughed and Kaito said, "I forgot where we were. And…and where we go from here."

Placing a finger on his chin and gazing into his eyes, she spoke the words he wanted to hear. "To my hotel."

Excited and nervous at the same time, he reached to help her up. "I'll give Manami a couple of squid, get Hokata to watch her, and we can go."

As they got into the car, Elizabeth snuggled up next to him. When she placed her hand on his knee, Kaito's doubts resurface. He knew from the movies; her invitation could mean and lead to intercourse. His fears fought with the desire. Up to now, he could only imagine being with a woman. What would she expect? *Could I do it?*

Driving to the hotel as fast as his fast-beating heart could go, he wheeled the car into a sharp turn. "Ooops," he said as Elizabeth's body swayed away from his. "Sorry. I almost missed the exit."

She held onto his knee. "Hope you're not having second thoughts," she said with a smile.

"No. But I'm thinking about where we go tomorrow."

"We don't have to go there now. Stay with me tonight."

She was right, but the *now* kept him gripping the steering wheel. "You should know, I still have what you called—hang-ups."

She squeezed his knee. "I've got them, too, but…" she leaned toward him. "We can both let them go."

"I hope so," he said, pulling the car into the hotel parking lot.

She whispered in his ear, "Don't worry." Then kissed him on the neck.

Her kiss sent a shiver down his body. He tried to leave his worries behind in the car.

They rushed into the hotel, ignoring stares from in the lobby and elevator. At her floor, Elizabeth pulled Kaito out of the elevator and took him skipping down the hall. Kaito's heart beat with the same charge of anticipation, trying to keep up with her. When they reached the door, Elizabeth pushed Kaito through it. He became a disjointed puppet being tossed around in a *Bunraku* show.

She tugged him into the sitting room, pulled off his jacket, and eased him onto the sofa. Putting her arms around his neck, she bent over and kissed him.

The hot taste of her intoxicated him, sending adrenaline through his body and alarms to his mind. He fought back a shudder.

She stilled and asked, "Am I going too fast?"

"No, no, but can I tell you something?" He ran his fingers through his hair. "I...I have never been with a woman before."

"Don't worry," she said, staring lovingly at him. "I'll show you the way."

Her eyes spoke of desire for him. It was the first time he felt the power of another reaching into him. She brushed her lips along his, then darted the tip of her tongue in and out of his mouth. Kaito let out a soft moan from deep in his throat. She climbed onto him and straddled his lap. Their bodies melded with ease, their heat mingling.

There was no weight to her—only energy. He experienced both a great surge and loss of power. She slowly unbuttoned his shirt. He removed her blouse but struggled with her bra. She undid it, revealing her breasts to him. He sighed at their beauty. He fondled and kissed them softly, then buried his face in their already damp smoothness, discovering a taste and smell that heightened his senses.

Kaito ran his hands down her back and dwelled in the dimples, twirling his fingers in the delicate depressions. Reaching lower to gently grasp her buttocks, he became attuned to the tiny rhythmic motion of her hips.

She reached between his legs and touched the tip of his throbbing shaft.

He jerked back a bit.

"Don't worry, I think we're both ready," she whispered and wrapped her hand around it. Then, guiding his hand, she said, "Now, feel how ready I am for you."

Feeling her wetness and hearing her moans, he became submerged in a current of sensations—a receiving—not a taking of pleasure. His fears and doubts about being with a woman, this woman, wiped away. Nerves raging in intensity, he came to the edge of a billowing tidal wave. He breathed heavily and his body convulsed before he fully let go. His being became one with hers as they floated above the earth in rapture.

When Kaito opened his eyes, he couldn't remember where he was. A warm breeze crossed the back of his neck, and a smile of contentment came to his face.

"Kaito?" Elizabeth whispered and curled a soft hand around his waist.

He turned, facing her. "Elizabeth?"

She smiled, raising a brow. "Were you expecting someone else?"

"No, no." He placed his hand over her ear and kissed her forehead. "I am not used to having…" He wasn't sure how he was supposed to feel. "A beautiful princess in bed with me." His hand glided over the arc of her hip. Palming her bottom, he pulled her closer.

She moaned.

His hand retreated to his side. "Something wrong?"

"Not at all." Her eyes brightened. "Last night was wonderful."

His eyes widened. "Thanks."

She snuggled. "We really connected, Kaito Yamamoto."

Kaito wanted to hear more.

"You know. I was doubting I'd ever be with someone again."

"Hah! I never thought I'd be with a woman, let alone a crazy *gajin*." He smiled and tickled her thighs, trying to slip his hand between them. She feigned resistance and said, "Kiss me softly first."

They kissed and made love.

Chapter Sixteen

After a long nap, Elizabeth woke wanting to have a deeper talk with Kaito. She was falling hard and fast for this man, just like she had done once before, and lost. The small feeling part of her was swept up, no, overtaken by his love. She clung fast to it. Held onto it with a vengeance. But the thinking part of her had to know. She tapped his arm and woke him.

He pulled closer, kissed her, and began stroking her hair.

"Not now, sweetheart, I want to talk," she said, crossing her arms.

Kaito stiffened and his eyes became wide with worry. "About what?"

She slid her fingers through his hair and gazed into the soft darkness of his giving eyes. "What are your true—what did you call them—*honne* feelings, about me?"

He exhaled and glimpsed into her eyes. "My feelings are hard to explain, but I know you've made me a very happy man."

She patted his cheek but wanted more assurance. "You make me happy, too. So, what are your feelings about us?"

He furrowed his brow. "You mean in the future? That's harder."

She brushed her hair behind her ear. "I want to know where your heart lies."

"It doesn't lie," he said, making a joke and pulling her closer. "It needs you."

She gave him a quick peck on the cheek. "I'm asking about...you know...do you think we have something together?"

"A team," he said, touching the tip of her nose.

"One that stays together?"

"Elizabeth. What are you trying to get at?" He looked deep into her eyes. "I don't know what else to tell you."

Elizabeth couldn't quite describe what she wanted to know from him and came to understand why. He didn't have any track record, any direct experiences. It was too new to him, and he was too intoxicated with lovemaking. How could he sense a future together and its unexpected challenges? She thought that if she could learn everything about this man and his family that that would erase all doubts she had about his honesty and trustworthiness. Maybe even overcome the always nagging feeling that something was missing in herself. She tried again.

"Can I ask you about your family, your sister and mother? What you thought and felt about them?"

"I guess. Why?"

"Let's say it's just part of getting to know each other better and how these things might affect us."

He took a deep breath and laid on his back "Okay. I was deeply affected by my sister's life."

Elizabeth wrinkled her brow.

"Etsuko became a *pan-pan* girl."

"What's that?"

"It's a long story."

"Can you start at the beginning?"

"If you want me to." He took a deep breath. "My sister had to get out, away from Father, anyway she could. Father had arranged her marriage with the son of a wealthy merchant—a village boy who would provide for Etsuko and bring status to our family. Etsuko refused and told him she would only marry for love—a boy from Tokyo named Horito. So, she left home."

"Is that it?"

"Pretty much. A young woman on her own during the occupation was tough. She only wanted *ninjo,* I mean, love." Kaito grimaced. "We heard she may have moved to Okinawa, where the U.S. military bases are. Maybe sold her body to the American GI's. But we were never able to find her or Horito. It's possible she committed *shinju*—a lover's suicide."

"Oh my god!" Elizabeth turned from shock to sadness. "What is that?"

"It's when parents won't accept the union of two lovers, they commit suicide to show their true feelings, be together until the end and avoid being disloyalty to their parents."

"That's crazy."

"No, it's an honorable way of solving the conflict between duty and love. The theme is still popular in Japanese literature, including *Bunraku* puppet shows."

"Unbelievable. So, how did her experience affect you?"

He sighed. "I was eight or nine. She was a teenager when things got bad. Etsuko was my best friend. When I had trouble at school or with Father, she helped me understand and feel better about myself."

"She was very special to you, wasn't she?"

"She was," he nodded, and propped the pillow behind his shoulders.

"Are you telling me the whole story?"

Kaito inched his hand toward her. "I told you what happened to her."

She held his chin. "But what about your feelings?"

He put his hand on top of hers. "When Father found out, he disowned her. *Okaasan* was heartbroken." Kaito swallowed hard. "And so was I."

"How did your father find out?"

Kaito took a deep breath. "I told him."

Her jaw dropped. "What?"

He frowned and nodded. "I was weak. Bound by duty to obey him. I had to be a man like him who would someday take care of and *control* his women. And I believed my father when he told me women were emotional and untrustworthy. If they didn't follow the ancestral *ie* traditions of the head of household, great shame would come to the family."

Elizabeth shook her head. "Not too many American families are like that, but I can see how her experience affected you."

"I was very confused. Etsuko was only following her heart. But I sided with my father, and it wasn't because I wanted to avoid a beating."

"And now?"

"I realize the shame was his alone. He was mean, selfish, and wrong. Etsuko's life was ruined. Hiroto left for Tokyo. She gave up the baby; none of it had to be." He lowered his head. "It was my fault. After that, the family fell apart."

"You were just a kid. You were not to blame; it was your upbringing." She ran her fingers through his hair. "Are you able to let that guilt go?"

"You know," he said, still looking down. "Etsuko stood by what she felt and suffered for it. I don't know if I didn't already. I honored her courage to stand by what she felt, even though she suffered for it in the end."

She stroked his neck. "That's a hard lesson."

"Uh-huh," Kaito acknowledged. "But when Etsuko left, she told me I had to someday decide whether or not I would stand up to my father and be my own man." He lowered his head. "I never did."

Kaito sighed. "My mother tried so hard, but she couldn't stop Father from beating me. Father was stuck in the past, but she was able to see the future."

"How?"

"Ha. It was you 'damned' Americans." Kaito tried to wink like his English language teacher did.

She wrinkled a brow. "The war?"

"Yes, and after the war, during the occupation, she began sewing Hawaiian print blouses and shirts to sell them."

"You told me before, but not what happened, really."

"*Okaasan* did it to supplement a fisherman's unstable income. She loved her work, but kept it hidden from *Otosan*." He lowered his voice and waved his hand. "He would have stopped her if he knew, he'd see it as bringing shame to him—unable to provide for his family."

"So, he blamed the Americans?"

"He did." Kaito narrowed his eyes, "The occupation forces rewrote our constitution, giving women and children more rights. Most Japanese have the ability to adapt. We call it *iitiko-dori*. But my father fought against change, including my mother's encouragement of my bookish ways."

"What did she do?"

"She told my father she would leave him unless he allowed me to go to university."

Elizabeth smiled. "What a woman."

"I know. She was prepared to sacrifice her life for me. That's when she bought me books, had a tutor come in and enabled me to go to university. Then Mother left him."

Elizabeth jerked her head back. "She did? Why?"

"He found out about her sewing business and gave her an ultimatum."

"I bet she took it. Smart woman."

"I don't blame her, but it devastated Father. She started a new life with a man from Osaka. He used to buy the shirts she made. Her sewing business is doing well. My *otosan*...In a way," he added, "It was a clash between individual goals and those of the marriage." Kaito looked down, "Is now a shell of a man, full of anger and regret."

Kaito let out a mournful sigh. "Sad, isn't it?" He threw off his bed covers. "Let me get a drink of water," he said and gave her a quick kiss on the cheek.

As soon as he got up, Elizabeth felt a tightening in her chest. She was distraught over Kaito's retelling of his parent's break up. So different from her own experience. But how could she blame Kaito's mother when the situational dynamics were so intolerable for one parent, and the chips and the children were to fall as they may. Elizabeth would have done what's right, just like his *okaasan*. But that didn't make her feel any more hopeful about the permanence of any relationship, no matter who left who.

Kaito got back into bed holding a fistful of pocky sticks to share.

"You'll get crumbs all over, you know."

"That's okay," he said, "We won't even feel them when we're in the throes, you know."

She picked one out of his hand and took a bite. "You're right. Now, you were going to tell me your feelings and relationships with girls."

"Huh," he feigned a laugh. "I never had any, until a princess…" he stroked her head…"Came to save me."

"Go on, prince," she chuckled.

"I guess that between my parent's troubles and those with my sister, I came to believe relationships with women were hardly worth it. In school, I was a serious, studious kid and didn't care about girls."

"You mean you were what we call a nerd?"

"A big one for sure, because the girls picked on me a lot and I…I got a—"

"Complex, maybe?"

"Maybe that's it. But even in college I avoided them, and they avoided me." He ran his hand over his face. "I even got hives when I sat next to them in class. Then, more studies. Then, the job at OceanWorld, then Manami and all-consuming training and…" he raised his hands in the air…"hanging out in my apartment alone every night. You know, I could never, ever imagine knowing a girl, let alone being with one. And here I am."

Elizabeth put her arms around his neck. They leaned into each other. "I'm beginning to understand you better. You've got a lot of broken pieces in that handsome head of yours."

"You're helping put them together, Elizabeth."

She tilted her head to the side. "How do you mean?"

"You are someone who sees me for who I am. Accepts me. Understands me and what I need. I am so lucky to have met you."

"Likewise," she said, thinking she didn't feel she deserved to find such a wonderful man. Especially when she felt she could never give back the amount of love she received.

Kaito buried his head in her chest. Elizabeth's fears about trusting him started to lessen. His honesty and willingness to share his feelings were endearing. His strong moral fiber comforted her. *But could I ever give enough love to him, knowing I won't get it back.*

She put her hand to his chin and pulled him closer. He lifted his head while she lowered hers. She kissed him deeply; Kaito breathed heavily. They swam.

#

In the middle of the night, Elizabeth felt a tap on her arm. She inched closer.

"Who's that knocking?" She placed her hands on his face.

"It's me." He gave her an eager smile.

She kissed his lips softly.

He moaned and cupped her breast.

She laughed and grasped his muscular shoulder. "I remember the first time I saw your body at OceanWorld."

"You thought of *us* then?"

"No, but I was surprised to see your athletic build. But mostly touched by your closeness to Manami."

He traced the outline of her mouth. "Yeah, well, we do need to go and see her soon."

"You've got gentle hands," she murmured. "Each time we do it, you become more attuned to what makes me feel good."

He ran his fingers through her hair. "Thank you." He squinted, then ran a finger down her cheek. "Compared to other men you've had?"

"By far," she nodded. "They were all takers. You are a giver."

"Well, I'll take that, but I sense there's something deeper in what you said. You know my dear, you asked me all those questions about my family and my feelings, and you say so little about yours."

She averted her eyes and reached for her hair. "As I told you, there's little to tell that I hadn't already told you." She turned onto her back.

"You did. Only that your father left your family. Your mom was an alcoholic and your sister, well, had trouble with drugs and tried committing suicide. You never told me really about your relationships with boys other than Greg abusing you badly." He gave her an encouraging pat on the shoulder. "What about your feelings? Your *honne* feelings. Please I'd like to hear them."

She laid motionless, struggling with how not to ruin what she may have with this man. Certainly not dig up and throw her fucked up past at him. Yet, he had shared so much with her and wants to know me better. She must tell him something. Her mind drilled down into the pit of her stomach. Dark images of her childhood and recent past ran across her mind in a blur.

She shook her head. "Now is not a good time, Kaito to hear about my shitty past."

"Well, okay," he said softly. "If you don't want to now, but it might be good for you and for me?" He looked to her for a response. Getting none, he said, "Could I ask how you felt about me when I told you about my screwed-up past?"

She turned to face him, thinking she did feel she understood him better and felt closer, but would he feel the same about my messed-up life? "I…I just don't want to spoil what we've got going. You know, burden you with my crap."

He shook his head and smiled. "You're so thoughtful, Elizabeth, but you wouldn't burden me at all. I promise. You didn't freak out or judge my crazy past. I was glad to have someone listen and understand."

She glanced at the ceiling and pulled her knees up to her chest. "Sorry, but I hate being needy."

"You're not being needy one bit. I want to know you better, that's all. Even if it you think it's negative."

She gave him a stern expression. "Look, Kaito I buried my past and want to forget it. Get on with a better new life." She swallowed hard and cleared her throat. "I don't want to be weak anymore—like some victim." She pleaded, placing her hand to his mouth. "I just want to be strong and safe and loved. Okay?"

He gently took her hand. "Okay. I'm sorry. Maybe another time. Just feel you can always express your true feelings to me." His eyes spoke with kindness. "The more I learn about you the more I like you and…and we become closer."

"Maybe," she said.

"Alright," he concluded, and reached over to swipe some hair off her forehead. "Can I ask you a favor?"

"Sure."

"Now that we are, umm, personal? Can I call you by a different name?"

She raised her eyebrows. "Why?"

"You know the Japanese have a hard time pronouncing English *L's*. I am embarrassed when I say Elizabeth."

She put her finger over his mouth. "I...I actually find it cute."

"Please, I have an idea for a name that refers to someone dear and special. We add *chan* to a girl's name, much like we add *kun* or *san* to a man's out of respect."

"Okay." She licked her lips. "What do you have in mind?"

"You told me your sister called you Lizzy. So, if you drop the *L*, I'd like to call you...Izzy-chan?"

"Izzy-chan," She sprung up on the bed. "It makes me sound ditzy."

He tilted his head. "What is that?"

"Someone who's off-balance. Maybe a little woozy."

"You mean like, crazy?"

"Sort of, I guess, and well, I can be at times."

"And I love when you are."

She kissed him. "Izzy-chan. I like it. But I want some breakfast. Do you realize that we never had dinner?"

"No, I didn't but it's only four o'clock. Don't know if they have room service at this hour."

"Wanna check while I wash up a little?"

The food came before Elizabeth was out of the bathroom. Kaito lifted the warming cover, enjoying the steam and scent of the *shishamo* and *natto*. She reappeared, wearing the hotel robe and scrunched her nose. "What is that smell?"

"Breakfast." He smiled in anticipation, pointing at the table. "I got some eggs and toast for you, broiled fish for me." He gestured for her to sit.

"Thanks." She grabbed a piece of toast, bit off a corner, then laid it back down.

He narrowed his eyes. "I thought you said you were hungry. Is your food cold?"

"No," she said, staring at his plate. "I guess I wasn't as hungry as I thought."

Kaito dabbed a slimy brown sauce over the fish and picked it up by the tail. Her eyes widened. He bit the head off with a crunch and chewed with delight, until a grimace swept across her face. Swallowing, he set the tail end down. "Something wrong?"

She held her nose with her fingers. "Are you going to eat the whole thing?"

"Sure." He shrugged and took another bite. "Oh, you're wondering about the innards?" She nodded.

"The bones are tiny and the roe inside is delicious." He held it out to her. "Want to try it?"

"No, thanks." She forced a smile. "After you're done, do you mind leaving the dishes in the hall? That brown stuff really smells. Maybe someday I'll get used to it."

He nodded. "It is *natto*, you know, fermented soybean, almost as good as my mother made." Taking one last bite, he caught her scowling. "Okay, okay," he smiled, "I'll take these dishes out now."

Watching him—his cute, tight butt heading to the door—she felt a flicker of fear. If we ever became a thing, would he someday leave me? She quickly scrambled back into bed and Kaito followed. She could see he was ready again.

He slipped under the covers. "We should think about getting ready to visit Dr. Endo. Make sure she's in health to perform again. You'll come with me, right?"

"Sure, but it's still very early," she said, running her foot up his leg. "Do we have time for an encore."

He smiled and she closed her eyes, waiting. His hands stroked slow and sure. By day's first light, Kaito woke fully satiated wanting to wake her and make love again. But this time, he needed more from her. He wanted to know what this all means to her. Where it was going. In just a few days, she was supposed to go back to America. How could he keep her here?

He tossed and turned in bed wrestling with his side of their growing relationship, forming dozens of questions he wanted to ask her.

Elizabeth finally blinked open her eyes and groggily lobbed an arm over his shoulder.

Kaito stiffly held back his first reaction. He spoke, "Izzy-chan. We need to move along with things."

"I know," she said, "We have to visit Dr. Endo about Manami."

"Yes, we do and I feel guilty not hardly thinking about her. Only thinking and feeling…" he reached over and stroked her head…"about you, and us."

She rubbed her eyes and stared at him. "You look so serious. What's up?"

"I want to talk, that's all."

"Please. Not about my past again."

"No. Your future and mine. Our future."

"Okay," she said with a smile. "What are you thinking?"

"Lots of things. But let me ask you, who are we?"

She looked confused.

He flicked his hand toward her. "Give me a word or two."

"Two people enjoying each other?"

"For sure," he concurred. "Incredible joy. What else?"

"Good friends?"

"And?" He leaned closer.

She offered, "Short-term partners? Is that what you're trying to get at? I agreed and really want to help you try and sell management on a dolphin sanctuary."

He clasped his hands together. "For sure. That means so much to me. Especially working with you. Anything else?"

"I…I can't think of anything. You?"

"How about…are we a pair?"

"Yeah. You could say that the two of us share our love of dolphins and have a mutual goal."

"That too," he said, "But let me ask it somewhat differently. Where are we going from here?"

"Oh. I get it," she said. "You want to know if there's a future together beyond the next few days."

"I…I do."

"Well, that depends on how things play out during that time. Don't you agree?"

"Yes, that's true, but where do you *want* our relationship to go?"

She narrowed her eyes at him. "Geez, Kaito. I can't say other than that I love being with you and want to more and more."

"Ah ha," he exclaimed. "Now we're getting somewhere."

"What do you mean?"

He pointed behind him. "Back to the first question. Who are we?"

She wrinkled her brow. "Thought we answered that question. What in the world are you getting at?"

He cleared his throat. "Are we..." he struggled with the words..."are we lovers?"

"Whoa!" She exclaimed and got up on her elbows.

Kaito pulled back, startled at her response, fearing what she might add.

"Well. In the sense that we in America use the term making love for intercourse. Yeah, it was great sex. Better than I had with any other man." She reached over and kissed his forehead. "You're not ready to go at it again, are you?"

"Not at the moment," he said, still trying to perfect the wink. "But I'm wanting to learn how you feel about us as lovers."

She sat straight up serious. "Kaito. You're not saying something more about love like those three words they end up saying in the Hollywood movies."

He sprung to her side and hugged her. "You got it!"

"Hold on," she said too loudly and nudged him away.

He slumped.

She caught the sadness in his face. "I'm sorry, Kaito. Please don't get me wrong. I like you very, very much. But I'm not ready yet to go there."

"How come?"

She twisted the ends of her hair. "But you hardly know me. I...I don't know myself sometimes."

"We can learn from each other." His eyes pleaded. "Don't you believe that the heels overhead thing can happen?"

She smirked.

"What's so funny?"

"It's head over heels."

"Okay. Same as swept off your feet and lovesick, isn't it? It happens to people not just in the movies, but right here in Japan too."

She nodded. "They say it does. But in the movies, the director compresses time, sets it to soaring music and can ignore reality."

"I understand that," Kaito said. "But when I watched those great old American movies, and they kissed, I could dream that someday I would fall in love like that."

Elizabeth looked stunned, eyes riveted on Kaito, her mouth held open. *Was she perplexed or scornful?*

"Aww," she uttered. "Me too."

He edged his hand across the bed toward her. She placed her hand on his.

Kaito's heart quickened. "So, you *do* believe that all people need a partner, and if they're open and ready and the right person shows up, you should embrace them?" He moved his hand up her arm.

Suddenly, Elizabeth seemed to snap out of her reverie. "I do believe that, but it requires both people to embrace at the same time. Right?"

"Right," he acknowledged with a sigh, "But I have this incredible strong feeling between us."

She took his hand and squeezed it. "I know, but how do you know it isn't your penis talking?"

His face warmed but he smiled. "It is finding its voice alright, but this is more than physical. It's *unmei*."

"I suppose that's intuition in Japanese."

"Sort of, but more like serendipity or destiny. When we say *unmei on no hito*, it means carry me to my soulmate."

"Oh, Jesus, Kaito, this is getting heavy."

Feeling both dejected and determined, he said, "In Japan we have a belief in the Red String of Fate." He could almost see Elizabeth's eyes roll. "No, Izzy. It's for real. My cousin in Kobi got the string and his wife of twenty years on their first date."

"Alright," she said, "You want to tell me."

"I will," he said, matter-of-factly. "It's rooted in the ancient belief that human relations are pre-destined by a red string that the gods tie to the pinky fingers of those who find each other. Once they do, the string will never break. Stretch, tangle even knot, but never break." He looked expectantly into Izzy's eyes.

Elizabeth seemed to search in vain for a response, then finally said, "That is very romantic and well-meant and for someone who believes in a guardian angel with fins, I understand, respect and cherish your endearing feelings."

"You mean?"

"I will be open to and wait for my end of the red string. In the meantime, will you wait for me? We'll find out more about who we are and where we're going as we work together to secure the dolphin sanctuary. Then, we'll see how we communicate, build trust, deal with challenges and all the things that point to the possibility of a loving, long-term relationship. Okay?"

"Yes. I got it. As long as we share our feelings, we can grow together." He gave her a kiss and jumped out of bed.

Chapter Seventeen
Kamogowa Hotel

Still in bed, Kaito woke to a dream of Manami in stress; his heart beat rapidly, and causing him to worry. Opening his eyes, he found Elizabeth lying beside him, sleeping soundly.

Last night was real.

He relaxed and closed his eyes to recapture their night together.

'Yes, yes,' he could almost hear her cry out in between the groans of pleasure. He had held firm until, from above, she reached her precipice and called out, 'Oh my god,' then shuddered and cried. At the time, he worried he hurt her.

So, once their breathing slowed, he asked, "Did I?"

"No, you didn't hurt me," she had said. "These are love tears. Kiss them."

He tasted her salty joy. Now, picturing her body under the sheets, he pulled closer. His reverie and reality collided. He tapped her shoulder.

"What time is it?" Kaito asked as he still found Elizabeth with her eyes closed a contented smile on her face.

She opened them, groaned and stretched an arm around him. "Quarter after eight. Kiss me."

He bent over and gave her a quick kiss. "Izzy. We need to talk to Dr. Endo about the hormone therapy, and I have to meet with Tanaka about the upcoming shows." He sat up on the side of the bed.

She put her hand on his shoulder. "We haven't forgotten Manami, we've just been busy."

He ran his fingers over his chin. "Yes, we have, my *koibito*. I think both of us were lost in the other, but we should get going."

"Just getting to know each other don't you think?"

"Yes, and the most…" he drew quotes in the air…"exercise I've ever had in bed."

"The best kind," she added.

"I don't have a razor or a toothbrush. And I must shower."

She sat up. "I have a spare toothbrush. What's a *koibito*?"

"Ah, think it would be lover."

She smiled. "Good, so we can save time and shower together, American style."

Elizabeth jumped out of bed and bounced past him, blowing a kiss. A few moments later, she yelled, "Shower's ready. Come on in."

Moisture beading on the glass door, Kaito stood and gazed at her form. "Izzy-chan, you are so beautiful."

She stuck her arm out the door and pulled him under the showerhead. "You've mentioned that, Yamamoto."

"I have?" He put his hand to the side of her face, thinking. "Rain falls on ocean eyes."

"Ha, a new haiku." She kissed him and grabbed the shampoo bottle. "We've got to wash that mop of yours." She squirted a blob into her hand and began soaping his head. "Mm, it's so thick."

"You told me that before, Worthington." She handed him the bottle.

He gingerly soaped her head. "Never washed someone else's hair."

"You can do it every morning." She wiped suds from her forehead. "Just don't get soap into my 'bee-uutiful' eyes."

Between his palms, he washed her hair until the ends reached the top of her breasts. Swiftly, his soapy hands swirled around both. He let out a long sigh.

She looked at his erection. "Down boy, remember we've got work to do. Now, let's scrub up."

Soaping each other's bodies, Kaito paused at her belly and stopped.

"What's wrong?" she asked.

"I have a hang-up I have to tell you about."

"Jesus, Kaito." She smiled, thinking it wasn't serious and kissed him. "Tell me."

Kaito was torn by what this could mean and lowered his head. Her long-term expectations might crash up against Nakayama's attack in the swimming pool. "Remember when I told you I had a water polo accident?" His heartbeat rose with his fears.

"Yes, you mentioned it."

"Well, the doctor told me, the injury might affect my, you know."

"Fertility? It certainly didn't affect your ability."

He smiled. "Thanks, but I'm referring to maybe not being able to make a baby."

"Oh, Kaito." She kissed him. "I think I told you when you we were in Miami—I have never wanted kids. I couldn't handle parenting." She pulled him under the showerhead and ran her fingers through his hair. "Don't worry about that, let's rinse off and get dressed."

Kaito and Elizabeth stood at the single mirror and jostled for position. She nudged him over to put on her make-up; he nudged her back, shaving with her pink, oval-shaped razor.

"I just had a thought," she said. "Maybe we should ask Dr. Endo about not giving Manami hormone treatments."

Kaito dropped his face towel and looked at her reflection. "Why is that?"

She turned toward him, putting her hands on his shoulders. "If you could build a sanctuary, maybe there's a way you could find a mate for her, and she could have a family?"

Kaito gazed into her eyes, looking for the words. "Izzy-chan. A dream goal of mine, too." He kissed her bare neck.

She laughed and finished pinning her hair into a bun. "I've got lots of ideas."

Kaito listened intently, mesmerized as he watched her put on mascara.

"Things I've learned from my summers working that 'Snorkel with Dolphins' tour boat. I've been thinking, once you train the dolphin pods in the shallows, the tourist families could not only have their close-up encounters, but you could have classes that teach kids a lot about how they behave in the wild."

Kaito turned away from watching her in the mirror. "Look at me, beautiful." He put a hand under her chin. "You continue to amaze me. How you've come to be such an inspiration." He kissed her deeply.

She cocked her head. "What kind of inspiration are you talking about, Mr. Yamamoto?"

"Not that kind, at the moment," he said. "We better get some clothes on."

"Right," she acknowledged, opening and scanning the closet. "Will jeans be okay?"

"Sure. I'll change into OceanWorld sweats when we get to the office."

Kaito finished dressing and sat on the edge of the bed to watch Elizabeth tie her sneakers. "You know, I can't help but think you seem to be having a change of heart."

"Ha," she laughed, then came to his side and poked a finger into his chest. "I followed it right to you."

Kaito pulled her close. "Glad you did, you crazy *gajin*." He kissed her.

"You're getting better at following yours too. We could make a good pair."

Excited to think she could also be a work partner, he asked, "Does that mean you might be willing and able to stay longer?"

Elizabeth's eyes turned downward. "Possibly, I guess, but it depends on a lot of things: Catherine, my family and whether or not we ever get a go on the project. I am supposed to leave in six days." She glanced at her watch. "But we'll have to discuss that later since we're already late for our meeting with Dr. Endo, and you with Tanaka."

"Kuso!" Kaito cursed. "We better run."

When they pulled into the staff parking behind the stadium, Kaito noticed a group of men walking along the restricted area at the shore of the bay. It looked like they were using surveyor's instruments. He'd have to ask Tanaka when they met.

Hand in hand, Kaito and Elizabeth headed toward the overnight dolphin pens. Before they even got there, Manami's *heaack-yip* call echoed loudly.

"She sounds happy," Kaito said. "I sure missed her."

Seeing them both, Manami's excited fluke sent waves splashing over the edge of the pool.

"Her pool is so small," Elizabeth remarked. "Now I know why you didn't want me to see it the first time I came here."

"I know," he said and flipped a gate lever. "Let's get her into the big pool. We need to see if she's ready to perform again."

She was. And Kaito was now convinced Elizabeth's presence had a lot do with her behavior. They watched with joy as Manami completed every aspect of her routines perfectly. After a spot-on circle/jump finale, Kaito was ready to check in with Dr. Endo. At the vet clinic, Dr. Endo smiled as soon as they entered her office.

"Manami's back to her best," Kaito announced.

"That's good to hear," the veterinarian acknowledged, making a note in Manami's record. "And more good news. This morning's urine sample showed her progesterone is down to normal levels."

Still a bit worried, Kaito asked, "Do you think she might act out the next time it spikes?"

"Good question," Endo replied. "It's possible, and a girl her age can ovulate anywhere from two to ten times a year. So, you would be taking a chance." She looked over her half-rimmed glasses at both of them. "I'd recommend we put her on hormonal suppression therapy."

Elizabeth asked, "Does the drug effect fertility if she were to be bred later?"

"No," Endo answered. "Our experience and limited studies suggest it doesn't."

Kaito looked at Elizabeth. "What do you think?"

"Well, I hate to mess with her natural rhythms, but if she hurts herself or someone in the stands, it could be disastrous." Elizabeth looked to Kaito. "Do you agree?"

Kaito nodded and sighed. They quickly returned to his office.

Picking up the desk phone, he said, "I'll call Tanaka now, see if he's ready to meet." He dialed.

"Be there in five, Tanaka-san," Kaito said into the phone, hanging up and turning to Elizabeth. "Wish me luck, Izzy-chan. Would be great if you were coming with."

"No." She waved him off. "I'll just be in the way. I'll wait here."

Kaito reached out to shake Elizabeth's hand. "You know, I want to say how helpful you were with Dr. Endo, your good sense back there."

Looking puzzled, Elizabeth asked, "What's with the handshake?"

"You'd make a great partner, Izzy."

Elizabeth stood silent for a moment.

Kaito's face warmed.

"You know. I like that," she said and smiled. "What's next?"

"You mean with us? Like maybe you'll stay in Japan for a while and help me with this project?"

"I wasn't meaning that now, but you know I would like to and could help, but that brings up all kinds of problems. Problems we haven't solved yet. I meant your meeting with Tanaka."

"You know you could stay rent free in my apartment, maybe do your writing for *Mother Ocean* from there. Tell Catherine she wouldn't have your living expenses." He looked for her response. "When are you going to call her?"

Elizabeth slumped. "I will, soon. Your meeting?"

"Right," he said looking at his watch. "Whatever you want or need to do, princess, I'm with you." He smiled broadly. "Should be back within the hour. Have to pick something up, too." He kissed her again and headed out the door.

"Stay cool," she yelled. "With Manami's prognosis, Tanaka ought to be happy."

Live with me. Stay in Japan? His words and seeing him leave struck panic in Elizabeth's throat. This wonderful man with such giving ways was asking for more than she was ready to give. *It's all happening so fast. Dammit, Liz, you have to face the facts, your fears and act.*

A haunting feeling of aloneness came over her. She had no one to help her sort through the jumble of contradictions between her heart and her mind. She felt small, weak and lost. Not worthy of his love. The same feelings she had as a child. Would he be another man to leave her? No one was there for her when she most needed it. She closed her eyes and asked her guardian angel.

"Rhonda," she said out loud. She knew Elizabeth better than anyone. Ever since childhood. Knows only too well her screwed-up family and relationships. *Could I just call and bother her with my shit?*

She turned to the only way she knew how to deal with these dilemmas. Write them down. Put the facts down on paper in a neutral, objective way. Then, if they made sense and got to the heart of the problem, she could ask Rhonda her opinion.

She wrote:

1. I think I love this man.
2. He wants me to move in with him, live in Japan.
3. He wants me to be his partner, help him on a worthwhile project.

There are cultural differences and challenges.

4. He is sincere and of good character.
5. We share many values with slight differences that could be overcome.

6. I worry about leaving my mom and Crissy.
7. I worry about cutting short my writing career, goals and ideals.
8. I still fear I may be making a big mistake.

She stared at the list for several minutes. Then, with a trembling hand, she picked up Kaito's desk phone, got the international operator and dialed Rhonda.

"Rhonda, it's Liz."

"Lizzy, are you alright? Shit, it's two o'clock in the morning. Where are you?"

"Tokyo, Rhon. Sorry for bothering you but I need your help. I have no one else to call."

"No problem. Let me go into the kitchen so we won't bother Jimmy or Arnie. What's going on? You sound in a panic."

"I am. Look, I'm in the middle of the biggest turning point in my life. Can I get your opinion on where I can go? You know me better than anyone else does."

"You got it," she said with the sound of her pulling up a chair.

"Thanks, my good friend. I don't want to bother you with all the intricate details of my predicament, so let me be as simple as I can and ask you to be as direct as you've always been with me. I've written down my key issues and if it's alright, I will start with number one?"

"Shoot."

"I think I may have found the man I love."

"I knew it! You couldn't hide that from me when we met."

"Rhon. You're the best. The kind of empathy I need right now."

"Okay. How do you love him?"

"He's such a wonderful man. Treats me like a princess."

"Oh Jesus, Liz. You sound like a silly pre-teen. How long have you known him?"

Elizabeth hesitated, counting the days. "Over three months," she said, then clarified. "I met him in Miami way back, but we've been seeing each other every day for the last six days in Tokyo."

"Hell, that ain't much time to fall in love, is it? Have you slept with him?"

"Yes."

"Was he that good?"

166

"He was more than fine physically. It was what he gave me. He's a giver not a taker."

"Oh. Okay?"

"No. Listen, Rhon. I cried after an orgasm. Tears of joy. It was like all my anger, doubts and fears poured out of me. To this man."

"Whoa. That is something."

"Strange?"

"No. For you, just right. That shell of yours is cracking a bit. You're on the right track. I buy it you love him. Is he in love with you?"

"That's the next item. He wants me to move in with him. Live in Japan."

"You mean you'd leave California. You'd do that?"

"I would. It's different here, maybe difficult in ways. But with him, I would adapt."

"What would you do there?"

"Good question again. He wants me to work with him. Be his partner."

"Is that what you want to do?"

"I could."

"I sense some hesitation here. Does it involve writing about marine life, your chosen field? Using your skills as a writer? Your ideals?"

"It does, but in a different way. More direct. More personal. More meaningful."

"What are you going to do about your job at *Mother Ocean* magazine?"

"Yeah. I'm sweating that as there's no viable way for me to work on *U.S.* issues from here. I've sort of led Catherine on asking her for more time on a bigger story and would be leaving her in a lurch and burning my bridges too. I have to call her soon and come clean with her if I'm staying."

"Maybe she'll understand if you're honest with her. Even save a spot for you just in case. There's a lot of demand nowadays for ecology and environmental reporting."

"I guess, and thanks for the perspective."

"What's next?" Rhonda asked.

"Kaito's character. He is very sincere, compassionate and respectful and we share a lot of values."

Rhonda asked, "So, he'd allow, no, *want* you to have the freedom to express yourself beyond the project?"

"Yes. He's the one who brought that up to me without me even asking. He's so kind and considerate."

"That makes him sound nice, but so was Greg at first, how can you be sure—?"

Elizabeth stiffened, then shuddered. Rhonda's suggestion was what really bothered her. Not only that he might hurt her someday, but that he'd leave her.

"Lizzy are you there?"

"Y…yes I am."

"Let me ask another way. Did you ever have signs that this guy wasn't trustworthy? You know, like Greg was abusing the dolphins at SeaWorld."

Elizabeth pondered her question and racked her memory for any clues. "No," she said. "Quite the opposite. Nothing aggressive at all and he's loyal to his family, including the father that mistreated him."

"Okay," Rhonda said. "I think your sensitive antenna would have picked that up. What does this guy do, basically?"

"He has a big job as a dolphin trainer and showman. Earns good money and is well-respected by his boss and the public."

"Ah! There's the connection I was looking for. Dolphins. But wouldn't training and showing them be contradictory to what you're fighting for?"

"To a small degree, now, but it could be an opening with a different angle. The same results, maybe bigger ones, written into a different story."

"What about kids?"

"I knew you'd ask that. We've talked and neither of us want our own children."

"That's sad."

"I don't think so. We're looking at helping dolphins and the children of Japan."

"You know, Lizzy, it sounds to me like your mind is more made up than you think. So, what's the panic about?"

"Leaving Mom and sis."

"Yeah, that's a tough one. But as I see it, if you truly want that new life, you've got to figure out a way of dealing with them from Japan."

"Mom's relapses, demands. Needs to stay in treatment. Pay for it. Crissy's ongoing difficulties. How can I help them from here?"

"Look," Rhonda said sternly, "They have their own lives to live, just as much as you have."

"But I couldn't be there when there's a crisis or to bail them out. They always need help."

Rhonda stayed silent for several moments, then said, "Hey. How about telling your dad to spend away your inheritance on keeping your mom in therapy. And you know what? I could visit her once a week, right down the PCH. Give you a frequent report. In a way, I think they'd be better off without depending on you."

"You'd do that for me, Rhonda?"

"It's done. If you're ready. What else have you got?"

"The big one for last. Am I making a mistake?"

"Ha, that one's the hardest, but if you want my opinion, I'd say go for it. But you have to weigh your current known life with the potential of a new one in Japan. One pulls you backward, the other forward. Take the fear and ask yourself which is greater—the fear of leaving Malibu behind versus the promise and possible failure in Tokyo, including the regret for staying in Malibu. Look, sweetie, you've just begun to open up your life to another, I wouldn't hold it back. You know, there are no guarantees in love or in life."

"I guess," Elizabeth managed to say, thinking of her father, the boys she dated and hated and Greg. Along with their images she felt a shudder of fear. The cold fear of living with Kaito, then him leaving her.

"Wait a minute, Liz. What does your guardian angel say?"

After a short silence, Liz answered, "That's easy, she is right here with me in Japan. Her name is Manami and she's Kaito's leading show dolphin. It was she that brought us together."

"Well, I guess that's your answer." In the distance, a voice called, "Rhonda what gives, it's two-thirty in the morning!"

Rhonda said, "Just an old, faraway friend, Jimmy."

"Rhonda. I'm sorry. You are a blessing. I'll let you know and thank you so much for being there for me."

"You're welcome. Maybe I'll visit you in Japan one day. Bye, Liz."

Getting off the phone, Elizabeth's heavy heart felt lighter, and it burst for joy when Kaito came into the door. She ran to him. Planted kisses all over his face.

"Mmm, I love it, but what gives?" he asked, holding her at shoulders length.

"If I stay, will you let me take the lead on the sanctuary design and proposal?"

"That's a question? You've got the job if you want it, but staying? You're not kidding me?" His eyes widened. "You've made a decision? What about your mother and sister?"

"Well, not completely yet, but my mom seems to be getting help now and my old friend Rhonda who lives nearby offered to check in on her and report. And I've never been able to help Crissy. Think they can live without me."

"You'd be willing to work around your career?" He took her hands and waited nervously for her reply. "You'll leave the job you love. Your writing?"

"I love my job," she said and thought, *but I have strong feelings for you.* "And for Manami and what we can do together as long as we take it one step at a time." She squeezed his arms. "Maybe there's a way I could still advance my writing career beyond the job. Here I could learn more about dolphins directly. It might give me an edge in my understanding and being able to write more in-depth about them. Sort of work on the inside—just doing my work in another way." She swiped a tear. "Who knows, maybe I'll write our story."

"But what about Nakayama and Japanese dolphin and whale hunting?"

"I'm thinking your go-slow approach is better. Better to understand the culture and the people first so I can be more effective."

Kaito's eyes shone. "So, you think the challenge of the dolphin lagoon is exciting to you? We can make it work?"

Elizabeth smiled and bumped him with her hip. "Yeah. I do. Together as a team, I think we can."

He took her into his arms. "You make me so happy, Izzy." He swayed her into a teetering waltz and began humming a tune.

Then he stopped. Froze. "But what happens if we don't get the project approved?"

Laughing, she said, "Worry about that later. American grit, remember? Clock's ticking. Let's get to work. What did Tanaka say?"

"He was happy, but—" Kaito's face turned grim.

"But what?"

"The first show is tomorrow morning."

"That's good, no?"

He frowned. "Tanaka also told me that Himura, the Director of Amusements, is working with some consultants to finally develop the bay area of the park."

Elizabeth cursed under her breath.

Kaito ranted, "How on earth are we going to pre-empt that with a dolphin sanctuary? I'll be doing three shows a day."

"Don't worry. I got it. For now, we need to call your friend, Naoki, and a meeting."

Kaito ran his fingers through his rolodex.

"Naoki Makuri-san," Kaito started the call, "How are you, good friend?" Kaito listened. "Sorry, Naoki. I can't chat. I need an urgent, big favor."

Kaito nodded toward Elizabeth, then went on. "I desperately need a talented professional to draw up a rough plan for a dolphin lagoon at the undeveloped bay. You remember it? Good." Listening, Kaito added, "Could you work with my American consultant who'll be leading the project and draw it up by no later than this Tuesday? I know it's a scramble, but I'm needing your help."

"Oh," Kaito uttered, digging his fingers into his scalp. He listened for a few minutes and nodded toward Elizabeth.

"You would?" He raised his arm in the air. "You're a savior, Naoki! Tomorrow at nine then, before my first show."

Forgetting to hang up, Kaito hugged Elizabeth and they cheered.

"Kaito! Kaito!" Naoki shrieked, still on the line. "You have a woman with you?"

"No, no," Kaito replied, "Sorry Naoki. That was my dolphin. I'll see you tomorrow." He hung up and turned to Elizabeth. "I had to say that or else, he'd go on and on about only that."

"Ha!" Laughed Elizabeth. "Wait till he meets your dolphin."

"Don't worry. He's a cool guy. You'll like him." Letting out his breath, he added, "He wants us to first tie-down rough goals and parameters." He pointed to his desk. "Let's sit and start noodling."

They looked at each other for a moment, then Kaito said, "You go ahead. You're the inspiration."

She twirled her pencil in the air. "Alright. I think the lagoon should mirror the dolphin's natural environment as much as possible."

"Agree, but not being in the open ocean, that'll be tough."

"As much as possible, okay?"

He nodded.

"It needs to be as large and deep as we can make it." Looking wistful, she continued, "I can see Manami and her pod, calf at her side, milking, freely exploring the sea floor, gliding between the beds of kelp and chasing fish."

"Yeah, but we'd have to have fresh fish catches brought in daily. That would be expensive, requiring the fish to be kept alive in holding tanks. We'll have to find sources and get quotes."

Elizabeth interrupted. "Didn't you say the bay was already alive with fish?"

"It is, but with adult dolphins consuming twenty to thirty pounds a day, that's a lot of fish. They also eat crabs, and they would be easier to catch and preserve. We could also go to fish farms and stock the bay with fry that'll grow into prey. But we could also supplement with our usual sources."

"Kaito," Izzy interrupted. "Let's not lose sight of the other part of the bay. We need a good audience revenue stream in order to convince management we have a better plan than ticket sales from rides. And don't forget, we need to set aside areas for dolphin/public interaction and health monitoring and training."

"And for your research," Elizabeth continued, "I see penned-in areas near the shore for the public and floating docks and house boats for you to conduct your dolphin-human intra-species communication studies. I see two-thirds of the bay for deep-water free swim and one-third shallow water, and specialized gates allowing dolphins to be moved in for handling."

"Sounds good, Izzy. I see you've been thinking about this."

"I dream about it."

"It will be a challenge for Naoki to develop some kind of under and above water gating system, but one step at a time."

For the next couple of hours, Elizabeth wrote out an itemized list of what they wanted and hoped to have for the lagoon. When they were just about spent, Kaito raised a concluding point. "We need to give you cover of some kind."

Elizabeth notched an eyebrow.

"We need to keep you and the work under wraps until we're ready to present. Yamaguchi sits in his office tower, checking out everything with binoculars, and if he were to see a tall beautiful *gajin* wandering around the bay, the old soldier is sure to be suspicious."

"So, what are you proposing?"

"We need to take cautions." He ticked off each on his fingers. "First, we can try and keep you out of the bay when the CEO is in his office. I'm good friends with Emiko, Yamaguchi's assistant secretary in charge of communications. She owes me for giving her family front row seats for years. I'll ask her to stay in constant touch with Hokata."

"Second, Hokata will always accompany you when you're in the park. He will let you know when it is safest to be in the bay. Third, I will get in contact with the head of our security department, Hitoshi Enatsu, to let him and his staff know that you, Hokata, and Naoki will be doing official work for me."

"Geez, Kaito. Does it need to be that elaborate?"

"I think so," he said, bending back his fourth finger. "People might ask what you're doing. You are a consultant in dolphin show production from SeaWorld San Diego on special assignment for me."

"Okay, okay. I'll be a spy again. Now, can we go swimming?"

He looked at his watch, then kissed her. "Tonight, my *koibito*, tonight."

Chapter Eighteen
OceanWorld

Saturday

Kaito was on edge. He worried his old friend Naoki might not show up in enough time to be able to complete the lagoon drawings. But, fifteen minutes before Kaito's eleven o'clock show, the office door blew open.

"Sorry, old salt," Naoki hollered, barging into Kaito's office, "Got stuck in Tokyo traffic."

Elizabeth smiled when she saw the short, rotund man spread his arms toward Kaito. Disheveled and sloppily dressed in a khaki safari jacket over well-stuffed cargo pants, he barreled over to Kaito, a slide rule hanging from his belt slapping against his thigh.

"Glad you could make it, Naoki," Kaito said. He relaxed with a big sigh and smiled.

Hugging Kaito with gusto, Naoki fixed his eyes on Elizabeth. "Great to see you, again, Yamamoto-san. You look like a changed man." He nodded toward Elizabeth. "Wouldn't be that pretty new dolphin, would it?"

Flustered, Kaito pointed to Elizabeth. "Naoki, this is Elizabeth Worthington from California. She's leading the design of this project."

"Fantastic!" Naoki declared and toddled over to Elizabeth with opened arms. "Congratulations!"

Elizabeth accepted his embrace while anxiously looking at Kaito.

Naoki said, "I knew it, Kaito always dreamed of American girls, right, old buddy?"

Kaito coughed. "Naoki is a real jokester, Elizabeth, but a great friend and engineer. We go back many years. But Naoki..." He held up his hand. "Elizabeth's my work partner for this project, and I've got a show in fifteen minutes, can we please get started?"

"Yes, sir, captain Kaito." Naoki saluted. "Let's get underway."

Kaito called Hokata into the office. "Let's go over the list of parameters we put together for the lagoon."

After they did a quick review, Hokata got on the phone with Emiko. "Good news," he said after hanging up. "Yamaguchi's across town for a conference until mid-afternoon."

Kaito excused himself and the team headed to the bay.

"It's much bigger than I remember," Naoki said after surveying the area. "Unfortunately, we can't use traditional surveyors' tools if we are to maintain a low profile. We'll need to walk the entire circumference of the bay to get the total length. Then, I'll be able to roughly triangulate it and draw up a scaled plan in square kilometers. Hokata, I need you to count your steps and mark each 100 in this notebook, while Elizabeth and I talk about issues along the way."

As they began the walk around the bay, Liz was bothered by something Naoki had said. "Naoki, mind if I ask you a personal question?"

"Okay. What?"

"What was that about Kaito and American girls?"

"Ha. He always rebuffed the Japanese girls who went after him. Think he watched too many American movies."

Elizabeth kept walking.

"Until apparently…" Naoki added.

"Uh, what do you mean?"

"Ha, I could see the way you looked at each other. I think he's falling for a real American beauty."

Elizabeth smiled and followed him to the water's edge.

"Looks like a sandy bottom," he said, then glanced at the list of parameters. "We'll probably have to dredge the upper two-thirds to get the fifteen meters depth for the natural dolphin section. We can reuse the sand to broaden and level the public beach area." He took notes as they continued the walking survey.

Naoki's demeanor changed when they approached the narrow neck of the bottle-shaped bay. "You're going to need the help of an ocean hydraulic engineer. He will have to analyze the tidal flushing rates. We may have to widen the neck. Waste and pollution are only one factor. An aeration system will have to be installed as well. With natural marine foliage, there's a risk of toxic algae blooms."

Naoki went on. "The gates at the entrance and in between the natural and public areas will be tricky too, not only in their mechanics and powering, but they will need to be custom-made. You'll need a saltwater proof material and porous design that allows the water and small fish to flow freely, but still provides a movable barrier that keeps the dolphins separate from people and sharks." He spread out the fingers of his two hands and crossed them. "Maybe like this."

"Makes sense," commented Elizabeth. "Do you think it's doable?"

"Excuse me," Hokata interrupted. "I don't think we've reached the halfway point yet and it's almost two o'clock. We'd better head back before the CEO returns."

"Right," said Naoki. "Put a wooden stake here in a pile of rocks to mark the spot and note it in your step count. You'll need to step out the rest of the bay while I'm gone and call me tomorrow with the numbers so I can make calculations."

On return to the office, Elizabeth reiterated her earlier question of Naoki. "Is it doable?"

"Doable? Yes, but it's a big, never done before undertaking. My only caveat is that we are up against laws of nature that we can't control."

"Always," Elizabeth concurred, "Respect mother nature."

Naoki checked his watch. "Sorry, but I've got to head out to my assignment in Nagoya. You've got my number. Get those measurements to me ASAP. Tell Kaito I'll do everything I can. It's been a pleasure, Miss Worthington."

That night, after Izzy moved into Kaito's apartment in Shibuya, the pair shared their progress.

"Manami's performances were flawless in all three shows," Kaito said in a joyful tone.

"Super," Elizabeth said, adding, "Naoki seems very knowledgeable and perceptive, I might add."

"Yes, he knows me quite well." They smiled at each other. "We ought to celebrate," Kaito said, kissing her neck.

"Yeah, but I didn't call my editor, and I'm worried."

Kaito softly pressed his fingers to her lips. "I know it's difficult for you. You won't be able to find a work around until you get her feedback. Tomorrow, right?"

She nodded, "I have to."

Sunday

It was still dark when Kaito groggily reached for the ringing telephone. It was before seven a.m.

"What the hell's going on, Yamamoto?" Yamaguchi shrieked. "I got yesterday's security brief about people wandering the restricted area of the bay yesterday. I called Enatsu, and he told me those people were under your direction. What are you doing out there?"

"Some people are helping me devise new routines for my dolphin shows," he answered, wondering what happened to his understanding with security.

"Out in the bay?" the CEO questioned.

"Ah…yes, sir, I wanted to give them a quiet place to come up with ideas."

"A tall *gajin* woman with that engineer, Naoki?"

"Yes, sir. That's Elizabeth Worthington from California who has a lot of experience with dolphins at SeaWorld San Diego. Naoki, of course, has vast knowledge of our facility."

"That woman's name sounds familiar, but I never approved a consulting contract with either of them."

"No, sir. She and Naoki are doing me a favor."

"An engineer?"

"Yes, sir. Maybe some related facility improvements could enhance the shows and increase revenues."

The CEO went silent for several moments, then said, "Sounds strange to me, Yamamoto. You better send me a detailed memo describing your ideas today."

"Yes, sir." Kaito hung up.

"He found out, didn't he?" Elizabeth asked, rubbing the sleep from her eyes.

"Somehow. Maybe one of the security guards didn't get the word or got scared. The CEO is suspicious, wants me to detail my so-called new show ideas."

"Shit!" Elizabeth sat up with him. "Naoki can't proceed without the rest of the numbers."

"I know. We can't afford to lose another day." He raked his fingers through his bed hair. "Do you think we could safely walk along the shore at night?"

"Maybe, but the guards would see a flashlight?"

177

"There's only one guard on night shift on our side of the park which covers the lagoon."

"But what if your boss puts the word out?"

"It may be a risk, but what else can we do, Izzy?"

"I should call my editor. Now, actually, it's three in the afternoon, LA time. Come clean with her about me staying in Japan." She shook her head. "Why don't you go ahead and shower?"

She dialed. A woman answered.

"Oh, Gabby," said Elizabeth. "Is Catherine there? Oh, no, I'm fine. When will she be back? Oh geez, nothing urgent. Tell her I'll call tomorrow morning, her time."

When Kaito came out of the shower, he could see by the look on Elizabeth's face she had gotten nowhere with Catherine.

"Mm, mm," Elizabeth groaned, shaking her head. "I couldn't get her. She's up in Capitola investigating the beaching of dozens of pilot whales, laying on the sand dying. That's a beat I should be there covering." She gazed up at the ceiling. "I won't be able to reach her again till late tonight our time."

"You can call her from my office after you and Hokata have finished walking the bay..." he paused. "That's assuming I can rely on the night-shift guard."

"We've got to, Kaito. We're running out of days. What are you going to do about Yamaguchi?"

"I'll try and put him off. You should stay out of sight during the day, work on how you're going to convince your editor to give you more time. Save your energy for a long night out on the bay."

Monday 3:00 a.m.

Elizabeth pried open the covers and crawled into bed. She didn't want to wake Kaito.

Half asleep, Kaito gave her a sideways hug. "How did it go?"

She kissed him on the cheek. "Good news. Hokata and I marked the rest of the bay. It came in at roughly six point eight linear kilometers. We never heard a peep from the night-shift guard. I'll call in the numbers to Naoki in a few hours."

"Great job, Izzy." Kaito sat up and propped pillows behind their backs.

"Yeah, but I'm tired. How did you fare with Yamaguchi?"

"I was able to put him off. But he's now expecting me in his office at nine, no excuses." He looked at her as she yawned.

He stroked the side of her head and tucked her hair behind her ear. "Maybe we could—?"

"Not this morning, lover boy. Just hold me. I'm worried and exhausted." She closed her eyes.

"Sure," he said. "Sleep in late tomorrow. I'll call you later in between shows."

9:00 a.m. Yamaguchi's office

Kaito arrived a few minutes early and bowed to the CEO's secretary. "Thank you so much, Emiko, for your special help," he said in a low voice. "Here are some more show tickets for your family."

"Thanks, Kaito," she whispered. "The CEO's doing his calisthenics now and told me to tell you he's running late."

Kaito relaxed and sat reading the morning newspaper. He figured Yamaguchi must have considered the intrusion into the bay a low priority.

"He's ready for you know, Kaito," Emiko said.

The CEO stood, erect, cold, and in command as always, acknowledging the dilatory bow.

"Yamamoto, sit. This will be quick."

Kaito let out a sigh of relief.

Yamaguchi pointed a stiff finger at Kaito. "You and your pals will immediately cease and desist from whatever your silly ideas are including hanging out at the bay."

Kaito flinched. "Sir?"

"Your shows are back up and in shape. If you have any further ideas on improving them, work through your chain of command and Tanaka. And stay out of the bay. I have other plans and I don't want you to get in the way. Understand?"

Kaito stood tall, hands behind his back. "Yes, but can I ask what other plans?"

"They do not concern you. Director of Amusements, Himura, is in charge, working with a team of recreation equipment consultants. He expects to have a formal proposal on my desk in the next few days. If there's nothing else, you're dismissed."

Kaito stood and bowed with precision, happy he at least got the lead. He rushed back to his office, called Elizabeth, and filled her in.

"We won't let that man beat us down, will we?" Elizabeth said in defiance.

"No, we won't," he agreed. "Even though his authority stings, you're right, we can still somehow beat him."

"Yes. We haven't finished. We still have a chance to make our proposal work. I know you won't give up on Manami and her opportunity for a better life."

"We've got today and Wednesday to make our case—even if it's rough." He glanced at his watch. "Izzy-chan. I've got to get ready for the show. We'll talk later. And thanks for your confidence. You mean so much to me."

"Thanks. Bye."

Chapter Nineteen
3:40 p.m.

With only fifteen minutes before the next performance, Kaito inhaled deeply to center himself and control his nerves. He could not ignore his anxiety about Izzy and Naoki. The dolphin park was a monumental project—one they dreaded to lose. He took a deep breath again, forcing himself to exhale slowly.

The phone rang, startling him and he choked. "Hello?"

"Kaito," Izzy exclaimed, "We've got good news. I think we have an edge over the other proposal. Cementing in the bay for a swimming pool is ridiculous. The customers would just move from the old smaller rides to the new ones, something in marketing they call cannibalization. And the bungalows surrounding the bay on the rocks are very expensive, and the return-on-investment would be decades away."

"Good points. And the drawings?"

"I was afraid you'd ask," Liz paused. "With our lost day getting measurements and the demands from his paying client in Nagoya, he's barely started. And, after talking to a hydraulic engineer, there are major health concerns. He recommends building a concrete wall to separate the water between the public beach and dolphin areas at considerable expense."

"Probably got to do it, Izzy. Will he be able to get us a drawing by tomorrow?"

"God, I hope so. See you after the evening show. Kisses."

9:40 p.m.

Kaito opened the apartment door and laughed at the sight of Elizabeth running to him for a hug. She was wearing his favorite baby doll nightgown and her perfume captivated him. "Izzy. You are so good for me."

"And you for me. I bet you're hungry."

"Starving for food and you. I smell something delicious."

"Good. I picked up some *oyako-don* from the *Nakau* shop down the street—your favorite."

"Rice with chicken and egg?"

"Yep."

"I'm really hungry." He kissed her. "Like they say in American movies, you're a doll."

In between wolfing down mouthfuls of his dinner, Kaito asked, "Any further word from Naoki?"

"No, not really. We can only assume he'll show up tomorrow with something to cause Yamaguchi to hold off."

"I know, but presenting it is what I dread. Especially without you."

"Right. But he doesn't like Americans, let alone a woman."

"I worry he may not even give me a meeting."

"If he balks, I've got an idea."

"What's that?"

"I saw that recent letter you got from Mr. Stickle on SeaWorld stationery. You left it on your bureau." She lowered her head. "I hope you don't mind, but we could tell Yamaguchi you heard from the U.S. Marine parks association president, and he'll want to listen."

"You could bring it. Maybe use it as a last resort." He set down his chopsticks. "But you know, Izzy, I'm afraid this whole grand plan will blow-up in our faces. You, Manami, our future."

She took both of his hands in hers. "You'll just have to dig deep and bring up the courage I know you have."

"Yeah, bucking the system, as you call it," he jabbed his chest. "Is not in my blood."

"Kaito. Just draw from your courage in the face of danger when you were fishing with your father."

"Maybe I can."

They were both deep in thought as they cleaned up after their meal, moving quietly until they found it was time to retire.

After washing up, they moved into the bedroom and propped up pillows for a long talk.

"Don't look so glum," Elizabeth held the tip of his chin. "There's always hope." She fluffed the pillows behind his head.

"I guess."

"Come on now. Tell me a seafaring adventure story. Naoki told me you have many."

He gazed at the ceiling for several moments. "There was this time on the *Yoshi Maru* when my father praised me. I was sixteen then."

Holding his hands, she said, "Tell me."

"We were setting our nets off the Ryukyu Islands. Our fish hold was about half-full and the bluefin were still running. But Father said we had to head back home. It surprised me because there seemed to be no reason to leave."

Kaito shrugged his shoulders. "Father said, *I smell a storm—I can feel it in the wind, the moisture on my skin.*"

He glanced at Elizabeth. "But the seas were calm, the skies clear, and there were other boats fishing in the distance, so I was confused. Father patted me on the head and said, 'I know son, but I have to trust my *yama ga li*. We're turning back.'"

"From the western sky, black clouds formed with sheet lightning coming toward us. It was like fire and smoke from a dragon's breath. I became frightened when the gales picked up and the swells soon reached four meters high. The *Yoshi Maru* had to climb to the top of the waves."

Lifting his hands, he slapped them together.

Elizabeth flinched and sat up.

"That was when the boat slammed down hard, shaking me to my bones." He clenched his fists.

Elizabeth tightened the grip on her knees. "Oh my god," she exclaimed. "I can't imagine."

"We heard a horrible grinding noise, and the engine sputtered and stopped. For the first time in rough conditions, Father told me I must take the helm, keep the bow always heading into the swells. Then he left me to find out what happened to the engine."

"Without engine power, the boat tossed around like a stick. I had to keep the rudder steady and pointed the bow into the wave or risk swamping it. I was a tiny speck floating between an angry sky and a hungry ocean that wanted to swallow me."

Elizabeth gasped, holding tight to his hand.

"Father came back with bad news. It was not the engine. A trawler's long drag net was wrapped around the propeller. If it was not cut loose, we could lose the boat." Kaito let out a breath.

"I was a strong swimmer. Father was not. When I told him, I would cut it free, at first, he refused, but his *yama ga li* must have told him I could do this. I saw it in his eyes."

Kaito got out of the bed and paced the floor.

"You, okay?"

He turned to see Izzy's concern on her face. "Yes, sorry."

Kaito continued, "Struggling to keep plying into the swells, Father managed to tie a bowline loop around my waist and secured it to the gunwale. He gave me his fillet knife, and I jumped in the water."

"At first, the cold shocked me. It was difficult to get my bearings, but I swam hard. The waves slashed at me, trying to rob my air. I choked and spit." He coughed. "But then, I felt the net under my feet. I clawed myself up, only to be thrown hard against the boat."

His breath became ragged as he relived the cold and swell of the waves. "I had to dive underneath to reach the propeller."

Elizabeth put her arms around him.

"With the boat rocking above me, I sliced and hacked at the rope until it was free." He dropped his arms. "I surfaced and yelled to Father, but he couldn't come and get me until he had the engine powered up and boat steadied into the next swell."

Elizabeth inhaled sharply. "I looked up and Father's strong hand grabbed mine. He pulled me in."

Kaito let out a deep breath and wiped the sweat from his brow, his hair damp against his skin.

Elizabeth took his hand in hers and kissed it. "Incredible."

"Wait," Kaito said, "Before we got home, Father told me I showed great courage. *Now we are men together*, he'd said. Then he told me that we must never tell our *okaasan* about what happened."

"That is an amazing story," said Elizabeth. "a testament to your *yama ga li* and courage within you."

"Thanks for your faith in me, Izzy."

She slid her hand behind his head and pulled him closer.

Wednesday 9:20 a.m.
Kaito's OceanWorld office

Elizabeth watched nervously as Kaito dialed Naoki at his client's office in Nagoya.

"Sorry, mate," Naoki said, "I couldn't get back to you sooner, but I should be there by four."

"That's okay. And the drawings?"

"I'll finish them, even on the train, if necessary. I'll call you when I get closer."

Hanging up, Kaito said, "Four o'clock," and dialed again. "Let's see if I can get an appointment with Yamaguchi." He nodded to Elizabeth. "His secretary is checking with him." Kaito frowned, then said. "Okay, thanks Emiko, tell him I will try again later in the day."

"Not surprised, Izzy. The CEO said he was tied up all day, and unless it was critical, it could wait until tomorrow."

"We can only hope Naoki makes it now with the drawing. I've got the five-year construction plan done."

Kaito sighed and glanced at his watch. "Okay. I've got to get ready for my next show."

"Go ahead. You need to focus on Manami." She blew him a kiss. "It'll help. We've got a long afternoon ahead of us."

2:45 p.m.

By the time the applause drew to a close after the two o'clock show, Kaito's nerves neared the breaking point. Waving to the audience as they departed the stands, he headed to the office.

He had to talk with Izzy. She wasn't in his office. He checked the locker room.

With his heart pounding faster than the passing seconds, he raced along the back of the stage.

"Izzy?"

No answer.

He found Hokata. "Did you see Elizabeth?"

"No, Yamamoto-san."

He jogged to the holding pens. There she was, petting and talking to Manami.

"Izzy," he said, breathing heavily. "I worried about you."

"Sorry, Kaito. I thought I'd sneak in a couple of minutes to talk to my guardian angel. Ask her to splash a little luck on us." She tapped Manami's nose. "Look at her."

Kaito sat next to Elizabeth and they both rubbed the dolphin's nose as she squeaked through her toothy smile.

"I think she understands us," said Kaito.

"If only she could talk," Izzy said.

"She can. We just need to understand *her*."

"You're right. I forgot."

"Yamamoto-san!" Hokata hollered, "Naiko's calling on the other line."

"Let's go," Kaito said, and they jogged into his office.

"Good news, Captain," Naiko announced. "I've arrived at the *shin-fuji* station stop. Should make it there around four."

"Thanks. See you then, my friend."

He hung up the phone. "He's on his way, Izzy."

The phone rang a moment later.

Picking it up, Kaito looked puzzled at first, then glanced at Izzy. "Oh, yes. Just a minute." It was Catherine. He handed the phone to Izzy and walked behind the stadium stage and waited.

Within a couple of minutes, Elizabeth finished the phone call and ran to find him.

Kaito was sitting, head in hands in worry. Hearing her call his name he looked up and tried to gauge her expression.

She stood in front of him, smiling. "I've decided," she said, and let out a big sigh.

They held each other at arm's length.

"I'm going to stay," she said.

They hugged and held each other, softly swaying.

"Yamamoto-san!" Hotaka cried out, "You've got to get ready."

On his way to the changing room, Kaito asked, "What did Catherine say?"

"She was understanding and basically said she knew things had changed for me and that's okay. She was very happy for me and gracious as always. Said she hoped we could still work together at a later time. Then, she wished me luck." Izzy gazed into Kaito's eyes. "We're good."

"Five minutes, sir!" Hotaka yelled.

As Kaito rushed backstage, Izzy shouted, "See you after the show." Then she plopped down into the canoe bench she remembered sitting in after her first swim with Kaito and cried tears of relief and resolve.

After his last show, Kaito rushed back to the office and found Elizabeth pouring over the drawings Naoki had just left. They took a moment to review his beautiful work then Kaito said, "Let's hurry and catch Yamaguchi before he leaves. You'll be presenting with me Izzy."

"Yes!" She cried out and pumped her fist in the air.

They gathered the drawings and scrambled to the car. Parking at the admin building, Kaito reached over, opened the glove box and rummaged around.

"Stay in your seat," he said, then ran around the front of the car and opened her door.

"Kaito. What the hell?"

"I've seen this in the movies." He got on one knee and looked at her. "I know it's not exactly proper but—"

He dropped on his other knee and opened his hand to a blue plastic ring in the shape of a dolphin he had bought at OceanWorld's gift shop. Holding it up like a ten-carat diamond, he mustered the depths of devotion and took a deep breath, "Will you marry me, Izzy-chan?"

Her eyes widened. She held her hand over her mouth. "Kaito. This is crazy. Don't we need time to know each other better?"

"Yes, we'll have plenty, but we can promise now, and marry when we're sure of ourselves," he said, wobbling on his knees and offering the ring.

She got out of the car, cupped his face with trembling hands and said, "You mean it, don't you?"

"I do." He stood and dug his fingers into his hair. "Live in Japan with me and we can grow together, pursue our individual goals, go back to the States anytime you want."

Breathing rapidly, she reached one arm across her body and clutched the other. "But we haven't even gotten to the 'I love you' stage."

"Right, but I think we both want to say it." He tugged her hand to his chest to feel his thumping heart and said, "I love you."

Helpless, a tiny cry rose from her throat. "I love you too," and she timidly opened her hand.

Kaito fumbled to fit the tiny ring on her finger. Finding it too tight, she stuck out her pinky. He looked up to the heavens, held out his pinky finger and said, *"Whoosh!* Feel the red string thing?"

Smiling, she helped him slip on the dolphin and bowed. "I'd be honored to be your crazy American wife."

They kissed, and he lifted her and swung her back and forth. Parting, Kaito looked into her eyes. "Now we're ready Mrs. Yamamoto-to-be. Let's go to the meeting."

Grabbing the drawing and the five-year plan, she asked, "But what will Yamaguchi do when he sees me?"

They headed up the stairs. "In Japan, other men must respect a man's wife as he would the man."

When they arrived at the waiting room, the CEO's secretary buzzed into Yamaguchi. "He'll see you now Mr. Yamamoto," she said and smiled at Elizabeth.

Kaito entered the doorway and turned to put his arm around Elizabeth's waist and guide her to his side.

"What's going on, Yamamoto?" Yamaguchi asked with the crooked smile Kaito hated.

"Sir, I'd like to introduce my *konyakusha,* Elizabeth Worthington."

Yamaguchi stood speechless for several moments. Then, he scowled, bowed slightly and said, "Pleased to meet you. Please sit." He looked at the smiling couple. "So, this is about working with the Americans?"

"Sort of, Sir. You see, Mr. Stickle, representing SeaWorld Miami, not the association, wants to hire me away, but I told him I have a much better long-term opportunity here at OceanWorld." He stood with the drawing in hand.

Yamaguchi's eyes snapped wide, and he jerked back. Kaito handed him the five-year plan for construction. Then, he unrolled the drawing on the CEO's desk. "May I present the first of its kind, anywhere. OceanWorld's famous, new..." He locked eyes with Elizabeth, "Swim with Dolphins Lagoon."

188

Chapter Twenty
Ten Years, Later 1985

OceanWorld's Dolphin Lagoon Grand Opening

Kaito and Elizabeth stood arm in arm, gazing out at the huge crowd of delighted visitors. "Think about it," Kaito recalled, "It took all those years to implement a plan that we thought might never see the light of day. And here we are celebrating a new era in marine parks."

Elizabeth kissed him. "And with Manami and her pod in this beautiful lagoon, visitors can really learn about dolphins in the wild."

"You know, between struggling with years of construction, the setbacks with hurricanes and management and disagreeing on stuffed dolphins for the gift shop, you and I worked things through, didn't we, Izzy?"

"We did," she agreed pulling him close. "We've grown right alongside each other."

"I thought we would," he nodded assuredly. "And now I can finally begin my study of dolphin language."

"And I back into some writing. I feel really happy right now."

"Yes, and after eight years of marriage, we ought to celebrate." Kaito reached into the pocket of his OceanWorld sweats and handed Elizabeth a small box.

She opened it to find a gold charm bracelet with figures of dolphins, whales, seashells, boats and one custom-made gold replica of the blue plastic dolphin ring he had put on her finger the day he proposed.

"Awww!" she said. "You're as sweet as always. I love you, my koija."

He hugged her. "So glad you stayed in Japan."

"Me too," she said as they looked up to the portable stage at the head of the lagoon.

The loudspeaker blared, "In a moment," CEO Yamaguchi proclaimed. "I will introduce you to the man that made this all possible."

"I know you're ready," Elizabeth said to Kaito. "Think Manami and her pod are for their grand entrance?"

"Hope so," Kaito nodded. I've rehearsed her for six months now. I think she'll pull it off for us. Don't forget to raise your voice for her cue.

"Ladies and gentlemen and children," Yamaguchi bellowed. "The man that created our grand opening, the former Acqua-bat, your showman extraordinaire…"

"Here we go," Kaito said as he tugged Izzy's arm. "At least my speech will be short."

"Kaito Yamamoto!"

The pair bounded on stage, hand in hand, and waved. The crowd went wild.

"Thank you. Thank you." Kaito placed his hand on his heart and looked at Izzy. "Thank you for coming. I'll make this very short. None of what you're about to see and experience would have been possible without the vision, grit and hard work of my dear wife." He raised her arm in the air. "Elizabeth Yamamoto."

After the applause died down, she held up her hand and said, "Thank you. I'll make it even shorter and let the dolphins speak to you. Please welcome your old friend. Here's Manami."

The sound of Copeland's 'Fanfare for the Common Man' built up over the speakers.

Out of nowhere at the foot of the lagoon, Manami soared an incredible fifteen meters in the air. One after another, dolphins followed. Eighteen of them leaped and dove to form a roller-coaster chain of silver bullets behind Manami. The crowds cheered.

Reaching the other end of the lagoon, the dolphins disappeared until they popped up alongside each other in marching formation across the lagoon and back to the center. Diving again, they shot up from a circle, one at a time, and 'knitted' their bodies in the air like never-ending blue angels. They finished by gathering in front of the stage and powering up on their tails, waving at Kaito and Elizabeth.

The Yamamoto's waved in turn and left the crowds cheering. Later that morning, when Kaito gave demonstration classes in the lagoon, Elizabeth was obligated to do a 'walk around' with the CEO's wife, Ahmya, and personally welcome school group leaders, politicians and moms. Elizabeth resisted, but Kaito tried to convince her to play the role.

He assured her that it was mostly just showing and extolling virtues of the lagoon, only requiring the exchange of pleasantries with guests. She agreed to try. However, she quickly found out that Mrs. Yamaguchi and the shadowing filming press that followed took their publicity roles quite seriously.

"Oh, you have such a wonderful husband, Mrs. Yamamoto. You must be so proud," one mother with three little ones at her side said. "And your children so lucky to have such a prominent father."

"We don't have any children," she answered. "Of course, I am very proud of my talented husband." Elizabeth wondered if this woman listened when Kaito commended her work.

"You have to learn to be your husband's best promoter," Ahmya commented. "Your success is your husband's."

"The gardens are so lovely," an important city official observed.

"Yes," Elizabeth answered. "I had a hand in sketching out the best varieties for color, texture and balance." Finally, an opportunity to showcase her contribution!

"Oh, yes," the man said. "I see you used Bakara Landscapers; they did an excellent job for our community center grounds."

After Elizabeth completed her obligatory derogatory lesson in spousal submissiveness, she met up with Chiyo, a secretary from the lead engineering firm whom she got to know during the construction phase.

"Say, Chiyo, we've known each other for a couple of years. Do you mind if I ask you some questions? I want to know how I'm perceived by the women and men here in the park?"

"Of course, Mrs. Yamamoto," the petite, always smiling woman answered, "But I should not speak of these things with you. You are an important woman."

"No, please, you will do me a big favor if you tell me honestly what people are saying."

Chiyo lowered her head. "Many women do not say nice things."

"Go ahead, please. I promise I will not speak to anyone about this. It stays between you and I, okay?"

"Some women think you show off. That you think you are better than them."

"How so?"

"Well, you strut around, ordering both women and men." She dropped her eyes. "Kind of loud and rude. You know, strange American ways we're not familiar with."

"The men too?"

"I only know they ask Yamamoto-san how he can stand your bossiness." Chiyo bowed her head and added, "I am sorry, Mrs. Yamamoto. But I am getting used to your ways."

Elizabeth thanked her for her help and went into Kaito's office to fume.

Later that evening

"Please, my dear *okaasan,* leave that for later," Kaito begged his mother. "Izzy, will you help drag Mother away from the dishes? The TV news recap is about to run."

Kaito ambled to his mother's side. "Can we watch it now?"

"Yes. Yes. Anything for my son." She patted him on the cheek and took off her apron.

Kaito offered his mother his elbow and escorted her into the sunken living room of their penthouse. They sat, sinking deeply onto the sofa next to Elizabeth.

The TV screen turns blue. Burbling sounds of water blend with the tinkly rhythms of Caribbean steel drums. Shafts of sunlight pierce the water's shimmering surface, illuminating a magical, sandy-bottomed lagoon.

Two divers appear, swimming past fluttering blades of kelp and over mounds of pink and white coral.

"Oh ho! it's you and Izzy," *Okaasan* said, her excitement filling the room.

Unicorn fish with orange bellies and blue tailfins chased schools of anchovies; silver bodies swoop together as one. Above, a dolphin slides and swirls like a mermaid in a slow-motion dance.

The divers surface and hug the dolphin. They laugh and squeal like children on a playground. The humans point to the sky, and the dolphin responds by soaring into the air with backflips and whistles. In the stands, families holler and applaud.

"Look at the kids with their dolphin balloons and stuffed toys," Izzy quipped.

"Watch *Okaasan,*" Kaito exclaimed. "Here's the next part."

The divers burst through the water, pull off their masks and grin. "Welcome to OceanWorld's Dolph-Fun and Learn Lagoon."

"Hi, I'm Kaito."

"And I'm Izzy."

Kaito's mother reaches over and plants a kiss on them both. "I'm so proud of you two."

The camera pans to Satoshi Komiyama.

"Oh, it's the lady from Nippon TV News," Mother exclaimed. "And she's with my two TV stars."

Satoshi taps his mic and smiles at Kaito and Elizabeth, standing with him in front of the dolphin lagoon.

"Kaito, turn it up," Izzy suggested. "Let's hear how well we did in this interview."

Satoshi taps his mic. "We are standing in front of the new dolphin lagoon at OceanWorld, Tokyo. With me are Kaito and Elizabeth Yamamoto, the couple you just saw in the grand opening commercial." He holds the mic in front of Kaito. "Mr. Yamamoto, as the creator of the lagoon, you must be very proud of its completion and grand opening."

Kaito smiles warmly at the camera, his arm around Izzy. "Yes. We are very happy today." He glances toward the lagoon. "It took five years of planning and hard work. We thank everyone involved and especially all those who love dolphins and the oceans. We're proud they can romp freely, something close to what they had in nature."

"I see that," Satoshi says as the dolphin's breach. He turned to Elizabeth. "And you, Mrs. Yamamoto?"

She looks at Kaito. "Most of all, we're excited to teach children about dolphins in Kaito's in-water classes."

"It's thrilling to see this new park in Tokyo," Satoshi says. "You've had a fantastic turnout. Congratulations." He looks into the camera. "Here's a recap of what our cameras caught earlier in the day, recorded from above OceanWorld."

Car horns from traffic jams at the park entrance mix with the sound of whirling helicopter blades. The large horseshoe-shaped blue lagoon comes into view, dotted with swimmers and paddleboats. Its high rock walls are lined with coconut palms, red and white-striped cabanas, and are crowned by a lighthouse.

"God, it looks so beautiful from the air," Izzy sighed. "All the years of work and setbacks to get there."

Kaito placed a tray with iced tea and glasses in front of them. "Yes, and Mother, see the large steel gates? They open to the ocean."

"Wow!" *Okaasan* exclaimed. "Look at all the people lined up to enter the park. What a success."

"A big opening day for the long-awaited dolphin lagoon," Satoshi says, "And throughout the day, there was fun to be had." Laughing tourists stand in the shallow water, watching as dolphins swim over and nudge them. The guests gleefully shake the dolphin's fins and give them belly rubs.

A mother glances down at her daughter. "Aya was thrilled to touch a dolphin. She even tried to talk to Manami, didn't you, honey?"

"Woooo! Look," a young girl in pigtails squeals as her older brother glides across the lagoon while holding onto the dolphin's dorsal fin.

A group of excited young people shadow Kaito's training session. A proud father dressed in a red and white polka-dot shirt and blue-striped shorts eagerly declares, "My son liked the submarine ride, but especially loved how Kaito bonded with his dolphins. He wants to be a trainer himself someday."

"There we go," Izzy said as she slapped Kaito's knee, "There's the essence of what we're accomplishing out there."

Reporter Satoshi stands next to CEO Yamaguchi. "I'm here with OceanWorld's CEO, Sato Yamaguchi. What are your thoughts, sir, on this big day?"

Kaito interrupts the broadcast. "We don't have to watch him, do we?"

Yamaguchi continued, "It's a great success, the very first sea-based dolphin lagoon in the world. Even beat the Americans—"

"For sure," Izzy agrees. "I'm exhausted looking back at our busy day." She turned to Kaito's mother. "You don't mind, Mrs. Yamamoto, if we shut it off now, do you?"

"Not at all," Noriko answered. "I would like to celebrate all that you two have accomplished."

"*Okaasan,* would you like some *saki* or I could mix you a cocktail? Elizabeth doesn't drink alcohol, you know."

Noriko shook her head. "Thanks, no."

Elizabeth said, "How about tea? I'll get the water started."

"Thank you," Noriko said. "It will have to be an informal *chakai* version without my kimono and the lilting string of a samisen." She asked Kaito, "Do you have *matcha* tea?"

"Yes, and I always have *wagashi* on hand."

While Noriko readied things in the kitchen, Kaito explained the ceremony to his wife. "We'll sit here on the tatami mats and remain silent as Mother prepares the tea in front of us. It's important to stay mindful of each movement and moment as it unfolds. She will be connecting art to life and the slowness of her movements will help us become self-aware."

"I can do that," Izzy said. "Now, let me prepare my mind." She folded her hands over her lap and closed her eyes as though she was meditating.

Soon, Noriko appeared, carrying a large lacquer tray. Elizabeth's heartbeat and breath had slowed by the time she opened her eyes.

Noriko bowed to each of them. She knelt and set the tray down in one slow, continuous movement. In the center of the tray was a large iron pot steaming with water. On each side of the pot, she had placed a montage of colorful utensils: a green cloisonne tea jar, a red maple wood scoop, and a feathered bamboo whisk. Elizabeth admired the tea bowls decorated with tiny blue butterflies which floated in a field of yellow flowers.

"How beautiful those bowls are," Elizabeth said, covering her mouth.

Noriko's long, slender fingers—skilled through decades of stitches and seams—took a maroon silk cloth and gently wiped each utensil. After placing each item back in their original position, Noriko picked up the tea bowls one at a time. She cupped them in her hands and gracefully ladled a little hot water into each, then washed them.

Noriko opened the lid of the pot and waved the steam curls toward the guests. Then, she scooped green tea powder from the jar and sprinkled the powder into each bowl. Picking up the wooden ladle, she trickled a full cup of hot water into the bowls. The liquid united with the powder, and the bubbling brew tickled the air and released a heavenly scent. Using a fine bamboo whisk, she swirled the mixture, rhythmically scratching the insides of each bowl.

Noriko bowed again, offering the little white bon bons of *wagashi*. She whispered, "Eat slowly first, while the tea seeps."

When the tea was ready, Noriko bowed for them to drink.

"Incredible," Izzy said. "Now I know why it's called a ceremony."

"How's that?" Kaito asked.

"When I drank from the bowl, the sweetness of the treat blended perfectly with the tartness of the tea. It brought a feeling of harmony to the family and inside me."

"That is the way of the tea," Noriko said.

"Yes, I was transformed by it," Izzy added. "I felt like a butterfly that knew which flower to light upon. So beautiful, and thank you so much, Mrs. Yamamoto."

Noriko smiled. "Please, call me Noriko or mother, if you wish. And thank you for inviting me to share this special occasion with you."

"Mother," Kaito insisted, "Your presence has made this day extra special, one that was only dampened by the comments people made to Izzy on her walk around."

"What happened?" Noriko asked.

Kaito glanced at Izzy, encouraging her to share this part of her story with Noriko.

She shrugged. "Most of the women think I lord over them and boss and diminish my husband," Elizabeth said with a deep frown.

"I say they don't know what they're talking about," Kaito interjected. "They're jealous and, how do you say," he paused, "'catty'?" Elizabeth nodded. "And Ahyma, don't fret about her. Her name means black water."

"Kaito's right, my dear," Noriko added. "Most Japanese women want to be passive, and men want them to be. Two strikes against both you and I, Elizabeth. Strikes we share and proudly display."

Elizabeth reached over and hugged her mother-in-law. "Thank you, Mother. I'm glad there's one person besides Kaito that understands me. I'm so happy to be part of this family," she declared, thinking she now finally had one.

"Yes," Kaito joined in, "This is a great little family." He reached a hand over to each of them.

Noriko and Elizabeth squeezed his hands. "I must tell you, Elizabeth, you are the best thing to ever happen to my son."

Elizabeth blushed. "Thanks, Mother."

Kaito kissed Izzy. "She is the best, alright."

They laughed and stood together, hugging.

"I better be off to bed," Noriko said. "I've got that flight to Milan, remember?"

Kaito bowed. "Of course, Mother. I'll clean up. We'll see you in the morning."

After Kaito washed the dishes, he sat down beside Izzy and sighed. "What a day, huh?"

"But we did it," Izzy concluded. "To the future."

They kissed and Kaito asked, "Now, what's this about our future?"

"Well, you seemed to like when I said the tea ceremony made me feel like a butterfly. So, this milestone is a good time for looking ahead. Find my flowers."

"Go ahead."

"Your focus, I think, will be teaching and research here at OceanWorld. For me, I need to look beyond this and pursue my mission. Not only for dolphins, but for all cetaceans. I want to advocate for their lives in the wild."

Kaito asked, "Isn't that what we've been doing?"

"In part, certainly," she replied. "But you remember when we first met, I told you of my vow to do whatever I could to help protect our cetaceans."

"Of course, Izzy-chan, what are you thinking?"

"Not sure exactly, yet, but if it's okay with you, I want to explore some outreach activities. Other, more proactive, ways I can help the species. Maybe it would lead to, you know, bring me back to my writing passion."

"Absolutely, my princess. I want you to pursue whatever that beautiful heart of yours needs to. Let me know any way I can help."

She wrapped her arms around him. "I love you, Kaito."

#

Ten months later

Hearing a wild knock on his office door, Kaito opened it and caught Izzy as she was about to fall. Her exhaustion from an all-night beached whale rescue had zapped all her energy. *Was she hurt?*

"I...I had to stay," Elizabeth said haltingly, not able to let go of the sounds of the slow deaths in her mind.

Kaito took her hand. "Let's get these wet clothes off." They headed to the locker room. Kaito undressed her gently, like she was a child, and sat her down on a cot. Sitting together, he wrapped a towel turban around her head and slipped a second bathrobe over her slumped body. He asked, "You didn't get hurt this time, did you?"

"No, only numb from spending the night kneeling in the shallows. Scratched and bruised a bit, but okay."

"Sounds like another futile rescue attempt."

She frowned. "But we had to try."

He nodded. "Why didn't you go to the apartment to shower and go to bed? I worried about you all night."

"I know, but it was easier for the Greenpeace van to drop me here."

"What's that?"

She kissed his cheek. "I…we…must do more." She looked into his eyes, hoping to see his understanding.

"Okay," he said, squeezing her hand. "But we can't be trying to rescue all the whales and dolphins in the ocean. You and I are doing a lot of good for the species right here at the lagoon."

"I know," she said, "But—"

"Izzy. Think about the thousands of kids we've taught over the years who now care about wild dolphins."

She patted his hand. "True, but if we can find ways to prevent all these strandings. Losing fourteen more pilot whales is breaking my heart. Something's killing them, Kaito. And I think it may be us."

He shook his head. "You know there are many reasons why a group of whales or dolphins beach themselves. Aristotle wrote about the mystery centuries ago."

"Kaito. Please hear me out. My instincts tell me there's more to it."

He sighed. "Okay. Tell me what happened."

"It was about four o'clock when the Greenpeace van arrived above the beach at Odaiba. I was shocked to see more than a dozen pilot whales on the shore. They were wobbling and moving their fins, digging themselves deeper into the sand. In the shallows, there were more swimming in circles."

"A local resident told me the first one beached around noon and the others followed soon after, most laying in the sun for hours. I cringed when I heard their distress calls and scrambled down to them."

She caught her breath. "When we got closer and stood among them, I heard their desperate gasps from their blow holes."

Kaito sighed. "Poor things. Their lungs and organs were collapsing under their own weight."

Elizabeth shuddered. "We formed a bucket brigade and splashed water on them to cool their bodies from the hot sun. I soaked my jacket and draped it over one."

"The team leader said there was little hope for those on the beach. Being only a few hundred pounds each and floating, we got ropes and tried to save the ones in the water. We had a hard time tying up their thrashing flukes, but working in teams, we were able to drag four to deeper water."

"Good that you could save a few," Kaito offered.

"No, it got worse. They'd come right back." She put her hand to her throat. "One of the whales was a baby, only about a meter long, and kept calling for its mother on the shore. A young volunteer, Kimmi, worked with me to tow it out, but the baby kept swimming back. Thank god for this dedicated teenager. Kimmi said she remembered you from an early lesson in the lagoon and wanted to become a journalist."

"That's something, isn't it? I'm glad she helped," Kaito offered a small smile.

"Yes, but it was so hard for us to look into its eyes as it cried out. That's when I concluded the pod leader, maybe her mother, was somehow sick, lost, or out of balance. Whichever the cause, I'm convinced she ended up committing suicide. You know, the family was so bonded to her they followed and died with her."

"Oh, Izzy..." he shook his head..."you don't know that."

"I do know. Just not why. My instinct, remember. Kimmi and I stayed with her talking through most of the night, until—" Elizabeth choked back a sob. "The baby died," she paused, "And part of me died with her. That's what I needed to tell you."

Kaito reached for Elizabeth and pulled her head onto his shoulder as she sobbed. He stroked her arm until she cried herself out and slept.

Moments later, she awoke with a start, flailing her arms. She looked at Kaito. "Sorry, I...I was back in the water."

He took her hands in his and said, "Look, Princess, I've got to get ready for my show. How about you take a shower and a long nap on my cot?"

Elizabeth opened her eyes at the sound of Kaito tiptoeing past her and opening the refrigerator.

"Sorry. Did I wake you?" he asked, holding up a *dorayaki* pancake.

Elizabeth yawned. "No, that's okay. I need to get up anyway." She stood in Kaito's drooping OceanWorld sweats and stretched.

"How did your class go?" she asked, stifling a yawn.

"Not bad, but sometimes, like you say, same old, same old."

"The lagoon is getting tired. The same way I'm feeling lately. Treading water. Not really accomplishing much."

"Izzy. It's only been five years. Are you suggesting the lagoon—the place you inspired—is not working?"

She lowered her head. "Sort of."

"Come on," Kaito grumbled. "The public loves us. It makes the park lots of money and for us, a new penthouse in *Shibuya*. We're educating thousands of kids and Manami roams free in the lagoon."

"Yeah. But she's swimming among concrete coral, dodging the submarine ride, the pirate's chest and mechanical mermaids." She threw her hands up. "It's all fake. And not enough for Manami without a family."

"Hey. It's still an accomplishment. You see, I convinced Yamaguchi not to put the submarine ride in this film, leaving that for the thirty-second ads. Come on, Izzy, what's wrong?"

"I guess you don't get it." She shrugged her shoulders. "I have to take a shower."

When she finished her shower, she said, "I'm going back to the apartment to give Catherine a call. I haven't talked to her in a long time."

"Come on, Izzy-chan," Kaito pleaded. "Let's finish our discussion. You seem to have greater doubts about our situation."

She pursed her lips.

He gestured to his desk. "Let's sit for a few minutes, okay?"

"I'm sorry, but to be honest, I've come to feel the lagoon is not the sanctuary I once envisioned. It's far from a natural home. Sure, they have more room and free time, but we're still asking them to give humans rides. We poke and prod them to learn how to interact with the customers. The whole thing is an accomplishment in human terms, but it's not enough for the dolphins. I feel we've been so busy building and operating this lagoon and program that we've both lost sight of our dreams."

Kaito studied his wife's face and listened to her concerns.

She continued, "I feel I've forgotten my goal of saving and protecting all cetaceans. And what about finding a language between the species?"

Kaito sat back. "Maybe you're just discouraged by last night's failed rescue."

"I am, and you're avoiding the big picture. For me, I want to know why these beach strandings are growing so I can do something about it."

Frowning, Kaito shut off the video and came around the desk. He placed his hands on her shoulders and softly massaged them.

She patted his hands. "I'm sorry. I know we've come a long way. You're proud and should be, but we both need to look beyond OceanWorld."

Kaito knelt at her feet and looked up to her. "I worry about you, Izzy. Are you saying you want to leave here, leave me?"

"No, no. Not at all. I'm just not fulfilled, I guess. We have to do more for the whales and dolphins."

"Maybe you should write again," Kaito declared. "Investigate the stranding phenomenon and write about it. Build awareness."

Elizabeth's face lit up and she poked a finger in his chest. "You may just have something there, Mr. Yamamoto." She smiled and kissed him.

"I could help you with your research. You could write under a Japanese pseudonym, and I'll translate."

"You are a prince," she said and wrapped her arms around him.

Four months later

"Kaito. What's wrong with these people?" Elizabeth chided, throwing a folded newspaper on the table in front of him.

Kaito picked up the copy of the *Odaiba Shoppers Weekly* and examined the photo of pilot whale carcasses on the beach.

Elizabeth jabbed a finger at the byline under the article. "That's my essay about strandings, isn't it? Haruki Hamada, that's the male pseudonym we chose, right?"

He nodded.

"And what are those people doing around the whales carving them up like that? They're not scientists doing necropsies, are they?"

Kaito sighed and shook his head. "No, they're not. They are townspeople."

"What does that headline say?"

Kaito translated. "Something to the effect of, citizen's waste not, want not."

"And this other column next to it?" she demanded.

"Oh, Izzy. You don't need to know. It's a letter to the editor from some local ignoramus asking why we should worry so much about these whales."

"What did it say?"

He shook his head. "Something about the whales being gifts from the seas. He took home several free, fresh meals, before the workers towed the bodies out to sea."

"Jesus Christ," Elizabeth cursed with a scowl. "I've heard that line a hundred times. I'm talking about this schlocky shopping tabloid being the only newspaper that ran my essay."

"Izzy. In Japan, we're just not where the rest of the world is on marine mammals. Let alone your level of concern."

"For sure, but it's not just that. Despite all the time you spent searching local materials for my essay, you've come up with almost nothing about whale and dolphin strandings. They don't care. When I talk to Catherine, she tells me there's a lot of interest in the States to learn of their possible causes."

He acknowledged. "I can imagine."

"The problem here is people don't ever question authority. They kowtow to it. No one thinks outside the box. A box filled with fixed and unspoken rules, only one of which is a blind adherence to a male dominated culture."

"Like me?"

"No, you're not part of that at all, thank goodness. But sometimes, you have a hard time questioning authority and fighting for what you believe."

"Like how?" he asked, straightening his back. "Didn't the lagoon come about with boldness from both of us?"

"Yes, it did, but we need to push further, like being willing to broach the idea to management about bringing injured dolphins into our lagoon and rehabilitating them."

He sighed. "Izzy, there are lots of reasons why it's not a good idea. They could bring in diseases and maybe even attack our show dolphins. Besides, we don't have the medical facilities and staff to handle healing outside animals. You know management would never go for it."

"But you could fight harder. Like you did before to establish the educational programs."

"I know I've disappointed you, but it's more than that. Isn't it?"

"Yeah. It's the whole damned culture." She held her hand to her neck. "I've had it up to here." Noticing the look on Kaito's face, she paused her rant and said, "I'm not talking about you."

"Thanks, but I am part of this culture. And I thought you had adapted pretty well over ten years."

"Yeah, but I've not been accepted. Everybody here is courteous, orderly and neat. Always smiling and bowing at you, whatever you say or do."

"Isn't that a good thing?"

"On the surface. But the men are condescending, and the women snicker when I pass, say things behind our backs. They call me *debu* all the time and I know that means, fat. I looked it up. And I'm sick of them staring at my boobs all the time."

"So am I," Kaito offered, trying to soften her anger. "They're just jealous."

"No, you know they're not," she said, grabbing a fist of hair. "Sometimes, I just wanna scream."

"I'm sorry this is making you feel that way, Izzy."

She shifted to curl onto Kaito's lap, appearing even smaller than she felt. Kaito wished he could take all her pain away.

"You know, I don't have a single woman here I can talk to. Except when we visit your mother. I have to call Catherine or my old friend Rhonda to share my feelings. I don't fit in anywhere here. I feel alone. Except when I'm with you, Manami or your mom."

Kaito kissed her hair. "You miss your country, don't you?"

She bit her lip and nodded.

"Maybe you need to go home and see your family. Catherine. Check out the research being done there. Write."

"Maybe," she said. "Catherine has been telling me about all the environmental issues facing America that need attention. Ones that the public cares about." She placed her other hand on top of his. "It's nothing personal, Kaito."

"I understand. Why don't you take a break for a few months? Get away from here. I'll take care of things when you're gone."

She kissed him. "You are so understanding and I'm such a pain in the ass." She placed her hands on the sides of his face. "I wouldn't be getting away from you. You are my sweetheart and I love you."

He gazed into her eyes. "I love you too. Promise me you'll take care of yourself?"

"I promise if you promise you won't forget me."

"How could I ever forget my crazy *gajin* wife?"

Chapter Twenty-One
Nine Months Later
9:00 a.m. Thursday. Tokyo

Kaito sat in OceanWorld's lagoon lighthouse, watching Manami swim in circles. He checked his watch. In five minutes, he'd call Elizabeth in America; she needed to talk early so she could make a meeting with a man she called Wilson. In the last four months, she seemed so happy and engaged. Kaito began to worry. Would she come back? He had to understand what she needed.

Elizabeth picked up on the first ring. "Hold on one sec, Kaito. I'm rushing to put on the coffee for Catherine. She loves a cup when she comes home."

"Not drinking tea these days, Princess?"

"No. Catherine loves French roast." The coffeemaker gurgled. "How have you been, sweetheart?"

"Oh, alright." He fidgeted with his key ring. He wouldn't burden her with his loneliness. "And you?"

Elizabeth frowned. "I'm fine. How's our Manami girl?"

"She's happier than ever. Breaching in front of me in the lagoon as we speak."

"How's Yamaguchi treating you?" she asked, stirring milk in her coffee.

"Managing," he chuckled, proud he'd convinced the CEO to bring the injured Rin into the lagoon. "How's the writing going?"

"Super," she slurped her coffee. "I'm working on a story about sea otters in Santa Cruz dying of microcystin and...uh...interviewing elders from the Makah Nation in Washington who are pushing for the lost right to hunt whales. Then there's Watkin's research on Alaskan finback whales, using radio telemetry to track their movements."

Kaito interjected. "I'd be very interes—"

She cut him off mid-sentence. "But the one I'm most excited about is interviewing the U.S. Navy about their use of sonar on ships. Research suggests it may not only cause whales and dolphins pain, but also dislocation and stranding."

She caught her breath. "This has been real good for me, Kaito. Exercising my writing chops again. Thank you so much for giving me this time."

"You deserved it," he said. *What if she goes back to her old job with Mother Ocean magazine?* He asked, "How's Catherine?"

"She's a doll, letting me stay with her all these weeks. Working freelance for my room and board plus salary. Makes me feel worthwhile again."

Stung by her insinuation she didn't feel that way working in Japan, Kaito kept his feelings to himself and asked, "How's your mother and sister?"

"Would you believe Crissy's clean these days? I actually spent a full day with her up in the Castro, and we purged a lot of our feelings about our childhood. Am much better now."

"Tell me about it," he said, continuing to avoid what was really bothering him.

Elizabeth nestled the phone under her ear, got up and poured more coffee. "That would take all morning, but you remember how I grew up under her wild shadow?"

"Yes," he said, glancing at his watch. "How you tried not to be like her."

"Right. So, here's what's funny. No, amazing. She revealed to me she felt like she lived under *my* shadow—me being the smart, creative and more loved child. And that's what caused her to seek love in all the wrong ways. Can you imagine, all this time?"

"That's good to hear Izzy, despite the difficulties."

"Yeah, and we had a good cry."

Kaito asked, "How about your mother?"

"Hah. She's with Paddy in Ireland trying to absorb what it's like to live in turn-of-the century Dublin. She wants to write seriously and enter a contest sponsored by the *James Joyce Quarterly.*"

Kaito's leg bounced, and he swiped his hair over his forehead. "So, this Wilson guy. Why did you say you wanted to meet with him?"

Elizabeth's cup rattled in the saucer. "He's on the forefront of the anti-whaling movement, that's all."

Kaito's stomach churned. "You mentioned he was a founder of Greenpeace International, what else have you heard about this guy?"

"Not much," Elizabeth said.

"What do you expect to learn from him?" Kaito asked, griping the phone.

"Just to pick his brains," she replied. "Nothing to worry about," she added.

Images of Izzy with Wilson formed in the back of Kaito's mind. With a dry throat and wet palms, he asked, "Will you be coming home soon?"

"It's so hard to say. I've got so many things going on right now."

Kaito struggled to find more words.

Putting on her heels, Elizabeth asked, "Can I let you know later?"

"I guess," he said, then added, "I've got some surprises for you when you get back."

"How nice," she said and walked over to the mirror.

"I bought a membership to the Tokyo American Club, so you can meet and make friends with other ex-pats."

She fussed with her hair. "How kind of you."

"They've got quite a facility. Big restaurant. Swimming pool. Tennis courts. And they put on classes. I thought it would help you settle in better here."

"Sounds good, but sweetheart, I have to leave. Catherine just pulled in. She's letting me borrow her car. Can we—?"

Kaito interjected, "I...I have another surprise, one you've always dreamed of, but it's in the works. You'll love it."

"I'm sure. Thank you."

She paused. "Oh. Hi, Catherine...Kaito, can we talk next week?"

"I love you, Izzy," he said, feeling she was slipping away.

"Love you too. Goodbye for now."

#

Elizabeth hung up the phone and Catherine sat down next to her. "Sorry for barging in on your conversation, but since it affects me as well, did you tell Kaito you needed to stay longer?"

"I did, but I don't think he was too happy about it."

"Did you spill the beans about Peter Wilson?"

"Not really. Just told him I'm going to meet him for the first time, not going to dinner with him."

"What are you going to do when Wilson asks you to become a crew member of Sea Shepard and sabotage whaling ships around the world? Then, Kaito will be really unhappy."

"I know, Catherine. But I don't know, you agreed, an inside look into whale wars would be the writing opportunity of a lifetime, making for a great series. That's all."

"It could, but please go into it with your eyes wide open. What getting the story would mean to the rest of your life."

"I got it, Cath," she said putting on her jacket. "I'm already late and thanks for the car. See you later."

Driving to Santa Monica to meet Peter, Elizabeth's excitement built at the prospect of writing an exclusive, engaging adventure series with deep, personal meaning. Using her best writing skills to expose the treachery of hunting whales and the opportunity to stop it was everything she could ask for. If Peter were to invite her to participate in and chronicle the Sea Savior's anti-whaling campaign, it could possibly lead to a book.

Finally, she'd be able to pay back the debt she owed to her guardian angel. By helping to save the lives of the dolphin's big brother cetaceans, she would be able to fulfill her sacred vow to her savior. Pulling up to the valet at the Pacific Dining Car, she recalled the last time she was there to meet with her father. An odd twist, she thought of the irony. How Father balked at continuing support for her mother's therapy and gave her none for her writing. Maybe she would be able to show him the power of her pen. How her work could make a difference.

"Good to see you again, Miss Worthington," the maître d' welcomed. "Your father was here last week, but today there is a Mr. Wilson waiting for you."

She smiled. "It's Mrs. Yamamoto and thank you."

He smiled back. "This way, please."

Peter, his mop of hair now showing gray, stood to greet her again with open arms. "Elizabeth. So good to see you again."

She gave him a proper friendly hug, but once again, could feel his natural sexual energy. He was so strong and alluring. The opposite of Kaito. Peter was wired like most men and was what most women seemed to succumb to. But Elizabeth was now a married woman, and she was there on business. "Likewise, Peter," she said, extending her hand. "Thanks for giving me the time."

He shook it and seemed to accept the focused bounds of the meeting. "Okay. Have a seat, let's talk."

Liz got out her notebook, raised her pencil and dug right in. "I've been reading about your latest exploits and although I personally applaud your efforts, the stories have been mostly top-line news accounts, but nothing in depth."

"Right, we've only recently learned to write and send out news releases, but how have you been Elizabeth? Heard you married that Jap dolphin trainer."

"Yes, happily married."

Peter scrunched his face as if to say, 'why are you here, then?'

Responding to his expression, she added, "I'm here to visit my family. Look for cross-country writing opportunities like this one."

He nodded. "I heard the dolphin sanctuary was a success in Japan."

"It was," she said, feeling defensive and protective of what she and Kaito had achieved. "Considering what we were up against."

Peter sat back in his chair. "I didn't mean to suggest that wasn't important. A bigger pool is good for a few show dolphins. I just thought you were more passionate about saving cetaceans in a big way."

"I am," she said, wiggling in her seat at his rude but partly true suggestion. "But it's more than a big pool, it approximates what they have in the wild."

"Sure, but not free."

Another dig, she realized. "I'm working on that too." Pointing to her notebook, she moved ahead. "But I'm here to see if you'd like to have your missions reach more readers on a visceral level. Have your personal story and that of your crew members display their courage and compassion for protecting sea life."

"I like that," he said, puffing out his chest. "And we need to build publicity for our cause. Raise significant dollars for our ships."

"Exactly, but also gain more favorable coverage of you."

He cocked his head and fixed his piercing blue eyes on her. "Say what?"

"Some of the stories depict you as a modern-day pirate. You know, with Greenpeace now disavowing you because of your less than peaceful tactics."

Wilson rapped his knuckles on the table. "I don't give a shit what they call me, Elizabeth. I'm fighting for our wildlife. They are the fucking pirates who are raping our seas."

Elizabeth made notes as the waiter appeared at the table.

"Can I get you started with another Pimm's cocktail, sir, and something for the Misses?"

Peter gestured toward Liz, then pointed at his empty glass.

"Iced tea please, with lemon."

"That's where changing people's attitudes come in, Peter. The public needs to get a more balanced view of you and your crew's selfless motivations."

"Wouldn't hurt, I suppose." He twirled the fruity remains in his glass. "So, how would you propose doing that?"

"Me being an imbed. That's how."

"Alright. How does that work exactly?"

"Well, I would be hired in as a crew member…a deckhand of sorts, that way I could really get to know your operations and, more importantly, the experiences and motivations of you and your crew—people willing to risk their lives."

"I love it," Peter grinned.

"Good. So, what and when is your next mission?"

"We sail in a couple of weeks to the North Pacific in search of some 800 or so factory trawlers doing drift net fishing—pillaging our oceans. Try to stop as many as we can. Ruin those monster thirty-mile-long monofilament nets that capture and kill everything in their path."

Elizabeth winced, then slumped. "Not whales?"

"Not on this campaign. Maybe the one after. I know it's not entirely about cetaceans, but the National Marine Fisheries Service reported that thirty-two Jap drift net ships caught three million squid and along the way 58,000 blue sharks, 914 dolphins, 141 porpoises, 52 fur seals, 25 puffins, and thousands more sea birds."

He took a breath. "And that's just a portion of the take. At this rate, our oceans will be depleted in decades. Dead bodies of water. With the passage of the U.N.'s 1992 act prohibiting drift net fishing worldwide, we have to stop their illegal practices by any means possible."

Elizabeth shuddered at the seriousness of the problem, then lowered her eyes to her notebook. She wrote furiously as Peter sipped his drink. She wasn't taking notes but poured out her feelings like it was her personal journal. She wrote: *his dedication is remarkable, and it rubs off on me. Connects with my ideals, but not exactly in line with what…?*

Reality and doubts bubbled up around his mission. Although full of merit, it wasn't quite what she was looking for.

"Elizabeth? A question. If the stories need to be more biographical, we would need to spend a lot more one-on-one interview time together, would we not?"

She nodded and kept writing. *What is he looking for? Does he truly want my writing, or me? Does he mainly want to enhance his cause, or his huge ego?*

He reached over the table, clutched and squeezed her arm.

Elizabeth felt the pull of his magnetism and strength.

"Will you consider it?" he pleaded with his eyes. "I could arrange for a private cabin next to mine. Much better than being crammed into bunk beds with dozens of rude and smelly volunteers."

She looked up at him. How different this man was than Kaito. Wilson mainly wanted a woman to satisfy his urges in between the long voyages. *I am lonely and missing Kaito. I can feel his gentleness, sensitivity and the respect of a giver not a taker.*

"Well," Peter asked. "What do you think?"

She thought about her own ambition. Could she find a way to rekindle her writing in Japan? What did she want? She would no doubt enjoy the short-term satisfaction of a good screw. But what about the long-term devotion of a giving husband? Was her shared obsession with saving sea mammals a blessing or a curse?

"I'll have to get back to you," she said, thinking she was crazy bad even considering becoming Peter's on-board maiden. Possibly losing Kaito.

"We'll be sailing in eleven days. This would be a great experience for you and the cause. I'd have to hear from you by tomorrow."

The waiter appeared. "Could I take your orders now?"

Peter returned to his menu. "You know what? I'm getting tired of the all-vegetarian fare on the ships. How about the twenty-ounce ribeye, rare."

Hearing Peter, she said, "Sorry, not hungry. I'll pass." She folded her notebook. "I should go, Peter."

"Let me know," he said and stood. "If not this mission, another one. I'd love to have you."

"I'll keep that in mind," Elizabeth acknowledged. "Thanks for your time. And good luck on the seas."

They shook hands.

Chapter Twenty-Two
Nine Months Later

Tokyo

Kaito pounded his palm on the steering wheel, cursing because he didn't leave earlier. Izzy had finally decided she needed to be home. He wanted to be at the arrival gate to welcome Elizabeth. Hug her home. Instead, he was stuck in Marine Day holiday traffic on his way to Narita airport.

He was pleasantly surprised when he finally pulled up to the Japan Airlines gate. There was Izzy coming out of the building followed by a porter rolling a dolly containing boxes. He double parked the Nissan and shouted, "Izzy. I'm coming!" and ran to her.

Kissing and holding her tighter than ever, he kept repeating, "I missed you so much." And he missed hearing the policeman's whistle.

"Kaito," Izzy said, "That's for us."

"What's for us?" he asked, still hugging her.

A tap on his shoulder and he turned. A uniformed airport cop squinted his scolding eyes at Kaito. "Say, buddy. I know you're in love, but you've got to move your damned car, right now."

Elizabeth slapped his shoulder. "You're becoming quite a scofflaw these days, husband."

"Ha," he grabbed her suitcase, popped the trunk, and found the porter standing right behind her.

"Oh, Kaito. We've got these too. They're light but too bulky for me to carry." They got into the car and Kaito asked, "What did you do? Replenish your wardrobe from Bullock's department store?"

"No," she grinned. "They closed in 1995. These are gifts for you."

Kaito pulled the car into traffic with one hand on the wheel, the other reaching over the console to hold Izzy's hand. "So how was the flight?"

"Uneventful," she replied.

"So, what event made you decide to come home all of a sudden? When we last talked, you were so excited about a big story you were pursuing."

"I know, but after I talked to a friend, I became convinced I needed to be here with you."

"Who was that?" he asked, thinking of that Wilson guy.

"Nobody you know, an old school friend, Rhonda. She yelled at me, cursed me, gave me a big piece of her mind. Told me I was such a big fool."

"Doesn't sound like much of a friend."

"She told me to get my sorry ass back to you. She made me realize I was being childish and selfish and obsessively ambitious."

"Oh, the good kind of friend," Kaito said as he merged into highway traffic. "Don't fret. You needed to work things out." Accelerating, he asked, "Are you in a hurry to get home?" Seeing her head shake, he said, "How about if we make a short stop at OceanWorld along the way? I want to show you a different kind of gift in your honor." She narrowed her brow but nodded.

Slipping past the long line of Marine Day visitors, he headed into OceanWorld's rear staff parking lot. Her took her by the hand and bounded toward the lagoon. "Come on. It's about two o'clock feeding time. We'll watch from the underground viewing area."

Reaching the high glass-walled room, they stood hand in hand peering into the dark waters of the lagoon. Kaito glanced at his watch. "Any moment now," he said as a waterfall of shiny fish descended from above; within a couple of seconds, a dozen or more dolphins swarmed and tumbled in front of them, gobbling their prey. "Ah," he said, "I bet you can spot Manami right away."

Elizabeth pointed and, instantly, Manami appeared nose to nose at the window to greet her. "She's such a sweetheart." Izzy puckered up and kissed the glass.

Manami nodded her head in laugher and began heralding Izzy with her favorite bubble trick. Blowing out a chain of bubbles and swirling them into a circle, she dove in and out of it until the bubbles rose to the surface. Elizabeth bounced on her feet and clapped. "So good to see her again."

"Look over to the kelp rippling on the left. Can you spot the male? The one swimming sort of awkwardly?"

"You mean the one with only half a fluke and deep scars running along his anterior?"

"That's Rin. Manami's newest pod-mate, and I think she likes him. Let me tell you about him while you watch, okay?"

"Only a few months ago, he was found injured and possibly dying in a shallow bay up the coast in Katsuura. He was apparently hit badly by a cigarette boat's prop and a group of school kids sort of adopted him. It was in the news." Kaito stood proudly and continued, "I convinced Yamaguchi that OceanWorld had an opportunity to look like saviors in the press and public's eye. So, we brought Rin into the lagoon, cared for and rehabilitated him. Something you always wanted. Since then, we've brought in four more. And here we are. A sort of living gift in honor of your vision."

With her hand to her heart, she said, "Thank you so much for thinking of me." Izzy's eyes remained glossy as she watched Manami and her new pod-mate swim in circles. She stood before the glass barrier for a long while, taking in the totality of what Kaito had managed while she was away. Eventually, she kissed Kaito and said, "Let's go home."

Struggling at the door with boxes and suitcases, Kaito burst into the apartment, dropped them to the floor, and hugged Izzy.

"Welcome home," he said. They kissed and gazed into each other's eyes. At the same time, they both said, "Swimming?"

Kaito nodded, but she said, "I want to show you the gifts first. Go ahead, open one of the boxes. I want you to know you can always find me."

He wrinkled his brow in curiosity and split open one box with his penknife. He pulled out a spherical rack of aluminum tubing, with a dangling cord at its base. "What in the—?" He examined it more closely. "I get it. It's a tracking antenna."

"Exactly," she said. "That's the rotating one. Open the other."

He pulled out another hand-held, oblong antenna. He examined it and smiled broadly.

"This one's omni-directional," she said, "And the signal mixer is in the bottom of the box."

"You are something else," Kaito remarked. "This is so fantastic. How did you…manage this?"

"I saved up my salary and didn't shop for clothes."

"I mean the technology."

"Oh. Well, I had met the guys, and one gal, I should say, at the Whale Research Institute in Sausalito. After I told them where you were at in your work, they assured me this is the latest stuff you'll need. But there's more in my suitcase. Go ahead, open it."

Kaito found two other small boxes and opened them.

She explained. "Those are the PTT transmitters, and the other box contains a selection of hooks to attach them to your subjects. Oh, and I forgot. That envelope contains the software and a two-year subscription for connecting to the Argos satellite tracking system."

Dumbstruck, Kaito's eyes began to flood.

"Ready to swim?" She asked.

He swiped at his cheeks. "Not so fast, Mrs. Yamamoto. You shower me with gifts without letting me give you mine?"

"Okay Mr. Giver, what are you giving me now?"

"Well, not actually gifts, but challenges for you. You know, after you left, I realized I got so wrapped up in my own research that I didn't do enough to help you after that disastrous article with the whale beaching. So, I've been working with some of the people I know in Tokyo and with Kimmi to set up some contacts and leads for environmental stories, including maybe an interview tomorrow with a resident in Chiba who claims a factory near her home is discharging waste into Tokyo Bay."

"You did that for me?" She lowered her head. "I guess I should have asked you to help earlier."

"That's okay and that's just a start. After you told me you were investigating the U.S. Navy's use of sea-going sonar on your west coast and its possible effect on cetacean echolocation, I got to thinking. I contacted the XO of the U.S. Navy's 7th fleet in Okinawa and spoke with a Captain Jacobi who said he'd be happy to meet with you regarding their ship-board sonar operations."

"Wow," she cheered, bent over and hugged him.

"There's more, but we can get into that tomorrow."

"No, tell me quick," she bounced in her chair. "I'm getting all excited."

"Well, there's trouble up in Nagoya these days. Been a lot of pent-up anger brewing with local villagers, sports fishermen and naturalists who live along the Nagara river regarding the federal plan to build another big dam to supply water to industry. These folks don't want to have their villages flooded and resettled, so they are planning to stop construction with hundreds of kayakers, boaters and fishermen showing up on the river. I've made a contact with their leader."

"That could be quite a developing story." She rubbed her hands together. "Is Kimmi onto it?"

"Yes, I talked to her this morning, she's awaiting your call. There's one more that I think will be a major story you could pick up on. Do you remember that I was involved in a Tokyo University research project to determine the cause of Minimata disease? Well, I talked to a fellow classmate who said many of the victims with sensory disorders in the limbs are considering accepting a hush-hush government settlement. They are interested in having the media explain their side."

Elizabeth appeared wide-eyed, as if in total disbelief. "Hold on," she asked, "Let me get my notepad." She scribbled some notes. "That's when you got to know Nakayama, wasn't it?"

"Yes," he grumbled, then continued in a bubbly tone. "One more gift. When you were gone, I came to better understand your difficulties in Japan, despite all we achieved together. Not only the difficulty of adjusting to the culture but being without real friends."

He reached into his wallet and pulled out what looked like a credit card and handed it to Izzy. "I joined this Tokyo American Club where we can meet new friends. Another real nice ex-pat American and Japanese couple, Marylyn and Masato Ibata, have already invited us to go dancing with them. You can also take Japanese language, art and gym classes, and they have a large, heated pool that we can go swimming in."

She bolted up and hugged him around the neck. "You are the greatest guy, Kaito Yamamoto. That could just be my ticket to feeling normal in this country." She ran a finger over his lips. "I want you to kiss me now. And go swimming, okay?"

After a long deep kiss, Kaito said, "Just you being here is the greatest gift I could receive."

They went into the bedroom.

A year later

It had been over a year since Kaito's mother paid them a visit. He was excited to have her see how well Izzy was doing ever since she got re-engaged in her writing career. So, when there was a knock on the door, he hoped Izzy was returning from her interview. But he was delighted to find his mother,

Noriko, when he opened the door. She looked vibrant in her neat gray bob and the black and *sakura* pink floral dress of her own design.

"You look beautiful, Mother," he said, hugging her aged, bowed frame. "I'm so happy you came."

"Sorry I missed last year's family gathering. The company just won't let me retire."

Kaito laughed. "But Mother, you *are* the company."

She playfully slapped his arm. "Like you are to your programs at OceanWorld."

"Ha. Not so much anymore. With Izzy's help and encouragement, I've been concentrating my time on dolphin language research, and Izzy makes all the TV appearances for the park. The audiences are delighted to listen to the cute American speak Japanese so lovingly. She also helps me when she can with operations at the lagoon, writing grant proposals and even making recordings of the dolphins."

"Where *is* that wonderful bride of yours?"

"Apparently running late…" he raised his eyebrows. "Like many evenings these days." He gestured. "Come, sit. I'll make tea."

"Water will be fine," she replied. "I suppose she's on interviews."

"Yes, often. Sometimes editor meetings or on some remote atoll investigating an oil spill. She's got many varied assignments these days, most of them working with her young protégé, Kimmi Matsuda."

"Yes, I read the feature series on the dumping of radioactive wastes in the Sea of Japan, using her pen name, of course."

"They're quite a pair. Izzy mentors Kimmi on American investigative techniques and Kimmi does most of the interviewing."

"So," Noriko leaned over and asked in a hushed tone, "How are you two doing? All those years apart."

"Just fine. We're both so busy in our careers. Some days we completely miss each other."

"Are you, you know?"

"Happily married? Yes, I am."

"Elizabeth?"

"I think so. We make sure we spend quality time together, not just working."

"Are you sure?"

He sat back in his chair and looked at her.

"Sorry for being nosey, but you told me you were quite worried when she had gone back to the U.S."

He lowered his head. "I was. She seemed so happy there when we talked on the phone. Back in her old job and all. I thought," he hesitated, "She might not come back." He rubbed his forehead. "I was scared for a while, to tell you the truth. Despite the continued success of my programs, I became depressed, and my classes got boring to teach."

He looked to his mother for understanding. "I came to realize how much she meant to me, kept me inspired." He cleared his throat. "How I needed to be more sensitive to her needs."

His mother patted his hand. "Now, that's a good husband. How—?"

"She wasn't happy in Japan, despite all we achieved. No friends, really, a hard time adjusting to the culture, being stymied with her writing. She needed more self-fulfillment."

"What turned things around?" she asked.

"For one, in the States, she was exercising her writing chops as she calls them. Challenging topics and a receptive audience gave her more confidence, and she became even more passionate about animal rights. Not like in Japan, being so far behind the environmental curve." He shrugged his shoulders. "I realized I needed to get involved. So, I promised I'd help her make contacts, get story leads, and translate. She took up the challenge of affecting Japanese awareness."

"You're a good man, Kaito Yamamoto," Noriko said, folding her hands together. "And, it's great that you recognized early individual growth has to be balanced with the growth of the marriage." She sighed. "A difficult think that your father and I never mastered."

Kaito continued, "To help socially, I joined the Tokyo American Club where we met new friends and became close to another ex-pat American and Japanese couple, Marylyn and Masato Ibata. After that, she took Japanese language classes, learned fast, and that opened up a lot for her."

"That's so wonderful," Noriko commented. "I can hardly wait to see her and speak with her."

"You know, Mother, I think the time away made us appreciate each other more. She gave me and Japan another chance. We take mini, romantic vacations up in Bandai and we often cook meals together. But frankly, we're both worker-types and don't play as much as we should. She now calls this her home."

The door buzzed. "And that must be her."

Kaito ran to the door and greeted Elizabeth with a kiss. "Mother's already here, Izzy," he said and kissed her again.

Dressed in an English trench coat, wet from rain, she threw off her bucket hat and coat and dashed to hug Noriko.

"Oh, Mother. I'm so glad to see you. *O genki desu ka?*"

"Very well, thank you, Izzy. Wow you speak Japanese so lovingly. My health is good, and I am most happy when I see you two. Your activities make me feel so proud."

"Thank you," Izzy said, holding Noriko at arm's length. "You look stunning."

"Ha. Maybe for an eighty-year-old trying to retire."

"Oh, come on, you look eternally young. Has Kaito offered you anything yet?" She put her arm around her husband and gestured toward the dining table. "Together, we've made *yakitori*, *sukiyaki* and at Kaito's insistence, *shabu-shabu*, his favorite. Let me change quickly and I'll join you in a toast."

"Kaito," Noriko turned to her son, speaking in a hush tone, "She does look happy and clearly devoted to you."

"She's been a great wife and working partner."

Sitting at the table, savoring the delicacies of *yakitori*, Noriko finished a shrimp and set down the tail. "Everything's delicious. Elizabeth, what assignment were you working on today?"

"Ho. Kimmi and I were in Okinawa meeting with the XO of the U.S. Navy's 7th fleet. Some fin whales had beached off Amami-Oshima Island, and we were monitoring their ship-board sonar operations."

"That's quite a distance away. Was the military cooperative?" Noriko asked.

"Yes, they've become so, even flew us back and forth from Tokyo. You know, it was your son—" Izzy placed her hand on his, "Who first suggested I contact them based on research in the States. After my article in *Japan Times* and further interviews, they agreed to minimize the use of sonar. I also got, in writing, a promise to release records whenever sonar was used so we can track the possible effects on cetaceans and strandings."

Kaito interjected. "Those articles were highly praised by the locals and kicked off her Japanese journalism career."

"That's great," Noriko added and asked, "So, the time you spent back in the States was worthwhile?"

"It was," she answered, looking past them and thinking. "I learned a lot about what mattered."

"Were you able to spend time with your family?" Noriko asked.

"A bit," she replied, "But my mother is always happily traveling with her husband and my sister in Frisco is heavy into volunteering with soup kitchens and homeless shelters. They're both doing fine."

"You no longer miss America?"

"Not really, especially the bland food." She picked up her chopsticks and asked Kaito if the *shabu-shabu* broth was hot enough.

"Yes, it is, and the Wagyu beef was perfect."

She dipped her tofu and cabbage. "Excellent."

As they speared and dipped their choices, Kaito said, "How about telling Mother of your dealings with the ministry of the environment?"

"Oh geez, Kaito, I'll go on and on and bore Noriko. Just know that I am a bit savvier about men in bureaucracies and I find workarounds to get the real skinny." She speared a carrot. "Husband, tell your mom about your progress analyzing voice recordings of Manami and Rin?"

"Yes, I would love to hear." She smiled at her son. "Kaito dreamed about dolphin language since he was a child. Who is Rin?"

Izzy said, "He was the first injured wild dolphin that OceanWorld rehabilitated. Kaito convinced management to take him in. Rin is Manami's boyfriend now, and since then..." she glanced at her husband..."You've rescued, how many so far, honey?"

"Only eleven, dear. And if it weren't for you bringing back the technology from the States, I'd be nowhere."

"That's my humble hero, and I love him to death."

After tea, Noriko announced. "Well, I'll leave you two lovebirds and head off. I don't want to be late for my evening meeting with the CEO of Shimamura. The clothing giant is interested in buying my company."

"Maybe you will retire soon, Mother," Kaito said, "And can visit us more often."

"I'll try," she replied. "It's so good to see you two again."

They showed Noriko out the door; Kaito turned to Izzy. "Oh, I forget, my Princess, CEO Yamaguchi called today and wants us in his office at ten a.m. for a meeting. He insisted on your presence."

"*Kuso*! Here we go again."

Next morning
Executive conference room

With one hand on the conference room door latch and the other holding Izzy's hand, Kaito hesitated. Things were going well with the dolphins and his marriage, but the CEO could stir up or dam the waters. And why did he need Elizabeth to be there?

Yamaguchi sat stiffly, smiling across the big table, opposite of a thirty-ish young man, dressed in a black t-shirt and jeans. Next to him sat an even younger woman with bleached-blonde pigtails.

"Mr. Sasaki. Ms. Himura," Yamaguchi pointed to the guests. "Please meet the creators of our number one attraction at OceanWorld—Kaito and Elizabeth Yamamoto."

Kaito and Elizabeth bowed.

The guests gave a perfunctory bow.

"Take your seats," the CEO gestured. "Mr. Sasaki and Ms. Himura are from Little Samurai Studios, a leading producer of TV shows. They've indicated an interest in producing a new series around you and the dolphins."

Mr. Sasaki began, "Thank you, yes. After viewing your infomercial, we saw great potential for a new show. Surveys indicate there is unmet consumer demand for the dolphin show and experiences. Not everyone can enjoy it live. The experience can be expanded virtually through television." He smiled politely at Kaito and Elizabeth. "We want to leverage the strong live entertainment franchise you've built with the young people of Japan and make it into a hit anime show for children." His voice rose with excitement.

Kaito and Elizabeth sat expressionless.

Sasaki continued, "We understand that teaching children is important to you, but we believe OceanWorld is becoming too heavy on the educational stuff—" he raised a finger. "So we feel the human and dolphin characters are perfect props for entertainment."

Kaito glared. "What do you mean too heavy on the educational?"

Elizabeth sat stiffly in her seat. "So, I understand. Are you suggesting we are props?"

"I didn't mean it that way. We love you two and want you and Izzy to be the lead human cartoon characters in the show. We want the show to tie-back to OceanWorld so the audience wants to come here more often. We can portray you as human parents of Manami and Rin who get into mischief in a make-believe world."

"Excuse me!" Kaito snarled. "That's not the message I'd like our youth to learn, nor am I interested in becoming a cartoon character. And what happened to cartoons that impart an educational message? We want children to understand how the species lives in the wild, naturally, not dumbing them down, making them into stupid human-like characters."

Elizabeth shot Kaito an approving smile.

"Hold on, Kaito," Yamaguchi interrupted. "You're doing plenty of the educational stuff with your independent research on dolphin language, on my time, no less. You need to listen to what these folks have to say commercially."

Sasaki tilted his head. "Can I ask what kind of educational cartoons you were speaking about?"

Kaito frowned. "I suppose you weren't born then, but back in the 60s, when anime first started, there was a successful and meaningful TV series called *Marine Boy*. The hero had a white dolphin named Splasher and they were on ocean patrol and fought against threats to world peace."

Producer Sasaki smirked. "Never heard of it—sounds preachy."

Yamaguchi interjected. "Kaito, I know you have strong feelings about the dolphin's intelligence and protecting their habitat, but this is for kids' entertainment and to build a bigger OceanWorld franchise."

"Pretty silly entertainment," Elizabeth said. "For an intelligent animal."

Yamaguchi glared at her.

Elizabeth glared back and said, "We don't want a generation of children growing up thinking dolphins talk and act like brats."

Yamaguchi jerked his head back. "I beg your pardon. What does an American know about Japanese children?" He muttered 'ama' under his breath.

Elizabeth stiffened, placing her hands on the table as though she was ready to leave.

Kaito glared at his CEO. "Civility starts at the top, and that requires we listen to each other. May I continue?"

Yamaguchi stiffened and nodded.

Kaito leaned forward, hand in the air. "Izzy and I do appreciate the power of television, and that's what worries us. Making the species into cartoon versions of humans is totally counter to all that we've taught the children for years. Dolphins are a species to be respected, not treated like our toys. It'll set back our work for a generation. We will not be any part of this sham."

Elizabeth's eyes sparkled with pride.

"*You* hold on, Yamamoto," Yamaguchi blustered. "You are employees under contract to OceanWorld." He turned to the producer. "Don't worry, Mr. Sasaki, we'd be happy to begin negotiations with your studio. We will work with you to make it a successful series."

Kaito and Izzy stared at each other, then stood.

On their way out, Elizabeth spoke loud enough to Kaito for the CEO to hear, "The better Japanese word for bitch would not be *ama*, but rather *baita,* or *aba-zure*. Whore is what he really meant."

Kaito turned to glance at the CEO's reaction.

Yamaguchi wiggled in his seat, his face bright red for the first time.

Seven months later

Carrying several large sheets of paper under her arm, Elizabeth burst through the door and stomped into their office.

Kaito looked up from his desk.

Elizabeth huffed. "Yamaguchi's secretary just dropped off copies of the storyboards for the anime TV pilot. She made a point of saying to me, 'it is a courtesy, and no feedback required.'"

Kaito frowned and leaned back in his chair. "The anime storyboards, right? It's really going to happen, isn't it?"

"I'm afraid so," she seethed. "Wait till you see how bad."

They spread the sheets out on their desks.

"Damn it," Kaito said, pointing at Elizabeth's cartoon image. "They've got you looking like an American Barbie doll."

Not smiling, she said, "And you look like Jerry Lewis from *The Nutty Professor*. Incredible."

"That's not the worst of it," Kaito added. "The dolphins are pictured as young students sitting in a classroom. Wearing clothes, no less." He shook his head.

Elizabeth was spitting mad. "Treating another species as cartoon characters. Is this what our work over the last twenty years has meant?" She swiped at the storyboards one at a time, flinging them to the floor. "How could they do this to us and the dolphins?"

Kaito slumped and sighed. "It's simple—they're in it for the money,"

"And what are we in it for?" She raised her hands in the air. "It's not right. Not what we, or the dolphins, are about."

Elizabeth put her arms around him, thinking this was the time to broach what she had been thinking for months. "I have a plan."

He looked up. "You have?"

"It's the dolphin lagoon. Although we worked hard and achieved progress, it's not enough."

He tilted his head. "What do you mean?"

She flipped her hand in the air. "It's not a real success."

"What are you saying?"

Elizabeth pressed her lips together and spoke out for what she vowed long ago. "We should set Manami and Rin free."

Kaito drew back in shock. "Izzy." He glared at her. "Tell me you're not serious. The risks to them in the wild would be tremendous." He gestured between them. "We would be cast out of OceanWorld as betrayers, probably sued."

"Maybe, but maybe not," Izzy said, thinking it would be worth it. "What's left for us here? And, for the rest of Manami's life, held captive in the lagoon?"

"Elizabeth." He paused for emphasis. "Manami hasn't the experience or stamina to survive in the open ocean. There are sharks out there. She lacks the know-how or speed to evade them. No familiarity with a territory to find prey, let alone catch enough to eat."

"There are risks alright, but she had a few years in the ocean before you captured her, and Rin was raised in the wild. He would help protect her and feed her. Dammit!" Izzy snapped, then lowered her voice. "They have a right to be free."

Kaito shook his head. "So, what's this really about? Have you been seduced by Peter Wilson and that old hero of yours, Dick O'Meery?"

She scrunched her brow. *Seduced by their thinking or their actions?* She said, "What?"

"I've been reading about him and these guys. You seem to be enamored by their risky quests. Wilson has been fouling the propellers of Japanese fishing ships. O'Meery's going around the world illegally freeing captive dolphins that cannot survive in the wild." Raising his voice, he added, "Are those the kind of dangerous activities you want to engage in?"

"Wait a minute," she said, thinking how dangerous it was to give in to Peter's advances. "You're jealous." Feeling guilty for almost succumbing, she added, "Do you think I had an affair with these guys back in the States?"

"I didn't say that."

"Well, if you even thought that…" she gave him a steely stare…"I didn't. But at least these guys are true to their causes."

"What does that mean?" He stood and stiffened. "You're suggesting I haven't been true to the dolphins? To you?"

Elizabeth took a deep breath, knowing she was being resentful, but didn't know why the feeling was surfacing now. "Sometimes you need to break the law in order to change the laws. Or at least get the government to start listening." She stood, hands on her hips. "That's what public protest has done in America. When was the last time you saw Japanese protesting a government action, authority of any kind?"

He lowered his head and muttered, "It's not in the nature of our Japanese character."

"Nor is captivity in the dolphin's nature."

Kaito dug his fingers into his hair, thinking. "What about the young people who marched for the first time at OceanWorld in support of Manami's freedom? Didn't that count?"

She nodded. "Sort of. There is hope for the young, more environmentally conscious Japanese, but the majority thought it was not your place to free her. And it wasn't against the government."

She let out a long sigh. "Look. Let's stop arguing and focus on the dolphins, okay?"

"Okay," he agreed and went to make some tea.

Sitting silently across from each other until they finished their tea, Elizabeth calmly suggested, "I feel we both have lost sight of what the dolphins need."

"What do you mean?"

"You've seen her and Rin lately hanging around the main ocean gates."

"Of course."

"They've been watching the ocean dolphin pods roaming northeast, following and feeding on the mullets that show up at this time of year."

"I know."

"And you've recorded Manami and Rin's repetitive signature whistles when they pass, right?"

"Right, but—"

"Shit, Kaito. They're calling out to that pod. They want to join them. Be free."

Kaito let out a deep breath. "Maybe they are. But your solution is ridiculous and wrong. Using aggressive tactics like O'Meery is risky and can hurt the animals."

"How about respect for the animal? And doing what is right?"

Kaito scoffed. "It sounds like your view about captivity when we first met. I can't believe you're saying that now after all these years."

The bad feeling kept gnawing at her insides. "Maybe it's obsessive, but I still feel that way."

Kaito's face burned red. He stood and jammed his finger into the desk. "I'm the one who first took Manami." He pointed to his chest. "And I'm the one to decide whether or not to let her free."

"Right. You're the sole authority." She stood and pointed at his chest. "Just like your *otosan*." Although she realized she was as hung up on her sacred vow as he was on his submissive ways, she struck out. "And you can leave me out of that cruel *ie* bullshit from now on. Head of household is not head of ocean wildlife. I'm through with this." She slammed the door before he could manage a word.

Chapter Twenty-Three
OceanWorld

Several weeks later

Kaito could hardly find the words to speak to Elizabeth for weeks. The anger in her voice when they fought affected his heart, his mind and soul. How could she justify throwing everything they'd accomplished and risk Manami's life for that elusive thing called freedom? His thoughts and feelings about the two most important beings in his life were tearing him apart. He knew he was disappointing Izzy, but he couldn't get a handle on what was right for Manami.

If only she could speak to me, tell me what she wanted for her life. He believed in her intelligence and, more than that, her will to survive. But how did she want to do that? If only he were more advanced with knowing her language, she would tell him.

Depression set in. During the in-water educational sessions with guests, they would ask questions and he'd often stare at the water for several moments before asking the person to repeat themselves. Gradually, he turned over all his public touring slots to his trainees. He was so lost in thought he hardly listened to his recordings of dolphin vocalizations and behavior.

Elizabeth confronted him one morning when he wouldn't get out of bed. "Maybe you should see a psychiatrist or something. This depression of yours is affecting the staff, the dolphins, and me."

He closed his eyes and shook his head. Her words hit him hard. "I'm sorry Izzy, I just can't do it anymore."

"Kaito. You need to quit moaning about yourself and focus on your dolphins. Manami is not being herself for several days and you don't seem to care about what's going on at the gates. When was the last time you monitored Manami and Rin's behavior? How about you get back in the game?"

Kaito's guilt shook him up. "You mean they're still hanging out at the gates?"

"Yes, and you haven't been paying attention."

Kaito tapped his feet on the floor, jumped out of bed and grabbed the binoculars. Looking out the window from the penthouse of the Dolphin Bay Hotel, he called to Elizabeth, "Look beyond the ocean gate, there's a pod of dolphins breaching along the coast near the channel. Maybe Manami or Rin know some members of the pod." He felt his heart beat faster. "They remember their original pod mates signature whistles for life."

He grabbed a windbreaker and headed to the door.

"Kaito, stop. I think you need some pants." Elizabeth nodded at his bare legs. "Then I can join you."

When they reached the mouth of the lagoon, fog had already rolled in, giving the lagoon a ghostly glow. It was too late. The dolphin pod was gone. Manami and Rin were nowhere to be seen.

Kaito rushed to check the hydrophone recordings. Izzy was right, not about the judgment of freeing her or not, but that Manami was trying to tell us something, and we needed to listen. At the same time, the dolphin pod passed by the lagoon, Manami and Rin repeated their own one-of-a-kind whistles. Kaito asked himself, was she expressing her will that way?

Each day thereafter, Kaito was kinder to Elizabeth. He was enthused again to educate the visitors about the dolphins. Every morning, he got up early and scanned the waters beyond the lagoon, looking for the roving dolphin pod, hoping to record their distant voices.

Before and after OceanWorld's public hours, he spent his free time working in the lagoon with Manami. When not with her, he was in his workshop electronically tracking Manami and Rin's sound-making in conjunction with their behavior at the gates. One especially long night, feeling the pain between his shoulders from bending over and listening to the slight variations of the sounds, he finally went to bed.

At two in the morning, a ringing telephone jarred Kaito awake.

"Yamamoto-san! So sorry sir. This is Hayashi in security. Alarms are sounding on both the inner lagoon gate and the outer ocean gate."

"Are the gates still closed?" Kaito grabbed his shirt from the chair while he waited for an answer.

"Yes, sir, both are locked shut. But the monitor doesn't show anything meeting the gates."

"Maybe an especially high tide?"

"It is high tide, sir. The system allows for waves and current. The light poles on the path aren't' bright enough. And the video monitor doesn't capture the tops of the gates. But I do see a shadow above the inner gate."

Kaito and Naoki's design of the two-sided, movable and electro-mechanical gates were powered to slide open when work boats needed to enter the bay. What or who could be coming in contact with both the inner and outer gate at the same time?

"Hayashi, I'm heading down on the north side. Get whoever's in maintenance to bring floodlights and a generator to the south side of the gates, and hurry."

"Kaito, what's going on?" Elizabeth asked, turning on the bed light.

"Something's hitting both the lagoon gates, setting off the alarm. Can you hear it reverberate across the bay?" He sat on the bed rubbing his neck. "I need to go."

"I'll come too," she said. They quickly dressed. "We can bring that new mobile phone with us."

They jumped into a golf cart and quickly headed along the cliffside pathway.

Within a few meters of the channel gates, Kaito brought the cart to a stop.

"What's that noise?" Elizabeth asked.

Kaito hesitated. "It's the call of a wounded dolphin." He shined his flashlight in the direction of the sound.

There, almost at the top of the inner gate, ten meters above the water, was the protruding body of a dolphin, its head wedged between the ornate grillwork. It was impaled on the gate spikes and hung, struggling to extricate itself.

Kaito retched at the streams of blood running down its white underbelly.

Elizabeth covered her face with her hands. "Oh my god. One of our dolphins tried jumping the gates." Elizabeth sobbed. "What have we done?"

"Izzy. We've got to keep focused. Can you go back to the vet's office and bring someone with a tranquilizer gun and medical supplies?" He jumped out of the cart.

Izzy jumped in. "Be careful, Kaito."

Hearing the painful cries of the dolphin, Kaito stumbled as he rushed to the channel gates. "Please, let it not be Manami."

It was Rin. The cuts to his head were made deeper by his struggle to pull out. There was little, if anything, Kaito could do for him. *But where was Manami?*

He scanned the channel between the two gates. A dolphin thrashed in the water. The half-moon notch of Manami's dorsal fin poked out of the water.

Manami kept looking up to Rin, wildly slamming her fluke on the surface and butting her rostrum against the outer gate. She must have been able to make the leap over the inner gate that Rin could not. Kaito had to get to her.

He called down, "Princess. It's me, Kaito."

Manami lifted her head, calmed and responded with her signature whistle, *iiyeekikittuiee*, followed by a low chirp—a sound that, between them, meant love.

"Yamamoto-san!" A shout came from the south side of the channel. It was Kenji from maintenance. "What's going on? I heard the alarm."

"Look down. It's Manami in the channel, between the two gates. Get the Hitachi crane here right away and a sling." He removed his jacket. "I'm going down."

Kenji held up his hands. "Stop, Yamamoto-san, you should wait until the crane gets here. The eelgrass on the rocks is very slippery."

Kaito stared at the precipitous ten-meter drop, then at Rin, who was drowning in his own blood. Rin's eerie wail did not stop; Manami continued to return his call. "No, I must go down to Manami now. Give me as much floodlight as you can. And tell security to shut off that damned alarm."

Kaito crawled feet first down the rocks, lowering himself over the clumps of barnacles; clinging to their surfaces gave him strong hand and footholds. Repeatedly, he called to Manami, "Kaito is here, Kaito is here."

Kaito slipped on the weeds. He fell hard against the rocks before landing in the water. Coughing and inhaling, he treaded water until Manami's nose was nudging him. She whistled. He smiled. The pain disappeared.

Kaito put his arms around her head and looked into her familiar eyes. Choked with emotion, he struggled to talk. "Are you okay, Princess?"

Her eyes were clear, and despite the abrasions on her rostrum from butting against the gate, she seemed okay. She wore the same expression on her face as the day he captured her. He stroked her head. Her whipping tail slowed and Kaito was comforted in the process. He ran a hand over her body, searching for injuries. Her girth had grown. *Is she pregnant?* Kaito wondered.

"We'll get you out," he told her. "Bring you back home…" The words no longer seemed right. "Into the lagoon."

Waiting for Izzy to arrive with the medical supplies, he stroked Manami's head. "You're one amazing dolphin, aren't you?"

Manami nodded and squealed. He had her attention. "I knew you could leap that high, and I know why you did." He nudged her under the chin. "You recognized the sound signature of a member of the roaming pod, didn't you? They called to you. You wanted to go home." He patted her head and sighed. *You finally told me what you wanted, and I didn't listen or couldn't understand. Someday, we will learn your language. Someday.*

"The crane is on the way," Kenji yelled from above. "But security says to disconnect the alarm from the control box."

"Do it then," Kaito said, cursing himself for forgetting that the alarm and gates can be opened from the controls located on the opposing left side of the channel.

Shouts and the rumble of the crane approached the gates. Kaito heard the voices of the work crew. He nodded to Manami. "We'll lift you out of here, soon. You can go back to the lagoon and be with your friends."

"Kaito, are you alright?" Elizabeth called down.

"I'm okay. Manami is too. Got the tranquilizer gun?"

"Yes. I brought the vet tech, Moto. He's getting the crane in position to lower the sling."

Kaito pointed up to a convulsing Rin. "Moto, give him a lethal dose of M99, there is no way he can survive. We need to stop his suffering."

The gun popped. The dart whooshed.

Rin was startled for a moment when it hit and sunk deep into his side. As the poison entered his bloodstream, his struggling movements lessened. After a wailing cry, his body quivered and shut down.

His life was over. Kaito saluted him. "Sorry it had to end this way."

Kaito's tears poured down his cheeks and landed below on Manami.

Elizabeth shouted, "We'll send Moto down with the sling. They'll pull you up."

"No. We don't need it for either of us. Just remove Rin as soon as you can," he directed. "Neither Manami nor I need to watch that."

"Is it over?" Izzy asked, then paused. "Is Manami okay?"

"She doesn't seem to be injured and we don't need to risk slinging her. We'll swim back." He looked up at Kenji. "Open the inner gate and Manami and I will swim out. Izzy, you and Moto meet us at the floating lagoon clinic to check out Manami. Have Rin's body brought to the animal clinic for a postmortem."

Kaito and Manami swam side-by-side toward the 'island' clinic.

Elizabeth was waiting and covered Kaito with a blanket. She dabbed the cut above his eye and hugged him until his shivering subsided. "She wanted to join that roaming pod, didn't she?"

He nodded. "Yes. I think she may have recognized signatures of old relatives."

"She was able to jump the inner gate but didn't have enough momentum in the channel to jump the second gate."

Kaito nodded.

She wiped her tears. "What are we going to do?"

"First, we must prevent her from jumping the gates again. We will place nets twenty meters from and across the harbor entry. She wouldn't jump over the nets and would never gain enough speed and momentum to make the leap."

Izzy watched the arrival at the clinic where Rin's body would be autopsied. She put her arms around her husband's shoulders. "Rin lived longer than he would have injured in the wild, thanks to you. And gave much happiness to Manami, but my love, we still have a dilemma, don't we?"

#

The following morning

Kaito came out of the shower, sat in his bathrobe and silently drank two bowls of miso soup. He let out a long sigh. "It's my fault, Izzy. The lagoon is a failure."

Elizabeth took his hand. "Not true. You've educated a generation about dolphins. Thousands of fans have given billions of yen to help protect the species. Always remember that. We have to move on from there."

He stared at her, then lowered his head. "The risks to Manami and to her calf would be tremendous."

"A baby!" Elizabeth cried out.

"I think so. It felt like she might be pregnant."

"Oh my god, Kaito. All the more reason she and her calf need to be returned to the sea."

"Only if she could join that pod," he declared. "And hopefully, they would help protect her baby once it is born. But still, the risk is high."

"Look, my dear husband," she said, lacing her fingers around his neck. "You have to come to the realization that you can't confine and control her life any longer. Her species, her genetic make-up, her natural ways dictate she needs to be free with her family." Kaito nodded as she spoke.

She added, "You also have to come to realize that your love and attachment to her are your feelings. I know you want to be her father and protector, but that's about you, not her."

"But what if we never see her again?"

"That would be an emotional loss, but put yourself under her skin and ask what she would feel."

"But...but she can't tell us."

"But she has. I once told you that one never knows for sure what another person is truly thinking or feeling beyond what they say or what they do."

"I remember."

"We have to understand and respect what these animals need."

Kaito nodded.

"Manami has spoken. She told you what she wants. She tried jumping over the gates at the risk of her, her baby and Rin's life. She has expressed to you her desire for freedom."

"So, just like that, we decide for her?"

"Yes. Give her a mother's chance to have natural-born offspring who would grow and live free. Join that roaming pod."

"It would be her best chance, if they ever show up again."

She brushed back his wet hair. "We could at least start planning how we could release her, *before* the calf is born."

Kaito took a slow breath. "I don't know, Izzy-chan. She still might suffer and die soon after."

"She might also live and prosper. But she can't do that by herself. *We* have to help her."

He closed his eyes and took in a deep breath. "I don't know if I could handle that."

Chapter Twenty-Four

As he had done for the previous seven nights, Kaito woke before dawn with Manami on his mind. He trudged to the lagoon and sat on one of the giant sea clam benches Izzy designed for the park. Manami circled endlessly near the nets now protecting the channel gates. He could feel her loneliness without her partner. There were no wild pods roaming along the coast to answer her pleas to join them.

Dr. Endo had since verified Manami's pregnancy, who was perhaps only a month away from giving birth. Depending on Kaito's decision, her calf would soon enter life either as a show or a wild dolphin.

A soft hand touched his shoulder. He gazed into Elizabeth's caring eyes.

"It's sad, Izzy," he said, pointing to the 'pacing' dolphin. "She's still at it."

Elizabeth sat next to him and kissed his cheek. "And so are you."

She tapped his knee. "Come to breakfast. I made *natto* for you."

He nodded.

She took his hand. "Maybe today you'll find some resolution, maybe even a plan." She stood and tugged him. "Let's go in."

At the table, Kaito breathed in the scent of Izzy's perfectly cooked *natto* and steamed rice with mustard sauce and smiled. She had made it almost as good as his mother.

Elizabeth chuckled. "Sorry, no broiled smelts."

He laughed. "That's okay. I appreciate you making it and putting up with the smell over all these years. We've come a long way, Izzy."

She sat down. "And a way to go, I hope."

"Yes." He scratched his head. "And I keep thinking, not only about Manami's future, but about ours." He reached over and grabbed her hand.

"I've been thinking too," she said, "And I think the answer lies beyond the dolphin lagoon and OceanWorld."

"Where?"

"Back to both our dreams," she replied, twirling a napkin around her finger. "Like when we first met. How you dreamed about decoding dolphin language."

He sighed and nodded. She took in a deep breath. "I vividly remember how excited you were, when you told me the more we learn about them, the better we're able to protect them. And what about all the new technology you were so gung-ho on?"

Kaito lowered his head. *I am as disappointed in myself as she seems to be in me.* "Maybe I got lost."

She shook her head and smiled. "But you'll find the way."

He'd have to come to terms with himself before he could see his way clearly and decide Manami's future.

"I hope so, Izzy. And what about your future?"

"Same as always," she laughed. "Saving every dolphin and whale on the planet."

"I know that," he said, smiling. "But as a practical matter, what do you want to do?"

"I've been evolving on that. Most immediately I'd like to stop the capture of dolphins for entertainment."

"You have been pretty consistent."

Elizabeth asked, "Does your *yama ga li* tell you anything?"

He closed his eyes and shook his head. "I've been thinking about the first time I swam with dolphins. Maybe return to my beginnings. Take a train ride back to Kushimoto. I need to get clarity so I can make the right decision."

"Is that what you need? From your *otosan*? Sure he'll help you with that?"

"He's ninety-four now. I haven't visited him in years."

She slumped and her face turned into a frown. "If that's what you want, but it might take you backward rather than ahead."

She looked for his reaction.

His head was still down.

In a brighter tone of voice, she suggested, "Why don't you visit your *okaasan*? She knows you better."

Kaito let out a deep breath. "She's too busy with her own life. Head of design now for that big clothing company. I already know what she would say if I asked her: 'You're a smart boy, Kaito. You have everything you need inside you. Use your mind but follow your heart.'"

"That sounds very American. Good advice, I'd say."

"Maybe she learned that from her business clients." He shrugged his shoulders. "I wish it would be that easy for me."

Kushimoto

The storm clouds darkened as Kaito walked along the bamboo-lined path to his boyhood home in Kushimoto. The bamboo was fully grown now, no longer the small rods his father cut and used for tools and buildings. They had also been used for punishment.

Kaito wanted to see his *otosan* again, but was he ready for the memories the visit would stir up? Memories of rejection and anger long repressed could surface.

His hands shook, but his perceived need for clarity drove him. He opened the front door.

Inside, he used to be greeted by his *okaasan's* hello and his sister's radio. Now, the sputtering static of a television blared from the living room and the musty smell of a closed-up house made his nose itch. When the door closed, his *otosan* jolted upright from his slumber in front of the TV.

"Kaito, is that you?" Ichiro's raspy voice called out.

"Yes, Father," Kaito said, reaching down and taking his *otosan's* blue-veined, no longer calloused hands in his own. "How are you doing?" he asked, already sensing the answer.

"Fine, for a man still alive after radiation poisoning."

Kaito winced at his father's almost forty-year-old grudge over the American's hydrogen bomb test. "Good to see you again, Father."

"Glad you came. What brings you here? It's been three years and four months since you last visited."

"Ah. Needed to talk with you and visit my roots," he said, becoming unsure of the result.

"That's very nice, considering how busy you are." He pointed to a pile of news clippings on the side table. "I've saved all the articles about you and OceanWorld, and I see you on the television from time to time."

Kaito's eyes shined. "I see you've had great success with your dolphin lagoon and education programs."

"Yes, but it's not only my doing. I owe a lot to Izzy. She was the inspiration for most of it."

Father flicked his hand in the air. "Izzy. Is that what you call the American woman these days?"

"Yes. And we're a very happy couple, you should know."

"Hope she'll stay loyal to you," he said and looked down.

Heat rose in Kaito's cheeks at his father's dig at Mother and his dismissal of Elizabeth. Izzy was the reason Father never came to see his shows or the lagoon. "Excuse me," Kaito said, "I need a drink of water."

Kaito needed to bridge the gap that had come to separate him from his *otosan*. "How about if I make some tea and we can talk?"

"Sure, Son. There's bean paste *anpan* in the cabinet if you are hungry."

At first, they chatted about his father's few remaining friends and neighbors, most of whom had died. They reminisced about the times they took in a good catch—how mackerel dropping into baskets was like money added to a purse. Kaito's thoughts returned to the future and his father's reaction to the ideas he toyed with. "Father, I'm thinking about buying a boat."

Father's eyes lit up and he put his hand on Kaito's shoulder. "You're going to fish?"

"Not exactly. Just thinking about buying a cabin cruiser to give me a break from the shows and routine. Be carried by the waves. Maybe take a different journey."

"Hah!" He threw his hands up. "You've got that independent streak like your *okaasan*."

Kaito fought back the urge to defend his mother. But he took a deep breath. "From you, I inherited my respect for our oceans. And now there may be other ways I can protect dolphins."

Father threw his head back. "Ah! Your beloved dolphins. I suppose you still think they talk."

"Yes. I know they do. I'm recording what they say. Someday, I'll find a way to communicate with them."

"Don't you get enough training them at OceanWorld?" He wrinkled his brow. "How is your Manami these days?"

Kaito turned his eyes downward. "Not good, Father. She recently attempted to escape from the lagoon. Her favorite male, Rin, died trying to do the same."

Father rubbed his chin. "Hmm, you'll have to fix up the lagoon so she can't escape."

"I've already done that." Kaito drummed his fingers on the table. "Maybe she belongs in the wild."

His father's eyes widened. "You're not..." he scowled..."that would be wrong."

"I know, and I worry she may not survive."

Father shook his head. "I didn't mean that. How can you forsake OceanWorld, your obligation to your employer? That would be dishonorable, maybe criminal." He jabbed a finger toward Kaito. "You cannot just abandon your life's work. You'd become an outcast."

It was like his lectures about being the nail that stuck out.

He took a deep breath and exhaled. "*Otosan,* maybe my life's work is bigger than what's at OceanWorld."

His father scowled. "Who put you up to these wild ideas? That crazy American woman?"

Kaito barked, "Father! How dare you speak of my wife that way."

Ichiro flinched.

Kaito continued, "Unlike most Japanese who are afraid of change and motivated by face-saving, Elizabeth speaks her mind. Her innovative ideas have made a big difference to OceanWorld and in public opinion."

Ichiro sneered. "Put the dolphin's pleasure before harmony? Destroying your career in the process?"

"Both Izzy and I speak out of respect for the rights of dolphins to live a natural life. We give voice to the hundreds of dolphins that are hunted every year out of places like Taiji, and not for meat."

"Kaito. Those fishermen are trying to make a living. How do you think I became head of the fishing cooperative? My *yamma ga li* ability to find fish was motivated solely by my caring for the fishermen and their families as a whole."

"I respect that, Father, but most of the money they earn is from selling live dolphins to dolphinariums."

"Maybe so, but you need to honor your people and your ancestors, not these animals and your newfound American ideas."

"These ideas are not so American. Both Buddhist and Shinto traditions say animals have their own spirituality and are capable of suffering. Say we should seek harmony with them. Have you forgotten?"

Ichiro rubbed his temples. "You have a point, but it doesn't erase the practical and personal consequences that would follow."

"Yes. I'm fully prepared to accept the results of my decisions. Thanks for your advice. I must get back to OceanWorld and Elizabeth."

"Leave already? I am a sick old man. I have nothing to live for but you."

Kaito thought that leaving his father might possibly cause Ichiro to commit suicide to, in his mind, restore family honor. He bowed his head. "I have a lot more to live for, Father. I will command my own boat and use my *yamma ga li* to set a new course."

#

Once Kaito returned to OceanWorld, he acted on his plans.

He bought a used, thirty-two-foot cabin cruiser, which he taught Elizabeth to pilot, and kept it docked in a nearby marina. He recorded and catalogued all of Manami's vocalizations. He trained Manami on a new series of commands, while carefully monitoring her increasing girth.

He installed both transmitting and recording hydrophones on the ocean side of the bay and connected them to a receiver in their bedroom. After meeting with a real estate agent, he arranged contractual terms for selling both their Dolphin Bay and Shibuya penthouses, pending his notice for listing.

He purchased the latest seawater telemetry equipment which he tested on Manami in the lagoon. He reviewed volumes of secondary research on undersea earthquakes with an eye toward writing research grant proposals. With Manami approaching her due date, Kaito began broadcasting her recorded signature along the coast, hoping to draw the roaming pod. Finally, he filled Elizabeth in on the details of his plans.

#

One night, weeks later, Kaito awoke to the hydrophone receiver's sounds of dolphins approaching the Bay. He flicked on the bed light and put on the headphones to pick up Manami's real-time response, hoping she'd communicate with a familiar pod-mate roaming the coast.

Elizabeth sat up, clutching Kaito's elbow. "Did Manami respond?"

"Shh," Kaito whispered. "Not yet." He held the earphones tighter. After several minutes, he shook his head. "Not the ones, apparently." He sighed, "But the mullets have returned, and other pods will follow to feed."

239

"What happens if—?"

Kaito turned to find tears hanging at the tips of Izzy's lower lashes. He reached out and she nestled into his chest.

"I'm sorry, Izzy. If Manami's calf is born in the lagoon, we'd have to keep them there."

"Oh, please no," she whimpered.

"Wait," Kaito said. "What was that?" He grabbed the headphone and twisted a knob on the receiver.

The static died down. "Hold on," he whispered, "I think this is Manami calling out now." Maybe the pod didn't like her recorded call. He whipped off the headphones and checked his watch.

"Three-thirty-eight a.m. Just enough time. Maybe the last time."

They looked at each other. "Let's go," they said in unison.

Throwing on his clothes, Kaito said, "I should be up at the gate control box by four-thirty, waiting for you to sail up the coast and meet us."

She pointed to the bags at the end of the bed. "Phones. Keys. Go bags. And don't forget to pack the telemetry equipment case."

"We can do this, Izzy."

"We have to."

Chapter Twenty-Five
OceanWorld

Dolphin Lagoon

Kaito waved to Elizabeth as the Nissan Z sped out of the garage. He couldn't turn back now. Manami's and their futures were at stake. He checked his watch. *She should get to the marina in sixteen minutes and launch the cabin cruiser.*

He had six minutes to get to the nets where Manami would join him. Jumping into the golf cart, he jammed the accelerator to the floor. He would coax her over the nets that kept her from the gates.

After leaving the cart on the hillside, Kaito called down. "Manami. Come to Kaito."

She emerged from the cool, black water with a *squawking* hello and a tail splash.

He dove in. When he surfaced, she was at his side. After a quick hug, he waved the other curious dolphins away. He called out one of the new commands. Manami balked away from the nets.

He swam over the net and waved, "Follow me."

Manami leaped behind him. The pair swam toward the gates, and in ten minutes they arrived at the rocky ledge by the left side of the channel.

Kaito searched along the rocks for the knotted rope he had buried between the outcropping weeks ago. It would help him climb up the slippery ledge. He couldn't afford an injury or the lost time, if he fell. Not finding it on the surface, he dove under a four-meter-high tide in total darkness and felt for the end of the rope. He couldn't find it. He jabbed his hand between the rock crevices, and a sharp pain shot up his arm.

He surfaced. The cut to his finger wasn't serious. Had someone removed the rope? Had it come lose? Diving again, he probed along the rocks.

"Ah," he said and grabbed the end of the rope and turned to Manami. "Stay here." He carefully pulled himself up the rocky ledge.

Once at the crest, he opened the gate control box, shut off the alarm and pushed the button to open the inner gate.

The gate creaked and groaned as it slid open, interrupting the quiet of the night. He winced and called toward Manami. She swam in circles in front of the channel.

"Manami. Come here!" He shouted, pointing into the channel below.

She chirped a frustrated 'no'.

Did she remember what happened to Rin? He searched the coastline for Izzy and the cruiser. Not seeing her, he turned to Manami. "It's okay, Princess. Please come in here."

She only looked at him.

He tried a stadium pool command. "Manami. In."

She cautiously entered the channel. He closed the inner gate. "Good girl. Now stay. We'll get you out soon." From where he stood, he could see far down the coast.

Nothing.

He glanced at his watch. 5:05. Based on trial runs, Izzy should be here by now. He untied the waterproofed sack with the mobile phone and dialed. No answer. His heart sank. The first glimmer of sunlight hinted at the horizon. He'd be visible within minutes. *Where is she?*

Manami butted her head against the outer gate. Kaito's gaze shifted from the beach to Manami and back to the beach. She didn't stop hitting the gate. *Does she hear the calls of the roaming pod?*

"Stop!" He yelled, then realized he could be heard by a night guard and would make Manami more anxious. "It's okay, Princess. Izzy will be here for us any minute. Be calm."

Manami stilled, no longer butting against the gate.

He dialed Izzy again. Still nothing. Did she lose the phone? No. The engine stalled? Maybe. Caught on a sandbar? Possible. *"Kuso!"*

The phone rang. He startled, nearly dropping it. "Izzy! Where are you?"

"Just pulling out of the marina. So sorry. I got hung up."

"What happened?"

Izzy caught her breath. "A large trawler was moored in front of our dock, unloading the night's catch. They wouldn't move. I tried ringing you on this damned new-fangled phone, but it didn't ring until now."

"Where are you?" he asked.

242

"Waiting for you. Manami's in between the gates. Are you at full throttle?"

"Yes. Should be there in eighteen minutes."

"Okay. Hurry." Kaito glanced at the brightening sky.

He crouched behind a boulder and shivered. *Was the dolphin pod still there?* "We'll have you out soon, Princess."

It wasn't long before the cruiser's bow lights came into view. The crest of the sun peeked above the admin building. Kaito bent down and opened the outer gate.

He searched for a safe spot to dive. "Follow me, Manami." He backed up a few steps and sprung into a high dive.

Manami met him when he surfaced. They swam to meet the cruiser.

"You made it!" Izzy yelled from the stern of the boat, "And Princess is right behind you."

Out of breath, Kaito climbed onto the swim platform and lifted himself into the boat. "Ah…okay," he said and took the towel from Elizabeth. "We need to move fast. I'll stay portside, calling Manami until we're out of range."

"You did it, Kaito," Izzy said and kissed him.

"Yes, we did. Full speed ahead, captain."

She snapped a salute and scrambled to the helm.

Kaito waved to Manami. "Follow Kaito, girl."

She jumped, flipped and twisted alongside the speeding boat.

They drew Manami far enough north to where the city's buildings blocked their view from OceanWorld. Kaito waved to the helm. "Izzy. Idle the engine and bring the telemetry case."

Manami slid onto the swim platform. He hugged her and planted a kiss on her nose.

"You're free, Princess. We'll find your new family. Don't worry, I bet you feel good to be back in your old home, huh?"

An eerie vibrato squeak meant something between a 'please' and a 'thank you'.

"Aww," Elizabeth said, "Manami sounds happy." She put her hand on Kaito's shoulder. "Remember the first question I ever asked you?"

"Yes. I do," he placed his hand over hers. "I think I can now say with certainty, she's happy. And she owes that to you, Izzy."

"And you," she added.

Kaito let go and attached a small battery-powered transmitter to Manami's dorsal fin.

"There." He gave the tag a pat. "Now we can keep in touch with her for maybe a month, as long as this thing stays on. Would you check the receiver?"

The receiver emitted a pulsing electronic beep.

"Fantastic!" He jumped to his feet and pointed to the water. "Go girl. Find your new family."

The next two days

They had followed Manami for more than 100 kilometers, almost to the Choshi peninsula, searching for the dolphin pod. The VHF transmitter emitted regular beeps.

Some 150 km north of OceanWorld, near the coastal city of Mito, Elizabeth screamed, "Kaito. There's a large pod at about two o'clock."

Kaito scrambled to the helm and checked through the binoculars. "And there goes Manami," he said. "She's 'flying' to catch up with them."

They held their breaths.

"Would the dolphin pod accept a strange female into their family?" Izzy asked.

"I don't know. We'll see."

The boat slowed near the pod. It consisted of over twenty members.

"They don't appear to be feeding," Kaito observed. "No squawking terns above them."

"Let me see," Elizabeth said, reaching for the binoculars. "Can we get closer?"

"A bit. We don't want to spook them," he said, and gently throttled closer.

Elizabeth held up her hand. "Wait. The pod seems to be circling around Manami, I can see her tag. What could they be doing?"

"Hopefully they recognize her, and don't reject or attack her."

"Oh. Wait a minute," Elizabeth whispered. "Here, I think I saw—"

Kaito took the binoculars.

"Yes...yes! It's a newborn about one meter long. She must have just birthed it and the pod family is protecting it."

Elizabeth yanked his arm. "My turn." Squinting through the binoculars for several moments, she let out a whoop. "Oh my god, Kaito. I see the calf jumping over Manami."

"She must be feeding," Kaito said. "We need to back off." He put the gears in reverse.

At about a hundred meters away and in calm seas, Kaito cut the engine. They stood arm in arm at the bow and watched the pod as the cruiser drifted in the dusky light.

Elizabeth chuckled at their playful antics. "Did you ever think we'd be blessed with a grandchild?"

"Ha." Kaito squeezed her waist. "I strained like an old man when I climbed up those rocks."

"Maybe you felt that way, but you performed like a Japanese James Bond." She nudged his hip.

They kissed, grabbed the radio receiver and went below deck.

Hours passed before the signal weakened. The pod was on the move again.

"Might be a long night," Kaito said as they followed Manami's adopted family.

Third day out

By dawn, the pod kept north toward Miyagi, a fabled rich fishing grounds for both men and marine mammals. Kaito scanned the nautical charts and shouted down to Elizabeth to come to the wheelhouse.

"We've got a problem, Izzy," he frowned. "We're getting close to empty on the auxiliary fuel tank and have to back up to Iwaki in order to refuel. We can't make it all the way to Miyagi."

He swiped the charts onto the deck. "*Kuso!*"

"What?" Elizabeth asked.

"We'll lose them," he replied, realizing he would have to let her go sometime.

She placed her hand on his arm. "Look, we can't spend our lives following her. She's free now."

While refueling in Iwaki, Elizabeth called her friend Marylyn Ibata from the club. She asked her to pick up her mail from the post office box and collect the local newspapers. They'd meet her in three days at the Mizuno Marina in Tokyo Bay.

Once refueled, Kaito pointed the bow north again.

"Where are we going?"

"Maybe we can catch up with them. Make it to Miyagi in a few hours. They must be foraging there."

Elizabeth took hold of his arm at the wheel. "Kaito, please. You have to let her go. That's what we decided. She has to live her own life as we live ours."

"I can't just abandon her, Izzy."

"You aren't. You're giving her and her calf their lives back. You're no longer responsible for her. She's responsible for herself and her baby. Take joy in that."

"I...I feel I've lost part of me."

"That's natural. But she's given you a gift. The opportunity to do bigger things. Greater things for her family and species. We have to go back, restart our lives. Research grants, write articles, remember?"

Kaito sighed, slumped into the captain's chair, and turned the boat around.

Chapter Twenty-Six
Three Days Later

Mazuna Marina Tokyo Bay

"Thank you so much." Elizabeth gave Marylyn a goodbye hug.

Engine idling, Kaito unhitched the boat lines from the dock.

"Wish I could say 'see you at the club'," Marylyn sighed.

"Don't think they'd ever have us back," Kaito scoffed. "Tell Masato it was great knowing you two."

Marylyn swatted the air. "It'll blow over, Kaito. OceanWorld hasn't even suggested they would press charges. Not wanting to look bad in the public's eye." She swiped her hand in the air. "I think they want to let things blow over. You'll bounce back. Got too many good ideas."

"Thanks for your kind words. Sorry we have to rush back to Kushimoto. And thanks for getting those newspapers for us." He helped Izzy onto the boat deck, threw the last dock line to the attendant and rushed to the wheelhouse.

Izzy waved goodbye from the stern, then joined her husband.

"You worry too much. Your father probably took a long walk or something."

"I think he may actually kill himself when he gets the news."

"Suicide? Really?"

"Yes. Not like America. In Japan, it is acceptable. It goes back to romanticized Samurai traditions of *seppuku,* using a knife to atone for public disgrace. Today, they call it *jiketsu,* an honorable act of self-sacrifice."

Elizabeth shook her head. "That's hard for me to understand."

"I suppose it is, but I believe he might do it, especially with nosey reporters asking him about me. Describing me as an outcast, even a criminal." He jabbed his finger into the air. "Why would the reporters track him down like that?"

"Here," Elizabeth said, spreading the newspapers on the dash panel in front of him. "Just look at the headlines. You're big news. It's normal for reporters to want to find you. Get a statement." She jabbed at each of the publications featuring photos of them and Manami. "The top papers in the country want to know where you went and why you did it. We shouldn't be surprised."

She read the headlines: ***"DOLPHIN FREE AS TRAINERS FLEE, DOLPHIN-NAPPING CHARGES FOR YAMAMOTO? OCEANWORLD DOLPHIN CAPER—WHY?*** And this one from the Asahi Shinbun: ***YAMAMOTO—SCOFFLAW OR SAVIOR?"*** Elizabeth pointed under the headline. "Look at the byline under this one. It's Kimmi Matsuda."

Kaito gestured at another headline: ***WHERE'S YAMAMOTO?*** **<u>Dateline Kushimoto</u>**. "That's the one that worries me."

"Think positive, Kaito. You can go to Kushimoto as soon as we get back." She held up a handful of envelopes and added, "And we've got these to look forward to. My editors want me to cover several stories. Here are the research grant applications we were waiting for." Shaking a letter in the air, she finished, "**A**nd I even got a letter from Peter Wilson asking if I could provide guidance on a documentary film that producers, including Dick O'Meery, are going to be making on Taiji. Expose the dolphin hunting."

"Guidance is fine," Kaito acknowledged, "But right now, I'm afraid for my father."

"Sorry. It's hard for me to understand that." She touched his arm. "Not having much of a father and knowing how badly yours treated you. Tomorrow, okay?"

Seven months later
Off the coast near Mito

Kaito's tears formed little black holes in the mound of gray ash as he reached into the urn. Tossing handfuls into the water, he watched the remnants of a life slide along the white fiberglass hull and swirl in the blue wake. He rinsed his hands and splashed seawater on his face. He looked up as the sun climbed high over the horizon, glad Elizabeth and his mother had convinced him to bury his *otosan* at sea.

A soft hand fell on his and his mother knelt beside him. Her arms closed around him. He forced a smile and sighed.

"Will you say the final prayer now?" she asked, handing him a towel. "It might bring an end to your guilt and grief."

He clapped his hands together three times and repeated *Jinsei no mizu,* the Buddhist 'Waters of Life' prayer—"after life is taken away, the body is returned to its elements. *"*

Tears drops streamed down his cheeks.

"Now, our tears can go with him," she said in between sobs.

Head down, Kaito mumbled, "I don't know, Mother."

"It was his time in his own way, Kaito. He was not only old, isolated and ill, but he died the way he lived, chained to his honor. He had caused all of us to leave him years ago and its finally time to let him go out of our lives. You need bear no guilt. *Sepuuku* or *Jiketsu,* it allowed him to erase his misdeeds in life."

"Maybe so," he said, admiring the wrinkles in her face and the gray hair framing her high cheekbones. "It was good of you to come, Mother."

"It was important for both of us." She gazed at Elizabeth standing above them. "I'm glad you called me."

Elizabeth took her hand and helped her stand.

Kaito stood and the three hugged as the waves gently licked the stern.

Elizabeth spoke, "I wasn't sure it was my place, but I worried if Kaito had a traditional funeral in Kushimoto, you might not come."

Kaito's mother patted Elizabeth's hand. "Have I told you, you are the best thing to ever happen to my son?"

Elizabeth blushed. "Thanks, *Okaasan.* You did."

Noriko chuckled. "I am getting old and forgetful."

Kaito kissed Izzy. "She is the best. And you're right. It would have been hard for us to face the cold stares of the villagers."

"Yes," agreed Noriko. "Now this little family must come together more often in happier times."

"For sure," Elizabeth said. "Let's go into the galley. I'll make some tea."

Elizabeth warmed up the Manju sticky buns she had bought in Mito Harbor the day before, then sat at the table with Kaito and Noriko. After pouring the tea, she raised her cup. "Let's toast and talk about the future."

"*Compai,*" Noriko said, and they clinked cups. "Let's start with that great news about OceanWorld dropping charges. The pressure your young students put on management must be very heartening."

"And humbling," Kaito added. "And don't forget the Greenpeace folks. They marched too."

Elizabeth nodded. "The power of public opinion, huh? And to think Yamaguchi agreed to quit capturing wild dolphins and start rescuing injured ones. It's remarkable how much impact you had on your students over the years. How they came to appreciate wild dolphins, way beyond those that entertained them in show."

Noriko tapped Kaito's hand. "Turns out you're both heroes. Now you two can have a fresh start. What are your plans?"

Kaito met Izzy's gaze. "Well, we're submitting research grant proposals to track the movements of cetaceans using satellite monitored telemetry."

"Wow, that sounds like one of your dreams might just come true."

Kaito gave a slight nod. "It'll be a challenge."

Noriko turned to Elizabeth. "And you? Will you be continuing your writing?"

"Yes. I'm in the middle of several stories, actually, under my pen name, of course. But I'm most excited about exposing Taiji dolphin hunting by helping produce a documentary film."

"Sounds important, doesn't it, son?"

Kaito glanced at Elizabeth, then to his mother. "A dangerous undertaking, I'm afraid. How about your work, Mother?"

"Well, my spring line of women's casual loungewear is set to launch in Europe almost as we speak." She glanced at her bejeweled Rolex. "Reminds me, I better be getting back."

"Please stay another day," Elizabeth pleaded. "There are some nice hotels in Mito."

"I am so sorry, but a buyer from the U.K. is making a surprise visit to see the new line in London tomorrow, and I have to leave. My driver's waiting for me in town."

Kaito's heart sank, then pleasantly warmed at the determined look on his mother's face, the same look she had sewing Hawaiian shirts on the kitchen table in Kushimoto. "Of course, Mother, I'll go and fire up the twin engines."

They said goodbye at the dock and promised each other they'd faithfully meet at least once a year for more than a day at a time.

Climbing back into the boat, Elizabeth declared, "So good to finally spend some time with…Mother."

"It was, but I already miss her. My heart feels," he swallowed hard, "Even more hollow."

She placed her hand gently on his chest. "I know."

"It's too hard. Too much to handle in a short time. Losing Manami, then my father. I can't get over seeing him like that." He buried his head in his hands as images flashed across his mind, of the plastic bag tied over his head with fishing line. He choked back a sob and looked at Izzy for understanding. "With the knot he tightened, there was no way to remove it."

"No one should have to see a parent die that way, but you told me his face was calm, as though he was sleeping." She wrapped her arms around him. "With time and work, things will get better, I promise."

"I don't know." He ran a hand over his face. "I hope so."

"I understand how you would feel that way," she said as she rubbed his shoulder. "I was depressed when my sister tried to kill herself, but with time, I came to understand it."

"You are one strong woman," Kaito said, kissing her. "And you give me strength."

She hugged him. "Keep thinking about what you have received from him that was good—your courage, your *yamma ga li*. Combine it with the good you inherited from your mother."

He cocked his head, eyes fixed on Elizabeth.

"I'm talking about Noriko's creativity and vision. Something you have a lot of but have trouble expressing." She tapped on the table. "Your mother told you right here you have to follow your dream. Complete your research. The future. Make your mark on science."

"Huh," he scoffed. "With Japanese' unbending ways and Nakayama, the head of the Department of Interior, I'd never get a grant for such a project."

"Never say never, Kaito. Maybe I can find funding in the U.S., a big foundation."

Kaito reached across the table and grasped her hands. "Please don't leave me, Izzy. Don't pursue that thing with Peter Wilson. I couldn't bear losing you."

"I won't." She held him under his chin. "We'll work things out together."

Part Two

Chapter Twenty-Seven
December 1995

Aboard the Umi-Kumiko
Off the coast of Yukawa

From his perch, sitting high on the flybridge of his new fifty-foot research boat, Kaito anguished over more than the red sky dawning in the east. He could handle a storm coming in from the west, but the risk of confronting his fellow countrymen, his beloved fishermen and the law, frightened him. If things got out of hand, they could lose everything they worked for over the last ten years: his grant funding and research, Elizabeth's writing career, the *Umi-Kumiko,* and worse. He let out a sigh, the wind snatching it away from him.

Thoughts weighing heavily on him when the ship's intercom rang and startled Kaito. "Ow!" Kaito yelled as he recoiled from banging his knee under the wheel. "That damned ringer," he cursed and picked it up.

"Kaito, I'm coming up," Elizabeth called from below deck. "Do you want anything?"

"Tea is fine," he answered, rubbing his knee.

"How about some Ogura toast?"

"No thanks, I've got an uneasy stomach."

Elizabeth climbed up and handed Kaito his tea and plopped down in the co-pilot seat. She removed her sunglasses and stared into the bright sun. "It doesn't look like they'll start the hunt today either."

"No," Kaito groaned, "They'd be out by now. The waiting is torturing me."

"You sound frustrated. Not having second thoughts, I hope."

"No." He shook his head, "I promised you, and we made a commitment."

"What is it then?" she asked, raising her eyebrows.

He took a long sip of tea. "Maybe because I'm fifty. Doubting my abilities to change."

"Come on, my *koijin*, you're just getting started."

"Huh," he scoffed. "With a major undertaking. For now, let's go below. I'll wake the crew, and we can call Louis to relax for another day."

After breakfast, the crew took their positions for more sport fishing. Kaito and Izzy sat at the galley table. He called Louis on the two-way radio. "Louis, are you there? Kaito here. Over."

"Copy, Kaito. Louis here. Any movement? Over."

"Nothing. Looks like we wait another day, but we're ready anytime. Over."

He glanced across the galley table at Elizabeth. "Tell Dick I'll keep her safe and below deck the whole time. I don't want them to think we're associated with the American spies." He chuckled to overcome the tension. "Over."

Elizabeth smiled.

Kaito continued, "From our position in Muriura Bay, we'd spot them going out." He shook his head. "No, I think we're well disguised. With the *Umi-Kumiko* flying a Japanese nautical flag and my captain and crew being Japanese, I think they're convinced I'm just a fat cat sports fisherman." He laughed, trying to break the tension. "Even caught a half-meter long skipjack— best eating tuna around."

Elizabeth laughed, holding her hands up one foot apart and shaking her head.

"I take it the local authorities bought that it wasn't you in the park last night above the secret cove. Over."

"No, all good. Over."

"I guess, the Fujinon night vision goggles worked well. Rock cameras, hydrophones all set. Over."

Louis answered, "Copy that."

"Great," Kaito added, "For sure Lois. Takashi's a good photographer. The camera's well-hidden under the tarp covering the dingy. Perfect camera angle from the stern. Okay. I'll call you the moment the boats head out. Over."

Elizabeth caught Kaito's attention. He put his hand over the radio phone. "Standby, Louis."

Izzy whispered, "Wish them well, Kaito."

Kaito nodded. "You and Dick and the crew take care."

"Thanks, we will. Over and out."

Elizabeth scooted next to Kaito and kissed his cheek. "You've turned out to be one cagey consultant, husband. I really appreciate what you're doing, and that you get along with Dick."

"Well, I know the routines of this place only too well. And I misjudged Dick until I found out he was wired like you."

"How's that?"

"All heart for the dolphins. No matter what the personal cost. Maybe jail time in his case."

"No jail time for me and you?"

He shook his head. "Even if they caught us, there's nothing illegal about Japanese nationals filming people fishing."

"But I worry they'll find out about you," Elizabeth pleaded, "And maybe the crew."

"That's what I worry about too, but only the coast guard or harbor police could ask for our identities, and we haven't seen them. As to the crew, they are all dedicated volunteers, and they know the risks."

Elizabeth sighed and ran her hand over the map in front of them. "I don't know how you can be so confident with your plans."

"I'm not without my fears. But once I plan something well, I stick to it."

"I can't help getting nervous about what might happen. Can you tell me again how this is going to work?"

Kaito pointed to the map of the harbor and coastline. "Once the fishing boats leave, from here, we will move our boat slowly into Taiji Harbor, trolling our fishing lines." He pointed. "We wait here on the southern end until we see the dolphins migrating up the coast migration. Or, hear the eerie clanging sound of the beater poles."

Elizabeth asked, "Do you really think they believe we are sports fishermen?"

"Yes. They've grown accustomed to us. Even waved that time, remember?"

"I guess."

Kaito continued, "The fishing boats form a semi-circle out from the harbor, and when the dolphins start heading past them, they stick long poles into the water and strike them with a hammer. The sound disorients the dolphins, and the boats close in, forcing the animals into the harbor."

Elizabeth ground her teeth. "Poor things. Must be frightening to them."

"For sure," he said, drawing his finger down the harbor. "As they drive them farther in, we'll be positioned here as Takashi films them dropping their nets. We need to record that, and when they start pushing them toward shore."

"Being close to the fishermen at that point, really scares me. What if they chase us away?"

"Well, we play unaware, slow-to-respond boaters, until I tell Captain Oba to rev up our 450 horsepower twin diesels. We can easily out-maneuver them at forty-five knots."

"Okay, but what about that secret cove you mentioned to Louis?"

Kaito stood. "That's not material to what *we* are doing here. That comes later. After we're gone."

"Kaito, you're evading my question. Where is the secret cove and what happens there?"

"Please Izzy. Trust me, you don't need to know."

"It's my business to know," she growled like a grumpy old movie character. "Investigative reporters uncover the truth."

Frowning, he placed his hand on her shoulder. "It's not about that."

"Then, what?"

He took a deep breath. "I just don't want to go back there."

She pointed to her temple. "You mean, in your mind? Like when you first captured little Manami?"

He slumped into his chair. "Yes. It...it was so simple for me back then. My first job. A chance to learn up close, work with the animal I loved." He stared past Elizabeth and through the cabin windows. The sparkling, evening waters of the bay transported him.

She tapped his hand. "Kaito."

He jolted. "Sorry, Izzy. I was at the shore waist-deep when I took her from her mother, screaming. That was bad enough. It was only after we had secured Manami into the waterbed I had rigged up in the truck for transport to OceanWorld," he paused, looking at Elizabeth, "When I heard men yelling in the distance along with the cries of dozens of dolphins."

"I had noticed all the dolphins were gone from what I thought was the end of the harbor. I asked one of the fishermen. He simply said, 'Oh, they're in the cove being harvested.' Harvested? I remember thinking what a quaint way of saying what they were doing, like bucolic rice farmers gathering grain."

Elizabeth gasped and covered her mouth. "You saw how they slaughtered the dolphins?"

"Not really. But when I headed back up the road, I looked down at a narrow, rocky, mostly hidden inlet and saw that water from it was flowing into the bay." He swallowed hard. "It was turning the harbor completely red."

Elizabeth's face contorted. "Could you see—?"

"No. I only learned later that those men in boats indiscriminately jabbed their long spears at the flailing, bleeding bodies until they finally stopped moving?" Kaito lowered his head.

Elizabeth gently stroked his arm. "You're a different man now," she said and kissed his forehead.

"Thanks to you." He placed his hands on her shoulders. "Just so you know, we won't be going anywhere near the secret cove. I believe they will be harvesting after the next round of fishing. By then, we'll be out of here."

"So that's where those rock cameras are hidden," Elizabeth said.

"Yes. They will be turned on remotely together with the hydrophones."

"Why them?" she asked.

"To record the horrible screams of being stabbed and dying underwater. You know, to make the film even more tragic."

Elizabeth held her throat. "Thanks. I couldn't bear seeing or hearing that."

"I know. We'll be leaving as soon as they start moving the dolphins into the cove."

\#

Next morning

A dark gray layer of fog crept in from the east as the *Umi-Kumiko* slowed into position. "Let's put her into idle, here, Captain Oba," Kaito yelled up to the flybridge.

Gliding into the southern end of the harbor, the *Umi-Kumiko*'s engines rumbled into a deadening drone, adding to the menacing mood of the entire crew.

"Let's have some tea," Kaito shouted to deckhand. "Shin, join me and Takashi at the stern. We'll have breakfast." He added, "Look casual, men."

From the cabin, Elizabeth climbed up the companionway stairs, keeping her head below deck, and asked, "Do you want me to make *tamagoyaki*?"

"That would be great," Kaito said. "Sorry you can't join us."

"That's okay," she replied. "Has there been any movement from the fishermen?"

"Not yet."

"You want your omelet with *dashi*?"

"Certainly. And Izzy, better to stay away from the cabin windows. I see another fishing boat heading out. Must be a late sleeper," he added, giving a little chuckle.

Shin brought up the tea, and Captain Oba and Takashi joined Kaito at the stern. They watched the last fisherman, a gray-haired gentleman smoking a pipe, pass by them on his way out of the harbor. Kaito and the crew smiled and waved, relieved that the man gave a friendly wave back and shouted, "*OiOi.*"

After a few hours of no action, Kaito set the poles to fish for flounder and went below deck to see Elizabeth.

"Might be awhile, Izzy-chan. Maybe they'll call it off. We'll just have to sit tight."

"Understood, but it is nerve-wracking," she said. "You know, it's incredible to me how the locals can rationalize."

"How do you mean?" Kaito asked.

"When we first drove through Taiji town, I was drawn into a Disney-fantasy land. Cute dolphin statures and fountains. Posters proclaiming the Dolphin capital of the world. Dolphin-shaped tour boats in the harbor. Stores selling dolphin hats. Dolphin lollipops for the kids. It's like the town glorifies killing dolphins."

Kaito shook his head. "No, Elizabeth. That's not fair. These are hard-working, decent people. This includes my fellow fishermen. I know them and love them."

"How can you honestly say that?"

"I can. Sure, the town fathers are glamourizing a grubby local business to attract tourists. Isn't that just like they do in cattle-ranching towns in America?"

Elizabeth rolled her eyes. "I get the comparison, but I just can't handle it."

"Come on, Izzy. These people see dolphins as big fish. Ones that consume a lot of the smaller fish we eat too. So, they're a competitor and a source of food. Not an intelligent, equal species. The dolphins provide a productive livelihood. They're proud of supplying food for their families."

"I know, but can't we get them to know dolphins are special and should be treated like any human life? Like you did?"

"Maybe eventually, but not by another culture insulting them. They have to be *shown* and see for themselves. Someday, their eyes will be opened."

"So, there's hope?"

"Yes." He nodded. "I can envision that day."

"To be honest, you've got a lot more of that vision thing then I have."

"It'll take time, Izzy, and a lot more than this movie, if…if it ever gets shown in this country."

"I guess we're back to whatever we can do as individuals—one person, one step at a time."

"That's it," Kaito concluded. "When this project is done, we both have more work to do. I have a serious, sea-going vessel for tracking cetaceans and more grant proposals to write."

"Yeah," she nodded. "And I've got dozens of articles in the works and dozens more story ideas to develop with Kimmi."

"Maybe tomorrow we'll be in the thick of it."

"Yamamoto-san," Captain Oba yelled down. "I see dolphins approaching between the fishing boats on the left side of the harbor."

Kaito grabbed his two-way radio. "Louis. Come in. Are you there? Kaito calling. Over."

Click Static.

"Copy. Kaito. Louis here. Have they begun? Over."

"The dolphins are heading along the coast. Stand by." He gave Izzy a kiss and scrambled topside. "Yes. I can hear them banging the poles. I'll fill you in as they get closer. Over."

"Takashi," Kaito yelled, eyeing the flybridge, "Get ready for filming. Captain Oba, keep sweeping the stern slowly back and forth over the line of fishing boats." He put his arm around Shin. "Let's bait the hooks and bring in some flounder. The boats will start closing in."

The strikes to the banger poles became louder. The sound wracked the dolphin's senses. The animals frantically leaped and charged to escape the acoustic horrors. The crew grew silent and stared wide-eyed at the hunt.

Elizabeth paced below, stopping at each window. The banging of the poles pounded in her head. She blew out a big breath and rushed topside. With her head protruding above the deck, she shouted, "Kaito. Can't we stop them?"

"Stay down, Izzy." Kaito set his fishing pole into the holder and hurried toward the companionway. He knelt and grabbed her by the shoulders. "Princess. Please. We're trying to make the film you wanted to show people."

"I know, but allowing them to bring these dolphins to their death when we could stop them?"

"If we interfere with this hunt, they'll be all the more vigilant on the next hunt. Dick O'Meery is right. We have to change people's minds. Think long-term."

He put her hands over her ears…"I can't stand the banging. How that sound barrier must hurt and frighten them. For Christ's sake, Kaito. It will be a blood bath."

"I know, Izzy. But it's too late now. We must film. Please, go below. Don't watch. Close yourself in the head, if you have to. Our job will be over in a short while. We can head home knowing we made a significant contribution."

"Yamamoto!" Shin cried out. "The fishermen are waving us out of the way."

"Izzy. I've got to go. Please."

She nodded and went below.

Shouts rang out across the harbor. "*Kiero! Kiero!*" The captain of the nearest fishing boat screamed.

"*Dete Iki,*" shouted another.

Kaito forced himself to walk steadily to the stern. "Tamiko, they're about to drop their nets. Are you getting them on film?"

"Yes, sir," came the muffled response from under the tarp.

The fishing boats closed in fast at the entrance to the harbor. They began lowering the nets.

Elizabeth let out a curdling scream. "Kaito, please. They'll kill the angels. You have to stop them."

He looked down the companionway and found Elizabeth sobbing, her body shaking with fear and anger.

"Izzy. Please get a hold of yourself."

"Kiero! Kiero!" the fishermen's shouts grew louder.

"Kaito, I can't bear it. It's so wrong!"

Elizabeth's cries shook in his gut, cut deep into his spirit. Her wail was a lament for the soul of the living.

A gap appeared between the last fishing boat and the cliffs surrounding the harbor. Kaito told Takashi, "Keep filming and hold on. The boat will be rolling."

He scrambled to the flybridge to see Captain Oba. "Change in plans. Oba. We've got the footage we need. The hidden rock cameras will later get the killings. We're now going to try and save some of the dolphins." He pointed toward the middle of the leaping animals. "Cut the pods in half and begin a zig-zag pattern, driving them to the leeward side of that last fishing boat. Push them through the divide."

Scrambling back mid-stern, he shouted down to Elizabeth. "We're going to give it a try, Izzy."

She put her hand to her heart. "It's not for me, it's for life, but my heart thanks you."

Kaito stood at the rail as the *Umi-Kumiko* quickly surged to thirty knots. Keeping his eyes on the pods of dolphins, some headed toward the opening while others scattered back.

Over the shouts of the fishermen and the roar of the engines, Captain Oba yelled down, "Sir! Look starboard. A harbor patrol boat is heading toward us."

"Can you outrun him?"

"I think so. He's a bit bigger, maybe fifteen meters, and has a steel hull, but we've got a bigger engine."

"Do your best, Captain."

Kaito gripped the rail as the boat swerved, the wake splashing over the deck. He lost his balance and dropped to his knees.

"Are you hurt, sir?" Shin asked, helping Kaito up.

"No. Thank you." Dozens of dolphins headed in front and alongside the boat. Kaito told Oba, "Keep zigzagging."

The two-way radio phone crackled on the emergency channel. "Attention, *Umi-Kumiko*. This the Taiji Harbor police. Identify yourself and stop your engines. We will board you."

"Full speed ahead! Cut hard to stern!" Kaito yelled back, ignoring the police order. As the boat swerved, he hobbled to portside. Looking down, he searched for the pod's backwash, worrying the sharp turn may have raked the propeller over the dolphins.

"Kaito!" Elizabeth yelled up. "Are you okay?"

"Yes, Izzy. Stay down and hold on."

Two pods of dolphins now moved ahead of the bow. Another pod swam unusually close alongside, as though joyriding on the wake. The lead dolphin breached the surface some three meters off the stern, a half-moon notch on its dorsal. Kaito blinked twice. *What had he just seen?*

He wiped his sea-mist covered glasses. It had been ten years, and they were hundreds of kilometers away from Tokyo. "It couldn't possibly be. "

With the piercing wail of police boat sirens ringing in his ears, Kaito held tight through the next swerve. The steel-hulled police boat charged directly at their mid-section. He shouted up to Oba, "Evade them!"

"Run to starboard, Kaito!" Oba yelled back.

Kaito leaped across the deck. The pod that had been breaching alongside stayed the course. They were now only some twenty meters away from escaping past the last fishing boat at the end of the harbor. The lead dolphin soared high out of the water.

He grabbed the bullhorn and waited on the stern for the pod to surface again. Sure enough, she had a shark bite on the exact same part of her dorsal fin. It was Manami. He bellowed her name. She turned, then circled back, followed by her pod.

"Izzy," he shouted, "It's Manami. Oba, Shin, Takashi, it's the dolphin I freed from OceanWorld ten years ago. She survived! Almost forty years old!"

"Oh my god!" Elizabeth cried out from below.

Manami breached again. Kaito waved at her. Their eyes met mid-air. Manami flapped her pectoral fin like he had taught her at OceanWorld.

"She's alive! She's free," Kaito shouted as the boat and pods slipped between the fishing boat and harbor cliffs, heading fast into the open ocean.

The air horn stopped. As the *Umi-Kumiko* pulled away, Kaito gave the police boat the peace sign. In short order, they were out of sight and reach. At five kilometers from the harbor, Manami and her pod continued to follow.

Kaito shouted down, "Come up, Izzy. And bring the champaign."

"My god, Kaito," Elizabeth said, "This is a miracle, and you made it happen."

"Yes, we did."

They hugged and locked arm in arm. Manami sped by with back flips and twists—all the time singing tunes from her old OceanWorld days.

"Do you think one of the others might be her calf?" asked Elizabeth.

"Could well be," Kaito answered. "When we get her up on the swim platform, maybe Rin Junior will follow her."

Elizabeth gave him a curious look. "What?"

Kaito shouted up to Captain Oba on the bridge. "Cut engines and drop anchor." He waved. "Come down for a toast."

"Compai!" Kaito bellowed, lifting and tapping his plastic flute with Oba, Tamiko and Shin. "Excellent work, gentlemen. Takashi got the shots we needed, and we saved a few from the hunt."

"And your Acqua-bat partner," Oba added. "I remember her well from your *Dolphins in the Wild* class at OceanWorld."

Shin chimed in. "A whole generation of kids learned from you, Yamamoto-san, me included. You left before I took classes, but OceanWorld still carries on the tradition."

Squeals broke out from below the stern.

"Manami hasn't forgotten either," Kaito said. "That's her saying 'let's play'. I'll get my equipment and mix in a little work."

"Kaito. You're kidding," Elizabeth said.

"Not one bit, my dear. Let's put on our swimsuits."

Like the old days at OceanWorld, Kaito and Elizabeth frolicked and danced in the water with Manami. The other dolphins remained distant, until Manami nudged a young male toward them. *Is that her son?* After Kaito petted Manami on the nose, Rin Junior led them to do the same.

Hugging Kaito, Elizabeth sighed, "It's a miracle, isn't it? To think we accomplished so much for her and others."

"Yes, and much more to do. Let's get her up on the platform."

Within minutes, Kaito attached both an acoustic recording tab and an ARGOS satellite tracking tag to her dorsal fin. After checking the receivers, he turned to Captain Oba. "Can you stay with me for another two weeks or so?"

"Only twelve days, Yamamoto-san. I've got piloting job in the Izu Island on the 14th."

"Okay. I'll fill you in after I talk to Elizabeth and Shin and Takashi."

Elizabeth wrapped her arms around her husband as they sat at the galley table. "You did it, Yamamoto, an incredible thing out there. You are an amazing man."

"Thanks but finding Manami is what is really amazing after all those missing years. But no time now to reminisce, we need to make some quick decisions."

"I gathered that, and I'm supposing you want to track her on the boat."

"Yes. Now that I've got the best possible research subject I could have, I can start proving out the technology. I can correlate her behavior in the wild with her recorded vocalizations and match them with my earlier recordings. Then, there will be new grant proposals. Manami has given me a huge boost to my big dream."

Elizabeth nodded. "For sure. It's like she's returning the gift."

Kaito kissed her cheek. "Now, the question is, what do we do? She's migrating and won't hang at our boat forever and neither will you. You can't really continue your writing—interviews, research deadlines with Kimmi—from the deck of the *Umi-Kumiko*. Better you use my old apartment for your home office."

"You're right, I couldn't, but why do I feel you're dumping me?" she asked. "How long will you be tracking her?"

"As long as I'm able, Izzy. Probably a week or more. If I can keep Oba at the helm or find some other pilot."

"And me?"

"I'll put you and Takashi into the dingy and you can make it to Nachikatsuura in about an hour. Bring the film and catch up with Louis and Dick once onshore. After that, you've got deadlines, no?"

"Geez, Kaito, I'm feeling like I won't see you for ages."

"Izzy. I have to stay at sea and follow Manami. Learn with these tools you gave me. See if she can survive with this pod at sea. This is a path I must follow. Not unlike your own path. But I will be back."

"But I worry. Pursuing Manami, the dolphins and your research is your dream alone. Like she's more important than I am."

"Don't be silly. There are times when both of us need to pursue our individual goals. Like you did in the States. That's okay, we still have our lives together."

Elizabeth tugged at the ends of her hair; her face set in worry. "It's like she's no longer our dream. I'm afraid we might drift apart in in our own separate seas. Please don't go."

"Izzy. I have to do this." He held her shoulders and looked deep into her tearful eyes. "I know this has been a very emotional experience for you. Evoking your childhood, I don't know. Bringing up your feelings of loss and safety?" He tugged her head against his chest and stroked her hair. "But I will be back, I promise."

She sobbed in his arms for a long time. When it finally seemed like she cried it all out, she looked up at him, fear still behind her eyes.

He told her, "Don't be afraid, Princess. We're a pair, remember?"

He kissed her. "Go now. I'll meet you back in Tokyo in a week or so."

Chapter Twenty-Eight
Thirteen Days Later

Kaito's apartment
Shibuya

Returning only hours ago from his successful tracking of Manami, Kaito stood at his apartment window and gazed at the night's street traffic twenty-one stories below. After spending weeks afloat on rolling seas, he wavered unsteadily between loneliness and anticipation. He missed Elizabeth and Manami horribly but remained excited about the discoveries that lay ahead. He hoped that Izzy had managed just fine with her writing while he was at sea. That the strength of their relationship held firm despite her unusual fear of a short-term separation.

Looking below, he trusted that Izzy was one of the beams of light heading home in the traffic; he sighed and dropped down into the easy chair. Next to him sat a smiling Buddha statue. He patted him on the head, flicked on the TV, and waited. A newsflash caught his eye. A young male reporter stood on a hill above a village harbor. Although the sound was muted, the fear in the reporter's face was tangible as throngs of panicked people carried babies and pushed bundles past him. With the sound off, Kaito fumbled to find the mute button and reconnect to the world.

"We all felt the earthquake here in Miyagi," the reporter said above screams. "As you can see, memories of the 1993 tsunami in nearby Sendai run deep here. But so far, there is no sign of an approaching tsunami." The camera zoomed up from the empty harbor. "Back to you in the studio."

"Thank you, Aiko. Stay safe," said the news anchor looking toward another monitor and adjusting his earpiece. "You saw that report, Environmental Minister Nakayama. Is there cause to worry?"

"Not really. It only registered 7.2 and our SeaGuard undersea warning system has not detected a possible tsunami." With a barely audible chuckle and a veiled smirk, he added, "No cause for media or public hysteria, especially in such a remote area."

"Bureaucratic idiot," Kaito mumbled. Shutting off the TV, he stared at the blank screen, fists clenched. He shook his head, remembering Nakayama's evil deeds at the university and cursed his malevolent rise to power.

Pulling his weary frame up from the chair, he shuffled again to the window.

A cell phone on the kitchen table buzzed and quivered like a dying beetle.

"Kaito. It's me. Sorry I couldn't get back to you sooner."

Kaito's taught shoulders relaxed at the sound of Izzy's voice. "Don't worry, my *koijin*. Where are you now?"

"Leaving the Times Herald office. Kimmi and I barely made the deadline on the Oshima fish farm story. Should be home in twenty minutes. How was your trip?"

"Exhausting. Left Mito yesterday morning. Docked tonight at seven."

"Oh geez. You're tired. I missed you, sweetheart. There's *shogayaki* in the fridge for you. Nuke it, okay?"

"Thanks. And hurry home."

"See you soon." She hung up.

Kaito's hunger re-emerged, and he added ginger to the pork dish and warmed it up. Watching it rotate in the oven, he winced at how American's used 'nuking' for microwaving.

Eating across the table from the stacks of data recording equipment, he pondered the long journey with Manami and her pod and the challenge of analyzing her vocalizations.

"Wau!" he exclaimed, realizing Manami and her pod would have been in the Miyagi area when the rock plates were beginning to slip against each other. Sensing an undersea earthquake would soon strike, she and the pod had left in a hurry. He could hardly wait to begin his study in the morning. Leaning back in his chair, his lifelong dream of understanding dolphin language gratified him.

Hearing the door open, his reverie broke, and he rushed to meet Elizabeth.

A quick kiss and a long hug later, Kaio said, "I missed you so much, Izzy."

"I can tell," she said, holding his chin and laughing. "Let me get changed and you can fill me in on your return voyage."

"Hungry?" he asked as she headed into the bedroom. "I'll make you a cheese omelet."

She glanced back. "Sure."

Returning in a three-quarter length silk robe over one of his favorite lacy baby dolls, she kissed the top of his head. "You're a prince." She sat and pointed to his tracking equipment. "And a dedicated scientist."

"That and more," he said as he touched her arm. "Eat now. I'll talk." He tapped his lips. "Three days ago, after watching Manami and her pod gorge on schools of sardines," he paused, "And nurse her calf, the audio D-tag recorder detached. Pretty much expected and with a signal, I was able to recover it."

"On that very night, lying in bed, the beeping became weak on the other satellite tag. Unusual for it to go so quickly. I got up. It was actually just before dawn, and I oriented the receiver to pick up directional movement."

Elizabeth set her chopsticks down and took a drink of milk tea. "I bet you worried."

"That I was going to lose her?" he asked, then answered, "At first I was." He sighed. "I sort of panicked. Wheeled the *Umi-Kumiko* in a wide circle trying to get a bead on where the signal was going." He blew out his breath.

"Then, the signal stopped. I wondered if the signal was interrupted or if the battery had given out. Did she bolt at high speed for some reason?"

Elizabeth pulled her chair next to him and put her arm around his shoulder. "I bet you were devastated."

He patted her hand. "For a while, I was. Then, I pictured you in my mind and heard you saying, '*There'll come a time when...*'" He swallowed hard. "And I knew I had to let her go."

He gestured to the telemetry equipment. "And accept what she has given me."

"I know," she said and kissed his cheek. "It was meant to be."

He ran his hand through his hair. "How about you now? What have you heard from Dick O'Meery?"

"He and the producers were pleased after editing the footage. They're planning to go back, confront the authorities and get their response. Still a long way from finishing *The Gulf*. They wanted me to tell you how grateful they were for your help."

"That's fine. Glad to have helped, as long as it doesn't get out to my fishermen friends. My countrymen would shun me."

"I know. Dick is cool. Speaking of fishermen," she added, "Remember when I told you about Dr. Murada's success at farm-raised tuna in Oshima?"

270

He nodded. "Yes, and how ironic. His cages are moored not far from Kushimoto. I know the bay."

"You know I loved working on a 'feel good' story for a change. Seems Japan is leading the world in aquaculture."

"Progress," Kaito concurred, "But what about continuing to use valuable forage fish for feed?"

"He's making progress there too with vegetable protein, corn especially. He thanked Kimmi and I for prodding him on that."

"Aha," Kaito laughed. "Blue fin vegetarians."

A smug smile formed on Elizabeth's face. "We've got a lot of work ahead of us." She looked into his eyes. "Ready for bed?"

He took her hand and trailed kisses up her arm. "Not that tired."

"You thinking what I'm thinking?"

He nodded, slipping his hand under the top of her nightgown.

Next morning

Watching Elizabeth leave the apartment to interview more Minimata disease victims, Kaito smiled thinking of how satisfying their lovemaking was after a long absence.

He made some tea and slapped on the receiver headphones. Turning dials to locate the most recent audio recordings, the crackling static faded into the burbling sounds of rushing water.

Kaito became submerged, swimming right beside the pod of dolphins. He was pretty sure he could already make out Manami's voice, along with what must have been the tiny voice of her calf. The timeline showed this was their first day in the Miyagi fishing grounds. For now, he most wanted to hear what might have led up to the abrupt loss of signal to try and correlate that with her vocalizations.

"That's Manami right there for sure," he cried out and marked her sing song on the timeline. "And yes, that must be Rin Jr.'s little squeaks," he mumbled, knowing that calves nurse for up to two years with their mothers.

As he listened throughout the morning, he made notes of the incredible diversity of sounds. Were they resting, maybe sleeping now? Did they just change direction? He was most amazed by what seemed to be conversational chatter among the family—a kind of call and response communication. One dolphin would let out a distinct sequence of clicks and squawks, and other dolphins would repeat it back. What kind of messages were they sharing?

By early afternoon, the headphones were making his ears sweaty and red, and he felt a headache coming. He didn't want to stop, so he took an aspirin and found a couple of *taiyaki* cakes in the refrigerator.

At 6:45, the dolphins were at the surface making loud tail slaps. To his ears, it sounded like a 'listen up' sort of warning. Manami then emitted a sharp, high-pitched, and fast pulsing cry—*ieeyipkoo, ieeyipkoo.*

Immediately, the whole pod repeated the call and, within seconds, the dolphins shot out of the area where they were feeding. After that, the only sounds were of rushing water and breaching.

At 6:49, the audio recorder went silent. Kaito concluded the dying battery signaled and released the D-tag off Manami's dorsal. That's when it floated to the surface. His heartbeat picked up as he strained to picture what might have caused those calls. Maybe a shark?

"Wait a minute!" he shouted to himself, wildly shaking his head. "That cry is familiar somehow." He got up and paced the floor, wracking his brain. A few paces later, he froze, whirled around and delved into the OceanWorld files.

Yes, it was a similar call she made in the lagoon years ago.

It meant danger, escape. He remembered he had a sonogram of that call so he could visually compare the sound waves.

Kaito followed a hunch that he was both excited and worried about. He rushed toward the closet where he kept his OceanWorld records and grabbed an apple along the way. He dug through a box marked: 'Voice Recordings 2004–05.' With the apple held between his teeth, he frantically flipped through the sonogram prints. Holding up the sheet marked "Rainstorm 2/4/04," he spit out the apple. Grinning, he said to himself, "Wait till I tell Izzy."

"Yes!" he shouted and rushed back to the table. He placed the old print next to the readout on the screen. The intricate wavy lines were almost identical. "That's it," he said and kept nodding his head.

"*Bikkuri!*" he yelled, unable to hold his excitement in. He laughed knowing that Izzy would have said, "Oh my god!" Then, he had to state his belief out loud, "In Miyagi, hours before the tsunami hit the coast."

He dashed back to the closet and slipped on the apple, catching himself on the corner of the file cabinet. Opening the drawer marked 'journals', he grabbed the volumes of Seismology Quarterly with the same anticipation he felt on his first day at college.

The phone rang. He hurried to pick it up.

"Kaito?" Elizabeth said. "Are you alright? You sound all out of breath or something."

He replied, "I'm actually out of my mind, right now. You have to come home. I have something spectacular to show you."

"Mmm, Kimmi and I were about to head back to the Times Herald offices."

"She needs to come with you." He raised his hands in the air. "This is going to be a big story."

That afternoon

Deep in thought, studying the physics of emerging cracks in the earth's crust, Kaito didn't hear the door open.

"Kaito. We're here," Izzy announced behind him.

He bounded up from his chair and bowed deeply to Kimmi.

The petite, young woman bowed as well and said, "An honor to work with you again, Yamamoto-san."

Kaito held his hand out. "My pleasure, Miss Matsushita. So happy you came. Elizabeth has told me of your vast talents and dedication to the environment." He cocked his head. "But I don't think we've met before."

"Years ago," she said, shaking his hand. "I was a student in your Dolph-Fun and Learn classes. It was you who turned me onto wildlife in the environment."

Kaito smiled and considered her looks. Her round face and bright eyes, framed by tortoise-shell glasses, reminded him of a tiny, but precocious student who asked too many big questions. Holding his finger to his chin, he asked, "Were you the girl who asked me, 'what do dolphins think of us humans?'"

She nodded. "Yes, and I still wonder."

"Me too," Kaito said, chuckling. "And that's a sign of true intelligence." He turned to Elizabeth; his chin raised high. "And the makings of a great reporter." He kissed Izzy. "Right dear?"

"For sure," she said then added, "Now that we've had our love fest, let's get to work. What have you got, husband?"

"Come, sit." Kaito gestured toward the table. "Now, Kimmi…" he placed his hands together…"has Elizabeth filled you in on my research involving dolphin vocalizations?"

"Yes, indeed, Yamamoto-san. It's wonderful that you were reunited with Manami and recently tracked and recorded her."

"Perfect," Kaito said smiling broadly at Kimmi's bubbly enthusiasm, "And here is the result." He held up the old sonogram print. "These voice prints of Manami were taken over five years ago and some two-hundred kilometers distant…" he placed the print next to the sound wave readout on the screen, unable to sit still. "Now, look at how her warning calls match."

"I see it, Sir," Kimmi remarked. "Same animal, same expression. It's uncanny."

Kaito placed a hand on his chest and sighed.

"That's great, Kaito," Izzy interjected, "But why is it important?"

Kaito jabbed his finger at the monitor screen. "This time, Manami was not warning about pollution entering the OceanWorld lagoon, because…" he raised his arms in the air and bellowed, "Because this time, she was warning her pod to leave Miyagi because she detected an undersea earthquake was going to happen." He paused. "Hours later, it did."

"Wow!" Kimmi cheered.

Elizabeth narrowed her eyes and questioned, "Are you saying she somehow knew ahead of time? Like predicted it?"

"Absolutely." He straightened his back, "Yes. I am. You did see Miyagi was hit by an earthquake and minor tsunami yesterday?"

"I did, but how do you know?"

"Well." He leaned back in his chair. "Let me take you through it." He took a deep breath. "For centuries, Japanese fishermen have reported the rare appearance of deep-water fish, like oarfish and Humboldt squid coming to the surface and being caught." He tapped on the table. "This happens every time, days before an earthquake strikes. It's anecdotal, but my father swore by it."

Elizabeth prompted him. "Go on."

"This phenomenon is also known with land animals. In 1975, a 7.3 quake hit Haicheng, China. One month before, hibernating snakes in the area abandoned their winter nests, months before usual. In that case, the government took it as a serious warning and ordered an evacuation, saving thousands of lives."

"Ha!" Kimmi laughed. "Wish our government had the same foresight."

Kaito admired Kimmi's willingness to question her government and noticed the piercing on her nose for a ring and a bit of tattoo peeking above her turtleneck sweater. She made him feel young again.

He slid to the edge of his seat. "What really got me excited was the Italian four-year scientific study of toad mating."

"Toad mating?" Izzy questioned. "You've got to be kidding."

"No. Their breeding behavior was the original purpose of the research. It was in 2009, in a lake near L'Aquila, Italy, during their spawning season. Five days before a 6.3 quake hit the area, the toads suddenly interrupted their breeding and abandoned the lake. Unheard of in the middle of the mating season."

"Were they horny toads?" Kimmi asked with a smirk.

Elizabeth shook her head.

Kaito chuckled. "No, they were common toads, but they returned five days later to re-commence their activity."

"Cool. I'm happy for the little guys." Kimmi narrows her brows. "But how do we take the leap from toads to dolphins?"

"Good question, Kimmi," remarked Elizabeth.

"Here's the exciting leap." Kaito's eyes widened, and he clapped his together again. "Just this last year, in New Zealand, some scientists believed that the beaching of 170 pilot whales, signaled the huge Boxing Day tsunami."

Elizabeth wrinkled her brow. "They fled to land to get away from it, right? Did they strand out of fear? Misdirection?"

"We'll never know," Kaito replied, "But what I do know is the disastrous Boxing Day tsunami killed thousands. And maybe the deaths could have been prevented."

"I see where you're going," Elizabeth nodded, then shook her head. "But I'm still hung up on what these early signs are and how the dolphins can sense them."

"I understand. It's complicated, but it all starts with the earth's crust on land or under water. Can I explain?"

She glanced at her watch. "Yes, please, but in laywoman's terms, Professor Yamamoto."

Gleefully, Kaito began by slowly sliding his hands together. "The earth's crust is constantly waxing and waning in places along these faults or separations. But when the plates begin to separate, there's a sharp forward thrust and an earthquake happens."

"That's the Ring of Fire that surrounds Japan, isn't it, sir?"

Kaito smiled broadly. "Yes. Japan has a large potential for earthquakes and disaster because the nation sits atop four huge slabs of the Earth's crust. Roughly 90 percent of all the world's earthquakes strike along this ring. The Japan Trench is where the Pacific plate beneath the Pacific Ocean dives underneath North American plate beneath Japan. These plates shift about 3.5 inches (8.9 centimeters) per year, and the movement has produced major earthquakes in the past nine earthquakes of magnitude 7 or greater since 1973."

Kimmi interjected. "That states the huge and ongoing magnitude of the problem."

"Yes, indeed. Now, *before* that separation, there are non-seismic, pre-earthquake signals that occur days or even weeks before an event. And, because dolphins and whales navigate partly by following geomagnetic contours of the sea floor, they are very sensitive to changes. This has been demonstrated by Dr. Margaret Klinowska from Cambridge University."

"Whoa, hold on Kaito," Elizabeth interrupted. "I'm losing you. How about we take a little tea break."

"I hate to stop now," Kimmi said, "But I do need to go to the bathroom."

Elizabeth sat back in her seat.

"Sure," Kaito said standing up and stretching. "I hope I'm not boring you."

"Not at all," Kimmi said.

While the ladies chatted in the kitchen, Kaito was studying notes he had taken from the seismology journals.

"Boy," Kimmi said to Elizabeth upon her return, "He's really onto something significant."

"Might be a little farfetched," Elizabeth said.

Kaito slumped when he heard Izzy's comment.

Sounds of dishware being pulled from the cabinets filled the room. Water running. The burner being lit.

Kaito held his breath, waiting for Elizabeth to say anything that might support what he was doing. *What is going on with her?*

Carrying a tray of tea, the girls sat down, and Elizabeth repeated her question. "So, we were talking about the dolphin's sensitivity to these slow changes in the earth's crust."

"Right. And we well know dolphins are very sensitive creatures. Let me take the specific senses that come into play with earthquakes, although we don't fully understand the physiology of how these senses operate. First, dolphins have magnetoreceptors in their bodies which make them sensitive to the geomagnetic fields in the ground. Second, they have chemoreceptors which sense all kinds of substances carried in the water. Thirdly, they have keen electroreceptive abilities to detect an electrical field, such as the minute electrical current generated by prey fish constricting their muscles."

"Simply put, they are biological sensing machines, abilities that have kept them on this planet for millions of years."

"I always knew they were special," Kimmi offered.

"So, what do they actually sense before the earthquake?" Elizabeth asked.

Kaito licked his lips. "Okay. So, as the plates start rubbing together, prior to cracking apart, dolphins sense the resultant magnetic, chemical and electrical changes that take place. The minerals in the rocks discharge electrons. That's what scientists call a stream of positive holes. In other words, turning into a battery. When these electrons reach into the water, they oxidize the H20 molecules into hydrogen peroxide, which we know sea mammals feel and is a skin irritant."

"Fascinating," Kimmi said, jotting down notes on her pad.

"Interesting," Elizabeth added, "But they have to tell us somehow."

"Right," Kimmi concurred. "And I'm sure Yamamoto-san will figure that out too. For me, the issue is how well us humans listen."

Suddenly, Elizabeth stood up. "I need to get a glass of water."

"Are you alright?" Kaito asked. "You look sort of pale."

"A queasy stomach, actually," she replied, holding her belly and wincing.

Kaito frowned but being delighted with Kimmi's enthusiasm, he turned back to her. "It all leads to a missing link that allows days, rather than minutes, of warning for an undersea earthquake and can save lives."

"*Bikkuri*!" Kimmi gasped, "This is amazing."

"Yes," Elizabeth concurred. "Kaito gets all charged up when he feels he's on the brink of scientific discovery."

"Who wouldn't be," he said, raising his chin. "And that is the big news I wanted to share with you. This is the hypothesis for my research."

"That is a big step, alright," Elizabeth commented, shaking her head, "But would you be all alone and too far ahead in the field?"

"In Japan, for sure, but there are others like Dr. Simon Northridge of the Sea Mammal Research Unit at St Andrews University. He believes there may be a correlation between some whale strandings and geomagnetic anomalies."

"Could be promising," Elizabeth said, "But with big challenges ahead."

Kimmi piped in, "With big rewards, I'd say."

"Thanks, Kimmi," Kaito said. "It's both and I'm now, more than ever, up to it. Starting tomorrow, I'll be preparing a major research program to the Institute on Nature and Science to evaluate the abilities of dolphins to sense the early warning signs of undersea subduction earthquakes." Kaito looked to Elizabeth for her reaction, finding her head down, doodling and deep in thought.

Kimmi broke the silence. "That institute is the only department with the funds and authority to approve grants related to undersea tsunami warning systems."

Elizabeth closed her notebook. "Well, this has been enlightening. I sense great enthusiasm and potential here for the long-term." She glanced at the wall clock. "But what's the story?"

Kaito and Kimmi stiffened.

"Short-term, I have to concur with you, Liz," Kimmi said. "But I think the big story lies ahead."

Kaito nodded. Elizabeth stood. "Yes, and it's almost seven. Let's pick this up at a later date, okay? Want me to call a taxi for you, Kimmi?"

"That's alright, Liz. I'll catch a train to Harajuku from the Shibuya station."

"Well then," Kaito said, standing at the door, "It's been great."

Kimmi bowed deeply and said, "It'll be an honor working with you again, Yamamoto-san. I so admire your vision."

Kaito bowed at the waist. "Likewise. It's an honor to have such an ally."

Elizabeth reached over and hugged Kimmi.

When they parted, Kaito said, "How about me? I like hugs too."

Elizabeth seemed to frown as she watched their embrace, but then smiled politely. "Goodnight, Kimmi. I'll call you in the morning."

Kaito and Elizabeth started to clear the table. Washing out a teacup, Elizabeth observed, "Well, that was quite an evening."

"It was. And so glad you brought Kimmi. She's real intelligent and a ball of fire."

"She is and was certainly enamored with you."

Wiping a saucer, Kaito asked, "About my hypothesis?"

"That, and your passion."

Looking surprised, he responded, "I am, as you say, psyched, about the prospects. I'm feeling a renewed purpose in my sixty-year-old life. Don't get the idea that I'm...what do you say...infatuated by a woman thirty-five years younger."

"I get that. It's the practical requirements of the research and the implications I worry about."

"You mean the direction I'm taking?"

"Yes."

"Oh."

Kaito put the dish towel down and sauntered over to the refrigerator. Grabbing a bottle of Kirin Ichiban, he said, "Can I get you something? We should talk."

"Thanks, no. I'll put the dishes away and join you in a minute."

Elizabeth sat a seat cushion away and began, "I'm skeptical about your plan, that's all."

"Is it?" he replied. "Your earlier questions had a negative frequency to them. If I were to print your sound waves, they were at best flat, sometimes even jagged."

"Sorry, but I worry the direction is not right."

"Not right by you?"

"I'm sorry. I worry about what this might entail."

"Can you explain?"

"I can't right now. I'm just trying to take it all in. It's emotional, I guess."

He reached over and stroked her arm. "How about if we take your mind off things. Go swimming. You know under the sheets. Get some healing, like in that Marvin Gaye song you like so much."

She pulled her arm away. "Sorry, not tonight." Then she walked out of the room.

Kaito slumped, feeling opposite energy. *What have I done to make her glorious eyes, turn so sullen?*

Chapter Twenty-Nine

Elizabeth returned home, placed the key in the door lock, and took a deep breath. Tonight, she would come to terms with Kaito about his research plans. Hesitating to open the door, she would, once again, find him absorbed with his dolphin recordings or among the stacks of journals, furiously writing. Then, he'd tear away and rush to hug her. She appreciated the gesture but wondered how sincere it was. But a deep fear was rising up from inside. *Does he care as much about me, or is it just a force of habit?* His work had held his attention for so long as of late that she could not help but think his affection disingenuous.

She turned the handle.

"My *Koija*," he shrieked and came to her, "I miss you." He lifted her off the floor. "You wouldn't believe what I discovered today."

"I'm sure you'll tell me about it," she said, giving him a hurried kiss. "Let me change out of these work clothes, okay?" She trudged into the bedroom, thinking it wasn't so much that he forgot to ask about her day, but that his mind was always elsewhere. He was as passionate about his research as she was afraid for their future. They needed to talk.

"What's wrong, Izzy-chan?" he asked as she returned in sweats and sunk into the kitchen chair. "You seem out of sorts, ever since we met with Kimmi the other day."

"I know," she said, "And I'm sorry for being distant. I need to explain."

"Good." He placed his hand on hers. "And tell me how I can make things better."

She grasped his hand. "You're so kind. Wish I could be—"

"It's okay. Tell me what's bothering you."

She looked down, struggling where to begin. "Things started the day you left me on the boat to track Manami." A picture of her father leaving the family flashed across her mind. "I...I felt ignored. Left out."

"Now that you say that," Kaito said. "I'm sorry, but I did sense dread on your face."

"That obvious, huh?" She sighed. "I felt like I was losing you. Even though I knew better."

He patted her hand. "But we agreed we'd work things out together, didn't we?"

"We did."

"So, when I returned from tracking Manami, did you feel better?"

"Yes."

"How about when I announced my new research plans to you and Kimmi?"

"I felt unsure. You were quite captivated by each other."

"How do you mean? She is some twenty years younger. You don't think—?"

Elizabeth fidgeted with the drawstrings on her hoodie as an image of her father with the young starlet shot through her mind. "I...I don't know." She chewed on her lips. "Her infatuation and your puffed-up ego. It just bothered me."

"I'm surprised. I really liked your writing partner. She's a smart woman and I was pleased with her appreciation of my theories."

Elizabeth looked past him and said, "I wasn't jealous of her," she said, thinking she was angry for failing her. "It's that you were so excited, and all consumed with your desire to make scientific discoveries, on the backs of dolphins. It was like you no longer knew me. Forgot about my feelings."

Kaito got up from his chair, put his arms around her and kissed the top of her head. "I'm sorry you felt that way, Princess. I just assumed you'd be so engaged with your successful writing career." He bent down and caught her gaze. "Don't we support each other?" He gently squeezed her arms. "You could help me with the grant writing."

She returned a fake smile. "Sorry, I won't do that."

"I'm confused here, Izzy-chan. I thought we both wanted each other to be fulfilled with our own individual pursuits as well as do things together. Didn't we have that understanding?"

She nodded, realizing she had agreed, but now faced a personal dilemma. "We did, but there's a conflict. Getting to your goal presents a problem, and it's not right."

He pulled up the chair next to her. "Not, right? I'm surprised you would say that." He drew a long breath. "Do you mean you don't approve of what I need to do in my work?"

"It's not about…" she paused, fear rising in her throat…"about approving, really, but not supporting." *He'll never understand the role of my guardian angel.*

"Really? Haven't I supported you and your writing career?"

"You did."

"And after that, I agreed to release Manami. Helped produce *The Gulf* against my fishermen." He looked hard into her eyes. "I came to believe these were the right things for us to do. I have no regrets, but what are you now saying you want me to do, or not do?"

Choking up, she stammered, "I…I have to go to the bathroom."

Kaito leaned back in his chair. "Sure," he said and blew out a breath.

Elizabeth sat on the toilet and began to sob. *What is wrong with me?* She felt horrible distancing herself from Kaito, who had been so good to and for her. She had no right to deny him his dream. *But I cannot be a part of it, something I am deeply against.* She still had to dig up the courage to tell him.

She dabbed her eyes in front of the mirror. *Go and tell him what's aching in your heart.*

She returned to find Kaito's face contorted with worry. Still, she had to stick to her vow.

"Kaito. This is hard for me to say, but I must—"

"Go ahead, please."

She cleared her throat. "Your research, no matter how well-intended, would require tagging of dolphins…" she saw that he nodded…"in order to determine if they could warn us of an impending tsunami, would it not?"

"Of course," he replied, wrinkling his brow.

"Well, I consider that a form of abuse. Hurting them is hurting me. I thought you always knew that. Using them as tools for human exploration and exploitation. Depriving them of their freedom. Putting them at risk for our own selfish needs. I simply cannot allow that."

"Izzy. Come on. You know it's to benefit science and humankind."

"I understand, but it's abuse no less. No less than the U.S. Navy using dolphins for bomb detection. Or giving them drugs. Living intimately with them in a pool house."

Kaito shook his head. "But this is different."

She shook her head. "Not in my mind. It runs counter to the core of who I am, and what I believe. The vow I made as a child to my guardian angel. You know that," she said, feeling her guardian angel would abandon her if she agreed with him.

Kaito slumped in his chair.

She continued, sensing she was losing the battle, losing her man and her future. A part of her wanted to control him to stop, but she said, "It's simply not right for humans to dominate and control other beings, no matter how honorable the intention."

"Izzy-chan, I know how deeply you feel about dolphins, but are you being maybe too rigid?"

"No. Remember my life goal has always been to protect dolphins and their fellow species. I can't bend on that."

"Is that it then?" he finally asked, his chin starting to quiver. He put his hand to the side of her face. "Are you sure there isn't something deeper?"

Their eyes welled at the same time.

"No," she said. "My belief is as deep as it gets and runs right up against my deep love for you."

They embraced, stroking each other's heads.

When they parted, Kaito swiped off his tears. "Okay. We're at an impasse. Where do we go from here?"

"Knowing that I can't expect you to let go of your dream—"

He nodded. "You're right. And I won't."

"So, I think we need to clear our heads. Figure things out." She knew it was something deeper than that but was at a loss to understand the barrage of emotions that kept forcing her to act. "We agreed. Each individual has his or her own goals and we should be able to pursue them and still be partners."

"Like I did in Kushimoto," he said, looking to the floor. "Maybe we're both trying to escape our childhoods?"

"Yeah. Maybe going back to the States will clear a path—a better future for us."

"So, you're leaving me?"

"Not exactly but we need to agree on a separation."

He winced. "Just because of that one thing?"

"Yes, I'm afraid. But it's not like a divorce over irreconcilable differences. The separation is over a single difference. Just hoping that with distance and time you'll either change your mind or somehow drop using dolphins as tools. I cannot, in good faith, be anything but honest to you."

"But Izzy, I can't do that." He reached out for her.

She withdrew. "I understand that, but I can't be with, lay with, a man who abuses dolphins."

"This separation is final then?"

"Yes. It has to be. And I will be leaving tomorrow."

"Okay. As long as we both hold hope we can come back together," he said. "I still love you."

"I love you too. And I hold the hope."

Kaito reached for Liz first, and she fell into his arms, tears falling down her cheeks. She could feel his body quaking from his own cries, but he did not release her.

Chapter Thirty
Los Angeles

Arriving at LAX at 9:40 a.m. from a red eye overnight flight, Elizabeth didn't feel tired, so she figured she'd stop and visit her mother in nearby Westchester. Signing in at the modern and friendly *Passages* assisted living facility, she was directed to the unit she shared with Paddy.

Knocking on the door, Paddy appeared, holding his index finger to his lips. He whispered, "Hi, Liz. Ye be early." He ducked into the hallway, closed the door and gave Elizabeth a warm hug.

"Sorry," he said, "Ye Mom's sleepin' now. Had a really bad night. Let's go into the community room and chat." He held up a panic button hung from a lanyard around his neck. "If she wakes, she'll buzz me."

Picking up a coffee and juice from a cart, they sat.

"So, Mom's not sleeping well?" asked Liz.

"No," he said, eyes dropping to the table. "Her congestive heart failure is gettin' much worse lately."

"She has heart failure?" Liz said, glancing around the room, then narrowing her eyes at Paddy. "First I heard that."

"Been several months now," he said with a frown. "It's a slow process. They're treatin' her with diuretics but can't do much more for her. She has trouble breathin' and all."

"Geez, I call her every week from Tokyo and yes she sounded tired, but how come she never told me?"

He sighed and nodded. "I know but she didn't want t' bother ye with her condition. Wanted to keep it between her and me."

Elizabeth asked, "So, how is she taking it?"

"Well, considering the prognosis, she's being a real trooper."

Elizabeth continued to be amazed at what Paddy was telling her. It seemed so unlike Maggie. Maybe Paddy's devotion to her had made a big difference. "What is the prognosis then?"

"Better t' have the doctors explain it t' ye, but basically her heart isn't pumpin' well and fluids are enterin' her lungs makin' it hard t' breath. I keep her propped up in bed and all."

"Thanks, Paddy, for what you're doing for her. How long do you think she'll be sleeping for? I'd like to see her."

"Probably several hours, I'd guess. Maybe ye could come back tomorrow and talk t' her and the doctor. I could call ye about a good time."

"Okay, then," Liz agreed. "I'm staying with my editor in Pacific Palisades, so call me when you can."

"Will do," he said, "And mighty grand of ye t' come visit her. She'll be pleased."

After a nap and a shower at Catherine's apartment, Elizabeth made a fresh pot of French roast coffee and waited for her editor to return home from work.

Hearing a key in the lock, Liz headed toward the door.

"Ha," Catherine sniffed. "Fresh coffee. Liz is back in town."

They hugged, parted and gazed at each other.

"Good to see my best writer again," Cath said.

Liz chuckled. "My best editor as well. You don't look a day older."

"It's been a few, but neither do you," Cath said, running her finger through her hair. "Helps to dye away the gray."

They laughed and sat down for coffee.

"So," Cath began, "You've come to visit your mother?"

"Visit you too, Cath, and thanks again for putting me up."

"No problem." She lifted her coffee cup and sipped. "I like having you."

"How are things at *MO magazine*?"

"Going well. Circulation is up to thirty-eight thousand. Ad revenues are steady. Environmental stories never-ending. Wish you were here to help. Maybe you could pick up a few things—"

"I...I'd like to, depending on my mom. Her boyfriend, Paddy, tells me she's got congestive heart failure and it's getting worse by the day."

"Sorry to hear that."

"I'm waiting for his call so I can go and visit her."

Catherine studied her face and asked, "How's Kaito?"

"Doing well," she said, looking across the room and wiggling in her chair. "He's gung-ho on his dolphin earthquake detection and warning hypothesis and research."

"I take it you're not."

Liz sat back. "Not so much. I don't like him using dolphins as guinea pigs in and around the precursors of earthquakes."

"So, you're dissing him again?"

"I…I wouldn't say that. Just time and space away—an amicable separation."

"Not heading to a breakup, I hope."

"I'm hoping he'll give up on using dolphins as our tools."

"Like he didn't give up on your forays." Cath tapped on the table. "Sorry, Liz, but I don't think you're playing fair with him. One of these times you might lose him."

Elizabeth didn't comment at first. "Cath, you know my sacred vow and commitment to dolphins."

"I do, but maybe it's time to re-assess that as well. It may be hurting you."

"How could that be?"

"That your guardian angel is like a straw man standing between you two?"

Elizabeth cocked her head. "I don't get you."

"I mean is that just an excuse, an untruth for keeping you from finding what's wrong?"

"Geez, Cath, I love you, but I don't understand you."

"I think you have to work better to understand yourself."

"I…I can't," she said as her phone rang. "Sorry, Cath," Elizabeth said as she picked up her vibrating cellphone and glanced at the caller. "It's my mother."

"Go ahead, take it," Catherine insisted, "It might be important."

Elizabeth answered, "Yes. Oh, Paddy. What's up?"

She gave her editor an uneasy look, got up from her chair and murmured, "When?" Face turning warm, she asked, "Saint John's? What did the doctors say? Jesus." Jolts of fear, sadness and guilt struck her.

"Maggie was now in a coma and the doctors said she may have only days to live."

"Okay. Hold on," she said to Paddy, gripping her trembling hand over the speaker and turning to Catherine. "My mom's had a heart attack. She's in the hospital in Santa Monica. Critical it seems."

"You better hurry, Liz," Catherine said, taking her car keys out of her purse and handing them to Liz. "Go. We'll pick up on this later."

Elizabeth grabbed her bag, mouthed a 'thank you' and rushed out the door. "Let me know if I can help," Catherine yelled out.

Phone buried in her neck; Elizabeth turned the key on Cath's Mazda. "See you there, Paddy."

Heading south on route one, Elizabeth's mind and heart raced with the afternoon's commuter traffic.

What could I do for her now? What if she dies? What would I say to her? What would she say to me?

"Shit!" she yelled, slamming on the brakes as the cars in front of her came to a stop. "Watch it, girl," she told herself and took a left, veering east to catch the shortcut from Walgrove to Centinela.

Aloneness came over her. *Who did she have to call?* Father would tell her he'd make an appearance at the funeral. Chrissy, the even more estranged daughter, would say, 'you're the caregiver type. Let me know when it's over.' Kaito was the only person on earth who would listen, understand, and help her cope. She would call him tonight after he woke.

A young couple whizzed by in a Porche 911 convertible, reminding her of Father taking off in his new life with Vyma. Would she ever be able to toss the litter of her lost childhood out the window? *Stop it! You should be feeling for her now not dwelling on your past. You are worthy now. You are worthy.*

Reaching the St. John's parking lot, she sat in the car, breathing the conditioned air to clear her mind for the task ahead. Paddy and the hospital staff would welcome the dutiful daughter's presence and support. *But if I care for her, will she notice me? If I don't reach out to her, will I feel more guilty, more depressed?* With her hand on the door latch, she decided to open her mind and heart to her mother as best she could.

Peeking through the door of room 232, she found Paddy sitting alongside her mother's bed. He came rushing to her, arms open for a hug.

"So grand of ye t'come," he said as she took in his small frame.

Looking up to her with his impish Irish eyes and melancholy countenance, he said, "She's been a askin' about ye."

She glanced over at her mother's comatose body, wondering if Paddy was being ingratiating. *Doesn't matter, Liz, he's been good for her.*

"And what a wonderful daughter ye were," he added.

Elizabeth accepted his comment with a nod, thinking she at least tried to help her over the years. "I should have done more."

"Ah. Forget and forgive, I always say," he said smiling. "Do you mind watchin' her while I catch a bite to eat?"

"Well...sure."

"The doc will be makin' his rounds soon," he said at the door. "I'll be right back."

The door closed and Elizabeth froze—alone with incessant sounds of the oxygen machine feeding her mother's ragged wheeze. Seeing Maggie lying there with her mouth agape was how she often remembered her. Blacked out. Ready to yell, "What the hell do you want?"

Elizabeth slapped her hand to her mouth and closed her eyes. *She's dying, dear god. I'm supposed to be here for her even though she wasn't there for me.*

Snapping out of it, she traipsed to the other side of the bed and sat. Her mother's face, swollen and pale, seemed locked in a position of pain. He abdomen billowed the sheets, and the smell of an old unwashed body filled the air. *You can do it*, she told herself and reached over to take her mother's hand. Stopping at her fingertips, she drew back, afraid of waking her.

A knock at the door. "Misses Worthington?" A bearded, bespectacled man in a white lab coat entered. He waved. "Hi, I'm Doctor Branson. Is this your mother?"

Elizabeth stood. "Yes, I'm Liz."

"How are you holding up?" he asked, grabbing Maggie's medical chart.

"I just got here. A little overwhelmed, I guess."

The doctor placed a stethoscope on Maggie's chest, raising his finger for quiet. Moments later, he made a note in her chart and turned to Elizabeth. "So, what has your father told you?"

"He's not my father," she replied, adding, "Just that she had a heart attack."

The doctor took a deep breath. "I'm sorry but your mother is at stage four of congestive heart failure—the final stage. Her heart is scarred and enlarged, breathing is difficult, her lungs..." he pointed to her enlarged abdomen..."and body are filling fast with fluids, and the liver complications..." he looked at Elizabeth's blank expression. "I'm afraid she doesn't have long to live."

Elizabeth coughed and struggled to ask, "Is there something you can do for her?"

He pressed his lips together. "We've done everything possible. It's sad to say, but her aged body is simply shutting down. She may stay in a coma or wake at any time, but she'll be more confused and disoriented. I'd recommend you bring her into hospice care, where morphine will ease her pain and you'll get support for the family."

"Dr. Branson, Dr. Branson," the hospital intercom squawked, "You're wanted in room 346."

"Sorry," he said. "I've got to go." He turned at the door. "Be sure to keep her head elevated on the pillow."

Numb with feelings, Elizabeth turned to her mother and adjusted her pillow.

Maggie groaned and opened her eyes, "Oh, Crissy…" she coughed…"so good of you to come."

"No, Mom, it's Elizabeth."

"Oh," Maggie mumbled and fell back into a deep state.

When Paddy returned, Elizabeth filled him in on the conversation with Dr. Branson. It confirmed what Paddy already understood and they quickly agreed to the hospice option. After Elizabeth made the arrangements with SoCal hospice to transport Mother in the morning, she asked Paddy, "Did Mother express any wishes to you about a funeral or anything?"

"She did, sayin' she wanted t' be cremated, ashes spread wherever I pleased and no funeral services."

Elizabeth moved to the edge of her chair; eyes wide in surprise.

Paddy sighed. "I know."

Elizabeth sat back. "Really?"

"I thought it strange too. Asked her why." He shook his head. "She didn't want to talk about it. Only said she no longer wanted t' be a burden to ye or ye sister."

Elizabeth's throat hurt and she tried to swallow. "That's it?"

"Pretty much," Paddy replied with understanding eyes. "Besides sayin' she didn't want people comin' t' visit her body and make up good memories of her, you know, pretend t' be sad." Paddy put his hand to his heart. "I think she felt a failure—as a wife, mother and writer."

"What made you think that, Paddy?" she asked, feeling guilt for her mother's guilt.

"I don't know," Paddy replied, scratching his bald head. "I only sensed that her childhood was maybe troubled. And that she never felt or learned how t' be a mother from her mother."

"Oh Jesus, that's terrible," Elizabeth mumbled and lowered her eyes. Maybe Maggie could only live those roles as best as she knew how.

"Eh, what can ye do or say?"

"Right," Liz acknowledged, thinking she was glad she didn't have any kids. "So, Paddy, will you be spending the night with her? You know, in case she—"

"Wakes?" he said. "Sure. You?"

Hesitating, she blurted, "Of course."

Paddy offered, "We can take shifts and nod a bit in our chairs. Follow her to hospice in the mornin'."

While her mother barely stirred, the pair conversed for hours over Paddy's family in Ulster County, Belfast and their visit to Maggie's ancestral home in County Cork. Elizabeth shared her adventures in Japan. Later, they both began drifting off to the drone of the oxygen machine.

In between the frequent comings and goings of the nursing staff, Elizabeth dwelled on Paddy's admonishment to forget and forgive. Whichever came first, she wondered what might have broken in Maggie's life and made her the mother what she couldn't help but become. Scrunched up in the chair, she finally caught some REM sleep during the early hours of the morning.

Hearing what sounded like sobbing, Elizabeth opened her eyes to find Paddy half-lying on the bed, holding Mother's head and crying. She stood up and reached to feel her mother's cold hand. Margaret O'Malley Worthington never made it through the night. Walking to the other side of the bed, she rested her hands on Paddy's quaking shoulders.

He looked up and wiped away his tears. "Sorry," he said and moved aside for her.

Elizabeth pushed back memories of missing goodnight kisses from Mother and kissed Maggie's cold cheek, blessed by Paddy's warm tears. She couldn't say goodbye. Couldn't ever learn of the secret troubles Maggie must have carried with her, let alone a chance to reconcile. *Forgive and forget*, she tried telling herself.

After transporting her mother's body to the funeral home and leaving messages for her father and sister, Elizabeth returned to her bedroom in Catherine's apartment. She needed to call Kaito.

"Izzy-chan," Kaito answered as she warmed to his cheerful tone. "Worried I missed your call yesterday. How are you?"

Her own tone was somber. "Mother died last night."

A heartbeat passed before she heard his gasp. "Are you okay?"

"I guess."

"So sorry. What happened?"

"Heart attack."

"I feel so bad for you, Izzy. How are you really taking it?"

"I don't know yet. Right now, I'm feeling sort of lost and guilty."

"Guilty about what?" He asked. "Did you talk to her?"

"No. Not able to resolve anything before she died. So, I sat here thinking of myself as her lost child. Not about her life, as I should. Her own struggles as a person."

"Based on what you told me about your relationship, your feelings are understandable. Don't punish yourself, okay?"

"Thanks, Kaito."

"Have you grieved?"

"You mean like cry? Nothing's there. My feelings didn't matter."

"They matter to me, Izzy, and you need to grieve."

Elizabeth's feelings of guilt ebbed in her eyes.

He continued, "It's no longer about her. It's all about you now. Listen my *koijin*, you need to grieve for the childhood you never had. The loving mother you never experienced. The happy family you always dreamed of."

A well of sorrow began to emerge from deep in Elizabeth's belly.

She put her hand there and felt the hurt building around her heart.

"Izzy. Are you alright?"

"I was just thinking how lucky I am to have someone like you who cares about me, someone who can be so uncaring."

"Izzy. You're not uncaring. You're just trying to get past everything and you're making progress, like right now."

"You think?"

"I know."

Elizabeth broke down. Holding her phone and Kaito's voice up to her heart, she cried harder than she ever remembered.

"Hold on, Kaito," she sniffled in between the jagging sobs.

"Keep going," he said, "Let it all out. Your mother will not take away your hopes, your chance for a better future."

Minutes later, Elizabeth managed to control herself and said, "What would I ever do without you?"

"You don't have to be without me. You can come home anytime. When you are ready."

"I know, but you're so involved with your research."

"I am and about to save a few juvenile dolphins from death to use for tagging."

Composing herself in silence, Elizabeth said, "And I am happy and hoping for you."

"Thanks, and remember, I'm here for you. Maybe you'll figure out what you need and come back. By the way, Marylyn and Kimmi ask about you all the time."

"Say hi for me."

"I love you, Princess, and take good care of yourself."

"Thanks. You too, Kaito. Bye."

That evening while Elizabeth shared a quiet Chinese takeout dinner with Catherine, Paddy called.

"Hello, Liz. How ye doin'?"

"Okay, Paddy," she replied, stood and smiled at Cath. Moving to her bedroom, she asked him, "What's up?"

"I wanted t' tell ye, I made all the arrangements for her cremation."

"Thanks for doing all of that. You and Mom were very close. How are you managing with this?"

"Ah. Well enough. Bein' a young provo in Belfast during the troubles taught me t' tough it up when a brother died. I'm a tryin' me best to follow her wishes. I was a wonderin' Liz, if I could ask a favor of ye?"

"Sure."

"Well, despite ye mother's spoken wishes about a service, it's hard for a good catholic boy not to give someone from the old sod a proper send off. Not a sayin' an Irish wake er anythin', but somethin'. So, if it be alright with ye, I

293

thought I'd have a priest come to *Passages* and say a few grand words o'er her ashes."

"That's fine, Paddy. When?"

"Would this 'Trs-day' at one o'clock work for you. Farther Riordan could make it then."

Hesitating, she answered, "I…I guess so," thinking sooner is better.

"Then I be thinkin' after, it would be grand if I would read the will…" he paused…"as much as it be. And ye would be there with your father and sister? Have ye called them yet?"

"Yes. They haven't returned my call, but I will do that. One o'clock Thursday at *Passages*, then. I'll let you know and thanks, Paddy, for all that you're doing."

Elizabeth was relieved to have Paddy handle this but dreaded making the calls. She bit her lip and picked up the phone.

"Father, it's Elizabeth."

"You're back?"

"Yup, and I'm calling to tell you Maggie died today."

"Oh," he said. "Hold on a minute. I'm with a client." Moments later, he said, "May she finally rest in peace. How'd she go?"

"Heart attack. Paddy's having her cremated and planning a short service, combined with a reading of the will this Thursday at one o'clock at the Passages assisted living center in Westchester. Can you make it?"

A rustling of papers, then Leland answered, "I'm in court that day. Why didn't you call me sooner to arrange this?"

"Didn't think you wanted to get involved."

"Yeah. I got it. I'll see if I can change the court date. Anything else? I've got to get back to my client."

"Nah. See you later, Dad."

She hung up and sighed. Then, she called her sister. "Crissy, it's Liz. How are you?"

"Fine sis, but I can't talk. I'm at work."

Elizabeth could hear the clanking of dishes and the whoosh of an expresso machine. "It won't take but a minute, Crissy."

"I'm not allowed to be on calls on my shift. Want me to get fired?"

"Got it, so be at the Passages assisted living center in Westchester at one o'clock, Thursday."

"To see Mother? You kidding?"

"No. She's dead and you need to pay respects and hear about her will."

"Jesus, Liz, can't you take care of it?"

"I'm trying to, Sister. You should be there."

"I don't know. I have to call my probation officer and see if he'll let me leave town. Oh, oh!" she said. "Here comes my boss. I gotta go." She hung up.

Elizabeth returned to the living room to find Catherine at the sink, rinsing dishes.

"So, how are things going?" Cath asked.

"Let me put it this way, if I were a drinking woman, I'd have one now. I'm exhausted, Cath. Been a long day. Thanks so much. It's Sunday, right? Think I'll go to bed."

"It is. Have a good sleep, Lizzy."

Thursday evening

For the past few days, Elizabeth had stayed in her room locked in a state of depression. Seldom eating, seldom bathing and rarely even speaking to Catherine. When she did come out of her room, it was in pajamas, hair ratted from wrapping it around her fingers. Catherine would pester her to seek therapy—telling her she knew of an excellent counselor.

"Thanks, Cath," Elizabeth said each time. "Once this funeral is over, I can let her go and this whole fucked up past life with it."

This evening, Elizabeth returned to Catherine's apartment after a long walk at the beach.

"Oh, Liz," Cath welcomed her with caring eyes. "Good to see you're still alive." Studying her body from head to toe, she added, "Looks like you've been strolling along the shore."

Liz looked down at her wet pants to see, which she had not felt, the wet from the waves. "Yeah. I needed to try and make sense of what went on at the so-called funeral service. Maybe walk it off."

"That bad, huh? I can see it in your face. Want to talk?"

Elizabeth hung her head down and grumbled, "I can't do it any longer, Cath. And I can't keep prevailing upon your good graces."

"Don't be silly. What happened at the service?"

"The end. If I can help it." She took of her pumps. "I left my family the same way I joined it—broken. I'm finally through with them."

"It can't be that bad. Come and sit."

Liz slumped, dropped into a chair and let out a long breath. "Well, the priest's kind words were the best part. It was what or shall I say, who that followed."

"Go ahead, Liz. It'll be good to get it all out."

"Okay," she blurted out. "After the priest blessed her ashes, Paddy stood up with a sheet of lined paper with scratchy handwriting saying Mother's designated him in the will as executor of her estate."

"What did the will say?"

"It was scribbled and confusing, including leaving lots, possibly millions, to Planned Parenthood."

"Wow," exclaimed Catherine, "That's interesting. How do you feel about that?"

"You mean because she didn't leave me anything? Not mad at all, as a matter of fact. I think helping new mothers in any good way is meaningful and appropriate. It's everyone else's reaction that depressed me."

"You mean your dad and sister?"

"My sister didn't even show up but sent her lawyer to represent her interests. Neither was my lawyer father there. He sent his own lawyer. And Paddy's lawyer claimed his client had domestic partner status and had first rights on her estate."

Catherine groaned, "Oh, Jesus."

Liz feigned a laugh. "At least Paddy deserves something for caring for her and making her happy for the last part of her life. This whole thing will go on for months in probate court, and I want no part of it." She shrugged her shoulders. "I told them, it's all yours' and stomped out of the room."

"God, that is a bummer, and your reaction fully understandable, but are you sure you want to let it go like that?"

"Letting go is exactly what I want. Leave the family that left me. I'm done fighting with them and myself. I need to get out of my skin, fight for something else."

Catherine wrinkled her brow. "Like what? And what's this about not prevailing upon my graces?"

"My dolphins, my cetaceans, Cath. My sacred vow to save them. The same passion you hired me for. Now I will do more than write for them."

"How would you do that?"

"I'm going to join Peter Wilson on the Sea Savior. Directly fight to stop those whale hunts."

"You are?" Catherine asked, drawing back.

"Yes. He's been wanting me for years."

"Have you given up on Kaito?"

"No. But I want him to quit capturing and exploiting dolphins for his research. I don't like to be so blunt, but how can he love me and still hurt me like that?"

"Are you sure about that? It seems," if I can say, "Irrational."

"It's spiritual, Cath."

"Maybe, but it looks to me like you're dueling with the husband you say you love dearly." She raised her voice. "It's like you're playing chicken with your lives and happiness together."

Elizabeth stiffened at her words. "I know; I'm afraid of that too."

Catherine moved beside her and grasped her hand. "Please, Liz. You've just been through your mother's and your family's death. It's understandable you want to flee, but if you're too rash, you may be killing your chances of happiness again with Kaito. Think of him."

Liz took a deep breath and felt the tug of Kaito's love. She began to cry.

"Please, Liz, for me. Someone that knows you well and loves you. Please at least see this therapist I know before you leave. You can trust him. He may be able to help you work through this."

Elizabeth nodded and barely audibly said, "Okay."

They hugged and cried together.

Offices of Brian Koslov, M.S., LMFC
Venice, California

Sitting in the waiting room, Elizabeth twirled the ends of her graying hair, thinking she was wasting her time. She had already told Peter she was coming and booked a flight to Melbourne next week. It was mostly out of Catherine's heartfelt plea that she was even here, let alone expecting some shrink to change her mind.

A young forty-ish guy dressed in jeans and a Grateful Dead t-shirt popped out of the office door, said a few words to the secretary, and went back in. *A client*, she thought.

"Mrs. Yamamoto? Brian will see you now."

Elizabeth's eyes popped wide open when she entered Brian's office. The same young, casually dressed, average-looking guy, surrounded by walls hung with concert posters of her favorite rock and roll stars, rose from his chair. Smiling broadly, he greeted her with both her hands.

"So good to meet you," he said, then pointed to himself. "I know. This is my afternoon garb, reserved for the artsy, hipster types of clients. I thought, since you're a free-spirited writer, this time slot would be ok?" He looked for her response.

"Sure," she said, relaxing at the friendly welcome.

"Good. Have a seat."

She settled across from him in a comfortable armchair, looked up and chuckled to herself, remembering that same Jefferson Airplane concert she attended in Livermore, California. Next to her was a small table and a crystal vase filled with a bouquet of colorfully wrapped lollipops.

"Want a lollipop?" he asked.

"I…I don't think so."

He started selecting one for himself. "You sure? I love to share them with my clients. Got some great flavors, both with bubblegum and chocolate centers. Ah, root beer," he said as he unwrapped one. "I often find by the time we lick it to the center; we've gotten closer to a discovery. What was your favorite flavor as a kid?"

"Cherry."

"Perfect," he said as he dug into the bunch. "Chocolate or bubblegum center?"

"Chocolate," she answered, watching him roll his chosen purple ball between his protruding lips.

Licking her pop, she no longer felt silly. It had been a long time since she savored the so-good sweetness of sugar candy. How it used to soothe her over the shouts of her parents.

Brian held his grape pop in the air and asked, "Do you mind if I take a few minutes to describe how my therapy works and how it can help you? Then, together, we can lay out an action plan to get you feeling better about yourself and your relationships?"

"Of course," she said and thought, *what a caring, sweet-talking guy he is.*

"I can see you're going to be a great client. So, what I practice here is cognitive behavioral therapy, commonly known as talk therapy. It can be a timely approach for getting at and improving your life issues."

"Okay," she said, jabbing the pop into her cheek.

"The premise behind this therapy is that our feelings, thoughts, memories, attitudes and behavior...the whole shebang...are all interlinked. And the way we think about something will determine our emotional reactions and actions." He checked for her attentiveness and continued.

"When we're upset, we think negatively. You know, threats, failures and fears take over. But by identifying and working on changing negative thinking patterns, we can change our reactions and behavior."

"Simple enough," Elizabeth commented.

"Yes, and we can learn how to actively slow down your thinking, examine it and challenge your old ways of thinking. To do that," he counted on his fingers, "One, we look back and into your feelings; two, accept them as okay; three, devise new and better ways to handle them; and four, take better care of yourself and your relationships."

He took a breath. "How does that sound to you, Elizabeth?"

"Ha, those are the hard parts, aren't they?"

"It does require courage and work, which you seem very capable of doing." She nodded.

"So, can we start with the hardest difficulty you are facing right now? Just talk freely, trust my empathy to only listen and take notes. Okay?"

Elizabeth started with her reaction to her mother's funeral, then spent most of the time pouring out her life with Kaito, surprising herself over her willingness to openly share her feelings. She ended with their current rift and divulged her plans to take a breather, as she put it, to become a writing crew member aboard the *Sea Savior.*

When she was done, Brian began capsulizing Elizabeth's outpourings. She became increasingly confident and comfortable with Brian's diligent understanding and caring ways.

"What a great start," Brian said, "You've given me a good sense of your troubles. With the remaining fifteen minutes or so, may I ask you to continue being sincere and answer a few questions?"

"Why not? Sure," she replied, thinking *what's to lose?*

"How did you feel exactly after Kaito announced his new research focus to you and, Kimmi, was it?"

Elizabeth shuffled in her chair and sucked hard on her lollipop.

"Take your time."

"I...I felt left out. Sort of jealous."

"Okay, did you feel any fears?"

"What do you mean?"

"That something bad was going to happen to you?"

She stared past him. "Ah, I can't think of any."

"At the time, did you have any memories or flashbacks that ran across your mind?"

"Yes, I do recall—How did you know? I saw my father taking off in his convertible with his newest girlfriend and my mother sobbing."

"And what did you feel after you experienced those flashbacks?"

"That Kaito was going to leave me behind."

"That's it," Brian said, "You're working with me. What then did you tell him?"

"That he shouldn't use dolphins as subjects in his research." She held her lollipop in the air. "That's when we reached an impasse and a parting of our ways."

"Great work describing the issues, and your feelings, Elizabeth. Just note though that what might seem now to be an impasse to you, might be able to be salvaged with work and insight." He put his hands together. "So, please, you told me you love him and that he was the best thing in your life. Do you have any idea why you told him using dolphins was unacceptable?"

"Yes. My guardian angel told me I must save, not use dolphins and if he continues, I have to drop him before he drops me." She let out a deep breath and took the lollipop back into her mouth.

"Great. Do you have any idea where that ultimatum came from?"

She stared past him again. "From me. No idea."

"Do you think it possible..." he hesitated and asked if he could possibly guess.

300

"Sure."

"I'm suggesting something because last week you told me you didn't want to talk about your childhood. That made me think it may have come from there."

"What? My childhood affecting my adult behavior? Seems kind of farfetched."

"Maybe not. Can I explain? It's well-known that millions of adults have been scarred by childhood experiences. Many of my own clients face this. How we feel and act is shaped by our parents, unintentionally or otherwise."

Elizabeth narrowed her eyes at him. "You mean like abuse? My parents never hit me or worse."

"Good. But what were they like?"

She placed her lollipop on the table and reached behind her neck to find strands of hair to twirl. Then she said, "They were busy, had their own problems. I had a privileged upbringing. Just like many of my friends in Malibu did. You know, most parents were involved with booze, drugs, affairs and divorces. Just normal stuff."

"That might be, said Brian, but there are other forms of abuse, like emotional abuse that comes from neglect. That might possibly be your case. But you have to uncover it. Talk about it and understand it."

She shook her head.

He asked. "You can't do it? Or won't do it?"

"Same thing."

"Well, I'm not going to pester you, but I have an idea how we can move forward with a first step."

"How's that?"

"How about if you write a letter to your dead mother? You are a skilled and expressive writer. Would you be willing, as an assignment, to pen a goodbye, write down on all your feelings and beliefs about your relationship, things you wanted to say to her? You know, anger, guilt, sadness, love, understanding, misunderstandings, and everything about your childhood. Spill the whole can of beans. Bring that letter to me for our next session?"

Elizabeth stiffened in her chair; hand trembling, she set down the unfinished lollipop. It hit her. *We didn't even discuss my plans to leave all this and get on a plane to get on a boat.* She clenched her jaw and stuttered,

"How…how could I do that next week when I'll be gone? I…I mentioned I was torn about leaving."

Brain's face became sad and contorted. "Oh. Geez, Elizabeth, I'm sorry. I had forgotten that and forgot to emphasize that this therapy takes time, often many sessions to work through and find healing. If you felt I and these first steps were starting to help, perhaps you could postpone your trip to another time."

She felt the fear turn into panic. "That would be hard to do."

"Do you mean, possibly alienating your husband or canceling your flight?"

She swallowed hard. "Both, I'm afraid. Is there any way, based on what you know so far, you could offer your opinion?" She leaned forward, eyes pleading.

"I'm afraid I can't do that in all good faith based on my training and profession. It's my job to help you reach your own conclusions as to what you need and what is best for you."

"You're just going to leave it at that?"

He took a deep breath and rubbed his chin, thinking. "I'm afraid I have to, but you've given me and yourself a clue. Focus on those feelings of being left and your healing can begin."

Elizabeth felt she was going to cry.

A knock came on the door. "Your next client has been waiting, Brian."

He looked at his watch. "I am so, so sorry, Elizabeth, but I have to go. Please feel free to call me to set up another appointment whenever you can. I believe, with time and your effort; we can help you find your own good answers." He stood and showed her to the door. Before he opened it, he whispered, "Good luck, Elizabeth. And write that letter, okay?"

Chapter Thirty-One
January 2008

Aboard the Sea Savior
Southern Antarctic Ocean

With her sore legs cramping against the steel bar of her bunk bed, her bandaged wrists raw, gobbed-with-salve knuckles high in the air to relieve pain, Elizabeth took stock of the here and now of her life. After spending the previous five days in dry dock scraping the barnacles and rust off the *Sea Savior's* hull, she began to doubt her decision.

She had agreed to serve as a deckhand and clandestine chronicler of Peter's mission to stop the whale hunts. But the work ahead had to be worth it if it just saved one whale. With the drone and rumble of the engine slowly pulling the ship far into Antarctic waters, she couldn't dismiss the thought that there must be better ways to save them all.

Listening to the snores and groans of her eight bunk mates, Elizabeth already began the task of capturing with words the motivations of the characters who volunteered on this dangerous mission. Although she was initially despondent, she found that living close to this hardy group of selfless whale lovers made for quick and lifelong friends. Most fell in either the lonely vagabond or idealistic adventurer camps, but all were dedicated to saving sea life, the kind of selfless souls she related to and wanted to be.

When not writing about the crew, she started the letter to Mom Brian had asked for. But she ended up focusing mainly on its meaning relative to Kaito, whom she terribly missed. She would tell him about what she was starting to learn in therapy. There was a connection between her childhood and adulthood and the dark cloud that still hung over their relationship. She needed to find it and get out from under it.

Like in a dream, music erupted on the *Sea Savior's* speaker. A booming voice interrupted the tune, *Waltzing Matilda*: "Ladies and gentlemen. This is your captain. Rise and shine. It's time to rock and roll."

To hear his booming voice for the first time since she boarded the ship, she wondered when and if Peter wanted to be interviewed, or still wanted to 'interview' her. She believed—now approaching sixty, her body sagging and wrinkled—he would no longer have any physical interest in her. And, with her years of glorious lovemaking to Kaito, she had long repressed any interest in him, beyond his heroic exploits.

In this moment, his genial and lusty call to arms reminded every crewmate of how their passion would soon compel them to risk their lives. Laughing like school kids on a picnic, the men and women jostled to use the single shared toilet and dress in layers of wool, puffy down and Gore-Tex. Girding themselves with bravado, they hurried up deck and eagerly squeezed together in the bridge to worship their savior.

"Thank you, sailors," the burly, mop-headed captain said, placing his hands together and pointing to the crew in a blessing. "Our mission is clear. We are here to enforce the 1994 International Whale Commission's designation of this Southern Ocean as a whale sanctuary. Now, we face the enemy."

Elizabeth thought it better to call them misguided adversaries.

"And, we are in hot pursuit," Wilson continued. "I'll make it short. We're gonna need each of you to bring your big hearts, strong bodies and guts into action to defend our fellow mammals." He pounded his fist against his heart. "Are you psyched up, geared up and ready to go?"

Hearty cheers pumped arms and applause rang out. Elizabeth joined in as much as her weary body allowed.

"Alright. Man your stations, ladies," he charged, then winked and laughed. "Woman your stations, men."

Elizabeth smiled at her deck mates, donned her life vest and scrambled on deck. The icy winds bit through her recently close-cropped hair, so she pulled the hood up on her parka and took her position below the bridge deck.

From there, she had a clear view of the *Nisshin Maru,* the Japanese whaler sailing under the phony designation of RESEARCH. Their boat was three times the size of the *Sea Savior* and was there to carry back tons of poached whale meat. *Beware,* Elizabeth thought. The passion of the Sea Shepherd's crew, with its menacing shark's jaws painted on her bow and a black pirates skull flag leading the charge on the small boat, meant big trouble.

Although her heart beat fast with the fear of confrontation, Elizabeth methodically checked her weapon and waited for the command. Seeing the shadowy figures of the Japanese sailors high above her, she didn't see them as the enemy. They were Kaito's countrymen with families trying to earn a living. If Kaito knew what she was about to do, he would try hard to convince her it was too risky. In the end, he could only fear for her safety. Shivering from the cold, she watched the white ice mountains float past the hull and cast black shadows across the deck—a place far removed from the sandy shores of Malibu. Her life was about to take another course. Along the way, would she finally escape from her past and find a lane in the sea leading to happiness with Kaito?

Suddenly, Butch, the ship's bosun in charge of all the deck mates, stood above her. "Is the LRAD cannon in working order, Worthy?"

She looked up at the strapping woman with the stern demeanor yet maternal instincts and answered, "Yes. It's powered up and ready to fire, chief." Elizabeth was getting used to the lingo and to the moniker her fellow deck mates assigned to her, as it made her feel good things were to come.

Butch put her ear to the squawking on her radio phone, then turned back to Elizabeth. "How's your pitching arm, Worthy?"

"Fine, chief. I guess?" she replied, thinking it was no worse than any other aching parts of her body.

"Glossy's below with seasickness again," Butch reported. "We may need another hand to throw the Butyric grenades, before you fire your cannon."

Elizabeth whipped a salute. "Just let me know, chief."

"Good," Butch said, adding, "When you hear the captain over the ship's speakers, come to the portside rail, okay? We're closing in fast."

Within minutes, the whaler's huge stern came into view, its roaring engines belching foul smoke in its wake. Elizabeth held back a shudder, thinking how threatening it would be to a pod of Minke whales.

"*Nishan Maru!*" blared over the ship's speakers. "This is Peter Wilson. Captain of the *Sea Savior*. You are poaching in Australian waters. It is illegal and you must cease and leave immediately. This is a warning."

Sprinting a few meters toward the port rail, Elizabeth balked, doubled up and fell hard on the deck from an unknown gut punch. Dazed from hitting her head against the engine room door, she looked up at the source of the blow. The whaler's upper decks were dotted with Japanese sailors firing powerful streams of water from cannons. She looked to see her deck mates flattened and scattered across the deck. Some were trying to get up, only to be blasted down again.

The water and the fear hit her skin at the same time. Hoisting up her water-logged and shivering body, Butch appeared carrying several plastic buckets.

"Here," she told Elizabeth, handing her a bucket. "Throw these as close as you can to the Japanese crew, then return to your LRAD."

Elizabeth's adrenaline and anger overcame the cold fear. She grabbed a nerf football-sized grenade and wound up to throw. She gagged at the rancid butter stench of the thing and threw hard, knowing its scattered reek would sicken the enemy.

"Good throw, Worthy!" she heard as she picked up another stink bomb. Down the rail was Tiny, a three hundred plus pound New Zealand shot-putter, setting up a mortar like gun on a tripod.

"Thanks," Elizabeth shouted back, letting go of another grenade, feeling pushback from her sore muscles. "What's that?"

Pop! Whoosh! A projectile shot out of the tube and hit the whaler's pilot house and exploded.

"It's a soap bomb," Tiny said, loading another. "By the time I'm done, the entire deck will be flooded with gallons of soap and the crew will be a'slippin and a'slidin."

"Aha," Elizabeth laughed, and tossed her last grenade.

"Oww!" she cried out, covering her ears with her hands. A loud, screeching guitar sound shattered the air. It sounded like Nick Cave's headbanging screamer rock. Her hands did little to stop the pain.

"Here," came a shout and Glossy, the glamorous Australian model turned PETA advocate, handed her a pair of large earphones and pointed to the upper deck of the *Nisshin Maru.*

Two Japanese sailors were holding up a large conical dish, similar to the smaller Long Range Acoustic Device sound cannon she was trained to operate. Elizabeth hurried to her first station set the LRAD between her legs. Aiming it at the whaler's pilot house, she turned it on. The deadening blare of recorded whale sounds shot through the air. High-pitched squeals, and penetrating trills, drowning out their cheap rock. The Japanese sailors dropped their discs and scrambled indoors.

Satisfied with her performance, Elizabeth recalled filling out the volunteer application: 'No wimps need apply. Only selfless volunteers who will give their all to our cause.' She chuckled. *That's me, becoming a woman without a self. I'll have to tell Kaito how free I feel.*

She once believed that writing to inform and maybe educate a reader's attitude was enough in life. That work paled in comparison to putting your life directly out there for a cause greater than yourself. She pondered how the foibles of humans seem so trivial. How humans needed to give of themselves for others. All animals were born with the will to survive and be free.

Wasn't that what Kaito believed and was doing, just in a different way? *We gave ourselves to each other. Did I do so completely? Was there a new meaning for me?*

Several dark-uniformed Japanese men appeared and crouched on their deck. Sharp cracking sounds cut through the air.

"Take cover! Take cover! We're being hit by live rounds," came over the ship's speakers but it didn't sound like Captain Peter. The boat swerved and Elizabeth lost her balance and slid along the wet deck. Looking up, she was under the starboard side of the bridge and climbed up.

Through the window, she saw the navigator, the engineer and first mate, gathered around Peter Wilson in his captain's chair. From behind, he appeared to be delirious.

They were examining the vest that he was wearing. Engineer Duugy had a knife and was digging into Peter's chest.

With the pop of gunfire still raging, Elizabeth slipped into the pilot house.

"I think I got it," she heard Duugy say as he held what looked like the mottled head of a mushroom in the air.

"Lucky you had your bullet-proof vest on, Peter," quipped First Mate Chucky T.

Elizabeth moved closer. Peter wasn't delirious, he was laughing silly at the near miss. "They're not going to get this ornery bastard that way," he crowed and stood up. "Pull back alongside them. Launch the Zodiac. We're going into phase three."

"You sure, Paul?" Navigator Magellan asked.

"Damned sure," he replied and grabbed the ship's speaker. "*Nisshin Maru! Nisshan Maru!* This is Captain Wilson. Your soldiers have fired upon us with lethal weapons, and we have it all on film. We have reported you to Australian police authorities." He turned to Chucky T. "Get Wally and Doofus into the Zodiac. We're going to board them as planned."

Elizabeth watched as two men in helmets climbed into the motorized rubber dingy and were lowered down the portside. Once in the water, they powered up to the side of the whaler, threw rope ladders with grappling hooks onto the tender gangway in the hull, and climbed aboard.

Japanese crew members ran toward the men. They wrestled them to the deck and hustled them inside.

Elizabeth gasped. Magellan whooped and the men hollered.

"We did it!" They patted Peter on the back. He gave them a smug smile.

Elizabeth couldn't help herself. "But what will they do to them?"

"We're betting nothing, Worthy," Peter said with a wink. "Now it's about what we'll do to them."

Mission accomplished, and with the Sea Savior running low on fuel, it was time to head back on the long trip to Melbourne. Time to feed the publicity machine. Peter finally called Elizabeth to bring all her notes and join him in his private quarters. Elizabeth had seen some of the young female crewmates come in and out of his room, so she was prepared for his advances. On her way to him, notes and journals tucked under her arm, she recalled the role sex had played in her life and her now mature attitude. Sex wasn't love, like her sister thought and practiced. It wasn't used by her as an escape, like her mom did from a shitty family and town. Sure, she felt lonely and longed for the touch and union with another. But she knew it could only be meaningful if the other person gave him or herself to the other. Like Kaito did.

Although she admired Peter's contagious power and the love he gave to sea life, for him it was not the same with people. To him, they were tools and Peter took from them. He would not and did not take from her.

Two weeks later
Melbourne, Australia

"It'll be okay," Elizabeth told Glossy as they checked into the rundown harbor hostel, "As long as it has a shower and a phone. I need to call Kaito."

"Right matey. We have cell phone coverage now. This place is cheap. And later, Peter wants us to come together to celebrate near the boat."

308

Elizabeth cringed when they opened the door to the tiny room, walls of patched brick and two twin beds stood a foot apart. They sighed and plopped down on the saggy mattresses.

"Not much better than the bunk beds, huh."

"Want to shower first?" Elizabeth asked, staring at the phone.

Glossy stood. "Sure thing, Worthy girl. I wish I had a man to talk to."

After the fourth ring and no answer, Elizabeth nervously reached behind her neck to find she could no longer twist hair around her fingers. Kaito would not like her new hairstyle. She left the phone number.

"Izzy-chan, are you alright?" Kaito asked when she picked up. "Finally got cellphone coverage?"

"I am and I did."

"Sounds like you're off the *Sea Savior*."

"How'd you know?"

"You were calling from a 61-country code."

"Right," she said, "But how did you know I was on this one?"

"Based on when you informed me of your decision to go and later reading the news coverage in our papers."

"Yeah, it was a last minute, 'ship ahoy' thing."

"You weren't hurt at all, were you?"

"No. Why?"

"It's been almost two months since I heard from you. I was worried sick."

"Are you mad at me for leaving like that?"

"Yes, I was at first. It's hard to understand your need to find yourself, but I then turned to worry. I missed you so much."

"I'm sorry and I missed you too."

"So, did the mission succeed?"

"Yes, we definitely stopped your boat from taking any whales."

"Not my boat, Izzy," he said curtly. "And I meant your personal mission to become selfless."

"Ha, maybe made some progress bit by bit and getting to understand you and our differences."

"That's good. Just because of the trip?"

"Some, as Antarctica froze my mind in place for a while then slowly thawed out. But it was mostly due to my therapy I had before I left California.

It's starting to clear my mind. I'm actually looking into my past and how it may have affected our relationship, but it's hard and complicated."

"That sounds very hopeful. Would be great if it can help bring us back together. What about Wilson?"

"What do you mean?" She asked.

"The sham, I mean. That Wilson fellow is a cagey guy. Must have planned it all along. You know, get the Australian authorities involved to release them and ban the ship from those waters."

"Kaito. You sound like you're defending the whalers. They shot at us. Hit Peter with a round, for Christ's sake."

"No. Not at all. But don't you see how those campaigns can turn out badly? You could have been hurt."

"Sure. But what about the whales? We stopped them from getting a single one. Kept them from refueling at sea and they had to go home with an empty hull. How can you criticize that?"

"You're right. Up to that point. But it was counterproductive. The whaling industry, our government and public have strengthened their resolve. The ships will be back."

Silence, then Elizabeth said, "Maybe, but this time they didn't. We saved these."

"I know. That matters a lot to you, as it should. I honor and respect your feelings about that, but it's the means that I worry about."

"Don't you think the publicity and awareness will work to change minds?"

"Maybe eventually."

"I know," she agreed. "It is a slow, step-by-step process and I keep thinking there has to be a better, bigger way to end all the whale and dolphin hunting."

"I wish that too. Maybe we'll come to that someday. But Izzy, let me come back to how are you feeling otherwise? You know, personally? About us? I miss you so much. When will you come back?"

"I miss you too, but…I'm not sure."

"How come?"

Elizabeth hesitated, then said, "What I'm doing now despite the risk is actually because of the risk. I'm feeling better, I think."

"That's good. Do you mean you're no longer doubting yourself, feeling like you're missing something?"

"Sort of...I guess," she struggled to say, reaching again for her 'ghost' hair. "I've changed, Kaito. When I'm out there on the boat, directly fighting for the whales, I lose my stupid self and focus completely on them. I'm no longer nagged by what's wrong with me. After months of crewing, I feel stronger, lighter. Clearer too. Kind of free."

"Do you mean like an escape?"

"Sort of, and more alive."

"Have you had enough time to process your mother's death?"

"Mostly, but I still have a lot of work to do, putting this mission into words. I'm excited to do that and feel productive again."

"That's good and you need to feel you're making a difference. But when are you coming home?"

"I don't know, yet. I may join another mission."

"I'm sorry," he said with a voice sounding less than apologetic, "But you don't sound like you've changed that much despite what you say."

"What do you mean?"

"I want you to be free and happy, but what about me? I am not very happy without you. You've always been my inspiration. We were supposed to be a team, remember?"

Elizabeth couldn't find the words to explain.

"Izzy-chan. How long can a marriage last when we're not together."

"C-can't you just hold on a bit longer?"

"You've been saying that for months now. Look, haven't I been supportive of your endeavors and needs all along?"

"You have."

"What about mine?"

Elizabeth dropped the phone to the floor. The possibility of Kaito actually leaving her slammed into the reality of her contradictory behavior.

Glossy came out of the bathroom.

She picked up her phone. "Sorry, Kaito but I've got someone with me now and I have to go."

"Go then. Goodbye, Elizabeth."

She put her head into her hands. *What's wrong with me? I'm such a fool.*

Glossy spoke, "Sorry, bad time."

"No," answered Elizabeth and to herself, she said, *I am worthy, I am worthy, I am worthy.* She hung up.

Glossy fixed her eyes on Elizabeth. "I hope you don't mind if I ask you."

"No. Go ahead."

"What the hell are you doing in this fleabag with me and aboard that floating tin-can when you've got a man who loves you like that?"

Elizabeth sat speechless.

"I could tell by your face you love him too. If I were you, I'd be on a plane tonight for Tokyo and in his arms."

"I only wish it was that simple," she said, not wanting to explain the crux of their separation.

"I dunno sweetheart, but you better start simplifying it before you lose him."

#

Chapter Thirty-Two
Two Years Later

Melbourne

After a grueling third *Sea Savior* mission, Elizabeth was totally wiped out in body, but not in spirit. She had helped save what Peter estimated to be over forty-three whales and had gotten bruises, muscles and ten-pounds lighter to prove it. Still invigorated by the rush and satisfaction of direct action, she vowed from now on she would put herself on the front line. She'd never return to the slow approach of writing for incremental change of attitudes. In the time between every pitched battle with the whalers, and there was plenty, she came up with dramatic ways she could make a serious impact.

She was a warrior now, a changed and empowered woman. She would repay her guardian angel with her soul and her actions. Yet, she knew there were limitations in the numbers by placing yourself in between the whale and the whalers. She kept dreaming about a much better way. When she got back to the States, she swore she was going to get on the street, into people's faces. Whatever, wherever it took to stop any form of cruelty to her beloved dolphins.

Getting off the boat in Melbourne, she said goodbye to Peter, her dedicated brothers and sisters, and immediately tried to reach Kaito. She hadn't spoken to him since the last time she was in port, exactly seven months and two days ago, even though she wrote him long letters every day that never got posted. She kept dialing him on the way to the airport, but he did not pick up. Was he still super busy engaged in his work? *Waiting for her to return?* As with all these past years, his dedication to her was next to a miracle, but she always dreaded that her insular behavior would finally lose him. Through no fault but her own.

When she got off the plane at LAX, she didn't really know where to go or who to call other than planning what she had to do next. Because it was in the middle of the night for Kaito, she dialed Catherine.

"Hi Cath, its Liz."

"Oh my god, the *Sea Savior* pirate has returned? It's been ages."

"Two and a half years, I believe. How are you?"

"Good but missing you. Where are you?"

"LAX. Just flew in from Melbourne."

"You here to stay?"

"For a while. I've got lots to do."

"I want to hear all about it. You have a place to stay?"

"Not really. I was wondering—?"

"Of course. You know where the key is. I'm up in Santa Barbara but should be back by eight."

"Thanks so much, Cath."

"Sure. Oh. By the way. Paddy has been trying to reach you for months now as has that Dick O'Meery fellow. And Kaito, who called me often asking if I heard from you. Worried sick about you, of course. Okay, I've got to run. See you soon."

On the taxi ride to the Palisades, she tried Kaito again, deciding he wouldn't mind being woken up. No luck.

Getting a hold of Paddy, she was flabbergasted to hear the probate court judge had decided she and her sister would inherit almost a million dollars each and he was holding a check for her.

Dick O'Meery screeched with pride and joy announcing that *The Gulf* had just received an Oscar for best documentary. He asked her if she would ask Kaito to help get distribution and play in Japan. She'd have to get back to him on that. Finally, she called Steve Cornell, a contact given to her by a crewmate, hoping he might be able to help her plan an activist event she was thinking of. Steve was the founder of the *Undersea Railroad*, so named to help enslaved dolphins escape captivity. Not picking up, she left a message she wanted to meet with him. Moments after Liz opened the door to Catherine's apartment, her heart jumped, hoping the incoming call was Kaito.

"Oh, hi Steve. Thanks for calling back."

"Yes. Liz. Cora, from on the *Sea Savior,* mentioned you might be calling me. She filled me in on your amazing background. How can I help you?"

"Well, I'm the one impressed by your daring dolphin rescue at the University of Hawaii Marine Biology Lab."

"Oh, that one. Many years ago. I'm now with the Animal Liberation Front. Same motivation, just a bit smarter."

"Even more creativity and stealth, I presume."

"Yeah, well I almost got five years back then, being convicted of grand theft." He scoffed. "On the stand, I said the university stole the dolphins in the first place, couldn't own free beings as property, and I was just saving them back. Only got 400 hours community service," he added, chuckling. "So, what do you have in mind?"

"Some grand events I'm exploring in SoCal. You're here, right? Doing what these days?"

"I'm hanging out in Julian in the mountains. Releasing minks from farms, raiding puppy mills and just burned down a Sheepskin factory."

Elizabeth shuddered. "Well, I'm looking for doing more like media spectacles—no violence. Only publicity sabotage."

"Fair enough. I've got a good nose for that too. How big?"

She hesitated, remembering Paddy's phone call. "Big," she said, "Can we meet tomorrow in San Diego?"

"I guess. Whereabouts?"

"SeaWorld. Where it all started with me."

"Love to. My most favorite enemy. Sounds like you've got the big mo."

"I'm psyched. How about we meet at the South Shore boat launch, right behind the park's Emperor roller-coaster. About two p.m. I'll be wearing a red SeaWorld sweatshirt."

"Got it. See you then."

She dialed Kaito.

"Elizabeth? Are you alright? Sorry I missed you."

"I'm fine. Just got back to LA from Melbourne."

"Are you finally done with the anti-whaling campaign?"

"I am. And the experience has got me onto bigger and better things."

Silence on the other end.

"Kaito, before I forget. I've got big news."

"Oh?"

"*The Gulf* won the Oscar for best documentary film! Proof of all the good work you did to help film the hunting at Taiji Harbor." She went on without a breath. "Dick told me he received the award and held up a sign in front of the cameras for donations. He said he thanked us for our support. With all the publicity, it could be a game-changer."

"I'm truly happy for you and for the cause, but the movie's not playing here in Japan. Don't think the way the film portrayed our fishermen would be well-received by the public, let alone the government."

After a pause, Elizabeth continued, "Dick asked me to ask you if you'd get involved and grease the skids in Japan?"

"What does that mean?"

"You know, connect with the right people in Japan so we can raise awareness. Help the local film distributor, get it widely played. Change minds of the public and government. You want that, don't you?"

Kaito went silent until he blew out a long breath. "That's the only reason you're calling me, Izzy-chan?"

"No, no. Of course not. I miss you."

"Well," he hesitated. "As much as I'd love to help, I can't. It would be, as you say, kowtowing to U.S. interests. Besides, if I was to get behind this in the public eye, it would compromise my research. Now that I'm collaborating with Dr. Ogawa and slanting the premise more to fishing resources, maybe I'll have a chance."

"You mean you still haven't gotten funding?"

"No. After years of work on the methodology, tool refinement and focus, I still get turned down."

"Geez, Kaito. I feel badly for you." She did, but also held out hope he'd finally drop his research paradigm. "Maybe your hypothesis using dolphins for early tsunami warning just isn't practical, let alone a government priority."

Kaito took a long time to respond. "You're still holding onto that, I take it. You don't even seem like yourself, how we agreed to respect each other. Are my goals worth less than yours?" He continued his rant. "I think they are more similar than different. Seems to me you're dedicating your whole life to blindly saving dolphins and whales. I hate to say it, but maybe you're using that as an excuse."

"Kaito," she said sternly. "We've been over this. I've been wracking my brains to come up with a bigger and better way to do more."

"Izzy, I'm trying to help you. I worry that you're working off a self-limiting belief."

"What's that?" she asked, wondering if he was responding to her jab at his work.

"That you'll finally find happiness if you save the lives of every dolphin and whale on the planet. You think that is the missing thing in your life, the thing you keep preaching about."

"That's hogwash, Kaito."

"Only trying to help you, Izzy. You know how I love you. More than you'll ever know, but I have my own promise to myself and my dream."

A long pause, then she asked, "That's it then? You want me to keep sailing somewhere in the seas with Dick and Peter?"

Speaking in a grave tone, he said, "That is your choice, Elizabeth, but know I'll be here waiting for you once you're ready."

"I don't know, Kaito. I don't know how we could be together again. I've got a couple of big projects I must complete here, before I even consider coming back to Japan."

"Not surprised, really. Call me when you want to have a real talk."

"Goodbye for now."

Elizabeth hung up the phone with deep anger and hurt in her gut. It was that same feeling she felt as a child. Lost again. *Why can't I respect his efforts?*

First came a sniffle, then a sob, and she ended up weeping.

After taking a shower, Liz ordered in a pizza and waited for Catherine.

Rushing to open the door as soon as she heard her car pull up, she stood, ready for a big hug.

"My god, Liz. You look so good," Cath said taking her into her arms.

"Thanks. Lost a bit of weight, gained some muscle. You don't look so bad yourself for a gal of fifty."

"Huh," she laughed. "On the dark side of that decade, I'm afraid."

Liz gestured to the kitchen table. "Got a Sicilian margarita and Moretti beer. You hungry?"

"Sure. Smells good. Let me change quick."

After they clicked bottles, Cath asked the first thing on her mind, "Did you talk to Kaito?"

"You mean is he still waiting for me?"

"Yes. That's the important thing, isn't it?" she asked, then narrowed her eyes at Liz. "And you still wanting him?"

"He is thankfully, and I always hold out hopes, but sometimes I think he's on the edge of dropping off."

She added, "That wouldn't be surprising considering how you've held him at bay for all these years."

"Are you going back to Japan soon?"

"I think so," she answered, wiping some tomato sauce off her chin. "But I've got a couple of projects to complete before I go."

"What have you got planned?"

"Not sure yet. In a few days, I'll know if one of them is even feasible. I'll clue you in."

Catherine slowly munched on her pizza then came back to the topic of Kaito. "Do you still love him?"

"I…I do."

"Even after being without him for like ten years?"

Liz placed her hand on her heart. "For sure. He's been with me all along. I just have these problems."

"Seems to me, if you don't mind me saying, you've always been the happiest when you're with him, and well, knotted-up when you're not. Are you going to work them out before…before it's too late?"

Sighing, Elizabeth asked, "I know. What do you suggest?"

"Get back in therapy with Brian. You told me he was great and had made some progress. Get to the core of what's keeping you from him."

"Mmm, I think you're right." Liz finished her beer, "Want another? Let's move on about the rest of our lives."

"Sure," Cath said. "Let's finish the six-pack."

"Yeah, and I've got a full day tomorrow. Got to get a rental car, pick up a check from Paddy and drive to San Diego. I'm tired and I'll want to hit the sack."

Next day
South Shore boat launch

Getting out of her rental car in her red sweatshirt, Liz spotted a big, husky guy, wearing cargo shorts and a 'make love not war' t-shirt, walking toward her. Italian-looking with a Roman nose and hair poking out of the top of his chest, Steve greeted her with a warm smile.

"Briefly hugging a kindred spirit," Liz said, "Thanks for coming, Steve. Nice to meet you. How about if we take a ride in my car and talk along the way."

"A woman of action. I like it. Let's go."

Taking SeaWorld Drive east, Liz took the exit to Fiesta Island. They drove down the road nearing the Fiesta dog park and stopped where the park moored their fireworks barge. "Here's where I want a big sign to go up at least ten feet high, twenty across, making sure every visitor and venue on the north side of the park can visibly read it. I want it to be raised up at the same time we drop the main display in front of the entrance. Probably need to spotlight the large letters."

Steve took furious notes.

Back on SeaWorld Drive, they drove in and around Ocean Gate Way near the park entrance to find a public space where the cars coming in from both ways on the eight freeway would have to pass on their way into the parking lot.

"Right there, I think," Liz exclaimed. "Big, open and visible where you can drop me and the cage. Think it'll work, Steve?"

"Jesus, Liz. Think it'll require a helicopter. Big bucks. Draws lots of attention."

"Perfect," Liz said. "The kiddie pool needs to be filled after we drop the iron bar cage. With the signs pre-attached, as per this." She handed him a sheet with diagrams and notes. "I'll wait for you to tell me you have all the materials, equipment and manpower, so I can make tentative arrangements with my friends at KTLA-TV. Make sure the media is there at the drop with their broadcasting trucks."

"Yes, Ma'am." Steve saluted like the marine sergeant he once was.

"Oh." Liz added, "And we'll need a sharp internet guy at the drop to make sure he catches the action and makes posts on YouTube and all the other social media sites."

"Got it. That's me, too." Steve said. "This'll take at least a week to set up. How are we going to handle funds?"

Liz reached into her bag and pulled out a thick wad of one-hundred-dollar bills. "There's ten K there for starters. Let me know if you need more. Any questions?"

"Nothing at this point," Steve concluded. "I'll get to work right away, and we'll talk."

Ten days later

Carrying her wallet, keys, phone, cuffs and bathrobe in a plastic bag, Elizabeth ducked under the whirling blades of the Bell 206 Jet Ranger. Buckling into her seat alongside Joe the pilot, she glanced behind her and nodded to the crewman, twenty-year-old Reggie. Scanning the cargo area, she saw the pool, cage assembly and water bucket.

"We all set?" she asked Joe.

"Think so," he answered. "Steve radioed a minute ago he was on the target area and everything was clear."

They got clearance and lifted off. Elizabeth felt like she left her stomach on the tarmac. She checked her watch to confirm the short ride to SeaWorld would synch with the scheduled drop time of ten-thirty. Her nerves shook with the shaking of the helicopter, but the years of pushing past fears on the *Sea Savior* kept Elizabeth's adrenaline pumping steady.

Approaching the intersection of the five and eight freeways, Elizabeth could see the long line of cars heading into the SeaWorld parking lot.

Losing altitude as they approached, Elizabeth's gut sank with it.

"There's Steve," Joe said. "We're heading down. Reg get ready in cargo."

Suddenly, the copter stopped descending and Joe called Steve. "Who's that?" He turned to Elizabeth. "There's some guy approaching him."

Elizabeth worried, "He's supposed to be the only one there."

Steve radioed up. "It's just some homeless guy. Bring it down."

Reg opened the hatchway and a whooshing sound changed the air inside. Traffic below roared and exhaust filled the cabin and cockpit.

Reg lowered the cage and pool into the open hatchway.

CRAAK! The cage swung against the side of the hatch.

Elizabeth jumped in her seat.

"Steady," Joe commanded as the lift cable ground, and the pool and cage slowly dropped over the target.

Turning to Liz, Joe comforted her growing nervousness by saying, "It's a bit windy, but so far, no gusts."

"Almost there," Steve squawked over the radio. "Got it. Unhitching."

"Crank her up," Joe said.

Reg connected the water bucket.

CLUNK! It too hit the side of the hatch, spilling water as it swayed.

"Let 'er down, Reg."

Elizabeth eyed the ground as the copter turned. Steve gave a thumbs up. The pool and cage landed on the target; the two signs attached to the bars were straight.

The lift cable zipped back, and Reg attached the bucket of water and began lowering it. By this time, the traffic had slowed going into the park and stopped once Reggie pulled a separate line, releasing a fall of water over the open top of the cage.

"Jesus!" Steve screamed over the radio. "You got me soaked. And we better hurry. Here comes a guy in a SeaWorld uniform."

Joe looked at Elizabeth. She smiled stiffly, unbuckled and scrambled to the rear. Taking off her sweats, Reggie's eyes bugged out. When he saw Elizabeth's shapely body, he must have thought she was a woman of his young age.

Elizabeth grabbed her bag, got into the sling and began twisting around like a tilt-a-whirl ride as she descended. In the nick of time, the SeaWorld guy and the cars stopped and gawked. And coming in from the east was the KTLA-TV broadcast truck.

As instructed, Joe kept her dangling above the cage until the TV crews set up with cameras pointing up. Twisting dizzily on the cable, Liz kept smiling and waving to the gathering crowd. She smiled even harder when she saw the duplicate sign unfurl on Fiesta Island.

With TV cameras pointed at her, Reg slowly dropped her down. Before hitting the water, she threw her bag to the side and pulled the sling release cord. She landed with a splash on her butt to a round of cheers.

By now, the police were trying to get past the traffic jam, some leaving their cars and proceeding on foot. Joe took off in the helicopter at the same time San Diego area TV station helicopters circled the sky in live broadcast.

"Now's the time," Elizabeth said, and reached for the bag and attached both sets of chained handcuffs to the metal bars on inside of the cage. Then, she locked her left wrist into one handcuff, and with her free right hand removed her bikini top. Then attached her right hand to the other cuff and sunk down into the water.

Aaaahs and oooohs and car horns broke out. The cameras whirred as the police stood motionless with their mouths agape.

Elizabeth could pick out Steve from the growing crowds, still taking pictures with his cell phone. With another thumb in the air, he was, no doubt, posting them on the web. There she lay, bare breasted, splayed out with both arms locked on the jail bars. The signs above her read:

FREE YOUR DOLPHIN SLAVES BUILD THEM A SANCTUARY

Lounging in the warm sun and cool water, Elizabeth felt free. Almost sensuous. Strangely, she imagined she was swimming with Kaito again.

After maybe ten minutes more of media exposure, a cop arrived with bolt cutters and a portable metal saw. He cut the cuffs off the chain and Elizabeth put on her bathrobe and waited for the cops to saw an opening to the cage. While waiting, she heard her cell phone ring in the bag and picked it up.

"Liz. It's Catherine. You really did it. The coverage is phenomenal. Congratulations."

"That good, huh?"

"Even better. KTLA interviewed some bigwig at SeaWorld who said they had already looked into building a sanctuary. If you can believe that, of course."

"Hold on Cath, the cops are breaking through. Think I'll be here for a while. Maybe see you tonight."

The cop feigned a snarl. "You're under arrest, young lady."

"Thanks for the compliment, officer."

"Show me an ID."

She handed him her Japanese driver's license, saying, "I am a U.S. citizen."

"Citizen or not lady, you're under arrest for disturbing the peace, blocking traffic and who knows what else. We're going to take you down to the station."

"Yes, sir," she said as the press shouted questions at her. "No comment." She said back. Getting into the squad car, Steve caught her eye. She mouthed 'thank you'.

Released after several hours and posting a five-hundred-dollar bail, Steve drove her home to Catherine's place.

"Elizabeth Worthington-Yamamoto," Cath said opening the door and opening her eyes wide upon seeing her friend's sunburned face. "You are one incredible, crazy woman."

She laughed. "That's what Kaito says about me."

"Well, it was a perfectly planned and executed publicity stunt."

"Except for forgetting sunscreen."

"Hell. The video went viral. Wouldn't be surprised if Kaito gets to see it. And in that hot new bod of yours." Cath pulled her into the room. "Let's sit and you can tell me about your next exploit. You said there were two."

"Yes, I hope to have another one in a couple of weeks, but you know what? I can't tell you about it in advance. I don't want to compromise you or MO magazine in any way."

"Oh, Jesus, Liz."

"Don't worry. But you know, Cath, I'm really pooped. Do you mind if I crash?"

"Not at all. Did you get anything to eat?"

"Yeah. Steve and I stopped for In-N-Out burgers on the way. I had just the bun without the patty. I'm good. Goodnight."

The next morning, Liz's phone began to ring. She didn't really want to talk to anybody and screened the mostly congratulatory messages. She did return the KTLA-TV producer's call, thanking him and offering them another exclusive with a favor.

When she got to Kaito's call, she listened. "Elizabeth. I saw the video. It's playing all over Japan, to mixed reactions, I might say. But I loved it, and you are crazy beautiful. Even more beautiful than I remember. I hope the results are making you happy. Call me when you can."

Two weeks later

Elizabeth had her hair shortened into a wedge cut and dyed pitch black in preparation for another clandestine operation. She chose a venue that most resembled what Kaito was planning to do—use dolphins for meritorious purposes by capturing, confining and training them to do your bidding.

The target was the U.S. Navy's Marine Mammal Program under the Information Warfare Center in Point Loma, California, near Coronado. Since the 1960s, the Navy secretly trained hundreds of dolphins to do everything from confronting enemy divers to disarming underwater mines during the Gulf War.

Recently, they had declassified the program and kept some seventy dolphins in pens for scientific study and claiming they no longer trained them for military missions. Liz was skeptical, but her goal was to pressure the Navy to also build sanctuaries.

Convincing KTLA-TV to take one of the Navy's public and media tours of their facility, she would tag along as a reporter for *Mother Ocean* using her old Worthington press credentials. This way Cath would have no knowledge of the ex-reporter gone rogue. The tour was tomorrow at one p.m.

When Liz, the KTLA reporter and camera crew checked in, they had to sign a visitor's agreement and adhere to a long list of no-nos. Do not interfere with military operations, do not share anything with foreign governments, do not deface government property, stay with the tour guide at all times, etc.

The tour was white-washed and led by Junior Lieutenant, Groat along a web of floating docks enclosed by netting. He extolled the great care they received by experienced veterinarians and noted they were exercised regularly.

At one dock, the Lieutenant introduced the party to Dolly, a fifty-year-old female, one of his favorites, who clicked and squeaked wildly as he stood above her. "Would anyone like to pet her?" Groat asked.

Thinking of how she loved and missed Manami, Liz bent over and dove in. With cameras running and Dolly at her side, Elizabeth began speechifying about keeping dolphins confined to small spaces and the importance of providing a large, natural environment.

"For God's sake," Liz would say as the cameras recorded. "These honorable veterans are giving their lives to the country. They deserved to be treated with dignity."

Groat blew his whistle and commanded Liz come out of the water, saying this was a federal offense. After a good swim and a kiss for Dolly, Elizabeth climbed out before two hunky Navy seals took her out.

The reporter winked at her as she was escorted to the base commander's office. Sitting in an air-conditioned room in wet clothes became the least of Liz's worries during her interrogation. Having to provide further identification complicated the situation as did their recognition that she was the person the press labeled, 'the nude woman jailed for dolphins.'

"I'm afraid, Mrs. Yamamoto," the tightly wound Captain Maloney said, "You will have to be detained under the Animal Enterprise Protection Act as an eco-terrorist." After making several phone calls, the captain told Liz she would be investigated further by both a JAG officer from the San Diego Naval base and by FBI agents.

Given a men's jump suit to change into, she was escorted and locked into a storage room equipped with a folding cot. The next day, she would be transported to Pacific Fleet Headquarters.

She certainly would not call her lawyer dad, but she called Catherine and asked her to find a lawyer willing to defend her at the naval base. She wouldn't call Kaito either. *Now you've done it, Worthy.* What else could she say for the predicament? She was given a large bowl of Navy bean soup, which they swore was vegetarian, and a stack of back issues on the Navy's monthly, *All Hands.* She fell asleep feeling as lonely as the little unworthy waif she once was.

Four days later, coming out of the brig, Liz was notified that the Navy had dropped charges. They didn't say why exactly, but she assumed they didn't want further publicity and investigations about their handling of the dolphins.

However, she was placed, with photo, on the eco-terrorist watch list and she knew she was finished with this line of work. Without a clear path ahead, Elizabeth again felt lost within herself. When she was not occupied, her mind continued to play its dangerous tricks that had caused her to separate from Kaito three years ago. This fear alone made Elizabeth pick up the phone and set up a therapy appointment with Brian.

Chapter Thirty-Three
Offices of Brian Koslov, M.S., LMFC
Venice, California

Elizabeth's hand trembled as she gave Brian the five-page hand-written letter she had written on her overseas journeys.

"Wow. You've been busy. Almost three years' worth, if I remember."

"I edited some of it this morning in a panic," she said primping her mussed-up hair and wondering what Brian knew about her recent media escapades.

"Don't worry, Elizabeth. At this point, panicked is more helpful than polished. Relax, have a lollipop and let me read it. Okay?"

Digging through the bunch of pops, Elizabeth already regretted what she had written. Shared even with an almost stranger. She had penned a selfish and mean tirade and the guilt pounded in her temples. Unwrapping a pink watermelon pop, the first lick reminded her of hot summer picnics on Point Dume. *What will he think of me?* she worried as she watched how he read with intensity but without expression.

Finding her tongue getting sore from tightly circling the pop, she pulled it out and took a deep breath.

Brian flipped to the last page and glanced at her with an accepting nod. Stacking the pages, he smiled. "Well. You certainly poured your heart out on the page." He gestured to the letter. "And had a good cry doing it."

"How did you know that?"

"Not only from what you wrote, but from the little blurry blotches between the lines. Those glorious tears of hurt and pain. Bravo, Elizabeth. Just what I wanted to see."

"Really?"

"Really. So good, in fact, that after a few questions, I think we can move to stage one—understanding and accepting your feelings. Let me grab a pop."

He grabbed a lollipop, unwrapped it and asked, "Question. How did you feel when you finished writing it?"

"Ha. Wiped out."

"I can understand that, but any more specific feelings?"

In between licks of her lollipop, Elizabeth rattled off a litany of angers, guilts, shame, fears and confusion while Brian made notes.

"It's super that your able to recognize them so well. I wonder if you also reached any conclusions about your childhood?"

"How about, it was messed up."

"Yes, but what was the result? Like what did you take away from it? What it all meant."

"My mom and parents didn't love me?"

"Okay," he said and took a long note, then looked up. "Why did you think they didn't love you?"

She asked, "Because I didn't deserve to be loved?"

"I can see why you might feel that way, but were you a bad kid or something?"

"I don't think so. I was lonely and quiet. Spent a lot of time in the bathtub."

"Let me ask again why you thought they didn't love you."

She bit her lower lip. "They weren't there. I...I mean, Mom was either incoherent or passed out, my sister was long gone and my dad...he was never home."

"So, you felt—?" He waited for her answer.

"Everyone left me," she said as a slow pumping sensation grew in her chest, entered her throat and her eyes began to tear. "Would leave me."

"Hold onto that feeling if you can and tell me what that feeling means to you now." She frowned.

"I can see it's a powerful feeling, so I'm asking, have you ever had that feeling as an adult? Ever felt being left by anyone else?"

She sat back in her chair. Her eyes flooded as she pictured Kaito's sad and dejected face. She buried her head in her hands and sobbed.

Brian passed her some tissues and said, "Let it all out."

After several moments, Elizabeth dabbed her eyes and tried to smile. "I'm sorry."

"It's all okay. You're doing good. Enough for now. We'll come back to that when you're ready. Let me talk for a while. Ask questions if you'd like. Okay?"

"So, with time and your willingness, we're going to learn more about those feelings. You'll be able to identify them and understand them. Then, we'll teach you how to deal with them in helpful way."

"I'm ready, teach. I can see how these ghosts from my past still haunt me. I need to bust them like they did in that movie."

Brian made a pistol with his hand. "Poof! Poof!" he shot into the air.

She laughed. "What's it with men and guns in this country?"

"Ha. That's a socio-cultural malady I wouldn't presume to help. But back to where I can help you." Holding his grape pop in the air, he said, "One of the first things you've got to come to fully understand is that you can't blame yourself for what happened to you."

"I can't?" she asked.

"Absolutely not. Your parents, unintentionally or otherwise, are the ones to be blamed for what happened to you. You need to mourn for not having caring parents. Losing or never getting what you needed to be safe and secure."

She chuckled. "Funny, that's just what Kaito said after Mother died."

"Good man. He knows a child naturally loves the first people they know and trust, even if they don't return the same. Kids simply are not capable or developed enough emotionally to process and know what's wrong, so they blame themselves."

Elizabeth nodded repeatedly. "I always felt something was wrong with me. Missing, maybe." She shrugged. "Still do."

"You got it. The bugaboo with childhood neglect is that it's a sin of omission, not tangible, often repressed by those who experienced it. Then it sneaks up on you in adulthood and silently damages those who you love the most."

"Might that be what I'm doing?" she asked.

"Yes, but you have to find it in yourself and face it. Then you can zap it, like a ghostbuster."

Brian's smile made her smile. "Yes, and with time, you'll come to recognize that you weren't the problem. You were and are loveable. You can nip the old feeling in the bud, before it grows like a weed. When we move into the healing stage, we'll give you some pruning tools."

"Sounds too good to be true," she said.

"Aha! You just caught another one." She wrinkled her brow.

"That defensive posture you carry around with you."

She wiggled in her chair, sucking hard on her lollipop.

"I'm betting I'm not the first person who thought you were rude."

"Or a tough cookie?"

"Right. It's like you keep an armored vest around your heart, so others can't hurt you."

"Don't we all need to protect ourselves?"

"Yes, to a degree, but we also need to let people in—be vulnerable and trust them in order to lead a fuller, happier life."

Brian's desk phone rang.

"Excuse me a moment, Elizabeth. Oh, he's been waiting. Be right there." He checked his watch and looked to Elizabeth. "I'm sorry, I have another patient."

"That's okay."

They stood and he took her hand. "You are making remarkable progress. Must be your conceptual skills as a writer. Just keep thinking about these things, journal them if you like and next session, I'll introduce you to some tools that you can use to address your problems."

"I could use those alright. See you next week."

#

On her way home, Elizabeth stopped at the Santa Monica library and borrowed every book she could find on child abuse, alcoholism and narcissistic personality. Researching the topics like the intrepid reporter she was, she quickly filled four notebooks with anything that resonated with her upbringing. Sequestering herself in her bedroom at Catherine's, she spent most of the day and half the evening writing furiously to meet an internal deadline of understanding.

A knock on her door. "Liz. Are you awake? CNN is reporting a major earthquake and tsunami on Honshu, north of Tokyo. You better come."

She bolted out of bed. Standing side by side with Catherine, Elizabeth remained speechless, her hands trembling over her mouth as she watched the destruction unfold.

The CNN anchor's voice raced to catch up with the fast-moving footage of houses and cars being tossed around like toys in a rain gutter. "There are reports of waves towering one hundred thirty feet high and wiping out entire villages."

"Jesus," Catherine exclaimed, "Those are people there, moving along with the debris. How could you survive?"

"You couldn't," Liz added. "It's other-worldly. Like an upside-down waterfall tearing away at the surface of earth. And with the fires surrounding the floods, it's like the end of civilization."

"Waves of water," said the news anchor. "Have reached as far as six miles inland according to one report. Bridges have been washed out, trains derailed, and power lines and cellphone towers tumbled."

"Look," said Liz, "The water's reaching halfway up that building. I know it's at the airport in Sendai. All the people on the roof."

"Fears are growing," the anchor reported, "That the three disabled Daiichi nuclear power plant reactors in Fukushima may soon be releasing radioactive materials. Scientists have measured the entire island of Honshu moving eight feet and even the axis of the earth is shifting."

Elizabeth asked Catherine, "Earlier, did the report say anything about how much of the island was affected?"

"Yes, when I first turned it on, I think they said twelve-hundred miles along the coast. And they reported the U.S. Navy will be dispatching 25,000 marines from Okinawa to aid in the recovery."

"I have to go there," Elizabeth announced. "Find Kaito."

"Probably kind of dangerous, don't you think?"

"I'm not thinking, just feeling, and I know I have to go," she said and got on the phone.

Catherine went into the kitchen. "I'll make the coffee."

Liz returned and caught her breath. "I can't get through at all to Kaito or Kimmi, who might know where he is. Tokyo airports are down. I booked a Cathay Pacific flight to Seoul, onto Osaka on the unaffected side of the island and will take a train to Tokyo."

"When does the flight leave?"

"In four hours. I'll get packing."

Throwing clothes into her suitcase, she noticed the notebooks on her desk. *What am I going to say to him? What about our relationship?*

She dialed Brian.

"Geez, Liz. It's not even seven. What's up?"

"An emergency, Brian. I'm sorry, but I need your help. A major tsunami has struck the eastern side of Japan and I can't get Kaito on the phone. I have to go to him."

"You should."

"I've got a flight out of LAX in four hours. Can you help me?"

"How can I do that?"

"Meet me at the airport."

"Liz. I have clients all morning."

"Brian. I'm hurting, here. I've got a good grasp of my problems and screwed-up feelings, but it's as you said—conceptual. I desperately need some practical tools to fix up my relationship with Kaito."

"Elizabeth, that can't be done overnight."

"I gotta try. Or I'll lose him forever."

A long pause and Brian came back on. "I'll make some calls. Can't promise, but I'll let you know."

#

"There he is," Elizabeth called out as Catherine pulled near the Cathy Pacific sign. Brian stood on his toes and waved.

Catherine parked, popped the trunk and they got out.

"Great seeing you again, Cathy," Brian said, kissing her on the mouth.

"Likewise, Bri," she said, blushing red.

Brian turned to hug Elizabeth. "And my most favorite, short-time client." He grabbed her suitcase. "Did you get a hold of Kaito?"

"Not yet. The lines seem to be down."

"Hey, Miss!" yelled a security man. "This zone's for a drop off, not a love-in."

"Yes, sir," Cath responded and gave Liz a quick hug. "Take care of yourself and your man. Okay?" Getting into the car, she waved, "Good to see you again, Brian."

Elizabeth elbowed Brian. "You guys were friends, I take it."

"Yeah. She turned down my marriage proposal, but that's an old story." He wheeled her bag into the terminal. "Let's get you checked in, grab some coffee and choreograph your journey, okay?"

Setting down their trays in a quiet corner of Starbucks, Brian pulled a torn envelope out of his pocket. She opened her notebook. "This is not the proper way of conducting therapy, but with your exceptional progress to date, passion, and me figuring I'll never see you again, I drafted a tool of sorts in the car coming here."

"Wait," she tapped his hand. "Never see you again?"

"Yes, my gut tells me you're going to stay in Japan. Stay with Kaito." He tapped her hand in return. "All I ask is that you drop me a line when you're happy ever after, so I don't lose my license."

"You're the best, Brian."

"Wait till you see my acrostic."

Down the length of the envelope were the block letters PATHS, followed by jagged scribblings.

"This, my dear, if I had the power to give it to you, are the keys, simplified, for you to help yourself. But as you know, the power only lies within you. That's what the P stands for as well as pains of the past."

She made some notes. "I've got plenty of those, the big ones being untrusting, self-doubting and over-protecting my feelings."

"Right. And you've got a good accounting of most of them, but how you handle them depends on the next steps, as in A. That is, acknowledging and accepting that you own these hurts, and they are real. But these babies are still lurking inside you like a mountain lion ready to pounce. Always remember, 'I felt everyone would leave me'. That feeling won't lose its punch without constant monitoring and managing over time."

"For sure. Since the tsunami, I've been drowning in fears of losing Kaito."

He nodded and pointed to the T. "Now, here's the real tool. There's gonna be lots of times when these old fears will poke up their ugly heads: situations, arguments, perceptions, images, single words sometimes. We call them triggers. Stimuli that shoot off the explosion of past negative emotions. Your tough job is to be constantly on alert for them."

"Like the flashback I had of my dad driving off with that starlet. A big trigger for my fear of abandonment."

"Exactly, and it was very real, although irrational and it caused you to overreact and have even more pain. So, your challenge is to step back, take time and space to distance yourself from that feeling. Look at it in a new, more rational and positive adult way."

"You mean like self-reflect?"

"Yeah, walking therapy," Brian commented. "Let's move on to the H."

"For healing, I'd imagine."

"Right, and this one requires a lot more time since you spent a large part of your life thinking you weren't loveable. You wrote your own script and followed it. Now you have to rewrite it. Let's brainstorm a mantra that you can use to re-program your brain."

"I've got one," she cried out, pointing a finger in the air. "A mantra I used to get me through college, into a good job and even cropped up again when I crewed on that anti-whaling ship. It's a play on my name." She paused. "I am worthy."

Brian stopped walking and stared at her. "You're something else, Worthington-Yamamoto. And what is it you most need to be worthy of?"

Still facing each other as travelers wound their way around them, Elizabeth pointed to her heart. "I am worthy of love."

"Bingo! And a healthy and trusting relationship with Kaito. And this will be," he paused as he got jostled by a passerby, "Your biggest challenge." He pointed to chairs in a mostly deserted waiting area.

They sat, and Brian picked up. "Here's how I see it, based on what you told me about Kaito. That he is a prince and wants you back."

"True. Absolutely," she said and made another note.

"You, dear, must work hard to understand *his* needs and respect *his* feelings as much as your own."

"That's the hard part."

"Maybe, but for starters, you're already a caring, pretty much selfless person, now you have to come to trust him."

"I know. I know."

"But you keep holding back, don't you?"

"I guess."

"So, here's another script rewrite. You keep using the exploitation of dolphins as a bugaboo in your relationship. Right?"

She grimaced and nodded.

"Well, here's how I see it. When your mom began abandoning you, she gave you a scapegoat for her failings." He rubbed his chin. "I think it was a scape-dolphin."

Elizabeth jerked back, dropping her pencil. "What?"

"Yes. It's my hunch, and you will need to see if it resonates with you as truth and decide. But I think the name and role you used for your dolphin ended up giving you the armor, the excuse, for protecting your heart."

"Jesus, Brian. Are you dismissing my spirit animal, the passionate focus of my life?"

"No. Just trying to reframe it. You see, these things can sometimes become obsessions and always ask for more to be satisfied."

As he spoke, Liz wondered if he maybe her knew she had taken multiple missions on the Sea Savior, always needing to save more whales?

"So," he continued, "how about if we no longer refer to the dolphin as your guardian angel, but instead, your guiding or good angel? In other words, use your angel to bring out the best in you—what you really need. Have it show you the way, not save you from feeling hurt."

She took notes with a vengeance.

"Look, Liz. You're going to need to let Kaito fully into your heart. Be vulnerable to him. And if you let your new dolphin suggest a resolution, it may come your way."

She stared into his eyes. "Okay."

"Just try it. If it doesn't fit, don't wear it."

BING! "Attention! Cathay Pacific airlines flight number 101 for Seoul, Korea is now boarding."

"Let's go," said Brian, "Don't want to miss your flight." They got up and he reached into his pocket and handed her a small bag of rubber bands.

"What the hell, Brian?"

"You will wear one on your wrist until you are completely issue-free. As soon as one of your old scripts raises its ugly head, you are to pull it and gently snap yourself out of it. Not to hurt yourself or to make you feel guilty. It's just a wake-up reminder to catch your old ways and take on your new, healthy perspective."

"You're incredible. Suppose you've got a name for that too."

"Snap therapy."

They got in line and Brian kept talking. "We can't forget the S, which stands for self-care. With all the hard work you'll be doing, you owe yourself an outlet that renews your energy and keeps you feeling good about yourself. With you, that's easy. Write your heart out, girl."

"That I can do."

"Looks like I won't be able to go any further, but I have to give you one more thing." He reached into his briefcase and pulled out a zip-lock bag of lollipops.

"You're the sweetest guy. Don't understand why Christine wouldn't marry you."

"Huh. She told me I fall in love too easily." Pointing to the bag, he said, "They're half cherry and half this great new flavor, blue raspberry. One you suck when you're stuck in your childhood, the other you savor for when you're feeling your new self."

"Oops. I gotta go," she said, showing the agent her boarding pass. "Thanks, Brian, so much for the best instant therapy."

Waving to her, he cried out, "How about therapy on the fly? Good luck Worthy girl."

Chapter Thirty-Four
Tokyo

March 14, 2011

By the time Elizabeth arrived in Seoul, her nerves were still up in the air. What if he was in or around Fukushima, drowned by the tsunami or radiated? She had to reach him. It didn't help when she got into the terminal to dialed him and looked down at both of her red and raw wrists. No answer again.

She wasn't as gentle as she was supposed to be, snapping her wrists like that. She did it at first to acknowledge her childhood fears, but later mostly over the real-time fear of losing Kaito. Despite the stares from fellow passengers, she didn't feel the least bit embarrassed. It was a good sign of recovery. Although she cursed herself for not seeking therapy earlier, she knew he might have been lost at sea, and this was a normal mature adult worry, not an old one from my childhood. And hopefully soon she would reconcile with him. Be with him to love him.

On route to changing planes for Osaka, her hand trembled as she tried calling Kaito again on his mobile but with no luck. "Yes," she said to herself, hearing the ringtone on his apartment landline. Her heart flooded with promise until she heard; 'Sorry. This mailbox is full and can no longer take messages.' She had better luck catching Kimmi, who told her she hadn't spoken to him for weeks but offered to try and find his whereabouts. As soon as the plane landed in Osaka, Elizabeth tried calling Kaito again. Nothing. Fearing the worst, she snapped her rubber band and called Kaito's eighty-year-old mother.

Her hand trembled, worrying that his mother might be angry at her and skeptical of her sincerity. She rang. "Mrs. Yamamoto, this is Elizabeth. How are you?"

"Fine, but remember, please, to you I'm still *okaasan* or Noriko. Where are you?"

"At the Osaka airport. Came in from Seoul. I'll be taking the *Shinkansen* to Tokyo in a few minutes. Do you know if Kaito is alright?"

"I hope so. I last talked to him a week ago. He was in Okinawa training his dolphins. I tried calling him after the tsunami but haven't gotten through. Are you coming back to be with him?"

"Yes, if he'll have me." *Snap!*

"Are you sure this time? He's been so broken up over you."

Snap! "I am sure, Mother. Please, do you have any ideas where he might be?"

"No, but I worry he was on his boat. The coast was hit so badly. Death tolls are still mounting. Call me when you can."

"I will. Thank you *okaasan*. They're calling the train. I have to go. Hope I will see you again."

"Me too, we're due another family reunion. Take care Elizabeth and hug my boy for me."

Arriving at his apartment in Shibuya, Elizabeth began searching everywhere for a clue as to where he could be. As always, the place was super neat, but the totally empty refrigerator made her think he didn't plan to be home for a while. It also reminded her that she hadn't eaten anything since she left Los Angeles and wasn't even hungry.

Standing and staring at the stack of journals, portable file boxes and folders neatly laid out on the kitchen table, she figured he was still hard at work. But she didn't think pouring through and being baffled by all the scientific papers would help locate him. She flicked on the TV. The images of the destruction and dead bodies made her shudder.

Wait. She rushed to his phone and pushed play. The message was from her, starting from the last one when he rightly refused to help the Japanese distribution of *The Gulf*. She listened to her hurt-child voice; 'You'll do this for me if you love me.' How she tried to control him to not leave her.

"Dear God," she cried out loud. I was such a fool. Didn't even respect his work. She pulled on the rubber band and broke it. The old hurt turned into the new hurt. Would he give her another chance?

She pushed play. Maybe someone else called. It was her voice again. Back further. Again. Another. Seems he saved every message she ever left him. She felt another cry coming on but caught herself and reached into her purse. She put another rubber band on and called Kimmi.

"Nothing yet," Kimmi reported, "But I put a call into the Fleet Commander's XO, Captain Mandell in Okinawa, remember him? I'm waiting to hear back. At least the small island was unscathed."

"Kimmi, can you give me his number? I left my phone directory back in the States. I'll try him."

"Are you coming back, Liz? Work together again?" Kimmi asked.

"Maybe."

"Great. Hold on, let me pull up the number. Ready?"

"Got it. Stay in touch and thanks, Kimmi."

Calling Mandell's office, his staff assistant referred her to a Petty Officer Quentin, who oversaw Kaito's work in the dolphin research bay. "Officer Quentin. This is Elizabeth Yamamoto, Kaito's wife, and I'm trying to locate him, can you tell me when you saw him last?"

"Sure," he replied, "Let me check my calendar. It was last Wednesday the Seventh. I didn't talk to him just waved to him in his dingy."

"Do you remember what he was doing and when he left?"

"I do remember that day. He didn't spend much time, as usual, in the water with the dolphins, he was mostly putzing around with a new piece of equipment. He was towing it behind the Zodiac, the dolphins swimming alongside."

"What did it look like, this equipment?"

"Well, it was a long cylinder that he kept putting in and out of the water. He left around lunch time that day. He was gone when I got back from the mess hall."

"Thanks, officer. Please call me if he returns." She gave him her number.

Next, she called the cell phone service provider and entered three for service outage and restoration. Sendai and a 150 km surrounding area would not be restored for three days or more.

She let out a low sigh. New piece of equipment. A long cylinder. Elizabeth kept repeating until she stood and rushed to the kitchen table and opened the grant file box. On top was his Financial/Expense ledger. His last entry: Marine Magnetometer 07/05/2011 1,293,000 Yen.

She called Kimmi. "Sorry to keep pestering you, but does a marine magnetometer mean anything to you?"

"Not exactly. But when we met that time, Kaito described how dolphins navigate by the earth's magnetic field and changes to it might signal a pending earthquake."

Elizabeth's heart sank. She snapped her wrist for not paying attention to his research plans.

Kimmi asked, "You don't think he headed to Sendai in his boat, do you? There could be aftershocks."

"I know, and that's not all, there's the chance of radiation exposure from the Fukushima Daiichi plant failure. But you know how dedicated he is. Dammit. I'll call the Marina in Tokyo Bay. Hopefully he still docks at the Mizuna. They should have a log of his plans. Goodbye, Kimmi. Let me know if you hear anything, okay?"

She hung up and dialed. "May I speak with the dock master please?" Voice cracking, she added, "This is an emergency."

"This is Hamido, may I help you, Madam?"

"Sir, Kaito Yamamoto has been docking the Umi-Kamiko there for years. This is his wife. Is his boat still there?"

"No, Madam. I saw him leave yesterday himself at the helm, the afternoon following the tsunami. I radioed him because he hadn't logged out. I asked him where he was going?"

Elizabeth froze, suspecting what he was going to say.

"Fukushima," he said, "And I told him quite forcefully, you're crazy to do that. I remember he answered, 'Maybe I can help some stranded fishermen, or anyone carried out to sea and still alive.'"

"I just shook my head and told him they've got rescue boats for that, including the U.S. Marines. Do you want to get radiated, I asked."

"Would you believe he said, 'The winds are prevailing westerly and I'm staying many kilometers out to sea. Closer to the source of the earthquake in the Japan Trench.'"

"You know what he said after that?"

"I can only imagine," she said feeling dragged by an undertow of despair.

"He said, 'maybe I can learn how to give people more time to evacuate, the next time.' He's quite the savior, your husband."

"He is, alright. Thank you, sir. Call me if he should return."

She jabbed her finger into the table. *I've got to find him and fast.* Glancing at the TV screen, it showed a total of 8,630 total confirmed deaths and scrolled a list of coastal towns by the number of deaths. She spotted Mito with no deaths. Perhaps she could travel that far. Turning on her laptop and entering Japanese Government Railways, Tokyo to Sendai routes. Trains were running on schedule, but only as far as Mito, about halfway north. She would go there.

But how would I ever find him? There was only one way. She searched for boat rentals in Mito Harbor. Mitoyat had a sixteen meter, 240 hp Mercedes, three cabin, ship to shore radio, Sailor K for 53,000 yen a day or about 400 U.S. It would be like finding a moving dot in 35,000 square miles of water, but she could pilot that boat with a little help.

She could hire someone, but she needed more than a crewmember. Looking up to the ceiling, she pleaded to herself, "Come on Izzy. Think."

Noaki? A good friend with a big heart. A hard-working loyal trooper, not only to his Communist party. Created plans for the dolphin lagoon in one week. Would he be available, willing? Join me on what? She could only think of it as a risky, far-flung and farfetched ocean odyssey. *Whatever it takes, Izzy-girl.*

Finding his number in Kaito's phone file, she dialed him using crossed fingers. "Naoki? It's Elizabeth Yamamoto."

"Oh, gorgeous. Have you finally returned?"

"I have."

"To stay?"

"I hope to."

"Where's Kaito?"

"Wonder if you knew?"

"No, but I know he wants you back."

"I am back, and I have to ask you for a huge favor."

"Ask."

"But it's huge, and I'll understand if you can't do it."

"Come on, Liz. What is it?"

"Help me find Kaito."

"I'm in."

"You don't even know what's involved. He might be right in the thick of the disaster."

"Doesn't matter. Involved in getting you two back together? I'll do anything to stop him from moping over you. What's the plan?"

"We rent an ocean-worthy boat in Mito and go looking for him. I've got good evidence he's at or coming back from measuring the magnetic fields near the Japan Trench where the earthquake originated." She didn't think it would matter to him how difficult that would be.

"That sounds just like my brainy old roomy. When can you get to Mito?"

"Taking the 7:18 express from Tokyo, I'd get to the marina say, 9:30."

"I'll drive from Nagato tonight, stay in Mito. See you then there, gorgeous. And don't worry, your husband is no dummy and quite a seafarer. I'm sure he's fine. We'll draw up a search plan that'll find him."

"You're a doll, Naoki."

"No. You're the doll. I'm just a dude—a crazy one at that. Tootles until tomorrow."

#

On the train ride to Mito, Elizabeth finally began to take in the horrors of the tsunami. Until now, they were flickering images on the TV. Even though the train route was considerably inland, fires were everywhere and when they slowed down going through towns, she witnessed ambulances rushing north to save the injured while hearses drove south to deliver the bodies northern facilities could no longer handle. The depth and breadth of the destruction to Kaito's nation and to the broken spirit of his countrymen, finally sunk in.

When she arrived at the Mito station, she felt a slight twinge of hunger, so she bought a banana and some weird trail mix from a vending machine, finishing the banana. Most cabbies were unwilling to take her to the harbor. One elderly driver finally agreed and told her the whole ride she was *kureji,* in adopted English.

She was able to finally shake off her fears when the cab pulled up to the Mitoyat boat sales and rental. There was Naiko, dressed in a sailor outfit, strutting toward her.

"Good morning, Captain Liz," he said saluting and grinning. Before she hugged him, she stared at what he no doubt wanted her to stare at: A wide brimmed sailor's cap and outsized aviator sunglasses, a white kerchief tied around his neck, fitted into gold-buttoned, double-breasted navy waistcoat and white, bell-bottom trousers.

"Ahoy, Matey," she said and hugged him dearly. "Where on earth did you get—?"

341

"A great costume shop in Nagota. Captain Pinkerton's outfit is quite popular and for you, Madam Butterfly..." he reached behind his back..."a *tsunokakushi.*"

She shook her head and guffawed as he handed her a white boxy, silk helmet with butterfly horns, the traditional Japanese wedding veil.

"You can be Cio-Cio-san, our Madam Butterfly. A little slim maybe, but in our opera, you'll be an American playing her, while your American sailor, will be played by a Japanese. And he won't be leaving you."

"That's quite a twist alright, but slim as in too skinny?"

"Don't worry. Kaito will love every last pound of you." He eyed her from head to toe. "You know, more for him to squeeze," he said laughing.

She held him by the chin. "You are crazy, but loveable. So good to see you again, Naoki, or should I say Director." She pointed to the rental offices. "But not being a stage production, let's get going on the search mission, Okay?"

Renting the boat, they were required to put down a double deposit, opt for collision and liability insurance, promise the company they would not sail near the disaster zone and sign a waiver.

Soon after loading the provisions, Elizabeth had ordered for the boat, she was at the helm. Naiko was at the stern taking in the ropes and they pulled out of their slip into a morning fog. Heading up the coast, they waved down every boat they encountered, asking the pilot if they had seen the fifty-foot *Umi-Kumiko?* After being met with countless 'nos', they soon reached the Fukushima area where the devastation become even more frightening. Small boats and big ships were tossed about like toys, ending up on streets or on top of buildings.

When they encountered a vessel floating upside down in the water, Liz's stomach turned and she made Naoki get out and measure the length of the keel to make sure it wasn't fifty feet. On and on they went, seeing once colorful coastal cities reduced to a flat grayness. Fires continued to burn everywhere including in the middle of new bays cut by the tsunami, looking like islands from hell.

Backhoes and bulldozers clawed and scraped at the debris while desperate people scavenged the shoreline for flotsam of their lives or the bodies of the no longer living. Hour after hour, from dawn to dusk for two days, Liz and Naoki took turns with the wheel and binoculars, until exhausted and crestfallen, they headed back to Mito to refuel.

Sailing past the fuel dock and into the main channel to open waters, Naoki noticed a cruiser entering behind them from another slip, turning and slowing at the fuel dock. "Cio-Cio!" he shouted up to the bridge. "Heave to and turn around."

"What?" she screamed.

"I think I just saw Kaito. The *Umi-Kumiko*, right?"

The engine chugged into reverse, then lunged forward as Liz pivoted hard to the portside almost hitting a piling. Coming around, she ran over a buoy.

"Easy Captain. He's docking and taking on fuel. Head to the dock on the other side."

Heart beating in her throat, she wanted to scream Kaito's name.

"Careful," Naiko said. "Slow her down. I'll get the bumpers and ropes ready."

She gripped the wheel hard to stay focused on the tight maneuvering.

"Steady...Got it. Cut the engine."

She ran down. Naiko met her.

"Elizabeth." He held her by her shivering shoulders. "I need to now ask you for a favor. We've found him, and I'd love to surprise him, get back at him for the last practical joke he played on me."

"But...but," she resisted and nudged toward the dock.

"Please. Just stay here for a couple of minutes more so I can put an act on with him and introduce you. When I call Cio-Cio-san you come running in choppy little steps, okay?"

She nodded, but wasn't really up for the game.

"And leave your sunglasses on. And here, put on the veil. He won't know you until you remove it. Got it."

She nodded impatiently, not wanting to dismiss his efforts to help.

Naiko climbed onto the dock and sauntered toward Kaito, chatting with the fuel attendant. In a low, throaty voice Naiko teased, "Ahoy, Captain. You manage this big boat all by yourself?"

Kaito gave him a detached stare.

Undiscovered, Naiko persisted, "I bet an old fart like you could use one of my best deck hands."

Confounded, Kaito huffed, "I beg your pardon?"

"Cio-Cio-San! Cio-Cio-San!" Naiko yelled and waved.

Elizabeth went along with his trick, her heart beating faster than her choppy steps.

Kaito stared in wonder at the rushing figure.

"*Nantekotta*," he cried out, squinting hard at the crazy man and back at the rushing woman. "Naiko. What on earth are you doing here?" He glanced again at the running figure. "What is going on?"

"Captain Pinkerton," Naiko bowed and waved his hand to Izzy, now standing opposite Kaito. "May I present your bride. You may lift her veil."

Once Izzy got a look at Kaito she threw off the veil and ran screaming into his arms.

"Izzy-chan?" He lifted her high, swaying her as he did when she first said yes. "I can't believe this. Let me look at you again."

"Yup, it's me." she replied, planting kisses all over his face.

His hugged her some more, then asked, "How did you find me?"

"Scientific reasoning, I guess," then quipped, "I just followed your magnetic personality."

"Ha! I can't believe this. It's like a movie."

"An opera actually, but with a better ending."

"Meaning you'll stay in Japan?"

"Yes, if you'll have me."

"You're joking. Of course, I will." He ran his hand across the bottom of her short hair.

Elizabeth asked, "Are you disappointed?"

"You're kidding me again." He kissed the top of her head and glanced at Naiko. "And you brought the joker along with you. Almost gave me a heart attack." Holding Izzy at his side he reached out his hand. "Come here, old friend."

"My pleasure. Anything to bring you two together."

They all hugged.

"Let's have a celebration, eh?"

Kaito agreed. "Certainly, cause to."

"Great," said Naiko. "I'll leave the loving couple alone for a while. I brought some scotch whiskey and let me go foraging on the rental boat that Liz had provisioned. I'll turn the boat back in too."

"There's mostly canned vegetables, I'm afraid," Liz added.

"And I've got a nice halibut, freshly caught on the way here."

"Perfect," he said, heading down the dock. "Meet you aboard the Umi-Kamiko." He turned and shouted back, "After we eat, we'll have the ceremony."

Kaito and Elizabeth looked at each other, shrugged and kissed.

After eating, drinking and reminiscing old times, Elizabeth had to excuse herself and use the bathroom. She threw up all that she had eaten, attributing it to all the excitement. When she returned to the deck, Naiko directed them to the bow.

"Okay, Kaito, an inch to the left. Lift your veil slightly, Liz. That's it," he said and snapped the shutter on his mini-Minolta. "Perfect. Now let's do it. Hold both her hands and look into each other's eyes. You first, Kaito. Repeat after me, I, Kaito Yamamoto—"

"I, Kaito Yamamoto," he said, smiling.

"Ah. Liz, please help me."

She said, "Do solemnly swear."

"Kaito. Repeat that."

Looking at Kaito holding back a laugh, Elizabeth said, "To take Elizabeth Worthington as my lawfully wedded wife."

Kaito repeated, chuckling.

"I, Elizabeth Worthington, solemnly swear to take this incredible man—"

"Heh," Naiko interrupted, "You've got to say it right."

Amidst flubs and chuckles, it went on until Naiko finally said. "I hereby pronounce you, once again, husband and wife." He clapped and they kissed.

Holding the kiss, Naiko kept clicking the camera until Kaito reached behind Elizabeth's back and pulled her so close that Liz stumbled.

"Hello, young lovebirds," Naiko blurted.

They parted; faces flushed.

"Time for me to depart. Leave the newlyweds to their floating love nest and honeymoon cruise."

Naiko joined them, hugging together.

"Okay. I'm off." He waved. "Bon Voyage."

"Thank you," Kaito and Elizabeth said at the same time and waved back.

After Kaito arranged to rent the same slip for the morning and have ice delivered to the boat, the pair settled into the main cabin. The sat close, cuddling in the galley and had tea.

"Could I ask my new, old bride, if she'll will stay with me now?"

She fixed her eyes on his. "I will. I promise. Forever."

"Thank your God. What made you come now?"

"I needed to not lose you."

He nodded and inched closer to hear more.

"When the tsunami struck and I saw all the destruction to your country and people on TV, I knew. I knew how wrong I had been about your goal to save lives, even with the help of a fellow mammal."

"So, you're over that?"

"Mostly, I think, my therapist suggested I was sort of sick obsessed with my guardian angel wanting me to save more and more cetaceans."

"That's the reason you ran, then?" he asked, then added, "You'll have to tell me about this therapist."

"I will, but this other reason is harder to understand and I'm just starting to. Can't expect you to. But I had a fear I...I was losing you."

"That does seem crazy. You mean to my own obsession with my dolphin warning system? I'm sorry I just couldn't give that up."

"I knew that. You shouldn't have." She waved her hand across the water. "And what happened here certainly justifies it. It's just that your dedication felt to the little child within me..." she tugged at the ends of her hair..."like you were going to leave me."

She saw his puzzled look and continued, "I know. It's all twisted-up in those childhood things. I'm still trying to make her..." she pointed to her heart..."that little child in here understand." The guilt rose up to her throat. "Kaito I was so messed up and selfish. I am so sorry for the pain I caused you all those years. Will you forgive me?"

"Forgiven," he said emphatically. "You know, it wasn't so much the pain as it was sadness." He pointed to his heart. "But somehow I knew inside, our love could handle this."

"Me too, if you can believe it. You were always with me. The whole time I was doing my thing." She chuckled. "Wrote letters to you every day about my experiences, even at sea. Never posted them as they were so 'woe is me.'" She placed her hand on his face. "Somehow, I knew you'd wait for me. I took you..." She yanked at the ends of her hair.

He finished her sentence. "For granted?"

"Yes. Pretty bad, huh?"

"It was sad," he said, "But from our first days together and through all those years, you were my inspiration. Inspired me to be a better man—the courage do more. Your love was always with me too."

"Love and marriage in absentia," she exclaimed.

"Yes, and you know, for me, it was mostly about that vow. When we married, we agreed to respect each other's individual goals. And you, being a liberated American woman had your own career interests and personal needs. Sure, I worried I might lose you, but I knew you had to get whatever was bothering you out of your system. Needed to come back on your own. Like you did." He tapped her chin. "Maybe it was true love that sustained us.?" He held up his pinky finger. "Or?"

She held up her finger. "That unbreakable Red String of Fate, huh? You are one wonderful man, Kaito Yamamoto."

"And you a wonderful woman. You need to believe with all you heart that I love the little girl in you as much as the grown up one."

Elizabeth nestled closer into his shoulder and looked up into his eyes she felt what she needed someone to give her all her life. He not only made her feel worthy of love, but for the first time, *full of* love. "Thank you," she said, "Now I want to know all about your research."

"You mean like we did when we first got to know each other all night in bed?"

"Both kinds," she said.

"Let's go swimming now. We can talk about my research in the morning."

They kissed and swam.

The next morning after Kaito made French toast for Izzy and carried it on a tray to the bed.

Elizabeth was wide awake. "Good morning my koija. Smells delicious." She patted the bedside. "Come sit and tell me all about your research. What exactly were you trying to accomplish?"

"Let me have a bite first," he said dribbling maple syrup on his toast. "It was to establish a data base for the second phase and grant of my dolphin early earthquake detection system—the magnetic field unipolar peroxyl detection. That all depends on success with the phase one grant and research. I've formed a great collaboration with Dr. Isao Okawa, a leading marine biologist and now research colleague. As a co-researcher, he will enhance my credentials. I'm supposed to hear of my grant approval in the next ten days."

"So that's what the magnetometer was for?"

"Oh, it's pretty complicated."

"Tell me. I want to know. I want to help you if you let me."

Kaito smiled and gazed into her eyes. "For sure." He searched memory. "As I was saying, I was towing the magnetometer behind the boat to map the magnetic contours of the earth's crust at the Japan Trench part of the ring of fire where the Tohoku earthquake and tsunami originated."

"So how would that baseline help you with dolphin detection?"

He tapped her knee. "Good question. Here's a refresher on my theory. When the earth's crust/plates separate, they emit magnetic pulsations at significant amplitudes before, during and after the event. I believe dolphins can easily detect those pulses, so phase two involves a lab simulation of an undersea earthquake."

"How on earth would you do that?"

"You sure you want to know?"

"I'm sure. I want to know all about your work."

"Okay," he said with a narrowed brow. "We have partly submerged granite boulders lying in the research bay in Okinawa. By the way, thanks to you and Kimmi's entre to the top brass, I have an idea research setting."

"I'm so glad we could help."

"Anyway. By inserting Bustar into a fissure in the rock."

"What's Bustar?"

"It's a slowly expanding concrete. So, as it begins to break the rock apart at the fissure, it sends out those pulses I told you about." He raised a finger into the air. "The key is to measure the number of magnetic pulses as the boulder breaks apart..." he looked to her attention..."and correlate the amounts with the dolphin's sensitivity."

"Wow! That's incredible."

"It is. And could be the lynchpin of a huge breakthrough in earthquake detection."

"You're brilliant, husband and I see what a contribution you could make."

"Thanks," he said and kissed her hand.

"Long story and still being written. But your vision and what it could mean is so important, it might outweigh the temporary use of a few dolphins in a simulation, where no harm will come to them. All for the greater good."

Taken by surprise, Kaito asked, "What about your guardian angel? Isn't she telling you it's not, right?"

"She was, but I'm thinking she's evolving into a different kind of angel."

"Hmm. How does that happen?"

"It's as complex as your therapist's theory, but I've been experimenting. I'll fill you in later."

"And what goals does my Cio-Cio-san have these days?"

"I still want to write, of course. Use my writing to influence world opinion as you use yours to prove that dolphins can help save humans. Getting just a peek at the carnage coming up the coast inspired me to write about it. I'll work on the short term, you the long."

They sat on the edge of the bed. He picked up her hands and kissed them. "This is wonderful, but can I ask what happened to your wrists?"

"Ah, that's the therapy." She pulled him closer. "Getting back to my inner child."

"Yes..." he held up and looked at her hands..."but it looks more like torture."

"Ha. I call it snap therapy. I put a rubber band on my wrist and snap it when I'm having counterproductive thoughts and feelings. It's a trick this super therapist, Brian, taught me."

"Okay but let me get you some lotion." He got up and rummaged through a drawer and dabbed it on her wrists and gently massaged it in.

"Do you mind my hair?" She asked.

"Well, it is a little short," he replied running his fingers through it. "And I do spot a few gray hairs coming through the always beautiful auburn. Do you plan to let it grow?"

"For you, of course."

He ran his palm up her arm. "Feels like you've been working hard on those ships, and you're so trim."

"I have lost a few pounds."

"Seems like more than a few. You weren't dieting, were you?"

"No, just not eating as much these days."

"I love you anyway you are." He kissed her and rubbed her neck.

"That feels good."

He fixed his gaze on her. "You know your eyes captured me on the first day we met."

349

She placed her hand to the side of his face. "They're the same eyes, just a better pilot behind them. When we get back, I want to go swimming again with you and your dolphins."

"How about a swim now, like we used to?"

"Older, but better?"

They kissed.

Chapter Thirty-Five
March 18, 2011

Kaito's apartment
Shibuya, Tokyo

Hearing Kaito gently knock twice on the bedroom door, Elizabeth pulled back another sob. "Come in," she said, wiping her tears.

"Are you okay, princess?" he asked while rubbing her shoulders.

She looked up from her desk as the printer released the final page. "I finished it. Sixth friggin' draft."

He knelt beside her. "You've been crying. Are you happy with it?"

"It…it's okay, but it took a lot out of me."

"I told you. Making that risky trip to see the devastation first-hand would be hard. All reporters were told not to enter the radiation zone."

"Funny," she said, feigning a laugh. "It was much harder to write than it was to be in the misery. But I had to redeem myself. This piece is actually a love letter to your country and to you."

"How do you mean?"

She reached over for his hand. "Writing it made me realize what a creep I was to you."

He shook his head.

"No. I failed to appreciate the importance of what you wanted…no, needed, to do to help people. I…I was so wrong," she added, holding back her tears.

He took her into his arms. "It's okay now."

"Is it? You must have been so disappointed in me. Being so selfish. That your work for an advanced earthquake warning system wasn't important." She stapled the pages together. "Like saving lives didn't matter compared to my hang-up with dolphins. And…" she held up her essay…"and my paltry words."

"Come on, Izzy-chan. Your words will inspire a lot of people to act."

"We'll see. I sent it off to editors both here and in the States under the pen name, Elizabeth Hamada."

"Being one of the first Americans reporting from the scene can't help. Can I read it?"

She handed it to him. "Here. Enough about me. You'll be hearing about your funding soon, right? Finally get started on proving what you've been working on all those years."

"Yes, I should know in a week." He sighed, "Fingers crossed, as you say."

Surrendering to the Water
By Elizabeth Hamada

I drove up the northern coast toward the tsunami-stricken town of Fukushima, searching for stories about courage, not pain. Ambulances screeched past, wailing of injury and death. Trailer-trucks, heaped with debris, rumbled south. They shook the road and trembled up into my feet. Spires of smoke billowed between the red-tiled ruins and burned in my nose.

As I managed the curves of coastal Highway 6, I tried to remember how it used to feel. In the summer, when my husband and I took vacation in Bandai, the air was salty and sweet. Graceful seabirds glided above and dove into harbors below. Wings of the sailboats flapped in the wind as they slid over the white-capped, turquoise waves.

Now, I look at the destruction and think of the numbers: 19,000 missing or dead, 160,000 homes destroyed, 76,000 refugees from the Fukushima-Daichi nuclear meltdown. Some 440,000 are displaced and living in shelters. The destruction is impossible for me to imagine. And, like our nation, I am numb.

I needed to find some meaning beyond the numbers. Sitting high and safe in my Tokyo apartment elevated my guilt. Watching rescues on TV only added to my sorrow. My donations of money may help provide food and shelter but would do little to soothe the wounds of loss. I wanted to serve a purpose outside of myself, reach out from inside me to touch the hearts of survivors. Salve the bruised souls of grieving family members.

Even though I was deathly afraid of my vulnerability to the pain of others and doubted my ability to stay in control during an interview, I decided I must write a first-hand, first-person account of the disaster, so the reader can feel what the survivors felt. As a reporter, the only medicine I have are my words. Words that I can pour out onto the page like tears and share with those who are suffering. Maybe I can help them find understanding amidst the grief. Give them a cushion of distance between the impersonal power of nature and the personal power of human grace. Maybe I can help others start to find what it takes to move on and heal. And, along the way, redeem myself.

Winding my way around bulldozers scraping debris off the road, I came to Iwaki City, twenty kilometers south of the Fukushima nuclear evacuation zone. I knew there was an old Buddhist monastery that was converted to an emergency shelter. Outside, a large crowd was huddled around a signboard posted with long lists of the missing and the victims. Entering the door, the clamor and the smells overwhelmed me. Crying, from both babies and adults, reverberated in my ears and the stench of stale food and unwashed bodies clutched my throat. It pained me to think that the people jammed into the prayer room looked like a pen of frightened bellowing animals.

Spotting a man who looked like an official, I headed toward him. I had to pass through two groups of citizens. One group was lying or sitting on the floor, suffering in silence. I tiptoed gently in the tiny spaces between their tangled limbs to reach the second group. These people were walking aimlessly and mumbling the names of loved ones, or asking about rice, the radiation, cots, baths and when they could return home. Finally, I reached the gray-haired man wearing an orange vest and showed him my press badge. He told me I could try for some interviews, but no cameras, and asked me to respect everyone's privacy.

Scanning the large prayer hall, I noticed the walls had faded murals, which told of Buddha's life story. Walking through the crowd, I looked for faces that might tell their stories. A woman wearing broken, taped-up eyeglasses and a red bandanna smiled at me, so I approached. When I explained I was a reporter, she was only interested in what news I had. Telling her what I knew, others started gathering around, asking me how and when the authorities were going to help them. Their pleading eyes and tugging hands made me feel helpless. When I asked who would be willing to be interviewed, they shook their heads and walked away.

I felt uneasy, an interloper prying into their pain, but I had to write a human-interest story from a human perspective. I am a professional, but I was afraid of what I might find and feel. Walking toward what must have once been the altar, I saw an open back door. There was a man sitting outside. The flow of fresh air drew me toward him. He had a small scruffy dog in his lap which he petted in a mechanical fashion. As I approached, I noticed a splint bandaged to his nose, and a stubby beard surrounded several stiches. Gaps from missing teeth broke up his smile, but his face was somehow alluring. I bent down, introduced myself, and told him his dog was cute.

"Thank you," he muttered, unsure of my intentions.

I told him I had come here to learn and report personal stories of those who have survived.

He stood up, shook my hand and said, "It would be an honor to tell you my story. My name is Sachi Okada." Holding his dog toward me, he added, "This is Ginger, she witnessed things I couldn't."

Sachi dragged a wooden crate closer to him and gestured for me to sit. I sensed courage in this man's voice and a certain resilience in his heart. I showed him my audio recorder; he agreed, and I began. "Okada-san, thank you so much. Can you start by telling me where you were when the tsunami hit?"

"Yes. I was driving out of Iwaki in my Corolla when I heard the tsunami warning siren. The highway was gridlocked, but I knew a gravel backroad that could get me home. I was desperate to reach my family and head to higher ground. I have a little boy, you see…"

Sachi caught himself and cleared his throat. I wasn't sure why he paused, but I saw anguish in his face, and I feared the worst.

He continued, "When I got to the top of a hill, I stopped the car and let the dust settle. There, between the naked branches of apple trees, I saw the city below."

Surprised, I asked, "You stopped your car?"

"Yes, I know. But since my home was even on higher ground, I must have felt I was safe. Maybe I was stupid, but I got out of the car. At first, I blinked. In an instant, a black wall rose up at the shoreline. Not a wave. A wall. It must have been ten, fifteen meters high. At the top of the wall, I saw a whirling spray of white mixing with the gray sky. I was lost in a trance, Miss. I just stood there watching. I saw the office building that I worked in…snap."

"Snap?" I asked.

"Yes, the wave crashing against tons of concrete, wood and glass, a second before being engulfed by a much bigger roar of the water. A blast of air slapped me, shook me out of my trance and I got back into the car. When the wave climbed the hill toward me, I saw what the monster was carrying on its back— trees, cars, houses and bodies, many flailing but some only floating."

"How did you feel at this point, Okada-san?"

Sachi looked down for a long time, then he raised his head. His chin quivered and he answered, voice cracking, "I'm ashamed to say…" He looked at me as though he was seeking understanding, "I wanted to surrender."

"That's okay," I said. Although I was deeply affected by his raw emotions, I hoped he could continue his lucid account. His despair was visible in his eyes, but he seemed to have the strength to go on. "Can I ask what happened next?"

He nodded. "The wave slowed, reached the shoulder of the road and stopped. It seemed like it was trying to make up its mind before it retreated almost as fast as it advanced. When the wave pulled back to reveal downtown Iwaki, the city was no longer there. Gone. The tsunami created a new wide beach. What used to be filled with swimmers and umbrellas, was then littered with cars, pieces of buildings and dead bodies."

I could see by the distant look in Sachi's eyes that he was struggling to continue. "Are you alright, Okada-san?"

"Yes." He shook his head and coughed. "That was when I thought of my wife, Maduri, my son, Daewon, and my parents. I sped off. A few minutes later, I heard another roar. A second bigger wave smashed into my car. It rolled me end over end in the surf before the car righted itself. I floated along maybe thirty kilometers an hour on the surface. I was rammed by debris from every direction. But the car's body and the water cushioned the blows that could have killed me. Cold water lapping at my feet, I knew I had to stay in the car as long as I could."

Sachi's steady, vivid flow of words left me speechless. I nodded.

He continued, "I saw an upended school bus shoot out in front of me. My car slammed into it and my face hit the steering wheel. It knocked me out for a moment, but I came to and felt something clogging my throat. I coughed and saw my teeth scattered on the dashboard." Sachi put his hand up and covered his mouth, then added, "I looked down and saw water rising to my knees. My car could be my coffin."

"I kicked the passenger door window out with both feet. Water rushed in as I struggled to swim out. Once clear of the car, I tried to reach the surface, but I couldn't see where it was. The swirling dark water tossed me in cartwheels. A motorcycle surged past, missing my head by inches."

I couldn't help but interrupt. "That must have been terrifying."

"You know, Miss, my world was turned upside down, yet I can remember the bike was a red Kawasaki." He let out a little laugh.

"But somehow, just as my lungs were about to burst, I bobbed to the surface. I grabbed a corner of an old wooden signboard, pulled myself up and rode it in the surf. The air reeked of diesel fuel and sewage. But I was alive."

"Heading fast into a stand of trees, with only their treetops visible, I smashed into the branches. I struggled but managed to wrap both arms and legs around a tall tree trunk as the water drove me hard against it."

I asked Sachi, "How long did you hold onto that tree?"

"I'm not sure," he responded. "I was in a daze most of the time. But when the water receded, I slipped down to the muddy ground. I was amazed to find myself close to the road that led to my house. Running through the pain, I came across a woman's body. Twisted arms and legs. Face buried in the earth. She had waist-long hair like Maduri. My heart jumped. When I reached her, I dropped to my knees. Frozen. I couldn't recognize the clothes because they were blackened by filth. For that time, the fear it might be her kept me from wanting to know."

Sachi was now bending over and looking to the ground as though he was reliving the scene. Ginger began to whine. I didn't want to interrupt him. My recorder was capturing his moving account.

"*Please. Let it not be,* I said to myself as I put my hands gently to her head. I knew I had to. I turned her toward me. The mud rolled off and I saw her face. I jerked and dropped her head. It was not Maduri, but the bruised face of a young woman, maybe a teenager. Her left eye was protruding out of its socket. I sat back on my legs and cried."

At that point, I asked Mr. Okada if he might need a break. To my embarrassment, I was the one needing solace.

Sachi looked at me and watched as I wiped tears from my cheeks. He reached out, took my hand in his. Ginger barked. I felt embarrassed, showing my emotion considering what he must have felt at the time.

Sachi nodded and continued, "When I got to where my home was, I found it still standing. 'Maduri! Mother! Father!' I shouted and sloshed through a half-meter of water. Pushing aside toppled furniture, I went from room to room. Empty. When I got to Daewon's room, I thought I heard a cry. In a corner behind a pile of furniture, I saw something move. I pulled a chest of drawers aside and, calling for my son, I saw Ginger. I bent over and picked up our mutt, still wet and shivering. Wondering how she could still be here, I kissed her nose and asked, 'Where did they go, Ginger?'"

"What did you do next, Okada-san?"

"Ginger and I headed to the municipal hospital close by my home. If they were injured, that's where my family would have gone. When I got there, the hospital building was destroyed, but there was a gathering of people, many of them badly injured. They were waiting for a military truck to take them to a shelter. I pressed through the crowd holding up…"

Sachi paused, reached into his pocket and with a shaking hand, gave me a torn photograph. He continued, "This soggy photo survived in my wallet. One person at a time, I showed them and asked if they had seen Maduri and our two-year-old boy."

"Beautiful, aren't they?" he said to me as he took back the picture. Pointing to a spot under his son's legs, he said, "Look, you can barely make her out, but there's Ginger. Daewon and her were very close." Sachi looked down at Ginger in his lap and slowly stroked her back.

"It's been a week now, Okada-san, since the tsunami struck. Can you tell me what happened to your family?"

"Yes," he nodded several times, took a deep breath, and swallowed. His face went vacant. In a matter-of-fact way, he said, "No word yet on my son or my parents and they haven't found their bodies. Maybe they're buried under rubble somewhere or floating in the sea. Only the gods know. Four days ago, they found my wife's body. She was lying in a rice field. The rats and the crows had been feeding on her. We had to have her cremated and had a respectful funeral two days ago."

"I am so sorry for your losses, Mr. Okada," I said as I felt my heart beating in my throat. I had to show the same strength he did. "How are you managing to hold on?"

"Well, I'm just living here at the shelter. They won't let Ginger inside, but I made this cardboard house for her and keep her on a rope in the back. I visit her and walk her several times a day. You know, Miss Hamada, this dog is my connection to my family. She was the last one to see them. She's waiting, too."

Sachi shrugged his shoulders, gave me crooked smile and said, "That's about it." He looked down at Ginger, took her head in his hand, moved it up and down and said, "Isn't that right, Ginger?"

We sat there for a moment, looking at each other and smiling. Then Sachi asked, "Do you have any other questions?"

"No. You have been so gracious to talk with me," I said and shut off my recorder. "Thank you so much, Okada-san, for telling me your story. I believe it will help our readers better understand this catastrophe. I will send you a copy once it gets printed."

"I'd like that," he said, standing up and bowing. "I'm going to take Ginger for a stroll now. Have a good trip back, Miss Hamada."

On the return ride to Tokyo, I mused about how to end my article, what else needed to be said. By the time I got home, I decided Sachi had already given me the ending. I got my story and a better understanding of myself.

#

Four days later

"I told you it was powerful," Kaito told her as he slid a copy of the *International Herald Tribune* onto the kitchen table. "Congratulations," he added, giving her a quick kiss on the head.

She picked it up and smiled. "Let's see if they edited the crap out of it."

Her jaw dropped. "I'll be darned. They left it clean. Also heard from USA Today. They're running it tomorrow. Got a call from *The Asahi Shimbun,* they want to run the Japanese translation and publish with my pseudonym."

"I'm so happy for you, Elizabeth," Kaito said then slumped into his chair.

She lingered on his tone of voice and studied his demeanor. "Kaito. What's the matter? You don't seem yourself this morning."

He blew out his breath. "My research proposals for an electro-biological system for predicting undersea earthquakes were denied. It's over for me, Elizabeth."

"What? Oh my god. It can't be. With thousands dying on March 11, the government doesn't want to do everything they can to prevent another Fukushima. Something's wrong here."

Kaito sat in silence. She looked at him. "I'm so sorry," she said, hugging and holding him tightly. "I get angry at government incompetence. I forgot how much this must hurt you."

They remained quiet together until Elizabeth spoke, "We'll find another funding source. In the U.S., if I have to."

"Fund a Japanese. I doubt it. The folks at the Institute on Nature and Science are the only source authorized to approve grants related to warning systems. I'm finished."

"No, you're not. Just another bump in the road. Wait a minute! You never told me why they rejected it."

"They said it just didn't fit their funding priorities, nothing to do with my research design."

"Incredible. With the hundreds of aftershocks and the public outcry for a better system, it just doesn't make sense."

"I know. The southward migration of aftershocks including one near us yesterday at 6.2 suggests an increasing risk for Tokyo."

"You think another one is imminent?"

"Not necessarily. Although most often, one quake seems to lessen the pressure for another, sometimes one can and have triggered another. It's called dynamic stress transfer." He shrugged his shoulders. "I learned all of this with years of self-study and most recently, it happened with the 2004 Sumatra earthquake. But if I remember correctly in Japan's past, there were two. The 1854 Ansei-Tokai eruption followed in the same year with the Ansei-Nankai quake. That one caused huge fatalities. And then, the 1944 Tonankai quake spawned another one a year later."

"Didn't they know that?"

"They should have. I didn't think I had to put that in my proposal. Didn't feel it was germane at the time."

"Shit! But what about the government's less than effective SeaGuard early warning system? The agency only predicted ten-meter-high waves and they hit fifty in some places, and it took 30 minutes for the alarm to sound. Why in hell would they not be open to new and better ways."

Elizabeth's phone rang. "Hold on, it's Kimmi. Let me take this."

"Thanks, Kimmi. Yeah, it ought to be in *Asahi Shimbun's* morning edition. Sure, it'll give me and you a boost of recognition for future assignments, but I'm dealing with a big problem right now." She glanced at her husband. "Kaito's grant proposal was turned down. His heart is broken, I'm afraid."

Kaito could hear Kimmi screaming through Izzy's phone.

Elizabeth handed her phone to Kaito. "She wants to speak with you."

"Kaito. I just heard the bad news, but something stinks here. Did you know the Institute falls under Nakayama's environmental ministry???"

"No. It was always under the Ministry of Science."

"I guess you missed that. They moved it in 2001 to Environment. Ever since then there's been talk of Nakayama's corruption, but nobody ever came forward. He could have gotten wind you were the research principal and killed it. I know this guy, Mika Harada, in his department who, well, I used to date. Stay put. I'm going to call him. I'll get right back to you."

Kaito handed the phone back to Elizabeth. "Kimmi's trying to help but I don't think it'll matter. She tells me my grant application actually fell two bureaucratic layers below the environmental ministry, not any longer the Science Ministry. You know who's in charge of that now?"

"That bastard, Nakayama?"

"None other," Kaito scowled. "And Kimmi suspects Nakayama may have gotten wind of it and personally killed it. I don't how he'd be involved in the decision, but if he knew it was me, I wouldn't put it past him."

"You talked about him before. Is it all just personal?"

"Much deeper than that." Kaito closed his eyes for a moment and pictured Katsu Nakayama, his rival from their early days at the university. Felt how he intentionally injured him in water polo, and how Nakayama made him out to be a cheat, got him kicked out of the university.

"So, it was personal?" she asked.

"Yes and no. He doesn't really care about people or the environment, was and still is, I believe, a corrupted minister of the environment. Wouldn't be surprised he's in collusion with corporate contractors now."

"Do you know that?"

"Based on past history, yes. You probably never heard of Minimata disease. It maimed thousands of poor fishermen and their families back in the sixties. His family's firm caused it and he is still involved in its cover-up. That's how I know he's corrupted."

"It's not right then. We have to do something to stop him."

"Never do it. He and the government have all the power."

"Hold on. Kimmi's calling back. Ok, I'll put him on." Kaito listened.

"That dirty bastard," Kimmi growled. "Mika told me your research and grant proposal was solid and approved for funding until somehow Nakayama knew about it and he rejected it, saying it was not needed."

"I'm not surprised," Kaito said, shaking his head. "Maybe he found out I was involved with the Taiji filming."

"I want to nail that asshole, Kaito. If the Japanese public only knew what a power-hungry corrupt bastard he is, they'd force him out." Her words gained in speed and pitch. "Kaito, we can beat him. We can use the media to force him out. Trust me. Liz and I will come up with a plan of attack. Put Liz back on."

Kaito shook his head, handed the phone back to Elizabeth and listened to the two of them rant and rave.

As Elizabeth was about to hang up, she looked at Kaito and said, "He's still pretty shaken up, but I'll try."

"Try what?" Kaito asked.

"Please let Kimmi and I know what you know about Nakayama. If we can find evidence to expose him, maybe we can revive your grant."

"Kaito. You've got to give me some ammunition. A lead of some sorts. We'll figure out how to take him down in the press," Kimmi said.

Kaito could only feel the sting of his father's bamboo rod. How it became Nakayama's clenched fist. "Izzy. It's past history and very complicated."

"But maybe we can paint it in a new light, uncomplicate it."

Kaito stared out the window and spoke without looking at Elizabeth. "He won't give up. He knows what I have on him could destroy his career." He mumbled. "And destroy me in the process."

"But what happened in the past might be a clue to the future."

"No. The past taught me it doesn't pay to fight the system."

"Kaito. you're smarter and a better man than he is. Truth will be on our side."

Kaito lowered his head. "Don't you understand? I failed everyone."

"You didn't fail anyone, including me. Please let me help you."

He stood up. "I can't," he said and walked out of the room, carrying the pain of his youth on his backside.

Chapter Thirty-Six
Months Later

Kushimoto, Wakayama

Pulling his weary frame up from the chair, Kaito shuffled to the front window of his now empty family home. He gazed out over the harbor, and memories of a long, contentious life washed up like flotsam after a storm. Although he continued to bear great shame for having failed to secure the grant funding, he didn't return here to hide.

At Elizabeth's suggestion and patience, Kaito considered some time and space might enable him to reconnect with his childhood dream and recover his motivation. Elizabeth had told him what Marylyn came to understand about prideful Japanese men; they sometimes need to be left alone to think and brood when facing personal problems. Kaito wanted her to come with him, but she was having a bad bout of gastro-intestinal distress and he understood why she didn't want to travel outside the home. "Go ahead," she told him. "You might get some perspective."

He agreed, realizing how Elizabeth's journeys had helped her. He would discover what was holding him back, keeping him from fighting. Besides, he had left some old files there he needed to recover.

The morning sun lit up the masts and hulls of the moored wooden fishing boats, their torn nets hanging in neglect. His heart felt heavy as he thought about how he let down the village fishermen, his father and now his country. He sighed, then caught a glimpse of the little swimming hole where he first swam with dolphins and his heart lifted a bit. Knowing too that his caring wife would soon be calling to ask about his health and spirit, he would be cheered up.

Right on time, the phone rang.

"Good morning, koija," Izzy chirped, "How did you sleep?"

"Fairly good, but I still feel tired, princess, how about you?"

"Busy. Got two interviews today. One with the Fukushima Daiichi plant manager covering their headway on containment and the Mayor of Sendai's plans for temporary housing. The tsunami and threat of another big earthquake has consumed the press and the public, even with a national election in two weeks. Have you been able to make any headway?"

"Still can't shake the feeling I let my people down."

"I can understand that considering what you went through all those years planning and all. But you can't blame yourself. Remember what Mika said. Your grant was flawless and stamped for approval until it got to Nakayama's desk."

"Little solace, I'm afraid."

"I know but it doesn't mean it wasn't and isn't important and promising."

"Yes, I still try and hold onto that."

"Good," she said. "Something will pop up. How about your spirits?"

"Still in the doldrums, I'm afraid, even after one week."

"Understandable. It's hard to believe how great vision and hard work can be shot down by the vengeance of one bad man."

"You got that right. And I keep trying to get my motivation back but keep feeling these barriers."

"Maybe who, not so much what?"

"I know, Izzy. You're right."

"You'll get back the will, Kaito. I have great confidence in you. You've done great things in the past and will again."

"Thanks, Izzy."

"Think of what you built with the dolphin lagoon, overcoming all the difficulties."

He scoffed. "We built. Even after the difficulties with Yamaguchi."

"For sure. You showed great courage holding onto your dream and fighting for its success."

"Yes, and you were and always have been my inspiration." He gazed into the distance. "You know, I was thinking—" His voice trailed off as he considered it was standing up to his father that enabled him to stand up to his boss.

Elizabeth stayed silent for a while, letting him finish his thoughts, then said, "You were thinking? Maybe your hope to help the younger generation?"

"Yes. That's it," his voice raised. "The goal. It carried me through my doubts."

"And you achieved it," she said, "With thousands of young people in Japan now advocating for the dolphins. And they're still out there for you."

"I guess."

"You'll do it again. Your dream is still waiting for you. Someday, you'll find a way to accomplish that and even more. I'm sure."

"I appreciate your faith in me."

"Absolutely. We're a team, remember? And Kimmi and your mom are pulling for you too."

"Thanks, princess. You probably ought to get to your interviews."

"Yeah, I'll call you tonight as usual. Why don't you try to get out of the house today? It's going to be a hot one. Take a swim or something."

"Good idea and make sure you eat. You seem to be losing even more weight."

"Yes, my dear. But I just don't have much of an appetite these days. Must be 'cause I'm getting older."

"Are you still having those stomach pains?"

"Aah...just once in a while." She rubbed her tummy. "Thanks for caring. Love you, my handsome hero."

"Love you too. Tonight then."

Kaito slumped back into his chair and gazed at the photos he had brought with him. He smiled at the picture of the two of them, standing on the deck of the *Umi-Kamiko*. Elizabeth's denim jacket flapped in the wind as she smiled at him with her Irish-green eyes. He closed his eyes and tried to remember how she felt next to him, how the wispy strands of her long, auburn hair tickled his face. Then he picked up the photo of him with a cadre of students in his lab class, receiving the 'Lay Teacher of the Year' award given to him by the city of Tokyo. Feeling a jolt of pride, he stood up. *I'm going swimming.*

Arriving at the shore of the little cove, Kaito could picture and almost feel his mother's hand the day she took him. He stripped down to his swim trunks and slid into the water. The caressing cool of it triggered his muscle memory and he stroked and kicked as easily as he walked on land. Suspended in that liquid dimension, he was carried back to his free and innocent childhood, one without fears.

Reaching the exact spot where he first met and swam with the dolphins, he flipped onto his back. He felt like the clouds above, floating in another blue. He closed his eyes, and he could hear the dolphins chirping among themselves as they chased the mullet fish. He was captivated once again. He wanted to learn everything about them and someday talk with them. He remembered how that dream carried him through school and into Tokyo University, on his way to becoming…

His head turned to the side as he pictured Nakayama. He gulped water and choked.

A sense of drowning came over him.

He spit out the water and swam to shore. Sitting on the sand, feeling the hot breeze on his cool skin, he shook off the fear and gazed at the open water. He could see Manami's notched dorsal swimming out at sea, and he smiled. *I will share this swim with Elizabeth.*

Returning home, he heard his phone ring. It was Kimmi.

"Yamamoto-san," she shrieked, "The coast guard in Tokyo Bay just reported a pod of dolphins swimming erratically and barking like a chorus of harbor seals."

"What?" Kaito drew a fast breath, his strong swimmer's chest expanding as he jumped over to the window. In his reflection, he saw a surge of excitement. A smile reached up to his high cheekbones. Rubbing the cracked canvas of his sea-weathered skin, he asked, "Did you see them for yourself?"

"No but wait. Maybe I can get a live news feed on my phone." Kimmi screeched, "Yamamoto-san I can see them. A dozen or more, right near the Tokyo Gate Bridge, breaching back and forth toward the shore."

"What kind of sounds are they making?"

"No idea. I'm picking it up off a mounted TV camera. There's no microphone. You've got to come see and hear for yourself!"

"Why would I do that?"

"Isn't it unusual to have wild dolphins enter the busy polluted Bay?"

"It is that," he replied, "Never seen that in my life here. They wouldn't be feeding."

"What if it's Manami and her pod, warning us of a tsunami about to strike the city?"

"Well, come on Kimmi, that's a stretch."

"Maybe, but what if it was? Think about it."

"I have. And even if it was her and her pod, do you honestly think the government, Nakayama, would say nothing more than it was pure quackery?"

"Okay he might, but there may be a way."

Kaito stayed silent.

"What if? What if, Yamamoto-san?"

"Okay," he said, "What would you want me to do?"

"Come down here and find out."

"That's crazy."

"Is it? Are you telling me the great Yamamoto-san is giving up on his dolphins, his theories, and his people? Elizabeth will never let you do that."

Kaito clenched his jaw but did not answer.

"But if it is Manami in the bay, and you match her warning call from the one she made at Miyagi, wouldn't you have proof this time?" She raised her voice. "Yamamoto-san, please, think about this and what it would mean if it was her and you ignored it."

He could only shake his head.

"Look Kaito, this is potentially a big, no seismic-size story. Trust me. If it were true, I can get the public to demand action from the government." She continued, "You need to get on the local train to Osaka first thing tomorrow morning. I'll meet you at the gate when you get off and we'll pick up the local. We can make our plans on the train and be at the Shinagawa-Tokyo station by afternoon."

Kaito didn't respond.

"Yamamoto-san, are you ready to do this or not?"

"Is Elizabeth aware of this?"

"I have call into her, but I think she's in an interview now. I know she'd want you to go. So, are you—?"

"I'm...I'm thinking." He sat down to rid himself of those always present early memories.

"There's no time to think. You've got to stop letting your past control your future."

Deru kui wa utareru rang in his ears. The sting of the rod clutched at his throat.

"Yamamoto-san, you've got to give this a chance. Remember your dreams."

He closed his eyes and nodded slowly. Kimmi knew him too well, but he wanted to talk with Izzy. "I'll let you know," he said and hung up the phone. Gazing down at the harbor, he felt the push and the pull of emotions. Feelings that always tore at his insides and often made him back down. To remember they started in his childhood didn't help. He still couldn't wipe them away.

Walking over to a cabinet, he opened a drawer. Looking inside, he said to himself, *what will I do this time?* He pulled out two CD's. One had 'OceanWorld Voices' printed on the jacket and the other had red characters scrawled on the surface in his own hand: Miyagi the day of the earthquake of 2011.

The next morning

The gentle rolling and clacking of the old local train comforted Kaito. Gazing out the window at the rice fields and black pines lining the Wakayama coast, he gained some distance from his fear. He recalled the excitement of his first train ride as he made his way to Tokyo University—over fifty years ago. Knowing he might be reunited with his old dolphin friend gave him great joy. And of course, the thought of another tsunami filled him with fear and a sense of loyalty to his countrymen and women. Elizabeth would, no doubt, encourage him to go.

A sharp bend on the tracks knocked his equipment case over. "Ow!" Kaito grabbed at his arthritic knee and righted the case. The hard reality of what he needed to do hit him. He opened the case and checked the contents, making sure he packed everything. Underwater acoustic transducer, soundwave frequency analyzer, laptop, batteries, cables—all looked good. Old CD recordings, recent flash drives? He panicked a moment, then remembered he slipped them into his backpack with his binoculars, toothbrush and personal items.

The frequency analyzer was critical. If the dolphins in Tokyo Bay were led by Manami, he would have to prove it was her and it was a tsunami warning call. He needed the exact frequency and wavelength on the screen to match the Miyagi recordings to prove these dolphins were giving another tsunami alarm. Without it, government officials would only hear a scratchy mix of clicks, whistles and shrieks. The whole thing was a long shot, but he might save millions from dying. He had to try.

"Okay, Kaito," Kimmi had said on the phone. "After we meet on the train, I've got a spot in a park under the Acqua Line Bridge across from the airport. It's pretty secluded, but a good view of the entire bay."

The train whipped up to its top speed—three hundred kilometers per hour. The G-force crackled in Kaito's ears. The colors and textures outside blended together with a watery brush. The green, terraced rice fields blurred into fuzzy rectangles and the undulating red tile roofs of the houses became pink and gray pixels. The bullet train moved effortlessly over the rail, no bump or sway as it rode the contours of the land. Kaito is suspended between the past rushing by and hurtling toward a destination programmed by the forces of nature. Light-headed, he rubbed his eyes.

Kaito stared out the window and shook his head in defeat. *If Nakayama learns it's me, he won't give up.*

The train slowed down and entered the Osaka station. As planned, Kimmi was waiting.

En route, the two discussed plans and soon they were leaving Shinagawa station, and in a taxi heading to the Acqua Line Bridge and Toriizaki Park.

#

The campground was a little pocket of greenery in the busy city, but the overhead noise of the late day traffic on the bridge was still loud. Kaito worried the ambient sound might make it hard to isolate dolphin voices in the bay. They got out of the taxi, and Kaito wheeled the instrument case around the RVs heading toward the shore. Feeling out of breath, they passed through a gauntlet of political signboards—an equal number for Kobe and Hoiki. The election for prime minister was only two weeks away.

"At least Hoiki is more pro-environment," said Kimmi.

Kaito only shook his head.

They passed a park guard sitting on a bench and looking at his smart phone.

"Will the guards let us make a recording?" Kaito asked.

"We just need to find somewhere out of view."

Soon, they found a secluded tree-lined bank above the shore that had a view of the bay. Kaito took out his binoculars. "Yes!" he shouted as he spotted the breaching dolphin pod. "They're here. Maybe one hundred meters out." He carefully climbed down to the waterline to get a better viewing angle. "They're swimming back and forth like they did in Miyagi."

Kimmi let out a 'whoop' and put up her hand for a high-five.

"Let's set up the equipment quickly," said Kaito.

Together, they wrestled the heavy case down to the water, and Kaito pulled out a directional microphone.

"Halt!" They looked up the bank and saw the guard from before.

"What are you doing?" he asked.

Holding up the microphone, Kaito answered, "We're making a recording of the harbor sounds."

"You can't be here," the guard said. "Can't you read?" He pointed to the back of a sign.

Kimmi gave the guard a sweet, innocent smile. "So sorry. We didn't see it. Please forgive our carelessness."

"No problem, Miss, but this area is restricted. No swimming, no fishing, and no access to the water."

"But sir," she pleaded. "We're not going into the water. We're only making a quick recording. This is a part of an important scientific project of great benefit to the citizens of Tokyo."

"It is not allowed. You must stop what you're doing and grab your equipment."

Kaito slumped. *Rules! You can't get around them in this society.* He glanced at Kimmi and saw a flash in her eyes.

She gave the guard a demure smile. "I'll bet you're from Tokyo."

He held his head high. "Born and bred."

"You've been with the service for some time, right?"

"Thirty-two years, miss."

"Wow! That long? You don't look a day over forty."

The man sucked in his protruding belly and smiled.

"I'm guessing you must have gone to OceanWorld as a kid."

"Sure." He wrinkled his brow. "Every kid did."

"Great. Then I bet you know who this gentleman is." She gestured toward Kaito. Following Kimmi's lead, Kaito pulled out his old director, *OceanWorld, Dolpfun and Learn Center* card and handed it to the guard.

The man studied the card, looked back and forth at Kaito and nodded. "I remember that name. I know. You were that great dolphin trainer at the old OceanWorld." He stuck out his hand and vigorously shook Kaito's. "I loved your show, Yamamoto-san. Back in the seventies, my mother used to take me every year on my birthday. So glad to meet you." He rolled back on his heels.

"You could get that talented dolphin to do anything. I loved when it waved goodbye at the end and splashed us. What was her name?"

"Manami," Kaito replied politely.

"Yes. That's her." He narrowed his eyes. "OceanWorld Tokyo is closed now. What happened to Manami?"

Kaito worried he may remember what happened to her. "She's retired now, thanks for your kind words."

"Perhaps for you it would be okay, Yamamoto-san. I'll check with my boss as soon as I finish my round." He jumped into his three-wheel cart and shouted back, "Wait here. It'll only take a few minutes."

Kaito adjusted the binoculars. "Thank the gods. The dolphins are still here. How much more time, Kimmi?"

"Based on yesterday's visit, maybe another hour, if we're lucky."

"I can't stand the wait." He rubbed his head. "I'm going to stretch my aching legs a bit and keep an eye out for the dolphins."

"Go ahead, I'll stay with the equipment."

Kaito scanned the bay while glancing back to see if the park guard returned. *If it's Manami and she's making a tsunami warning call, I need to get that recording.*

"Kaito!" Kimmi called and waved. "The park guard is pulling up in his cart."

The man lowers his head toward Kaito. "I'm deeply sorry, Yamamoto-san, but my boss says you must have a permit from the ministry of the environment to make recordings in the bay. You are welcome to apply, but until that is granted, you'll have to put away your equipment."

Kaito shook his head and immediately started packing up his case.

"Hold on, Kaito." Kimmi stared at the park guard. "Is there another part of the campground that isn't restricted?"

"No miss. You must apply online with the ministry of environment."

"Shove it!" she said under her breath.

"Let him be, Kimmi." Kaito frowned and waved his hand. "It doesn't matter. The dolphins have left. Thanks for your time, officer."

"You're welcome, Yamamoto-san. It's been a great honor to meet you. Can I give you and the lady a ride to the gate?"

"That's all right, officer. We'll walk."

As soon as the guards left, Kimmi asked, "Why did you give up so fast?"

Kaito stared straight ahead, not wanting to reply. He mumbled, "I know when I'm beaten. It's no use. What did your friend Mika at the environmental ministry really say?"

"I'm sorry, Kaito. I didn't want you to be intimidated into giving up. He said that Nakayama was already expecting that you would show up."

"How did he know that?"

"The article in Japan Times, which was about the dolphins in the Bay. I mentioned you thought they may possibly have come here to warn us of new earthquake and tsunami that could hit Tokyo. Considering the heightened public fears, it's become a big story now. There's already a clamor for you to appear."

"Wait a minute, Kimmi. I didn't give you permission to use my name suggesting it was possible."

"No, but I knew that would raise public interest and get you back involved."

"Well, dammit, it did that, but without my say. I am very disappointed in you."

"Sorry, Yamamoto-san."

"I don't think Elizabeth would have approved of your lack of professionalism."

"Sorry again, but don't think we can turn back now. I'll find another place for tomorrow. It's that important. If she returns, we can get the recording in secret."

Feeling a storm of deception, Kaito closed up the equipment case. He remembered how Nakayama corrupted the Minimata research; that same raw power of authority was engulfing him once again. He dropped his eyes to the ground and shuddered. "I don't think so. I'm going home."

"You're going home? What if your dolphin comes to Tokyo to possibly warn us?"

Kaito glared at her and wheeled the case, walking toward the entrance. "I'm calling a taxi."

"And what about the Americans? They found increased seismic activity in the Kuril and Nankai trenches, nearer Tokyo."

"Yes, but there's no indication yet and no basis for panic." He kept walking.

In a softer voice, she said, "Give it one more chance that it is Manami?"

Kaito slowed his step but continued in deep thought up the driveway.

"Look, Kaito, this could be a Nobel Prize for you, and a Pulitzer for me."

Kaito stopped in his tracks. He turned and glared at Kimmi. For the first time, he realized Kimmi might just be out for herself and her career. That same kind of gut-wrenching feeling he used to feel about Americans—that you can't trust them—engulfed him now.

When their eyes meet, Kimmi's face turned red, and she looked to the ground. The taxi pulled up.

The driver loaded the case and backpacks into the trunk. "Where to?" he asked.

Kaito felt both fear of Nakayama's power and the pain of defeat. He answered, "The Shinagawa train station. Shinkansen gate, please."

"Kaito, if I may. You're in Tokyo. Elizabeth is here. Stay with her, talk it over and let me know first thing."

Kaito scowled and shook his head.

Kimmi narrowed her eyes. "6–15 Nishi Shinjuku."

On the taxi ride to Kimmi's apartment, Kaito's anger over Kimmi's behavior continued to fester. What she did was clearly premature. But what if it was Manami warning of a quake? Staring out the window as they passed through Shinigawa, Kaito knew he had to talk to Elizabeth before he decided. Knowing he could see her now comforted him.

Kimmi spoke up. "I am sorry, Yamamoto-san. I made a big mistake."

He nodded. "You did. Several."

"I know and I shouldn't have used your name in connection with the dolphins." She lowered her eyes. "And if the dolphins never show up again, let alone warn us, it will be a waste of time."

"Were you that naïve about Nakayama, Kimmi?" Kaito growled and jabbed his finger into his seat table. "Knowing that Nakayama and I were enemies and jeopardizing any hope, no matter how remote, that Manami was in the Bay."

"I was wrong, Sir." She pointed at herself. "Too enamored and blindly believing it had to be your dolphin. Be...because what it all could mean to Tokyo."

"Right," Kaito agreed, "And possibly too eager at the prospects of getting an exclusive lead on the story."

"That, too, Sir. I admit I was overzealous in pursuit of the story. One I still believe in with all my heart."

"Well. Thanks for being truthful," Kaito offered.

"I also should have told you in advance of the story, before I filed it."

"How's that?"

"Mika found out through Nakayama's secretary that he knew you were involved with the filming of *The Gulf*. Even had pictures of you on the fishing boat."

"That son of a bitch," Kaito cursed. "He's got long arms and minions doing his dirty work."

"I know, and I'm finding out more and more about his corruption. I've got a lead on his possible corporate collusion with SeaGuard. And get this." Her eyes widened and her voice raised. "There appear to be defects in his warning system. To be verified, of course."

Kaito perked up. "That would shed light on things. Keep me informed."

The taxi slowed near Kimmi's apartment.

"No. Next block," Kimmi said, "It's number 18020."

On the good side, Kaito thought, the article stirred a lot of public interest, and all the papers are covering it now. He was also heartened by the fact that Nakayama was being forced out of the bureaucratic shadows.

The taxi pulled up. "I'm hoping you'll reconsider about tomorrow, Sir." She opened the car door.

"I'll let you know, Kimmi."

Chapter Thirty-Seven
Kaito's Apartment

Shibuya Tokyo

Entering their low-lit apartment, Kaito was surprised to find Elizabeth lying on the sofa, sleeping.

He had called her from the taxi after he dropped off Kimmi, but he hated to now wake her, maybe frighten her. He made some tea and quietly sat near her and waited. He was torn up by both Kimmi's actions and the conundrum she had boxed him into. He set his teacup in the saucer.

Izzy blinked her eyes open. Looking groggy, she attempted to rise.

"Hi Izzy-chan. Don't get up. Are you okay?"

"And not greet my lover?" she said, groaning and standing with effort.

He rushed to hug her, then settled her back onto the sofa.

"Thanks. So glad you came. I missed you so much," she said, kissing his cheek.

He kissed her back and asked, "Are you sure you're okay?"

"Sure," she said. "Just feeling tired these days. Just like you." She chuckled. "Getting old together."

"Don't I know it," he agreed, rubbing his arthritic knee.

"How'd it go with Kimmi?"

"Not so good."

"I heard, actually. She called me a short while ago and filled me in."

"What did she say?"

"How she screwed up. How sorry she was."

"What do you think?"

"It was my fault."

He stared at her; eyebrows knitted.

"She's young, Kaito, and a woman in a Japanese man's world. I taught her a lot of the tactics American investigative journalists use to, you know, open up a witness or confront a subject in order to dig up the dirt." She looked at him for understanding. "Then, I went to the States and left her alone. Think she got carried away."

He studied Elizabeth's expression. "I'd say. That's it?"

"No. I scolded her. Told her she was too personally close to and invested in the dolphins. You know, part of what you taught her. And, too close to both of us, pulling for who and what she loved dearly. She wasn't able to stay objective and stick to the facts, become an advocate. She realizes that and has agreed to run everything across my desk like I'm her editor."

"I got it," Kaito said and let out a breath.

"I think a lot of it has to do with a young woman trying to be as good as all the men. Giver her a chance. We need her now more than ever. This whole thing could turn out momentous for your countrymen and women. Maybe you can put aside your worries about Nakayama until we know what we've got." She held his chin. "Maybe you'll get to reunite with your other princess again. You need to go with Kimmi in the Bay tomorrow."

"Will you come?"

"I'd love to join you, but I don't feel too well."

"What's wrong?"

She put her hand to her stomach. "Just digestive issues. That's all. A little constipation keeps me from wanting to be too far from a toilet, let alone spend a day in the field."

"That's not good. You look more sick than you say. Are you eating well? Drinking lots of water?"

"That's part of it. I fill up quickly and feel bloated."

"I think you ought to see a doctor."

"Nah. These things usually just pass." She smiled, "Been on edge, I guess."

"It's me. Isn't it?"

"No. No," she said, "I can tell. Being in Kushimoto has helped. You're getting clearer all the time. Now, tell me about your day."

Kaito hesitated, but she put her head in his lap like the old days and said, "Come on. Tell me." After a few minutes of his talking, he realized she was asleep. He was tired too and he had a day in the Bay to look forward to.

Under an early morning drizzle, Kaito and Kimmi walked into the skateboard park with *suketo-bodos* bungee-corded to the sides of an improvised picnic cooler cart. Kimmi wore a white, faux-fur cape over punked-out, fringed shorts—a pattern of stars on the top, stripes on the bottom. Kaito laughed at her disguise.

"Ha, this outfit makes me feel young again," she replied.

He pulled the drawstring on his gray Hanshin Tigers hoodie to hide his face but flashed a big grin. "Makes you feel young. Makes me want to breakdance."

Kimmi pointed to a spot between two concrete ramps that she said were a half-pipe and a grind box. She wheeled the cart inside and they settled in under the ramps in an area shielded on three sides but with a clear view of the bay.

"How do you know about this place?"

"I used to skate a lot. My friends and I would hide here and drink beer. But tell me, Kaito, what kept you from going home?"

Scanning the bay, he said, "I decided it was too much of a coincidence. Dolphins used to come into the bay periodically to feed or just look around, but to come to the same spot two days in a row, vocalizing and breaching back and forth to the shore. Too much like Miyagi."

"That's it?" she asked.

He lowered the binoculars. "Elizabeth made me realize you're loyal to our cause."

"She is a special woman," Kimmi said, reaching into the cooler and pulling out a thermos and plastic cups. "How about some tea, Yamamoto-san?"

Kaito clutched the cup to warm his hands and smelled the soothing vapors of green tea.

"Did you have breakfast?" she asked.

"Didn't take the time."

"How about some prawn crackers? This is all I had in my apartment. They might be kind of stale, sorry."

"You go ahead," he said, slowly swirling the tea.

"You seem sort of wistful, Kaito."

"I was thinking of how I met Manami in 1967, and how her life intertwined with ours."

Kaito stood up. He scanned the bay with the binoculars, but, after a while, stared down at the shoreline.

"Kaito. You alright?"

He uses his shirt to wipe away the mist on the lenses of the binoculars and glanced at his watch.

"Maybe she'll come back to you, right here."

"Yes, but it's still early. They're not commuters, you know."

The pair sat in silence. Loud shouts rang out from above. They looked at each other. Kimmi pointed to Kaito to lie down as planned and pretend to be sleeping. "It might be Nakayama's goons."

Kimmi rushed to the entrance of the ramp to distract them. Kaito winced at the sound of a long rumble. Then a crash. He froze. Kimmi scrambled out.

"Awesome!" a voice cried out from above.

"Skaters," Kimmi said. She grabbed her skateboard. "I'm going out for a bit."

"Hey, *Hippugaru!*" Kaito heard a group of men yelling, mingled with Kimmi's voice and laughter. Then, all he could hear was the incessant rolling roar of skateboards. After eleven, Kimmi returned with her cheeks glowing from exertion and sweat glistening on her skin.

"Looks like you had some fun."

"I did," she answered, panting. "Those guys were old skating buddies of mine. They got a big kick out of seeing their *Hippugaru* again."

"What kind of name is that?"

"Yeah, embarrassing or what? When I first started skating, I spent a lot of time on my rear end, so 'butt-girl' became my nickname."

He laughed. "Do those guys know what you're doing down here?"

"Probably dope or a boyfriend. They've agreed to give me the whistle if anything looks like trouble."

For the next couple of hours, the two sat quietly. Kimmi checked her messages and texts.

"It's almost noon," she said, "And I've gotten six messages from my boss. The campaign for prime minister is heating up. He wants me to look into PM Kobe's connection to a right-wing educational group. I told him I may have a bigger story. Heh! I'm starving. They've got one of those cool *Nichirei* vending machines up by the restrooms. Can I get you something?"

"No thanks."

"Why do you think they haven't shown up yet?"

"I'm suspecting food. A dolphin needs forty pounds of protein daily. Considering they had to travel over one hundred kilometers out of the bay to find their 'vending machine', they deserve a break, don't you think?"

"Sure. Sorry, Kaito. And this animal hasn't eaten anything substantial since last night."

Soon, Kimmi is back holding two steaming hot dogs and a large cup of fragrant French fries.

"Whoa. I thought you said they only had a vending machine?"

"Hah! Kaito, we're not in Kushimoto. Our machines can thaw frozen foods, microwave and dispense them before your eyes. Try it."

"Thanks." He chomped the dog down in four bites. "Not bad." He checked his watch.

"I'm sorry, Yamamoto-san. I worry Manami may not even be out there."

"You shouldn't be." He laid his binoculars in the case and placed his hand on his chest. "We'll hang in there as long as we can."

Kimmi smiled, flicked the tears off her cheeks, and kissed Kaito on the forehead.

A rolling rumble and a sharp crack signaled the return of the skaters. Kimmi jumped up and checked to see if her old friends had come back.

Cursing, she ducked back in. "I saw a couple of guys—stiff looking characters in raincoats—walking around. Could be narcs, but they could be Nakayama's goons." She grabbed her skateboard and kneepads. "Maybe you could put a skateboard under your arm and lie down like you're sleeping. I'll get a closer look."

Kaito kept an ear out for voices and watched the bay brighten up. The constant rolling of the skateboards made him uneasy, but he trusted Kimmi's ability to care for herself.

Kimmi poked her head in. "They're leaving. I heard one guy talking into his mobile. He said, 'It looks clear, let's make the other rounds.'" She frowned. "Have you seen any dolphins yet?"

"Nothing."

"Too bad." Kimmi pressed her lips together. "But I have a feeling those guys will be back." She reached into the cooler. "I'm better prepared today. I picked up a couple of bento boxes." She opened the cover of the first box, then sniffed appreciatively. "This one's got salted salmon with tamagoyaki and pickled apricots." Laying it down between them, she opened the second box. "Or, you could have the grilled eel?" She pointed at the compartments, "It comes with *gyoza* dumplings and pickles."

"I'd like the eel." Kaito split his chopsticks apart and dug in.

Kimmi's phone rung. Kaito overheard a male voice shouting through her phone.

When she was finished, she shrugged it off saying, "Just my boss bugging me."

"The fog has almost lifted," Kaito said. After a long look out at the bay, he gestured to Kimmi. "Come and have a look at this. You've got younger eyes than I do. See that line of boats just past the airport, to the right of the bridge? They look like coast guard cutters. Can you see what they are doing?"

She looked. "I see men on the deck holding up long poles."

"That's what I thought. That son of a bitch, Nakayama. When the park guards told him about me trying to record them, he ordered the coast guard to use banger pipes to keep the dolphins out of the harbor area."

"What?" Kimmi said.

"Remember I told you how the fishermen at Taiji used the pipes to frighten them and jam their echolocation abilities so they could herd and capture them?"

"He would go that far?"

"Against me, yes."

Kimmi furrowed her brow. "Is it that personal?"

"It's much bigger than that. He'll do anything to keep me from getting a story out there. He's corrupted and afraid of being exposed."

"Kaito, what are you not telling me?"

He looked to the ground. "Nothing."

"Come on, Kaito. I'm an investigative reporter. If you have something hard on Nakayama, it will help if you let me work it. With Liz's permission of course. I can't..."

Kimmi's phone rang again, but she hesitated to pick it up. On the fourth ring, she looked to see who was calling. "Shit! It's my boss's boss—the managing editor."

"Go ahead," Kaito said. Kimmi raised the phone to her ear and walked outside. Kaito wished Elizabeth could be with him. He wanted to hear her wisdom again, hear how her deep faith would inspire him. Yes, he could see her warm green eyes reaching into him. He worried about what was going on behind them.

Kimmi hung up just as Kaito shouted. "I got it!" He reached into the cooler and opened his case. He shuffled frantically through the instruments, then jumped up, holding a CD in the air. "I've got it! Manami's signature voice. My early 'conversations' with her when she was in OceanWorld, and later in Miyagi. I made a mix. There's a chance. Go see if it's clear out there."

"Okay, but I've got to tell you something. The managing editor told me if I'm not back in the office by tomorrow morning, I'm fired."

Kaito gently put both hands to the sides of Kimmi's face. "Please, Kimmi. See if you can hold him off for now. This may be our only chance."

Kimmi nodded and headed outside while Kaito started connecting the recorder and hydrophone to the battery.

"The coast is clear. What are we doing?"

"It's a long shot, but if Manami and her pod are not too far away, it's possible she will hear and recognize her own voice and my commands from the recording."

"You mean she could hear through the sound of banging poles?"

"I know our chances are slim, but these distinct sound frequencies travel far through the water. Given a dolphin's acute hearing and memory, she could follow the sound to its source."

"She and her pod would swim under the boats?"

"She could easily, if she knows it is my voice and believes I am here." Kaito handed Kimmi the hydrophone and they hurried toward the shore. "You know, Elizabeth used to tell me you have to let the forces come together. She called it synchronicity."

At the shoreline, Kaito dropped the crackling hydrophone into the water, inserted the CD, and started the transmission. "From up here, you won't hear much, but the sound travels many kilometers down the bay. We need to be patient and let the recording play. Can you keep checking the park for Nakayama's men?"

"Right away, Yamamoto-san." Kimmi gestured with a salute and left.

The coast guard boats pulled away. *A good sign*, Kaito thought. Maybe Nakayama had figured he's done the job.

Binoculars fixed to the head of the Bay, Kaito spotted some splashing at the surface.

"Kimmi, quick. Look just to the right of that tugboat approaching from the direction of Disneyland, Tokyo." He pointed and handed her the binoculars. "What do you see?"

She changed the focus. "I'm not sure, maybe you're right, but I can only make out a patch of rough water."

Kaito took back the binoculars. "Looks like maybe a dozen or so dolphins. Hold on...I can't seem to...Yes, wait. I saw some breaching."

"They're coming fast. Maybe only fifty meters out. Wait. Yes! It's her, Kimmi, the one in the lead. I can make out her notched dorsal. She must have waited till the pole-banging stopped."

"How do you know?"

Twenty meters.

Ten meters.

Kaito bent down, took off his shoes, and walked into the water.

Kimmi shouted, "Careful, Kaito."

"Come on in," he said, standing up to his knees in water, splashing it like a little boy.

Only a few meters away in the shallows, Manami stopped. She poked her head up, squealing and clicking.

"Yes, it's me." Kaito gestured for her to come closer.

She nodded her head and splashed her fluke. Behind, her family circled, watching the action with curiosity. Kaito moved waist-deep into the water. Manami swam up to him. Kaito gave her a hand signal, and she rolled over and exposed her almost white, but scarred underside. Kaito laughed and gave her a belly rub.

"Good girl, good girl, nice to see you again, my friend."

Manami clicked up a storm and nodded her head.

Kaito wiped the tears streaming down his cheeks. "Kimmi. Come, meet Manami."

When Kimmi reached them, Manami rolled upright and backed off. Her pod family made a nervous retreat.

"No, girl. It's okay," Kaito said and flipped his hand over. Manami returned, once again exposing her underside.

"Just like this, Kimmi." Kaito showed her how to use the palm of her hand in a shaking motion, just how he had showed Izzy years ago.

Kimmi felt her rubbery skin.

Manami chirped at her touch.

Kimmi watched Kaito. "Kaito, I've never seen you cry like that before."

Letting the tears flow around his smile, he said, "It's been a long time. I can hardly wait to tell Elizabeth."

He slapped the water with his right hand and Manami turned over and faced him. "Ladies. We've got work to do."

Kaito gave Manami the 'swim out' hand signal, pointed into the bay and swept his arm. Manami nodded and swam out some fifteen meters, a pool length away. She swam back toward the shore and flipped over for another belly rub.

"No, no, girl!" Kaito gestured with his open hand, shaking head. He repeated the swim out signal. Manami went further out, joined by her pod, and looked back. Stopping, she turned around and began singing a song she learned at OceanWorld.

Kaito stood, shivering with frustration in the cold water. She always sang that song after completing the three-hoop jump. Manami returned and looked for a command.

"What's wrong, Kaito?"

"She's totally distracted now."

For several moments, Kaito stood in silence. Then, he turned to Kimmi. "Can you go into my case and pull out the CD marked Miyagi?"

Waiting, he gave Manami the hold on signal.

He took the CD and inserted the recording of the Miyagi warning call into the recorder on the shore. Through the line, it began broadcasting to the hydrophone in the water. He placed his hands on his ears and told Manami to listen. When she seemed to recognize it, he gestured for her to swim out.

Manami dove. Kaito kept gesturing for her to go further until she was about twenty-five meters out. He pulled out the Miyagi CD and put in a blank and turned the receiver to record.

Looking at Kimmi, he said, "Check the park for the men."

Kimmi ran to shore and around the ramp for a view of the area. While Kaito adjusted the receiver, Kimmi shouted down, "That same black SUV just pulled into the parking lot."

Kaito waved to her and turned back to his instruments. "I'm getting her signal now. She understands! She's barking, just as she did at Miyagi." He adjusted the controls. "But I'm getting a lot of ambient bay traffic mixed in." He looked up. "Kimmi, can you see if the dolphins are breaching?"

"They are, yes."

"Good. We have to wait. I've given Manami the clear signal. Take some photos with your mobile and make sure there's a date and time stamp on them."

Kaito whistled across the water and pointed to his ears. Manami acknowledged with a nod and a series of chirps.

He gave Manami the 'wait for a new command' hand signal. She nodded. He waited then gave her the 'your turn to talk' motion with his hands. Minutes passed.

"Kaito. Kaito!" Kimmi shouted down. "I got the photos, but a goon is back. He's using binoculars and might have spotted the dolphins. He's alone and on the phone for now, but I also see a coast guard boat heading our way."

He glanced up. "I need more time." After pressing the headphones to his ears, he watched the soundwave pattern on the screen.

"Kaito." Kimmi's voice turned to a whisper. "The guy is now walking around the perimeter. He could reach our ramp in a couple of minutes."

"Come on, come on," Kaito said to himself. Hand shaking on the dial, he felt the pressure building. "Wait, we've got it. She's giving us the real thing." He ripped off his headphones, laid them on the ground, and looked up. No Kimmi.

He hurried to the edge of the ramp and peeked into the park. There was Kimmi walking with a tall man in a tan raincoat. Kaito cursed and headed back to the shore. He picked up the instruments and put them into the picnic cooler and attached his skateboard to the cart. Putting on his shoes, he peeked out again for Kimmi. There she was, standing close to the man alongside the restroom building, still holding her skateboard.

As the coast guard boat neared, the pod disappeared. Kaito let out a sigh and pulled the hoodie over his head. He grabbed the picnic cooler cart and rolled it out to the edge of the ramp.

Whack! A skateboarder landed on the ramp above him and Kaito's heart skipped a beat, but there was no pain this time. Kimmi and the man disappear behind the building.

His knees shook and hurt, but he walked briskly to Kimmi's car, then realized she had the keys. Waiting, he felt for the first time his wet, cold legs. He shivered. Finally, Kimmi reappeared on her skateboard, moving fast toward the car. Kimmi stopped next to Kaito, panting. She caught her breath. "Did you get the recording?"

"I think so."

Kimmi gave him a tentative smile, looked back into the park and opened the trunk. They lifted the cart and skateboards inside and jumped into the car. She was shaking too.

As she drove the Corolla out of the park, she seemed unlike her usually perky self. "How did you divert that guy's attention?" he asked.

"Well, let's just say I investigated his manliness."

Kaito said hastily, "All right, I don't need the details. But thank you. I couldn't have done this without you."

"At least we've got our story now."

Kaito shook his head. "It's only a good first step. I've got to analyze the data and make sure the recordings line up before we have clear proof. And you've got to get your editors behind you for a story."

They drove on in silence. Kaito let out his breath, believing the goons didn't see them.

"What?" asked Kimmi. "Don't you think that you can do it?"

"It's not that. It's Manami. I didn't give her the 'good show' sign. Didn't say goodbye to my close friend of fifty years. I'll probably never see her again, and I just took off."

"Sorry, Kaito."

"Brought back memories, that's all." He sighed, thinking of how he left her once before. Sad that she was gone from his life.

"I know. Those are what keep Yamamoto-san going."

"Right, and we've got a lot more work to do."

Chapter Thirty-Eight
Nikko Hotel

Tokyo, Japan
7 a.m.

Kaito sat at the hotel room desk, headphones pressed against his ears. He intently listened, trying to match the two dolphin recordings. His eyes slowly closed as sleep took hold of him, once again.

The phone rang. He jerked awake. Slowly, he reached for the phone, but his stiff fingers dropped it.

"Kaito, did I wake you?" Kimmi said. "I'm sorry."

"Hold on," he replied, rubbing his hand together. "I was just trying to—" He pushed his fingertips against his pulsating temples, looked at the equipment in front of him, and remembered. "I still don't have the match between Manami's warning call at Miyagi and Tokyo."

"Oh no. Our meeting with the managing editor is at nine. Without proof, there's no chance of a story."

"Evidence, Kimmi, evidence. But no, I don't have it *yet*."

"What happened? I thought you recorded Manami's call yesterday."

"I did and I swear I heard her making the same chirp, chirp, squeal, click repertoire she made on the Miyagi recording, but—" He reached over to the spectrometer and advanced the recording again.

"But what?"

"They have to match up exactly. I worked on it until after midnight and I'm still at a loss." He rubbed his hands together. "Something's wrong with the recording, or me. Maybe it's my old software interface. I don't know. Feels like I'm losing my touch. Without identical wave lengths and frequencies, we can't say Manami may possibly be warning of a tsunami slamming into Tokyo."

"But our meeting's in two hours."

"Can't you put it off?"

"I can't. Hamasaki is a hard ass. Barely gave us this chance."

Kaito sighed. "If I don't get it by eight-thirty, you'll have to meet without me." He waited for her response, wondering if she is doubting herself, or him. "Kimmi. You can handle it. I'll call you when I have it together."

"I—I can't."

"You'll do fine. Call Elizabeth. She'll give you some pointers." He toggled a button on his laptop. "I've got to get back to this. Call me after the meeting. Sorry." He clicked off.

10:35 a.m.

Kaito blew a warm breath into his hands, steeled his nerves and, once again, fine-tuned a dial on the spectrograph. Two neon green lines rippled on the screen and merged. The phone rang but he ignored it. Placing his other hand on top of the one shaking on the dial, he steadied it. "Hold on," he said to himself as he carefully twisted the dial. The snaking green lines came together in an electronic hiss and overlapped perfectly.

"Yes." He dropped his hand from the dial, wiped the sweat from his forehead and picked up the phone.

"Hi Kimmi. How did it go?"

"Pretty good. Hamasaki was skeptical, but he said he will meet with you. He can't promise a time, but he's willing to squeeze you in between production meetings."

"Congratulations, I knew you could do it."

"How about you, did you match the recordings?"

He tapped his aching fingers on the desk, still worrying he might not be able to duplicate the match in the meeting. "I think so."

"Kaito. You don't sound very confident. Will you be able to demonstrate it?"

Kaito stared in a daze at his equipment. It seemed to be in good order, but too many years had passed since he used it.

"Kaito." She raised her voice. "What's the problem?"

He clenched his jaw, worrying about his growing lack of fine motor control. "Technical glitch, that's all. Don't worry, I'll have it. Tell me about the meeting."

"Hamasaki's very leery about getting *The Times Herald* involved. You know, possibly inciting an evacuation based on a warning from a dolphin. But he told me I could have the lead if we can develop the story, reporting directly to him."

"Did you tell him you witnessed Manami in the Bay?"

"Of course. But he said the government will use their own evidence. They consider their current warning system completely reliable."

"What about our evidence?" Kaito asked.

"I went through everything, Kaito. He's keeping an open mind, but he's very skeptical. At first, he wouldn't even consider a meeting."

"What happened then?"

"I followed Liz's advice and it worked. Told him Nakayama must be trying to stop you and squash any story."

"Try to catch the bigger fish, I guess."

"Yes. When I showed him my pictures of the Coast Guard boats keeping the dolphins out of the harbor, that changed it. Hamasaki knew that if the boats were ordered under top-level authority, it was at least a lead worth pursuing."

Kaito dreaded an open battle with Nakayama but knew it might come to one. "Guess we've got to connect those dots."

"Right, can you get here by noon and set up for a one o'clock?"

"I...I think so."

#

As planned, Kaito called Elizabeth after his quick lunch of pocky sticks. He had to keep it short.

"How did it go?" She asked.

"It didn't, yet."

"Oh no," she groaned.

"I mean, I had a hard time matching the recordings, but I think I have it now. Had to put the meeting off until this afternoon."

"What's going on, do you think?"

"Typical stuff, that's all. How are you feeling?"

"My stomach's a bit sore, but then I finally went to the bathroom. So, I'm good."

"But I thought you said you were going to go in for a checkup. You hardly eat anything these days, and those stomach pains..."

"I already saw the doctor; he did some tests and I'm waiting for the results. I'll let you know."

"Did he say anything? Any idea about your pains?"

"Not yet."

"Glad you went and hope you're all okay. I better sign off now. See you tonight, princess."

Kaito gathered his equipment and materials, wheeled the cart down the elevator, out the lobby and across the street to the *Times Herald* building. By the time he reached the newspaper's conference room, his hand felt glued to the handle. He fumbled to tuck in his shirt before opening the door.

Swinging it open, he froze. The young woman sitting at the table wore horn-rimmed glasses, a business suit, and her hair was bound in a tight bun. She was barely recognizable.

Kimmi chuckled. "Sorry, Kaito, today I can't be your skateboarder bud."

"I know," Kaito mumbled as he rolled the equipment case to the conference table. To not appear disabled, he slowly, methodically, unloaded the spectrometer, battery, laptop, and CDs on the table. He fidgeted with the connections, then pointed and nodded at each part of the setup. Grabbing a technical manual, he sat and exhaled deeply.

Kimmi asked, "Is everything in order?"

He gave her a stiff shrug. "Just double-checking."

"Kaito, once you get those spectrograms up, he'll see the two warning calls match up, right?"

"Aha! Yamamoto-san," Managing Editor Hamasaki said as he barged into the room, followed by a bespectacled elderly gentleman. He bowed deeply at Kaito. "And this is our science editor, Mr. Yuri. I want him to closely analyze your findings."

Getting up to return the bow, Kaito stumbled.

"So pleased to finally meet you," the editor said.

Kaito bowed again. "I am honored to meet you and Mr. Yuri, and thanks for giving us this meeting."

"My pleasure, sir. Might I say, as a boy in my teens, I caught many of your dolphin shows at OceanWorld and I must admit, I was very sad when you and Manami left."

"Thank you again, Hamasaki-san, many more were *happy* when I left."

"Yes, it was controversial." Hamasaki agreed with a chuckle. "But that's what makes great press and I'm glad you're still making waves." He lowered his voice. "Sorry, no pun intended."

"None received." Kaito smiled and pointed to the equipment. "May we begin?"

Hamasaki nodded.

Kaito held up two CDs. "This first recording was made at Miyagi during that April 2010 minor earthquake and tsunami that preceded the major Tohoku 2011 tsunami. The second recording here, was made in Tokyo Bay yesterday with Miss Matsuda as a witness." He nodded in Kimmi's direction. With trembling fingers, he inserted the second disk into the instrument. "Now, when I play these two recordings on the spectrograph, you will be able to hear the similarity and see the two identical soundwave patterns line up."

He held a finger above a red button. "Ready?"

Hamazaki and Yuri leaned in closer and listened intently to the rapid clicks and chirps. Green lines resembling jagged mountains and deep valleys shot across the screen. The screen frizzled, popped, and went blank.

Kaito poked at his pockets, found a second pair of reading glasses, and frantically flipped through the technical manual. Putting his nose to a page and finger to a line, he tried to laugh. "The gain control's so counter-intuitive." He jabbed a key.

Hamasaki and Kimmi looked at each other.

Another pop and the display lit up. The jagged green lines of the two sonograms slowly begin to ripple and move toward each other. Kaito fine-tuned a dial. The two sonograms snapped together and overlayed perfectly.

Kaito held up a finger and smiled. "That identical sound could only be duplicated by that one animal."

"I'll be dammed," Hamasaki said and leaned back in his chair. "But how do we know what the squeaks and clicks mean? How can you say those translate into words that humans can understand?"

Kaito reached for another CD and glanced at Mr. Yuri to gauge his reaction. "This is only one recording of hundreds of vocal interactions, communications if you will, between Manami and me over fifteen years of training. This was just the start of a planned major dolphin language-decoding project."

Hamasaki nodded to Kaito. "Let's get to it."

Feeling rattled, Kaito faltered, "Stay with me, please. These vocalizations came directly from her experiences and behaviors in the pool in her own language. This is nothing like what the Americans did with Koko the gorilla, teaching her *human* sign language."

"Okay, but how does what she said in the pool translate into a tsunami warning?"

Kaito nodded. "Because whenever Manami encountered something wrong with the pool water, either being too hot or too chemically treated, she made the same exact combination of sounds which you heard. It meant 'bad water'."

"Okay." Hamasaki probed, "But bad water could mean other things, like, say, pollution."

He looked at Kimmi, then at Kaito. "But how on earth could she detect and know it is an approaching tsunami?"

Hamasaki listened intently as Kaito filled him in on how, prior to an undersea earthquake, the rubbing of the adjoining rocks of the tectonic plates changes water molecules into hydrogen peroxide.

Turning to Mr. Yuri, the editor asked, "Okay Yuri, what's your assessment?"

Kimmi leaned in. Kaito straightened in his chair.

"Well, sir, my analysis tells me the dolphin's recent behavior in Tokyo Bay is something much more than a coincidence."

Kimmi relaxed her shoulders and sighed. Kaito sat motionless.

"However, as a scientist, I cannot objectively extrapolate further in terms of what the dolphin calls actually mean, when or where the tsunami will occur, let alone understand the animal's motivations—if it has them. So, I'm afraid I can't give you what you're looking for." He took off his glasses, blew on the lenses, and cleaned them with a cloth.

Kimmi looked to Kaito and silently mouthed, "No, no."

Kaito held his hand up to her.

Hamasaki jabbed his finger hard on the table in front of Yuri. "Are you saying you believe we have no basis to ask for a government response?"

"Well, sir," Yuri said, sitting up straight. "Dolphins were trained by the U.S. Navy in the Iraq war to disarm mines and plant explosives on enemy divers in the Straits of Hurmuz." He nodded to Kaito. "It is not inconceivable that Kaito's dolphin is warning of an impending tsunami." He held up his index finger. "Now, what you do with that…" he raised his voice…"*possibility,* is beyond my expertise."

Kaito let out a breath.

Hamasaki jumped in. "Okay, Yamamoto-san. I agree with Mr. Yuri. What you've presented is plausible and interesting future science, but I need facts for a story, and we simply don't have enough of a solid case to bring it forward, yet." He gave a polite smile. "Your hypothesis is simply non-verifiable at this point." He jabbed his finger on the table. "*The Times—Herald* cannot publish conjecture like this and possibly incite the public to panic without thorough government and scientific review."

Kaito raised his hand, and voice. "What kind of panic do you think will happen when the tsunami actually comes, and we have only twenty minutes warning! That's all Nakayama's current warning system, can give. It's an imperfectly designed and limited system."

He stood and slapped his hand down hard on the file in front of him. The table shook. "We're talking about giving *days* of warning here and saving thousands of lives!"

Hamasaki pushed his chair away from the table.

Kaito realized his outburst had spooked the editor. Red in the face, his knees shook, and he slumped back into his chair.

Kimmi's eyes turned down.

"Look," Hamasaki said. "I understand, Yamamoto-san, you have had conflicts with Minister Nakayama in the past, but personal vendettas aren't sufficient cause to launch an investigation."

"It's not about a vendetta," Kaito argued tersely.

"Okay, Yamamoto-san, but I need something concrete to go on. If I were to go to Nakayama with your recordings and theory, you know what he will do." He glared at Kaito. "He will discredit you."

Kaito blew out a breath and nodded.

The editor narrowed his eyes. "You not only need proof your dolphin's call was a warning, but you need sources, witnesses, and material proof that he personally ordered those boats to stop the dolphins. And a verifiable reason that explains why he would stonewall your dolphin warning. Without that, we have nothing."

Kaito kept his head down.

Kimmi answered, "We will get that, sir."

Kaito glared at Kimmi, wondering why she would put herself out on a limb like that. He had not given her what he knew about Nakayama. Even if he told her, it would not be enough to prove his current corruption.

Hamasaki closed his notebook. "Until you have something concrete, I have a major election to cover."

Kaito mumbled. "The dolphin knows more than we know, and cares more than we do."

Both Kimmi and Hamasaki stared at Kaito.

Kaito whispered, "But only nature can show us the way."

Hamasaki stood. "We're done here."

"Please, sir," Kimmi pleaded.

A loud clacking of high heels echoed down the hallway. There was a knock on the conference room door. It opened a crack. A frightened woman said, "So sorry to disturb you, sir."

"Yes, Tamiko. What is it?"

Hamasaki's secretary said, "I think you need to see this." She passed him a piece of paper.

He read the note.

Hamasaki slid the paper across the table to Kimmi and said, "A 6.9 earthquake has been reported 60 miles off the Hokkaido coast. We can pick up after I check into this report."

Both of them looked to Kaito with a mix of fear and respect in their faces.

Kaito squared his shoulders. With the style and poise of a former high diver, he spoke calmly, "It's probably only a strike-slip quake. Not the big one."

Yuri stood up. "I'll check into it, sir."

Kaito looked across the conference table and sensed Kimmi's slipping confidence in what he had said.

Kaito hoped the surprise announcement of the 6.9 quake in Kamamoto might make the newspaper better appreciate the gravity of situation facing Tokyo.

"Let us know what you find," Kaito said as Hamasaki and Yuri bolted from the conference room to get details on the quake. The heavy paneled door slammed shut, leaving Kimmi looking at Kaito for an explanation. Kaito leaned back in his chair. "I don't think that this quake will result in a tsunami."

"How do you know?" Kimmi asked, eyes wide.

392

"Kimmi, I've been paying close attention to undersea quakes for many years now. Kamamoto's far from the Japan Trench and Tokyo and not where my dolphins called the alarm. It will likely cause some interior structural damage, but hardly a tsunami."

Kimmi let out a long breath. "Then we're exactly where we last left it. Hamasaki will want to know if we have any leads as to why environmental minister Nakayama wants to stop the public from knowing about the dolphins. The dolphin warning is connected to your past with Nakayama and his goons and the current warning system. Kaito, we need the basis for the whole story. What are you not telling me?"

Kaito averted his eyes.

Kimmi reached over and took his hand.

He pulled it away.

"Look, Kaito, we may only have weeks or even days before a tsunami might hit land right here. It's my battle too. You can trust me."

"You're right about the timing. The plates could be shifting fast or slow."

Kaito lowered his voice. Kimmi leaned closer. "I have good reason to believe the builder and operator of the current tsunami warning system, SeaGuard Shokan, has made bribes to Nakayama." He swallowed hard. "And he knows I would know."

Kimmi's eyes widened. "Can you prove it?"

"I'm sure Elizabeth will confirm, your best chance to prove it is to follow the money trail."

The conference room door swung open, and Hamasaki came back into the room.

"I have confirmed the 7.0 quake in Kamamoto did not produce a tsunami." He nodded at Kaito. "The government issued a tsunami warning twenty minutes after the quake hit with a projected wave of one meter. They lifted it an hour later with no wave. The strike-slip earthquake did only minor structural damage."

Kimmi smiled and extended her hand toward Kaito. He gave her a slight nod.

She asked, "Kaito, anything to add?"

"Only to say that the current system isn't infallible, and of course can only give minutes warning, not days."

"That's the big picture, all right," Hamasaki added, "And in the short term, that quake shook us into pursuing, very carefully, the possible Tokyo dolphin warning."

Kimmi straightened her back in surprise and said, "Yes, and besides, we need to look into Nakayama's dolphin cover-up. I have a promising lead on the Minister's corruption."

Hamasaki bent forward. "Just a minute, Matsuda. Proving corruption at that level is serious stuff, but you may be interviewing Nakayama sooner than you expected."

Kimmi and Kaito stared at each other in surprise.

"Yes. We just learned that the International Olympic Committee and several member nations, including the U.S., have made formal requests to the central government. They are worried about the safety of thousands of athletes, coaches and guests attending the approaching 2020 summer games, they are demanding a thorough review of all earthquake warning systems and evacuation plans within thirty days. We're awaiting comments from Prime Minister Kobe and maybe even from his challenger."

Kimmi raised her hand. "That means millions of Tokyo residents living in low-lying areas will also want their own assurances."

"Exactly," Hamasaki said, "And I've already put in a request for you to interview the environmental ministry. Matsuda, you may be able to work that new angle, but be very careful, Nakayama's a powerful, influential man. If we can find evidence that he tried to stop the dolphin warning, maybe we'll have a story. In the meantime, I have to put a paper to bed, if you want, I can come back later this afternoon."

As Hamasaki headed out the room, Kimmi said, "We'll let you know if we have anything else." She turned to Kaito. "Do you mind hanging out here for a while? I want to make a couple of phone calls. I'll be back."

Within minutes of Kimmi leaving, Kaito buried his head in his arms and fell asleep on the conference table.

Soon, he felt a nudge on his elbow, heard a muffled voice, and he raised his head.

"You okay?" Kimmi asked.

He stretched out his arms with a wince and a groan. "Getting old, I guess. Any luck in researching Nakayama's finances?"

She smiled and flipped through her notebook. "You won't believe it, and I'm just getting started. Once I found his dummy corporation, the money trail led to a treasure. He's got a ski chalet in Hokkaido and a penthouse on New York's upper west side, a yacht moored at the Yokohama Bayside Marina." She took a deep breath. "And, a Swiss bank account, all on a minister's relatively modest annual salary of twenty million yen. Shit, the yacht alone cost several times that." She flipped another page in her notebook and showed it to Kaito. "Here's his net worth so far."

Kaito looked at the almost three-billion-yen figure and shook his head. "Good work, Kimmi. Don't think it's from his father's bankrupt businesses either."

"Yeah, but unless we can tie that to bribes, we won't have a story. But Hamasaki's will have to decide and he's on his way here as we speak."

Hamasaki entered with a bouncing gait and focused his eyes on Kimmi. "Good news. Nakayama has agreed to give you a half-hour at three-thirty tomorrow. See if you can crack him, Matsuda. Find out if he's trying to cover up the dolphin warning."

Kimmi nodded. "Working on it, sir."

"All right, Matsuda," Hamasaki said. "After you get the minister's views on the Olympic Committee request, you can ask him about the dolphins in the bay."

Kimmi jumped in. "And his connection with SeaGuard Shokan."

Hamasaki narrowed his eyes. "You better be careful, Matsuda. What's the angle?"

Kimmi took a deep breath. "The possibility that he may have taken bribes from the builder and operator of the current cabled tsunami warning system."

"Based on what?" Hamasaki inquired.

Kimmi pointed to her notebook. "I've found that he's got a tycoon's lifestyle on a bureaucrat's salary. His net worth is over three billion."

Hamasaki held up his hand. "That is a serious charge, Matsuda. Nakayama is highly respected in Japan. An Olympic athlete, founder of a major children's charity and a big supporter of the LDP party. Better tread carefully until your findings are irrefutable."

Kimmi tightened her suit collar. "I understand, sir."

Hamasaki stood. "Have a draft of your story to me by six tomorrow. Thank you and good day, Yamamoto-san." He bowed and left the room.

Kimmi held her palm up to Kaito for a high-five.

Kaito shook his head and patted her open hand. "You're not skateboarding, Kimmi. We've got work to do."

"Like sniffing out the money trail."

"Yes, but that might be hard to prove in the short term."

"Of course, but what are you saying?"

"Can we trust your friend Mika at the environmental ministry?"

"I think so. Elizabeth reminded me we need an insider to corroborate what we've been assuming. Confirm if Nakayama personally ordered the coast guard to keep the dolphins out of the bay."

Checking for Mika's phone number, Kimmi added, "Elizabeth also wanted me to find out if Nakayama has a cozy relationship with the CEO of SeaGuard Shokan and to look for any budget abnormalities. If Mika finds anything, we might use it in the interview with Nakayama tomorrow."

"Good work, Kimmi. I'm going home to check on Izzy. She hasn't been too well lately."

Chapter Thirty-Nine

On the morning before her appointment at St. Lukes International Hospital in Koto, Elizabeth decided to make a few difficult phone calls.

First, she dialed Kaito's mother. "*Okaasan*. How are you? It's Elizabeth."

"Of course, my dearest daughter. How are you?"

"Well, I have some not good news to share with you. I have epithelial ovarian cancer."

"Elizabeth. No!" she shrieked. "How bad is that?"

"Pretty bad. I'm going to the hospital for a PET scan this morning."

"So the doctors aren't sure?" Noriko asked, her voice wavering.

"No, they're quite sure. Only not how long. Think I'll be saying sayonara soon."

"Elizabeth, why do you talk that way?"

"To make me accept things, I guess."

"Does Kaito know?"

"No. And that's why I'm calling. How do you think he'll react when I tell him?"

"Oh my, Elizabeth. Can't it be treated?"

"Doubtful. The cancer is in stage four. Spread throughout my abdomen, even in my liver and lungs. Seems surgery and chemo would only prolong the inevitable. I'm trying to face it now and get ready."

Okaasan started to cry.

"Please, Mother, can I ask what you think Kaito would do?"

"He'll be devastated. Do everything he can for you. Care for you every minute. He loves you so much."

Elizabeth sighed. "I thought so. Just wanted to be sure."

"But Elizabeth, can I do something?"

"No. You've already given me a lot. I'll let you know. I'm going to fill Kaito in tonight. I'd love to see you and say goodbye at some point."

Noriko sniffled. "This is so sad."

"No crying now, Mother. I'm trying to make it not be sad. I have to keep it together, okay? Bye for now, *okaasan*." She hung up.

Elizabeth dialed Marylyn Ibata. "Hi Marylyn. It's Liz."

"Yes, I was hoping to hear you're coming to the concert at the club on Saturday."

"I'll be there. But I have an important question to ask you. Tell me what you feared when you went through with your double mastectomy?"

"What? You have breast cancer too?"

"No. But what did you fear?"

"The surgery, of course. Catching any spread. Losing my womanhood."

"I'm sure," Liz said, then asked, "Was that all?"

"Well…" she hesitated…"I worried I'd lose Masato. You know."

Elizabeth sighed. "Yeah, men and those breasts. It worked out though, didn't it?"

"It did, but why these questions—you pretty much knew that already."

"I just wanted to hear it."

"Liz. What are you not telling me?"

"Nothing now, Marylin. Look, I've got to go. We can talk at the club on Saturday. Okay?"

Hanging up, she dialed Brian, hoping she'd get him with the eighteen-hour difference. It would be a short call.

"Elizabeth," Brian groaned. "It's five a.m. You're some client."

"Ha. Past client. Cured client. In the head, anyway."

"Where are you?"

"Japan."

"Still with Kaito, I hope."

"Yeah, for a while anyway."

"What do you mean?"

"I have cancer. Big time and need a little therapy. Teletherapy, we can call it."

"You're being glib."

"No. I'm not. Bear with me. Tell me how to handle death."

"Liz. I'm not a grief counselor."

"That's not what I want. How about a debrief counselor. Tell me."

"Oh, geez, Elizabeth, you're putting me on the spot."

"Just a few good words, that's all, Brian. Please?"

"Well," he sighed. "You've got to start by accepting all your feelings. Then, share them with Kaito. Get his. Then, find a wat to stay strong. Maybe write your own story of the illness."

"That's it. Perfect. Brian, you are a genius."

"It's not that simple," he said.

"It is, really, if I make it so."

"But Liz—"

"No buts and no time left. Using up my international minutes. Go back to bed sleepy head. Love you, Brian," she added, hung up and drove to the hospital.

Undressing and changing into a hospital gown, the PET scan tech, Mio, guided her into a small room. Mio then injected Elizabeth with the radioactive tracer—the cold metallic tasting liquid surging through her veins while she read the 'What to Expect When You Have Cancer' brochure the doctor had given her. With a pen in one hand and twirling her hair with the other, she made notes as to options for treatment. She needed to know the facts, be realistic and truthful to Kaito about the progression of her disease. No sugar-coating.

Since she could no longer significantly control the disease, it was all about her attitude and ability to handle the only part she could control—preparing Kaito.

As Brian confirmed, she was well on the way to accepting she didn't have long to live. Accordingly, she decided to deal with it pragmatically and with strength. If she were to appear weak and needy, it would greatly affect Kaito, her number one priority. She didn't quite know how she was going to get him to accept the inevitable, but she was determined.

Glancing at the clock and expecting the tracer to have completed its journey through her bloodstream, she girded herself for the claustrophobic experience many patients fear. She almost refused to take the test, but the doctors insisted it would help them and her have a better idea on treatability and how long she might expect to live. The amount of time was critical for Kaito and his countrymen.

She willingly following Mio into the exam room, smiling when she saw the huge piece of equipment that was about to swallow her.

Laughing, she said. "It looks like a giant Randy's Donut sign; you see them all over Los Angeles."

"That is funny," Mio agreed. "Donuts must be big in California."

Laughing again, Liz said, "Well, today I'll be eaten by a huge frosted one."

She was delighted to have her imagination stimulated at this time as creativity streamed through her heart and into her hand. She would write about it.

Mio helped her onto the narrow table and adjusted the pillows behind her head and under her knees. After giving Liz the rundown on how she would be drawn into the hole, Liz promised she would remain motionless and keep her hands tucked behind her head.

Wearing only a gown and panties, she felt naked and vulnerable when the scanner took her in. But she closed her eyes and listened to the whirring sound spinning around her and soon she felt like a towel in a dryer. Her mind cleared of fear.

She heard a repetitive clicking sound that made her think of a heartbeat inside a womb. And when Mio gave her gentle instructions over a speaker, she thought of an unborn child hearing the voices of her mother.

She began to envision being pushed down a birth canal. Heading toward a new breathing life in a cold, dry and confusing place. Like an old slide projector, still images of her young mother, father and sister clicked through her mind, aging by the minute. She was no longer a baby. Then, a lost child swimming. A hurt teen crying. A woman happily married to Kaito.

Just as her life began to feel full and meaningful, the whirring slowed and Mio spoke, "Okay, Mrs. Yamamoto. We're all done now."

Elizabeth began crying.

The tech rushed to her. "Are you alright?"

"I think so," she said, wiping her tears. "I was just worrying about how I was going to tell my husband."

Mio patted her hand. "I'm sure that is hard for you, but it's good that you have completed this." Helping her up, she added, "Your results should be available in a day or two and the doctor will call you to discuss them."

Leaving the parking garage of St. Lukes, Elizabeth considered taking the Rainbow Bridge back to Shibuya. Jumping off the bridge would in some ways be fitting for the occasion, but she took the shorter route through Ginza. Nearing their apartment and fearing the task of breaking the news to Kaito, she visualized snapping her wrist with an imaginary rubber band. Passing by Yoyogi Park, she stopped the car and parked. She was determined to handle all this in a productive way. She put on the emergency flashers and went for a walk. Strolling by a pond with children floating origami boats, she slid back into her youth. She asked her now guiding angel for help. Sitting on a bench, her hand reached into her purse and pulled out a pencil. One the mostly blank back of a brochure, she wrote a poem.

When she finished, she picked up her phone and dialed Kimmi.

"Oh, hi Liz. Glad you called. I need your help."

"How's that?"

"I need you to help inspire Kaito to get more involved and to face Nakayama. I think that's the only way I'm going to break this story wide open."

"I agree completely. Helping you and him do that is now my life's mission. And I'm going to extract that promise from him. I will need you to remind him of that promise."

"Which is?" She asked.

"To hold onto his dream and fight for what he believes."

"Wau. That's a big one."

"It is, and I need you to hold him to that for me. Promise on my promise?"

"You got it."

"Thanks, Kimmi. I'll stay in touch."

She got in the car and headed back to their apartment.

On the way, her phone rang.

"Izzy. W…what's going on?" Kaito stammered. "I got calls from my mom, Marylyn, even Kimmi. Are you alright?"

"Yes. I'm heading home right now. You?"

"On my way back from the *Herald Tribune.* Should be there in ten, fifteen."

"See you then."

Warming up some miso soup for Kaito, Elizabeth prepared her psyche for the onslaught of questions and pleas she expected to hear. He would need to know the details, fight the diagnosis and argue for the treatment plan. He would need and get that from Elizabeth.

The door slammed open and Kaito rushed to her. Held her. "What did the doctor's say?" He asked, guiding her to the sofa. "Mom said it didn't sound good but that you should tell me and I should listen."

"Okay," she confirmed, patting him on the knee. "I'll fill you in on the details, we can discuss it, then I want to lay out my plan. How does that sound?"

"Sure," he said, taken aback by her tone.

"For starters, my symptoms of many weeks—not eating, stomach pains and all were caused by a growing cancer in my ovaries and unfortunately it has spread throughout my pelvic area. So, the prognosis is not good." She glanced at his reaction. "And yes. I should have gone to the doctors earlier, but beating myself up for it doesn't help that."

"Izzy-chan. This is such dreadful news. How do they know? Are you sure?"

"Yes. One test after another. First, the blood test showed the cancer antigen in my system. Then, they did a laparoscopy exam where they inserted the camera and tool through my abdomen, took pictures and snipped some of the tumor. This proved to be a certain type of cancer cell that is very aggressive. The PET scan is only to confirm the spread and time left."

"All that in one afternoon?"

"No. This is my third appointment in as many days. Only a PET scan today."

"What's that? Why didn't you tell me?"

"Sorry, I didn't want you to worry, and I needed to get a handle on it first." She smiled. "The PET scan was a trip into a donut hole, a clothes dryer and a mechanical womb."

He gawked at her. "Come on, Izzy. This is serious."

"Come on, Kaito," she retorted, "We both need to be able to laugh."

"Sounds like you have almost rehearsed this."

"I did. Wanted to get past that so we can agree on what comes after."

He took her hand in his. "I will be with you. Care for you. Whatever it takes."

"I know you will, but this has to be about you as much as me. We're a team, remember?"

"This must have been so hard for you." He gazed into her eyes. "When you got the diagnosis, how did you manage?"

"At first, I was overwhelmed by the complexity of the disease. Sort of numb. Got a little angry. Fear of pain and sickness. But mostly lost and lonely."

She put her hand to his face. "Missing you. But having lived with these feelings all my life, I'm sick of woe is me."

She tapped his knee. "My life and death are now more about you and those who will be living." She stopped her spiel and found Kaito crying.

She held him and cried with him. Letting out her past, her pain.

Several moments later, Kaito cleared his throat and wiped his nose. "Izzy-chan. I don't want to lose you."

"I know, but you won't. And I'll tell you how."

"So, we can fix this?" He asked.

"The docs laid out a treatment team of specialists and multiple surgeries, chemotherapies, and immunotherapies that could possibly prolong my life."

His eyes widened.

"Could, I said. But not without a lot of side effects, in and out of the hospital, constant nausea, losing my hair, the list went on and on."

"There's hope, then."

"I don't call it that, Kaito, and I don't want to live my last days like that. I want to enjoy them with you and know you are doing your work as well. I want to enjoy the time as best I can with you, but only part of the time. I want to walk on the beach. Read together. Stay home. Go swimming. Love each other when we can."

"You mean no treatments?"

"Not entirely. I will need pain medication, and maybe you'll have to turn me over in bed so I don't develop bed sores."

"You mean just letting you die?"

"In a way. In a good way, yes. Death, like life, is what you make of it." She reached into her purse and handed him the brochure she had written on. "I wrote this in the PET scanner." She kissed him. "Please read it."

Poem for Kaito

By Elizabeth Yamamoto

Warm, dark and wet
I leave another womb
Born again, unbound,
to breathe freely

and see what I didn't know
I cry out my past
my sorrows, my mistakes
but not my dreams
I wait for other arms
Your arms
To take me in
Accept me
Join with me
Unite our dreams
Let them grow
into a great gift for all
And when
it is time for one of us to leave
Give their dream to the other
so it can flourish
Take it now
and swim in the womb
that carries the land
And waits somewhere
beyond the sea
to hold your hand

Kaito began crying again. "Elizabeth, this is so sad."

She wiped his tears.

He looked deep into her eyes. "What does it all mean?"

"That it doesn't have to be sad. I need to make peace with myself and can't do that without your help."

"I will help you. Whatever it takes, princess. But how can you do this? It's almost like seppuku, which you once said was so un-American?"

"Let me try and say it this way. You gave me your love many times over, and I didn't return it. You gave me hope, joy, direction, and adventure. I gave you grief."

He held up his hand. "That's not true."

"It's my truth. Kaito, you always stayed by me, even when I didn't stay by you. I hurt you badly the times I left you."

"It did hurt, and it was hard to understand, but I knew you didn't mean to."

"I'm sorry for having spent too much of my life trying to figure it out. How abandonment as a child caused me to abandon you, keeping me from being hurt and losing you. That self-sabotage thing is so backward." She looked into his eyes. "Do you forgive me?"

"Of course, I forgive you." He kissed her forehead. "I think I somehow knew that clinging to your guardian angel was over-protecting you. But that's done now. You know I'll never leave you."

"I do know and that's why it's my time to give back. I'm reminded of the old Bob Dylan song, 'If not for you.' You let me flourish as a writer and I need to let you be the dream doer."

"Oh, come on, Izzy. You gave me so much. The power to see my power. That I could do what I believed. What was right and good. Taught me that authority is my authority to overcome. Gave me the best of American culture into my own. I am indebted to you."

"Maybe, but I have only one thing left to give you." She held his chin. "But you need to promise."

"Promise?"

"Yes. Promise you will accept my dying wish. Take it to your heart and not give it up."

"I will. I promise." He kissed her. "What is it?"

"That you will carry on without me. Give your love back to your country and all that we dreamed of."

"Okay, but how can I do that with you being sick?"

"You can give me precious moments here and there in between your work. Important, pressing work that goes way beyond either one of us."

Kaito dug his fingers into his shaking head.

"Kaito. Like I wrote in my poem, it was beyond the sea that I found you, Manami, love and myself. Now my life is about you. And I will die full of love if you promise me that you will not stop your work, what you always dreamed of. When I'm gone, you will then have my spirit with you and the courage to keep fighting for Manami and your people. Okay?"

Kaito lifted his head and gazed into Elizabeth's eyes. "I promise."

"Good. Now, let's go swimming."

Chapter Forty

As the taxi pulled alongside the tall environmental ministry building, Kaito forced back a shudder. Nakayama's power loomed above him, but Elizabeth's entreaties and sacred promise grounded him. He hated to leave his sick wife, and fought back for a while, but she held up her promise and he was here with Kimmi. But he was with Elizabeth as well as she had prepped him on tactics for interviewing possible whistleblowers. Kaito kept her spirit in him and was ready.

Getting off at the pachinko parlor down the block, Kaito fumbled the door and cringed at arcade's sensory assault. The screaming slot machines, choking cigarette smoke and stink of fried food made him feel dizzy. But it provided good cover for what Mika might reveal about his boss, Nakayama. Kaito wanted to learn what they could and quickly get out this rotten place.

Mika, a slight-figured fellow in a well-tailored suit and a Yankees baseball cap, scanned the parlor. The man looked nervous, Kaito thought before he spotted Kimmi cracking a tiny smile.

"Hello, Mika," Kimmi said and gave him a one-arm hug and a peck on the cheek. Mika flushed, then beamed and bowed at the waist to Kaito.

Kaito smiled. "Can we find a quiet corner?" He gestured down the rows of clanking machines and shouting players. "The noise is overwhelming."

"Let's stand over there." Mika pointed to a corner by the restrooms. "I've only got a half-hour."

Kimmi glanced at her cell phone. "Okay, so can we start with the coast guard order?"

"First, let me be direct." Kaito leaned in. "Why are you helping us, Mika?"

Mika looked around the room. "Despite the fact that my boss personally contributes large amounts of money to environmental causes." He squinted and held up a finger. "He is not a friend of the environment. Done nothing with our waste management problem. Turns a blind eye to everything that isn't development. Under his watch, several animal species have gone extinct, and our clandestine whale hunting continues." He bowed to Kaito. "But most importantly, I've been a secret fan of your work ever since I was in college, Yamamoto-san."

Kaito stepped aside as a man exited the door of the restroom. Kaito coughed, narrowed his eyes, and considered Mika's motivations.

"Furthermore," Mika continued, "My boss is vengeful and demands total loyalty from his *kohai* employees. If you so much as challenge him," Mika shifted his eyes and lowered his voice, "He will demote you to waste treatment plant monitoring, or worse."

Kaito asked, "Hmm. How have you gathered your information without being compromised?"

Mika looked to Kimmi. "I'm embarrassed to say." He shot a quick glance at Kimmi. "Mostly from Nakayama's executive secretary. She likes me."

"Do you like her?" Kimmi inquired.

"No, not that way." He rubbed his chin. "She's twenty years older, and well...too needy. She told me her boss called Captain Kiagi directly and ordered a patrol boat with crew to the mouth of Tokyo Bay two days ago. Their office wouldn't have a record, but the Headquarters of the 3rd Regional Command in Yokohama would have."

Kimmi finished taking notes, then glanced at Kaito. "Kaito, you don't look well. Can I get you something?"

"No. It's just the bad air. Please go on, Mika."

Kimmi checked her watch. "Yes. Can you tell us anything about calls he made the day before that? Did he speak to the park authorities about someone trying to record the dolphins under the Tokyo Gate Bridge? And did he know we were in the skateboard park?"

While Mika answered Kimmi's questions, Kaito was finding it hard to concentrate. The bells and pinballs of the pachinko machines were all he could hear. The dueling anime cartoons on the screens all he could see. The room spun.

A burly man plowed out of the rest room and caught Kaito's arm. Kaito reeled, lost his balance and tumbled in a thud to the floor.

"Kaito!" Kimmi and Mika reached to help him up.

Kaito tried to stand and winced, crying out as his left ankle gave way.

Mika said to Kimmi, "Get a stool and a glass of water."

"I'll be all right," he said, pain throbbing in his foot.

"Are you sure?" Kimmi asked.

Kaito nodded and they eased him onto the stool. He took a drink and said, "Tell me about SeaGuard."

They listened to Mika. "SeaGuard's CEO, Akahiro Kodo, often comes to pick up Nakayama for a game of golf at the Yomiuri Country Club. They're big buddies." He smiled at both of them. "Maybe I could find something in the files—he keeps copies of his personal finances in the office."

"Thanks, Mika," Kaito said. "We really appreciate your help on this. Please let us know what you find."

Kaito reached down and removed his shoes. Rubbing his ankle, he mumbled, "My dammed foot feels more than swollen."

"Can you stand on it?" Kimmi asked.

Kaito gingerly set his foot down and cried out in pain as soon as it touched the ground. "Think you may have sprained or broken it," Kimmi offered.

"You're right," Kaito agreed. "We should go to a hospital. Have a doctor look at it, maybe get an ex-ray. I'll call Izzy and cancel our reading of *Moby Dick*."

#

Five hours after they first went to the hospital, they arrived at the door of Kaito's apartment. Kaito had trouble balancing, fumbled with the keys and dropped them.

"Here, let me do that," Kimmi said, picking them up and opening the door. "You're going to have to get used to others helping you."

"I know," Kaito said, shaking his head. He hobbled in on crutches, his left foot dangling behind him in a cast. "Have seat. I'll get Izzy and we can update her."

Tottering into the bedroom, he found Elizabeth sound asleep and the smell of feces attacking his senses. He managed to grab hold of a side chair and dragged it alongside the bed. He laid his crutches on the floor and sat. She didn't seem to even hear him, and his heart began pounding in his throat.

"Izzy, wake up," he said, gently tapping her shoulder.

She stirred but did not wake.

Looking at the stained bed sheet and blanket, he cringed. Panicking, he shook her shoulder.

She turned to face him. Her complexion was pale, skin wrinkled, and hair matted with sweat. "Kaito. Where are we?" she asked.

"You're home, dear."

"What's that smell?" She asked then glanced down her body and threw off the bedclothes. "Oh my god!" she cried out. "I've soiled the bed." Her face reddened with shame.

"It's okay, Izzy," he said, slowly stroking her head. "You just had an accident."

She sat up. "I've got to clean up. I didn't even know."

"Don't worry. I'll clean this up. Can you take a shower?"

"I think so," she replied and carefully lifted herself out of bed. Looking at the crutches on the floor and Kaito's foot in a cast, she gasped. "What happened to you?"

"Just fell. Broke my ankle. No big deal," he said, waving it away. "How about if you give me your nightgown and get in the shower. Kimmi's here waiting for us." He pointed to the bed. "I'll handle this while you shower, okay?"

"How bad is the break?" she asked.

"Multiple fractures but should heal in 2–3 months."

She persisted. "All that time to put on a cast?"

He didn't need to add to her worries. "The doctor just ordered some other tests. Not a big deal."

She stared at him for a moment, then removed her nightgown.

He felt nauseous seeing her increasingly gaunt, cancer-ridden body. How it must feel to her. "Take it slow, okay. If you need my help, just holler."

"I'm so embarrassed, Kaito."

"I understand. Shower now and it'll all be better."

Elizabeth shuffled toward the bathroom and turned, holding onto the doorframe. "Are sure you're alright?"

"I am," he said, gathering the soiled bedclothes and holding back retching. "Go now." Placing the soiled sheet, blanket and mattress cover into plastic trash bags, he was thankful the mess didn't reach the mattress itself. He would wash them later.

Hearing Elizabeth crying above the sound of the water, the realization of where her life was heading sunk in. This latest incident combined with her long sleep sessions convinced Kaito she was in rapid decline. He called the leading

Tokyo hospice organization and began a discussion of having a nurse make regular visits in the home. He took a deep breath to feel strong and heard Kimmi's phone ring in the other room. He hobbled over to the chest of drawers and pulled out fresh underwear, a nightgown and bathrobe from the closet and dropped them off in the bathroom.

Grabbing a room deodorizer, he sprayed and opened the door a crack and said to Kimmi, "Liz is in the shower. Give us a few more minutes, okay?"

Finding Elizabeth exiting the shower, he handed her a towel and pointed to her change of clothes.

"Thanks," she said, drying off. "Does Kimmi know?"

"Not really, but I'll go and fill her in. You come out when you're ready." Kaito swallowed hard thinking of her once full body, now shriveling.

He hobbled out of the bedroom and found Kimmi on the phone.

She raised a finger and mouthed 'It's Captain Kiagi' and continued to listen. Finishing up, she thanked him and told Kaito, "Kiagi said he'd look for the record."

"Good work, Kimmi," Kaito said, "If we can trust him." He sat at the kitchen table and leaned his crutches against a chair.

"How's Elizabeth?"

Kaito took a deep breath. "I've been avoiding telling you on Izzy's orders, but she's got a serious case of cancer and the prognosis is not good."

"Oh no." She sat back and covered her mouth. "You mean not curable?"

"Seems so, but she's got an amazing attitude."

"Kiato. I feel so bad for you and for her. It's tragic."

"Yes," he coughed, not wanting to say the words. "She may have only weeks, maybe days to live. We're going to have a hospice nursing come in. Her mentation is good and spirits high, considering and she doesn't want anything to get in the way of your story and our mission. She asked me to ask you to treat her as normal as possible and wants to continue to help."

The bedroom door swung open, and Elizabeth came out in blue jeans and a green oversized sweater. Kaito noted Kimmi's wide eyes and open mouth.

"Hi, Kimmi," Liz said, rushing to hug her. "So good to see you. Heard about your meeting with Nakayama."

"Good to see you too. It's been weeks. How are you doing?"

"Okay, Kimmi. But we need to focus on the task at hand. How was your meeting with Nakayama?"

"It was a short meeting, same long story I'm afraid."

"Tell me, but first tell me about Kaito's foot. I feel he's not sharing everything."

Kimmi explained how they were at the pachinko parlor meeting with Mika, when the rude guy knocked him over, he fell hard and the foot fractured and they took him to the hospital. She left out what she promised Kaito not to divulge, i.e., the doctor's concern over Kaito's weak and painful hands, the MRI, and all.

"So, I take it you went to your meeting with Nakayama when Kaito was in, what do they call it, central casting? How did it go?"

"Sorry to say, but I got nowhere with him." She lowered her head. "He's everything Mika said he was and worse. Fucking modern-day, sexist ninja. In a battle of wills, it was hard to maintain my cool."

"I'm sorry, Kimmi," Liz interjected. "These kinds of guys can rattle anybody."

Kimmi took a banana clip from her hair and shook her head. "When I asked about the adequacy of the tsunami warning system, he handed me a written public statement and told me to read it. He sounded like a recording when he stated his system was fail safe, that even if a tsunami started at the coast, it could never reach Tokyo. And, he said, the press and public have nothing to worry about." She exhaled.

Kaito shrugged. "Not surprising."

Kimmi picked up her notebook. "From that point on, he balked, deflected, or denied every question I asked and never even blinked." She flipped a page. "He denied knowledge of any coast guard boat sent to the bay. He even claimed he had no knowledge of any dolphins appearing in the bay…" like he didn't read the paper…"let alone people attempting to record them."

Elizabeth chimed in, "These kinds of guys lie through their teeth."

"Yeah, and when I told him that the Times science editor had reviewed recordings made of the dolphins and they duplicated the warning calls made before the Miyagi quake, Nakayama laughed and called it 'hogwash'."

"Then I asked Nakayama if he was aware you were involved in working with *The Times Herald* to resurrect the dolphin warning story." Kimmi jabbed at her notebook. "He showed no surprise, but said, and I quote, 'I thought the old walrus dropped dead in his little fishing village years ago'. And when I told him our in-house expert feels there may be support for a near term tsunami, he said it was gibberish, that there is no science behind those who talk to the animals and think a dolphin is smarter than we are."

Elizabeth's eyes were beginning to close.

Kaito took a sip of water. "That son of a bitch. When he rejected my 2011 proposal for a dolphin-based warning system, I knew that would be his attitude if he ever got involved."

"Do you want me to go on?"

Kaito nodded.

"When I asked him about all his assets and lavish lifestyle, he seemed to be a bit taken aback. But he smiled and answered that his father died with considerable wealth, and he draws from his estate. I'll try to verify that."

"For sure," Elizabeth said, "Check the probate court records. And follow up with the Greenpeace director about that member who worked for SeaGuard. I gave her your number to call." Elizabeth wiggled uncomfortably in her seat. "So, what else happened in the meeting?"

"Yes. When Nakayama told me my half-hour was almost up, I was getting pissed off. So, I brought up his relationship and dealings with Kaito back in your university days—you know, the research project you both worked on." Kimmi fixed her eyes on Kaito. "And you know, for the first time, I could see a break in his fierce demeanor. Up to that point, I felt we had no chance to crack him." She squinted. "But then, I swear I saw a flash of fear in his eyes— like we were onto something."

Kaito coughed. "I know why." He glanced at Elizabeth and smiled. "I didn't have the courage to tell you before what actually happened, but back at the university, in 1966, Nakayama rigged the results of a study." He steadied his speech. "To hide the cause of Minamata disease and government malfeasance and collusion with industry." His voice became hoarse. "The corruption continued for years. Hundreds died." Kaito struggled to continue.

"That is incredible," Elizabeth said, shaking her head and patting his hand. "Keep going, Kaito."

"I have proof that could help bring Nakayama down. Maybe if the public knows about his past corruption, they'll doubt his word now." He took a deep breath. "We can challenge him on this, but there may be a downside."

Kimmi asked, "Why the hesitation, Yamamoto-san?"

He shook his head. "I could go down *with* him."

"What are you saying?"

"I was complicit."

"Kaito, come on," Kimmi said.

"No, he could ask why I didn't do anything about it then, but it's okay. My skin doesn't matter anymore compared to his. If it comes down to breaking him, we can play that card later."

Kimmi's phone vibrated. Looking at it, she said, "It's Mrs. Ogawa from Greenpeace. Let me take it." She stood and went into the hall.

Kaito reached across the table for Elizabeth's hand. "How are you feeling, my *koija*?"

"Not too well," she replied, rubbing her stomach. "I feel like I need to rest already, and I napped for three hours."

Kaito asked, "When is the hospice nurse coming?"

"Six-thirty."

"We can ask her about the...you know."

Kimmi returned. "Great news. Mrs. Ogawa says that fellow is willing to meet with us and I called him right away and he can see us this evening. Funny, his surname is Nakayama, Toshio Nakayama."

"It's a pretty common name," Kaito said, "But I do believe Katsu had a son."

"Irony of ironies if it was, heh? He said he can meet us at an *izakaya* bar called Mukashi, not far from *The Times Herald*. Should we all go?"

"How about you handle it, Kimmi?" Kaito said. "Think Elizabeth and I ought to stay home."

"Of course," she said. "Why hobble around on crutches?"

Elizabeth interjected. "No, I think it's important for Kaito to be there. I need to rest anyway. The nurse will be here soon."

"Are you sure?" Kaito asked, fixing his eyes on her. She glared, then smiled at him. "Absolutely. You go." Kaito froze. The prospects of him, possibly soon, living without her, hit him in the gut. *How could I ever keep going without her?*

Kaito lowered his eyes. "Okay, but when I get back, we'll read about Ishmael's thoughts on human's burning too much whale oil."

Elizabeth nodded.

Sitting at a small table at the neighborhood *izakaya* bar, holding a plum nigori drink, Kaito caught his hand trembling and set the glass down. Kimmi pointed toward the door where a small, stubbly-bearded man entered. "That's him," she whispered, stood and waved the young man to the table. Toshio bowed politely, sat down, and cracked his knuckles. "Sorry, I am very nervous."

"That's okay," Kaito said, pointing to his crutches. "Sorry I can't greet you properly. Would you like some sake?"

"No thanks." He rubbed his neck. "I need to get right to why I've come. When I told Kimmi on the phone about SeaGuard's maintenance operations, I left something out."

Kaito smiled. "Go ahead, son."

"This is hard for me." He glanced at Kimmi. "But after we spoke, I realized I can no longer keep it buried."

"Thank you, Toshio," Kimmi said. "We really appreciate anything you can reveal that will get the truth out."

He lowered his head. "Yes, it's not right that people's lives could be at risk if the SeaGuard system fails in a major event."

"Could you be more specific?" Kimmi asked.

He straightened in his chair. "Of course. There have been problems with the sensors at the tip of the Beso Peninsula, from 35 degrees north and between 140- and 142-degrees east, close to the mouth of Tokyo Bay." He gulped a breath. "As Yamamoto-san knows, the seismic and pressure sensors along the quake-prone faults are very sensitive."

Kimmi raised her hand. "Slow down, please, Toshio, I have to get this right."

"There has been an ongoing problem of shrimp boat netters interrupting the fiber optic cable that connects to the monitoring stations." He waited for Kimmi to finish her notes. "These sensors need to be calibrated on schedule to make sure they do what they're supposed to and not send false alarms—and that is a labor intensive, hugely expensive operation."

"So, what you described isn't happening?" Kaito finally asked, happy to have had Kimmi lead the questioning as he was distracted thinking about Izzy.

"Exactly," Toshio nodded. "This area has not had coverage for several months and the ministry has ignored it. My former boss, Mr. Morita, recommended immediate repairs be undertaken, but he was turned down for unspecified reasons."

Kaito narrowed his eyes. "Would you know who at the ministry turned down the request?"

A bead of sweat formed on Toshio's upper lip. Kaito put his hand out toward Toshio. "It was your father, wasn't it?"

Kimmi gasped. Toshio closed his eyes and bowed his head.

"It's okay." Kaito patted Toshio's hand. "I know this must be very difficult for you, I too, had a major falling out with my own father that ended very badly. I understand what you're going through." He turned to Kimmi. "Why don't you get back to *The Times Herald* and see if you can track down Morita for a statement. I'll be up shortly."

Toshio exhaled deeply and nodded to Kimmi as she left the table.

"There's more, isn't there, Toshio?"

"Yes." He took a deep breath.

"Once, many years ago, when I was living at home, I overheard a conversation my father had with Mr. Kodo, the SeaGuard Shokan CEO." He closed his eyes for a moment and said, "My father was taking bribes from him."

Kaito spoke softly. "Did your father know you heard it?"

"Yes, I remember asking him what he was doing. He got very angry and told me I better wipe it from my memory forever."

Seeing the anguish on Toshio's face, Kaito was reminded of the last time he spoke with his own father and what happened afterward. Kaito leaned in closer. "Would you be willing to share details of that with *The Times Herald?* You could do that anonymously and they would follow up." He put his hand out toward Toshio. "But I know that might be impossible for you to even consider."

Toshio rubbed his chin. "My father got me that job at SeaGuard because of my desire to help people. It was the last kindness he extended me. My father disowned me because I came out as gay. That's when I quit SeaGuard and later joined Greenpeace."

"I know how you must feel, Toshio. I'm sure Kimmi would agree that none of that has to be in *The Times Herald* story. I can only ask you to help us for the same reason I am trying to help our country. Will you tell the details about the system problems and bribes to Kimmi for a published story?"

Toshio pressed his lips together, thinking.

Kaito's phone rang. He put up his hand. "Ah, Naiko. Let me call you right back." He hung up and looked at Toshio.

Toshio lowered his head. "I will."

Kaito patted his shoulder. "You're an honorable man, Toshio. You have showed a tremendous amount of courage."

"And that information may help convince my editors that we have the basis of a story." Kimmi stood and shook his hand. "Thank you so much, Toshio."

"You're welcome," he said, smiling for the first time.

"Okay, Kaito," Kimmi concluded, "Let's see if I can convince Hamasaki to print the story, subject of course to Nakayama's comments or denials. We will need to interview him again and I think your presence would be critical."

"Don't know about my participation," Kaito said. "I've got to be with Izzy."

"Please consider it. Your evidence and challenge to his power could make a big difference."

"Elizabeth may need me."

"Understood, and that is up to the two of you, but I'm betting if she's well enough, she would want you to go."

"Probably," he said, rubbing his scalp. "Call me in the morning if it's a go. Right now, I have to get back to Izzy."

Chapter Forty-One
Kaito's Apartment

That evening

Returning exhausted from his meeting with Kimmi and Toshio, Kaito rushed as fast as he could, on crutches, into the bedroom. Elizabeth was still awake. Although her eyes were closed, the gentle swaying of her head meant she was listening to the music pouring through her headphones. Probably Dvorák, she loved the American rhythms in his *New World Symphony*.

He tapped her shoulder. "Izzy-chan?"

She opened her always beautiful eyes, smiled and removed her headphones.

He took them. "Don't you want to get some sleep?"

She smiled. "Good morning. Give me a kiss."

He kissed her. "It's a little before midnight," he said, almost not wanting to tell her.

"Ah, now I remember you were meeting with Mika."

"Yes, I was with Kimmi but it was with Toshio."

"Who was he again?"

"How about we talk in the morning, so you can get your rest?"

"Maybe," she replied. "But I do want to watch that special on TV about the Fukushima aftermath. It airs at midnight."

"Hmm, I forgot. Sure that's a good idea?" He patted her hand so as not to touch the IV line the nurse had inserted yesterday. "You need your sleep, you know."

"Please, Kaito. It's important for both of us to watch."

"You know I don't want to." He rubbed his thinning hair.

"But will you, with me? To keep me company?"

Taking a deep breath to stifle the sadness, he slowly nodded.

She glanced at the nightstand, picked up the remote and turned on the TV.

A half-hour later, the program wound down with the heartfelt testimonies of survivors interspersed with images of workers rebuilding and children playing. Ending with an uplifting melody on a *samisen*, Kaito shut off the TV. Elizabeth silently sobbed, her hands together as if in prayer. He reached for a tissue to dab her cheeks. "See, that program upset you." He got up from his side of the bed. "We need to change your position now, make sure you don't get bedsores."

"Okay, but after we talk."

"Come on, Izzy. Why do you want to relive all that misery?"

"I guess because of the survivors. I love stories about courage."

"Like your own. Not everyone, let alone an American woman, would take the risk to go days after Fukushima to interview survivors."

"You're so kind. It was a good human-interest piece, wasn't it?"

"Indeed. But I'm thinking thousands more may die in a Tokyo version."

"I know, so you gotta keep trying. You're still on the brink of a major discovery." She coughed.

"Need some water?"

She shook her head.

He glanced at the night table and saw an unopened container of yogurt. "I can see you're not ready to sleep. Have you eaten anything?"

She didn't answer.

"How about we have some apple sauce? You like that."

She shook her head.

"Izzy." He held up a scolding finger.

"I love when you say that," she acknowledged.

He went to the fridge, opened a baby jar and filled a spoon. He propped her up on the pillows. Holding it to her lips, he scowled as she didn't open her mouth. "Izzy."

She opened her mouth halfway, and he eased the spoon into her mouth. She took it in, gagged and spit it out.

He wiped her chin. "Come on, Izzy. Try again. You've got to eat."

"I'm not hungry."

He tried another spoonful. She balked.

"Look. Unless you eat some, I won't tell you about Toshio."

She held up a single finger and took in the sauce and forced a swallow.

"Izzy. You have to promise me you'll eat."

She smiled. "Yes, Doctor Yamamoto."

He shook his head. "Funny. I never told you; we had another nickname for you, besides Izzy-chan."

Her green eyes flashed, looking at him, waiting for the good name.

"At OceanWorld, my colleagues and I used to call you 'the wolfhound'."

"A dog?" She screeched, then smiled.

"Yes. You were relentless. Wouldn't give up until you had me cornered, then brought me down."

"No. It was more like wrenching your individuality out of a thick shell. What do Japanese call it?"

He sighed and whispered, "'*shudan ishiki.*' It's so easy for Americans to judge." He chuckled. "You never get hammered for not being humble and going along."

"I know, I know, but you've stood up to the group-think before and you can do it again."

"Maybe." He touched her cheek. "But I couldn't have done it without you."

She placed her palm on his chest. "But you will need to. Now, tell me about Toshio. Who was he again?"

"It turns out he was Nakayama's son. Though now estranged and disinherited."

"He's going to tell on his father?"

"Not directly. But when he worked at SeaGuard, he learned of a defect with the earthquake detection system—a weak link in the Tokyo segment. He gave us the name of the Regional Director who has personal, first-hand knowledge of Nakayama's decision to ignore the defect."

"That could be a pivotal anchor for the story."

"Yes, and Kimmi is following up and she's convinced that with that ammunition and with my…" he caught himself.

"My what?" she asked.

"Nothing," he mumbled.

"Come on, Yamamoto. I know when you're keeping something from me."

"She just wants me to stay involved."

"And you told her you needed to be with me, didn't you?" She gave him that knowing sideways glance of hers. "Come clean, mister. Remember I'm the wolfdog. What does she want you to do?"

"It's conditional."

"On what?"

"Only if Hamasaki approves an article and Nakayama is given the chance to dispute the charges. She's seeing her editor in the morning with a draft."

"Then?"

Kaito let out a big breath. "Kimmi wants me to be in the meeting and confront Nakayama directly with my evidence and expertise."

"Why wouldn't you do that?"

Kaito looked at her in silence.

"You know you have to go."

"To get back at him?"

"No. To expose him for who he is, get the press involved to build support with the public. Get your dream back. Prove what dolphins can do. You have to go."

"But Izzy," he pleaded, the guilt dragging at his heart.

"Look, the hospice nurse will be here in the morning." She put her hand to the side of his face. "You promised, remember."

He put his hand on hers and shook his head. "I promise. Now, let's go to sleep, okay?"

Minister Nakayama's Office
Next morning

"You may go in now, Miss Matsuda," said Nakayama's secretary.

Kimmi smiled at Kaito, then at the secretary. "Thank you for allowing my dear grandfather to wait here while the minister and I talk." She tugged at her suit lapels and walked confidently into Nakayama's office.

Left sitting in a wheelchair in the antechamber, Kaito ignored another call and message from his doctor saying something about 'slowing the progression' and concentrated on the challenge ahead.

He worried that their ploy would not work. Kimmi was a savvy investigative reporter, but could she really fluster Nakayama into making mistakes? And when she introduced her surprise card, could he find the courage to confront his old enemy? They needed to find a crack in Nakayama's defenses in order to get their story out about the dolphin warning.

Kaito could not see into Nakayama's office, but he heard Kimmi say cheerfully, "Thank you, minister Nakayama, for seeing me again on such short notice."

"Leave the door open. It'll be quick, Matsuda," Nakayama barked. "I have little patience for the prying media."

"I will get right to the point, sir. *The Times Herald* only wants a clarification on your earlier response to the Olympic Committee's request regarding earthquake safety during the upcoming games."

He grunted. "I've already told everyone that our SeaGuard earthquake and tsunami warning system is failsafe."

Kimmi's tone remained confident. "I understand, sir, but an informed source has told *The Times Herald* that your tsunami warning system might be compromised. That there have been defects left uncorrected. Tokyo could be vulnerable."

"That's ridiculous," he yelled without making eye contact. "It's the most sophisticated system in the world. Anyway, a tsunami could never come all the way up the bay and reach Tokyo."

"So, you are stating to the Japanese public that there are no flaws in the current SeaGuard warning system?"

He hissed, "That's my statement. Yes."

"Thank you, sir. If you don't want to dispute the details of what our source is saying, you'll have an opportunity to respond after *The Times Herald* story runs tomorrow."

"You're being insolent, Miss!"

"Perhaps you'd like to meet my source yourself," Kimmi said.

That was Kaito's cue. Ignoring the secretary's shock, he rolled his wheelchair through the door and found Nakayama standing behind his desk, mouth agape. Kaito smiled. "Aha, Katsu, haven't seen you since our university days. Do you have a minute?"

The minister's face turned red. "He's your source? I should throw both of you out right now." He regained his composure and snickered. "Sure, come on in. You think the old man with the wacky dolphin theories is going to win over hard science and high technology, Matsuda? He's a dreamer, just like he was back in university."

Kaito shrugged his shoulders and said, "Maybe, but I understand you are guaranteeing the public that a tsunami will never hit Tokyo."

"Yes, it is a ridiculous notion, *kohai*." The minister rocked in his chair. "Tokyo lies eighty kilometers from the coast in a sheltered bay."

"True," Kaito said with a nod. "But the 1923 Kanto earthquake brought ten-meter-high waves into the bay, killing one hundred forty thousand residents. And that was way before massive land reclamation formed the low-lying Odaiba areas where the summer games will be held." Kaito gave him a half-smile. "With millions now living in those areas and hundreds of thousands attending the games, a lot more could die."

"Stupid, hypothetical," Nakayama snarled.

Kaito held up a finger. "You ignore geological history and recent advances. If you were aware of Takagi's work, you'd know we could easily have three simultaneous quakes along fault lines south of the Japanese trench. That would generate a huge tsunami, making a direct hit to the mouth of the bay. And the waves would bounce off the seawalls up the bay until they engulf the low-lying city."

The minister waved his hands in the air and shouted, "Ridiculous, that's a once in a thousand-year event."

Kaito narrowed his eyes. "Could be a *three-day* event."

"Hah!" Nakayama laughed. "I knew it. The dreamer boy is only trying to promote his imaginary dolphin tsunami warning again." He looked over at Kimmi. "Your newspaper will never do a story on that quackery; I'll make sure of that."

"So," Kimmi said. "I'll note that the government is threatening to censor the press."

Nakayama mouthed the word 'cunt', then quickly focused his rage on Kaito. "You stupid asshole. When are you going to understand? You and your dolphins don't matter." He pointed a finger. "I knew it was you trying to record in the bay."

Kimmi made a note.

Kaito nodded to her, acknowledging how her gamble was working.

Nakayama flipped his hand in the air. "You're never going to make a difference, Yamamoto."

"It's not about me," Kaito replied. "If you had approved my research, it was possible my dolphin-based system could have saved thousands of lives at Fukushima in 2011."

Nakayama sputtered, "You don't have science behind you, *kohai*. No one could ever prove those dolphins knew and were warning us. And where are those genius dolphins now? Have they changed their minds?"

Kaito shook his head. "You've always been an ignoramus. My tsunami warning system could give people *days,* not minutes, to evacuate."

The minister threw his head back. "Huh! Your proposal was flawed."

Kimmi interrupted, "I'm sorry, minister, that's not what our source inside your ministry tells us."

Nakayama threw his pen down on the desk. "That's it. You have nothing substantial." He pointed to the door. "Leave, now!"

Kimmi looked to Kaito. Kaito wheeled his chair right up to the minister's desk. "We'll gladly leave, but not before discussing your history of industry collusion that continues to betray and harm the public."

"What are you talking about?" Nakayama clenched his jaw.

Kaito swallowed and said, "You rigged the test results on our 1966 university research project that sought to find the cause of Minimata disease." Kaito shook his head. "And all to benefit your father's business."

"You stupid son of a bitch!" Nakayama moved from behind the desk toward Kaito. "You and your lab partners signed off on the results."

Kaito did not flinch. When the public finds out about Nakayama's earlier collusion with industry, they would demand an investigation of his dealings with SeaGuard. "We did sign off on that research," Kaito said. "But I have a separate document—a printout of the actual readings and results. All the research participants signed it. It proves you falsified the published findings."

Nakayama was spitting with rage. "You lie. Let me see it." He bent down and pointed his finger in Kaito's face. "If you did have it and you made it known, you'd go down with me."

Kaito batted the finger away. "I am prepared to suffer the consequences." He smiled. "It will be a pleasure to take you down with me, my old *sempai* friend."

Nakayama raised his fist as if to strike Kaito. The hatred in his eyes reminded Kaito of his brutal attack in the swimming pool, but he managed a smile. "That may have worked in university, but it won't work now."

Kimmi quickly moved next to Kaito and glared at Nakayama. "I don't think that would be a good idea." Nakayama pulled back, face still raging red.

"Thank you for your time," said Kimmi. "We will leave now."

Kaito added, "And now that you deny there are any faults in your system, your fate will soon be in the public's hands. The public that you never honorably served." He started turning his wheelchair, then looked back. "You

still have a chance, Katsu, to redeem yourself and start an orderly evacuation."
He nodded to Kimmi and wheeled out the door. Kaito was in the taxi on the way back to his apartment when his phone rang.

"Kaito, somebody broke into my trunk," Kimmi cried out. "The only thing they didn't take is the wheelchair."

"What do you mean?" Kaito asked.

"The CDs and your equipment are gone."

"That son of a bitch, Nakayama!"

"Hold on, let me get into the car."

Kaito heard the car door slam and the engine start up. "Did you get anything from Captain Kaiji?"

"I think he's stonewalling. Nakayama must have gotten to him. The Captain is about to retire and he might be worried about his pension. And I still haven't been able to reach Mika. He doesn't answer my phone and I worry something's happened to him."

"This is getting quite serious as I know the lengths that man will go, but Kimmi, I have other problems to attend to. Liz is not eating, and the nurse told me she's getting much weaker and we'll have to feed her intravenously. Now that you tell me about your break in, I worry he might try our apartment next. Look, I've got to go."

There was a fast revving of a car engine.

Kimmi cried out, "Hold on for a moment."

The call broke up. A loud roar. "Kimmi, Kimmi!" he called out. His heart jumped into his throat. There was a screeching of tires.

He shouted, "Kimmi, are you there?"

Minister Nakayama Accused of Receiving Bribes
Tsunami Warning System Integrity in Question

By Kimmi Matsuda

Tokyo. The city of Tokyo and the entire bay may not receive sufficient warning of a possible tsunami. An anonymous whistleblower has revealed to *the Times Herald* that the SeaGuard Shokan undersea earthquake sensors near the mouth of Tokyo Bay are not being maintained properly and might not give citizens time to evacuate. Environmental Minster Nakayama denies the accusation and States he has full confidence in the ability of the system to detect undersea earthquakes in the area and give residents the greatest amount of advance warning possible.

The Times Herald investigative staff spoke to the system's Regional Director, Mr. Tadashi Morita, who verified that the ministry turned down a request for the needed repairs on 16 October of last year. Minister Nakayama has fully denied his agency ever received such a request, as well as denying an accusation that he had received bribes from SeaGuard. The *Times* has put in an official request to the Public Prosecutor's Office to investigate Minister Nakayama's actions under the Unfair Competition Prevention Act (UCPA).

In a related story, Kaito Yamamoto, famed OceanWorld dolphin trainer, has come forward with an allegation of fraud against Minister Nakayama that dates back to 1966 when both men were students in the Tokyo University marine biology program.

Yamamoto has revealed his own involvement in the study but States that, at the time, he was not able to disclose the fraud. *The Times Herald* has opened an investigation of university personnel and records concerning these matters.

Recent Dolphin Appearances in Bay
No Cause for Alarm, Minister says

By Kimmi Matsuda

The Times Herald has learned that the information about possible failings of the SeaGuard tsunami warning system may have a connection to the recent sightings of dolphins in Tokyo Bay. This reporter directly witnessed the highly unusual dolphin appearances in the Bay, where they repeatedly breached toward the shore in behavior similar to that documented in Miyagi in April of 2010, prior to the Tohoku quake. Recordings were made by renowned dolphin trainer, Kaito Yamamoto, of a pod of dolphins led by a former OceanWorld dolphin star, Manami.

Yamamoto has claimed that the dolphins were detecting early signs of an undersea earthquake and has attempted to convince the environmental ministry of their importance. Minister Nakayama dismissed the claims as quackery.

Previous to the March 2011 Tohoku quake, Yamamoto submitted a research proposal to the ministry to fund a long-term study of the potential for using telemetry attached to dolphins to identify possible early signs of developing undersea earthquakes, monitor their locations, and give many days warning of major events.

On 22 January, this reporter verified the identification of the dolphin Manami by known physical characteristics and witnessed Yamamoto making recordings of the dolphin's specific calls. *The Times Herald* scientific staff have since reviewed the recordings and verified they were identical to warning calls made in Miyagi in April of 2010.

The *Times Herald* has interviewed Minister Nakayama, who confirms he knew Yamamoto attempted to make recordings of the dolphin's calls on January 16th. In addition, *Times Herald* staff witnessed a coast guard boat with crew members banging large poles in the water to keep the dolphins from re-entering the Bay. Despite Nakayama's claim that he did not order the boat, witnesses have been interviewed by the Times Herald, and records of the Coast Guard activities suggest otherwise and will soon be made available to the public.

The Times Herald has requested comments from SeaGuard Shokan CEO Kodo as well as requesting a formal response and interview with Prime Minister Kobe on the investigation. Due to the sensitivity of this matter, brought on by the International Olympic Committee's request for detailed warning and evacuation plans for the coming Tokyo games, *The Times Herald* expects a quick response.

Chapter Forty-Two

It was seven in the morning when Kaito felt confident enough that Elizabeth was finally sound asleep. After a night spent waking every few minutes to make sure she was still breathing and not in need, Kaito slipped quietly out of bed to contact Kimmi. His worry between Elizabeth and Kimmi was at a breaking point. Kimmi was pretty sure her near miss with the tractor trailer truck was random, but Kaito knew what Nakayama was capable of. He needed to check his phone messages that he earlier ignored.

Reaching for his crutches and rising, he felt dizzy and grabbed hold of the bedpost to steady himself. He mentally began counting 'one, one-thousand, two, two-thousand, three-three thousand...' until he got to ten-ten-thousand and stepped off and hobbled with pain to the window. He pulled open the drapes and the morning sun washed over his face.

Seeing crowds of people jamming the streets, he grabbed the binoculars and scanned twenty-four stories below. Marching in every direction were mobs carrying signs that he could not read, but the red banners must have meant the Communist Party of Japan was at it again. Could this only be a campaign rally? He would call Naoki, a lifelong party officer, and find out was going on.

Gazing down past the Tokyo Tower toward the Hamariku gardens, a barely moving line of cars blocked the Rainbow Bridge and jammed the major roadways leading away from the harbor. In dismay, he stood in front of the TV, turned to the all-news channel, while keeping the volume low so as not to wake Izzy.

A young, spike-haired male reporter spoke over honking car horns, "As you can see behind me, we have a three-car collision with a metro bus." He pointed and the camera zoomed into a crash blocking a line of cars. "These desperate motorists are hoping to get through this mess and north on Highway 306."

The reporter continued, "Earlier, I spoke to Mr. Saito, who has abandoned his car on the road, and begun walking north toward Sumida." The screen showed both men. "Can you tell us, Mr. Saito, why you left your home?"

The man wiped his mouth. "I got a text message from a friend saying the government warning system isn't working and a tsunami could hit any day."

The reporter asked, "Mr. Saito, had you heard any evacuation orders from emergency officials?"

"I don't need official word—I heard some dolphins signaled a tsunami was approaching." Mr. Saito shuffled his feet and looked off camera. "Look around you—I'm not taking any chances." He forced a smile, bowed, and left.

Kaito felt like a tsunami was smashing into his gut. His knees felt weak, and he backed up and dropped into a stuffed chair. Tokyo was in a panic over the story he helped Kimmi write. All begun by his hypothetical assumption that Manami might possibly be warning of an undersea earthquake that might strike us sometime in the future. He sat in shock, watching more coverage.

"That's it from Koto Ward. This is Takumi Ueda reporting. Back to you in the studio, Jun."

The woman at the anchor desk shook her head. "An incredible turn of events only days before a major national election." She turned to a balding and scowling commentator next to her.

"Turmoil, that is the only word for it, Jun," he said. "Look what has happened since the story broke last night in *The Times Herald*." He narrowed his eyes. "People are rushing to get away from these low-lying areas any way they can." He sighed. "Where is Prime Minister Kobe?"

There was no official evacuation, but a random panicked evacuation was already underway, and people would be hurt. There should have been emergency officials in the streets directing traffic through the planned evacuation routes. A throbbing pain built in Kaito's head. He shut off the TV and called Kimmi. No answer.

He lurched over to the answering machine and played the first message: "Kaito, it's Naoki. You've made waves again, old friend. The Tokyo chapter is about to take to the streets, calling for Nakayama's resignation. Give me a call."

He dialed. "Hello, hello. Haru, is that you? Kaito here."

Shouting and chanting assaulted his ears: 'Nakayama *Dete kimasu!*' 'Come out!' 'Do your job!' 'Fire Nakayama!'

Haru's voice came in. "Kaito is that you?"

"Yes. What's going on?"

"*The Times Herald* story went viral—that's the power of social media. We're going to finally get that bastard Nakayama."

"Are your people being peaceful?" Kaito asked.

"Hah, no more helmets or staves—just public pressure. Mostly, the crowds are worried about a tsunami. They want PM Kobe to explain—tell them what to do. Kaito, maybe you should come down."

"Maybe later." There was no way he would leave Izzy.

"Okay, I've got to go. Peace, comrade."

Kaito hung up the phone and stared in a daze out the window. Did he hear Izzy stir? He staggered into the bedroom. He looked at the clock. It was almost eight and Mrs. Ishihara from hospice would be here soon.

Elizabeth was kicking her legs and waving her arms.

"Easy now, Izzy," he whispered.

"She's so beautiful, Kaito," Izzy murmured, her eyes open but staring at the ceiling. "It's like I'm swimming with my guardian angel. Look at her."

He gently took hold of her arms. "Izzy, you're dreaming."

"It is like a dream, isn't it, Kaito?" She fixed her eyes on him. "Oh," she mumbled. "Where are we?" She reached to touch him, her hand shaking. "Where's your costume?"

"We're at home, princess. In bed."

She looked around the room. "It was only a dream? I saw you doing your act with Manami and then we went swimming."

"We sure did, didn't we?"

"That is when I saw something special in you."

"Hah! And later you took most of your clothes off and jumped into the pool with her. I wasn't sure what I was in for."

"Think it took you longer."

"I was enchanted at first, but for me, it was after management closed the show, remember? You came to console me, and we sat on a rock looking out at what would become the dolphin lagoon sanctuary. It was your eyes. Still is." He put his hand to the side of her face. "When we first met, the gray-green color enchanted me, but on that day, the waters of the lagoon reflected and danced in them. They were different and deeper—the color and depth of the ocean."

She placed her hand on his. "Keep going, you romantic boy."

"I saw a genuine quality of someone who acted upon what she believed. What I saw in you was something I didn't have and wanted." Kaito stroked her balding head, caused by the increased dosages of morphine. He remembered the soft curls that once covered her ears. But he soothed her just the same.

Kaito realized he needed to check her diaper first, a task he had come to regard as a loving chore. Elizabeth said her home health aide was a little rough. To keep her mind off the changing, he said, "How about if I take you east of the harbor tomorrow? They say the *sakura* trees are almost in full bloom and as fragrant as ever. Would you like that?"

She managed a slight smile. Looking at her emaciated body, he caught himself before he winced at her blotched, wrinkled skin stretched over protruding bones. She nodded, trying to lift her hips, letting out a short groan of effort and pain.

"Sorry. Are you okay?" he asked, looking at her mostly dry diaper. "You still haven't been eating."

She gave him a tiny nod and began crying. "I'm sorry, Kaito."

"Nothing to be sorry for." He grabbed a tissue and dabbed her eyes. "Now hush."

"I'm sorry for interrupting your life's work."

"Come on now, it was *our* work." Not wanting to upset her, he stopped talking, opened the jar of salve, and gently rubbed it on her irritated skin. Finished, he eased her onto her left side.

"You know, I'm not going to last much longer," Izzy mused. "Mrs. Ishihara said you might want to put me in the facility and not have to bear the pain of my pain. She's a very experienced hospice nurse."

"Please, Izzy. Let's not go there."

"We'll have to, Kaito, sooner than later. My life has no point to it anymore other than for you. And I no longer want to be a burden."

"Nonsense."

"No, it's not. You don't need to watch me suffer any longer. I want to die with good memories. Talking to you. Remembering our good times together. Swim forever with you and Manami. Not lying unconscious, rotting away from the insides."

He lifted her bony hand and kissed it. "Hey. Let's take off your charm bracelet. You might smash it into your eye swimming in bed again."

"Good idea. I was thinking you could take off the blue plastic dolphin ring for yourself and give the gold charms and bracelet to Kimmi. Okay?"

He nodded.

"And by the way. I don't want any services to be held for me. Just cremate me and do with the ashes as you please."

"Don't be silly, Elizabeth. There are dozens of people wanting to honor your memory."

"That's the problem," she said.

"You mean because you didn't return their calls? Ever since the word got out about your illness, everyone's been trying to reach you. Kimmi, Naoki, Marylyn and others from the club, your editors. Even Catherine and Brian from the States. Mrs. Ishihara has a call log of several pages."

"The problem is, all that rigamarole would take time. Time away from the bigger crisis facing the city. From your long-term research work."

"Let's not decide that now."

"There might not be much of a later," she said with a stern look. "Will you contact everyone on my behalf?"

"Sure," Kaito said, lowering his head and holding back a sob.

"Hey. Enough of that. Tell me how things are going with the news story." She pointed a finger into the air. "The threat of a Tokyo tsunami is what matters now."

"Well, as we speak, the story hit and Nakayama and Prime Minister Kobe are standing firm, but the people living in low-lying areas are dangerously evacuating. I'm beginning to doubt myself, my work and even Manami."

"What do you mean?"

"I mean, what if I was wrong about her appearance in the Bay. Did I really understand her vocalizations? Many people could now be hurt and worse because of my..." he began, choking on his words. "My possible misinterpretation of her chirps. What if there's no actual plate movement occurring? No tsunami?"

"Come closer, koija," she said in a faint voice as she crooked a finger.

He bent his ear down to her mouth and closed his eyes. Faltering, she lifted her head and kissed him. She whispered, "I have faith in you. The same faith I am asking you to have in me."

Kaito kissed her lips and laid his head alongside hers.

"Listen Kaito. If Manami is sensing an earthquake, she will return to the Bay. She knows you are here. She will tell you."

Kaito nodded. "Thank you, princess. You always lift my spirits."

The phone rang. Kaito wiped his tears. "I better get this," he said and hobbled into the living room, just as Mrs. Ishihara appeared at the door. He let her in and answered the phone.

"Kaito, can you hear me? It's Kimmi. How are you? How's Liz?" She asked over the din of the crowd. "Sorry I couldn't call you earlier, but I'm here now with Toshio on the lower deck of the Rainbow Bridge."

"We're fine," Kaito lied and pressed the phone to his ear. "Toshio at the bridge? I saw the crowds."

"Yes, his father is perched high on the bridge rail attempting to jump in the harbor."

"Doesn't seem to me like what Nakayama would do. Are the crowds just onlookers?"

"No, everyone here is terrified trying to escape the tsunami—they're in a panic to get past the police barriers. One woman told me everyone in her Odaiba neighborhood has abandoned their homes."

Kaito glanced into the bedroom checking on Izzy. She was asleep and Mrs. Ishihara sat at her bedside reading. Kaito was glad his wife didn't know what was happening.

Kimmi continued, "The light rail and bus lines are jammed, many have come this far on foot. And two school children were killed during the mayhem. Kaito, I'm afraid our story has not generated the government response we need. What can we do?"

Sitting down, head in his hands, he mumbled, "I don't know. I figured Nakayama would be advising the prime minister to order an immediate evacuation, not be attempting to kill himself."

"Hold on Kaito. I'm getting closer. Wait. Toshio wants to speak with his father. I'll call you right back."

"Okay." Kaito hung up, thinking Nakayama was always a coward. Ending his life by *jisatsu* would save his son a lot of anguish. Maybe this dishonorable man would be finally brought to justice. Seeing Izzy still sleeping, he turned the TV sound back on.

A Nippon News *Live at the Kantel* caption appeared below a long shot of Prime Minister Kobe sitting behind a desk in his flag-draped office. The camera zoomed in, revealing his flustered face. He bowed sharply to the camera.

"Good afternoon, citizens. There is no, let me repeat, no earthquake or tsunami currently threatening Tokyo or anywhere in Japan. My government has analyzed the reports and rumors, and we find them to have been promulgated by an unqualified individual. There is no scientific basis for these dolphins being able to warn of a tsunami."

Kobe shook his head and continued, "Now, in terms of our current scientific tsunami warning system, we have the most sophisticated system in the world. There may be a short-term, small gap in one area of the network, and we will be addressing it forthwith. Be assured, you will receive the earliest possible warning to evacuate, when and if it is necessary. The last thing I will mention on this matter regards environmental minister Nakayama, who, it has been alleged, may be culpable in allowing the system to be minimally compromised. You can be confident that your government will make a thorough investigation."

Kaito let out a sign and covered his face with his hands. Alleged. Minimally compromised. He cursed. His phone rang. It was Kimmi.

"Kaito. At least we may have gotten Nakayama."

"What happened at the bridge?" he asked.

"Nakayama did not jump. The police took him away. Toshio was too upset to give me an interview, but he told me he would be a witness in court proceedings against his father."

"Poor Toshio," Kaito said, feeling little satisfaction with his old enemy's demise. "But what about the tsunami story?"

"I'm sorry, Kaito. Hamasaki will no longer cover the dolphin warning. The *Times Herald* will not be responsible for inciting further public panic."

"I'm not surprised. We're done. The government and the press have retreated to the status quo." He sighed.

"Maybe there's something…"

"With Izzy getting much worse, I can't fight any longer."

"What will you do?"

"I haven't decided. It'll be up to Izzy. Bye, Kimmi."

In a daze, he stared at the TV.

The news anchor announced, "We'll be going live any minute now to Democratic Party headquarters for PM candidate Hoiki's equal time comments on recent events and a rebuttal to Prime Minister Kobe's statement. With the polls showing them neck and neck, this could be a game-changer."

Kaito sighed and stood in front of the TV, finger on the power button.

"In a moment, we will hear from Asako Hoiki, in what could be a pivotal juncture in a hard-fought campaign. And, to some, a historical change election."

The camera zoomed in on a tight grouping of animated volunteers dressed in blue jeans and T-shirts and holding up red carnations, a symbol of their party and their movement. It then focused on a middle-aged woman with a short bob, wearing a yellow polka-dot blouse.

Asako Hoiki gave a little wave to the viewing audience. "Thank you. Let me first join Prime Minister Kobe in asking for calm. We hope your family and neighbors return safely to your homes. There does not appear to be a basis for calling a tsunami alert or evacuation. However, I am asking for Kaito Yamamoto, the famed dolphin trainer, to come forward to help calm any remaining fears."

Kaito let the TV remote drop to his side. How, under the circumstances, could he do that?

"However, I am in disagreement with Prime Minister Kobe on his handling of the allegations against environmental minister Nakayama. I am calling for Nakayama to be fired immediately and taken into custody for questioning."

She nodded. "In conclusion, I wish to thank the media for giving me the opportunity to speak with you."

Reporters shouted and held their hands up.

"Madame Hoiki, Madame Hoiki. Atti Jano, from *Natural Science Japan*. Do you give Yamamoto's claim about the dolphin's tsunami warning any credence?"

Kaito leaned into the TV.

Hoiki looked steadfast into the camera. "I must trust what our government scientists have concluded. However, I would like to learn more about any theory or ideas that have the potential of giving us days rather than minutes warning of an approaching tsunami." Kaito gasped and put his hand to his mouth.

The phone rang. On the fourth ring, he reached into his pocket. It was Kimmi.

"Kaito? Did you see Hoiki's address? Can you believe it? She's given you a chance, now you've got to meet with her. She could be our next prime minister. I gave her your number."

"What?"

"Yeah, I'm sorry. I know how difficult this must be for you and Liz, but Hoiki told me after she talks with her staff, she may call you."

Kaito put his hand to his chest. "Kimmi, it's no use. I can't speak to her. Goodbye."

He rushed into the bedroom to check on Izzy. She was sleeping and deep in between breaths. He worried and placed his hand under her nose. Relieved to feel her breath, he sat in the chair next to the bed.

He was deluged by doubt. Did Kimmi really think he would appear in public and denounce his beliefs? Did he blindly trust Manami, a trust that went way beyond their bond and her uncanny intelligence? Was he just motivated by hubris, wanting his theories understood and honored? A circling storm of thoughts and feelings battered him from all directions.

What would Izzy say? Want me to do?

Every time he stayed with her, she'd ask him what was going on with the tsunami, Nakayama and Kimmi. Although he tried fighting back, she reminded him of his promise, and he always relented.

He decided to wake her. He tapped her shoulder. No response.

"Izzy. Izzy. It's me." He squeezed her shoulder. "Izzy, please wake up."

He shook her.

She woke, turned to him with frightened eyes and screamed, "No. Don't touch me. Get out of here. Go, or I'll scream again."

"Izzy. It's Kaito."

She screamed.

Mrs. Ishihara came rushing into in the room. "Hold on, Elizabeth. It's me okay. You're safe." She pulled out a hypodermic needle and filled it. "She's having a delusion, Yamamoto-san. The sedative will calm her down. Maybe you can come back to her in a couple of hours. Okay?"

She didn't know me? Kaito was devastated by Elizabeth's response and kept squeezing her hand, "It's me, Izzy. It's me, Izzy."

Dreaming of swimming with Manami all those years ago was one thing, but mistaking him for her abusive ex? He was losing her more and more. His throat closed; breathing was becoming more difficult. All the tears that were constantly on the brink of falling raced to the surface.

It was even hard to accept the nurse's explanation, even though he knew it was probably true. Elizabeth was fading fast, and he was torn by the thought of letting her go. He still needed her. He sat and closed his eyes, trying to get a handle on what he needed to do. His exhaustion kicked in and he soon fell asleep.

Chapter Forty-Three

The telephone rang. Kaito realized it was early morning, and prime minister candidate Hoiki was calling. He let it go to voicemail. He turned over and studied Elizabeth. Last night was very difficult for her, struggling for breath and all, but she now seemed peaceful. Hopefully only deep in sleep, not losing consciousness as the nurse suggested she might be doing. One part of him wanted to ignore the phone call and have it all go away, but Izzy's faith in him continued to give him courage. He vowed he would fulfill his promise to her.

He just had to figure out how he could manage going in front of the panicked public and calming their fears, when he believed in Manami's warning and the need for an immediate, orderly evacuation.

The doorbell rang. It was the hospice nurse's morning appointment. He threw on a bathrobe, mounted his crutches and painfully trudged to the door.

"Hello, Mrs. Ishihara. Good to see you."

She bowed. "And you too, Yamamoto-san. How did Elizabeth do last night?"

"Pretty good, as much as I can tell. She got up several times asking for water. But when I gave her the straw, she had great difficulty swallowing."

"That's a typical sign, I'm afraid."

He gestured to the living room. "Come sit. Tell me what you mean."

She sat on the edge of the sofa and blew out her breath. "I know how difficult this must be for you, but we have to face the facts no matter how devastating. I believe she is in rapid decline and very close to the end, sir. And I think you ought to prepare yourself for that eventuality."

"Just tell me what I can do for her."

"Keep helping her as you have. Tell her you love her. Be with her. Above all, listen to her and her needs. She may not have many lucid periods left."

He lowered his head. "It's so hard. She keeps telling me she's ready to die and for me to move on. How can I be with her then?"

"She told me she wants to leave her life for you, the living, so you can continue with your work. That memory and promise is what she needs to take with her and die in peace. I would recommend you accept that and honor her wishes while you still can."

He put his head in his hands and rubbed his face up and down. He looked up. "Thank you, Mrs. Ishihara. I'm trying."

"That's all you can do, Yamamoto-san." She stood. "I better go check on her now."

Kaito sat there for a while, feeling he wanted to cry when he caught the flashing red light on his phone answering machine.

He played the message: "Yamamoto-san, this is Asako Hoiki. Can we talk? I could meet you at your apartment anytime soon. This is my private number. Please let me know."

He pushed the redial button. Hoiki picked up. "Yamamoto-san? I am so glad you called back. Can we meet now?"

He took a deep breath. "Do you mean what you say about advancing my research?"

"Yes, I will try my best. Can we discuss it?"

Kaito took a deep breath and remembered Izzy's words about her maybe providing a pathway. "Can you hold for a minute? I'll let you know," Kaito said, putting the call on hold and turning to Mrs. Ishihara at Izzy's bedside.

"Do you think Izzy's stable now?"

"She's still sleeping soundly now. Heartbeat is strong."

"Do you think it would be okay if I head downstairs for a few critical moments with candidate Hoiki?"

"I think so. I could call you in case there's any change."

"Thanks, I'm an elevator ride away."

He clicked on the call. "Madame Hoiki. Can you give me about half an hour? But we can't meet in my apartment. Do you know where I live in Shibuya?"

"Yes. I live three blocks away."

"Okay. There's a small café in the lobby of my building. Good. See you then."

Kaito hurried into the shower and got dressed. When he went down to the lobby, there was a bevy of photographers on the street outside the door. Sitting alone in the café was Mrs. Hoiki, wearing a floral print dress topped with what Elizabeth once called an Eisenhower jacket. Her eyes were steady and engaging.

She stepped quickly toward Kaito with an outstretched hand. "Honored to meet you, Yamamoto-san, and thank you for seeing me."

Her hand still in his, Kaito saw the sincerity in her eyes. "Thank you, Madame Hoiki. Can I order you some tea?"

"Yes, green please."

Kaito ordered and they sat.

"Yamamoto-san, if I may say, I attended your dolphin shows at OceanWorld as a child. And to this day, I remain amazed at the complicated tricks you taught your dolphin, Manami."

Kaito shifted in his seat. "Thank you, but it was her high intelligence and our bond of communication that made everything possible."

She nodded. "Yes, I am only starting to learn of your great love for your dolphin and the potential of the species." She leaned forward in her chair. "I also heard from Miss Matsuda about the treatment you received over the years from Minister Nakayama. Maybe someday he will apologize to you and the public from prison." She took a deep breath. "Also, at Miss Matsuda's urging, I have reached out to Mika Harada from the ministry, and Dr. Isao Ogawa, your colleague and research co-author."

Kaito sat back feeling relieved, but worried about Izzy. "That's good," he said. "But can we make it quick? I need to get back to my wife."

She continued, "Yes, sorry. I believe there is merit in the potential of cross-species communication using advanced radio biotelemetry on dolphins. May I be straightforward with you, however? The country needs you to come forward and clarify the reports about the dolphin's tsunami warning. Many people living in low-lying areas of our city are not heeding PM Kobe's call for calm."

Kaito moved his trembling hands to his lap. "I never expected my theories and findings to be so problematic. I only hoped the government would be prepared to order a full and orderly evacuation once I had firm indications from my dolphin that a tsunami could be imminent."

She nodded. "I understand, but with the government now deciding not to call a tsunami alert, we are left with a problem. Simply, many people believe you and the dolphins. Like me, many citizens that attended your shows and children that were a part of your classes came to believe in your ability to communicate with them. Unfortunately, the chaos is resulting in injuries and deaths, and it will continue if you do not state publicly that your theories are unproven."

Although she spoke the literal truth, he couldn't help feeling the anger along with the hurt. His whole life—his father's domination, being dismissed by the university, overpowered by Nakayama and defeated by corrupt authority—played like a movie across his mind. He mustered control and spoke, "Madame Hoiki, it took me a long time to speak up and fight for what I believe, despite the consequences. I must stand for what is right."

She held her hand up in the air. "Please Yamamoto-san, I respect your beliefs, but we are in a crisis now and the consequences extend beyond *your* beliefs."

Kaito closed his eyes and nodded. "I do…do understand how others can't know and trust what I do. But I hope you also understand what the consequences will be without an evacuation. When Manami reappeared in Tokyo Bay days ago and made the identical call, the call that I had known for many years at OceanWorld to mean 'bad water', I knew it could happen again. The only question is when and how strong the earthquake and how high the tsunami."

"Isn't it possible the call could have meant something else at Miyagi and it was just a coincidence that a tsunami followed?"

Kaito knew she had made a point. Hoiki's intelligent questioning created doubts in his mind. And it was possible Manami mimicked the warning call from his playing of the Miyagi recording on that day in Tokyo Bay.

"What do you think?" she asked.

He rubbed his temples. He had trouble finding the words, let alone speaking to them without stuttering or slurring them. When he made the Tokyo Bay recordings, he was under great pressure from the approaching goons. Maybe he should have allowed more time after asking Manami to talk to him. Was his zeal to believe in her so great that it clouded his judgement?

"Yamamoto-san, are you okay?"

"Sorry, yes. T…technically, her call could have meant something else."

"Look," Hoiki added. "I understand that your recording of the dolphins in Miyagi before the tsunami hit offers a promising base for further research, but if there were current indices occurring in the plates now, why isn't Manami in the Bay warning us again that it's imminent?"

Kaito took in a deep breath. "I don't know. Nakayama was keeping them out of the bay after I arrived. He may have had them killed."

"Can you be sure, Yamamoto-san?"

Her rationality and understanding sent a shock of cold fear sweeping through him. Was he holding too stubbornly to the thin thread of possibility? He could not respond.

"Please, Yamamoto-san." She leaned out from the edge of her chair. "The citizens of Tokyo need for you to come forward and explain yourself, before there are more deaths." Her voice was strong and steady.

Torn between the current panic and potential carnage, he answered, "I can't say."

She asked, "What is it that you want, Yamamoto?"

Kaito took a deep breath. "I...s...simply want the research on dolphin language and intra-species communication to go on."

"I am with you in theory, but I will have to learn more about the methodology."

"The methodology is known. We would not capture and hold dolphins and treat them like the Americans treated Koko the gorilla. My research called for tagging free-roaming dolphins in the wild and watching, listening and recording how they interact with their environment. This way we can learn *their* natural language, not forcibly teach them *ours*." He put his hands out to her. "And they can teach us about our planet so we can better protect it." He let out a deep breath.

She gave Kaito a broad smile. "I like what you say, Yamamoto-san, and if I am elected, I think we can continue your research." She paused, then nodded. "No, I *will* support that kind of research. In the meantime, I will ask you again to please come forward with me and calm the public."

Kaito sat in silence.

She stood up. "I only hope your best and truest nature will decide what's right." Exhaling, she said, "I will await your call. We would have to arrange an ad hoc press conference right away as the election is tomorrow. You have my number."

"Yes, thank you."

After Kaito said goodbye, and he entered the elevator and the door closed, he was left with one outstanding question—could he trust her? He already knew the current PM's position was against him and he had little faith in politicians overall; maybe she was his only hope. Watching and feeling the floors rise, he hoped he would find Elizabeth awake and get her advice.

His phone rang. Kimmi.

"Kaito, you won't believe this, but a pod of dolphins has shown up in the bay."

"What?"

"Near the Bay Bridge at Haneda airport."

"Is it Manami?"

"Only you can tell."

The elevator door opened to his floor. "I can't right now, I have to be with Izzy."

"I understand," she said. "Call me when you can."

When he reached Izzy, he found her 'directing' the music on her headphones.

As soon as she saw him and took in his facial expression, she asked, "You're in a panic, husband. What's wrong?"

"Nothing. How are you feeling?"

"I'm fine, but not fine seeing you troubled. Tell me the truth, Kaito."

"Kimmi called, that's all."

"That's not all, Yamamoto. I can see it in your face. Give it up."

He hesitated, holding her hand tighter. "I will not leave you."

She gave him the old 'evil eye'. "What if it is Manami? You must go. I will wait for you, I promise. Remember I cannot die happy otherwise."

He could only shake his head.

"Shit! Yamamoto-san. You know what that might mean to Tokyo, let alone me. Get your damned ass over there now."

"But—"

She pulled her hand away. "Look, Manami might be the key to the better way we always sought. Please go. The promise, remember?"

He looked deep into her eyes. Beyond the gray-green beauty that he first saw, he was now able to see sadness and pain. And beyond that, he saw her still burning love and determination.

She puckered her lips.

"You're incredible, Izzy."

"So are you. Now split. Mrs. Ishihara will be here any moment."

He kissed her, got up and dialed Kimmi.

"I'll head out right away to the Yokohama Bayside Marina near the bridge. Can you arrange a charter boat to pick me up at the public dock?" He pushed the button for the ground floor.

442

"Got it. You want me to get the TV news crews there too?"

"Bring every station in Japan. I'm taking a taxi. Just let me know what dock."

"Will do and good luck."

He got out of the elevator, waved to Mrs. Ishihara, and grabbed a taxi.

At the marina dock Kimmi had arranged, he found a throng of TV trucks and cameras on the road outside the dock gate. He gave the cab driver his credit card, who agreed to wait as long as needed. Before the press converged on him, he held up his hand and said, "Thanks for coming gentlemen and women, but I haven't a minute to spare and please don't interfere with my mission, okay?"

The charter boat captain was waiting and opened the gate. Kaito hobbled along the dock as fast as crutches could carry him. Once on board, he pointed to the breaching pod and told the pilot, "Take it slow, Captain, I don't want to spook them."

Twenty meters from the slow-moving pod, a TV news helicopter dove above, whirling blades whacking. Kaito waved it off, hoping his whistle could be heard above the din. He yelled out, "Manami!" and blew the 'come here' command on his old OceanWorld whistle.

The pod turned toward the boat.

"Cut the engine!" Kaito yelled. His adrenaline surged along with his hope.

The dolphins breached wildly. The fluke of one large female slid under the surface close to the boat.

His phone kept ringing. He shut it off.

"Manami!" he screamed as he recognized the distinguishing notch on her dorsal.

She poked her head up, squealed, and nodded.

"Come here, girl. It's Kaito. What have you got to tell me?"

Manami blew out her signature whistle and gave her familiar raspy greeting. Neither she nor any of her pod mates seem to be making any kind of a warning call. Manami confirmed what he suspected with her familiar click, click burble chirp call, meaning, 'I'm good'.

Kaito was convinced the tectonic plates must have stopped moving. The undersea earthquake threat was gone for now and they were safe.

"Yes! It's you, girl. Elizabeth knew you'd come back."

Kaito stretched his arm, leaned as far forward as he could, and commanded, "Jump!"

He waited.

She dove, shot up through the surface with another dolphin. Was that a full-grown Rin Jr. at her side?

He gave them his open hand and a smacking kiss. Kaito's heart pounded with a renewed energy and the need to act fast. "You are beautiful, princess. Your return means everything to me, but I have to leave now and tell our people." He gave her the 'goodbye' signal.

She flapped her fluke.

With tears forming, he put his hand to his heart and told her, "I love you and…and so does Izzy."

The pod moved away, and Kaito watched as she did a high backflip and a double twist, just like he had taught her.

"Let's head back fast, Captain," Kaito commanded from the stern. His heart soared as Manami and her pod breached in the distance.

On the way back, Kaito noticed he had a voicemail. He played it. "Mr. Yamamoto, this is Doctor Harari, head of the neurology department. My colleague has been trying to reach you. We believe that your weak condition in your hand may be serious, and you should call us back to—" Kaito stopped the message as the boat slowed into the dock.

The TV news crews had multiplied in size but were still behind the high dock gates. The taxi was waiting for him at the access road. He had to get back to Elizabeth.

Opening the dock gate, the reporters jabbed microphones into his face.

"Was that Manami?" "Is a tsunami coming?" "What is happening, Yamamoto?"

Pushing his way past them, he opened the cab door. "All clear gentlemen. All clear. I have to go."

The taxi steadily honked to divide and pass the reporters, the shouts were muffled, and the chasing bodies blurred in the car windows.

"Back to my Shibuya apartment," he told the cab driver, "And hurry, please."

Moving past the press hordes, Kaito picked up his phone, worried there might be a message from Mrs. Ishihara. He played them. They were from the press. One after another.

He called the hospice nurse. "Hello. It's Kaito. Is Elizabeth okay?"

"Yes, Yamamoto-san. She's still sleeping. Are you coming home?"

"Yes. On my way."

He dialed Kimmi. "Kaito. I saw the live news feeds at the boat. Was it Manami?"

"Yes, and the coast is clear."

"Thank goodness. But Kaito, the public will need more. They're still in a panic."

"I already told them, all clear."

"Kaito. Clear for what? An evacuation? You need to speak to them directly. Explain things."

"Okay. Maybe later. I've got to see Izzy first. Okay? You can tell your editors and the rest there is no tsunami threat." He hung up and the phone rang.

It was PM candidate Hoiki. He hesitated to answer. Girding himself, he clicked on.

"Yamamoto-san. It's Asako Hoiki. What did you find out in the Bay?"

"There is no dolphin warning at this time. You can tell your supporters and the media you spoke with me. I need to get home."

"But Yamamoto-san. They saw you on TV. The people and the press want to know from you what happened. Stop the panic. Please. You need to explain in person."

"I…I can't right now."

"Please. What's more important than your countrymen?"

"Right now. My wife. That's who," he responded with a snarl. "She's dying," he added and hung up.

Another crowd of press people surrounded the entrance to his apartment building. He instructed the cabbie to drive into the rear alley and he'd take the garage elevator. "Right there," he said, pointing and handing him a nice tip. He grabbed his crutches and opened the door.

"Yamamoto!" they screamed.

"Please. I have to go. There is no tsunami," he kept repeating until he got into the elevator.

Getting off on his floor, more reporters were waiting in the hallway. He pushed past them as fast as he could go on crutches and opened the door. Mrs. Ishihara sat at the kitchen table.

Relieved to find her relaxed demeanor, he asked, "How is she?"

"Good. In light sleep now," she answered. "Seems more content actually and asked about you."

"Do you think she'll recognize me?"

"I think so. Just wake her gently. Use your soft voice. Oh, and before I forget. That Doctor Sukari called for you again and left his number."

"Thanks, later," he said and headed to the bedroom.

"Oh, Izzy," he squeaked, "Are you awake?"

Her eyes popped open. "There you are," Elizabeth said, raising her hand a few centimeters off the bed.

"I'm right here, princess. How are you?"

"Happy to see you, koija," she said with a radiant smile. "How are things out there?"

"Beautiful. Thanks to you, my dear," he said and laid down beside her. "Manami and her pod came back in the Bay. Just like you said they would. I talked with her and there's no longer a warning. I touched her once again for both of us. Izzy. She was full of joy. I could tell." He gently kissed Izzy's forehead. "Joy with the freedom you gave her."

"We gave her," she corrected.

"Yes, and I believe I even saw Rin Junior, full size now. Gliding at her side. It was so beautiful."

Tears poured down Izzy's cheeks.

Kaito caught the streams with his finger, their wet warm feeling of joy.

"I know, I know," he said. "It was like you say—a miracle."

"Yeah, like my guiding angel guided me to you. I am so happy for you and our people."

He tapped her nose. "You played the central role in that, Izzy. If it weren't for your American grit and vision, none of this could have happened. And there's more."

"Tell me."

"There's hope that if Hoiki wins the election, she will get behind my research. Provide the pathway you suggested she might. What will I ever do without you? Without that love and courage?" He took her hand and kissed it.

"Hah," she laughed. "I gave you mine..." she poked his chest..."on top of your own."

He ran his hand through his gray hair. "Hoiki wants me to speak tonight at a press conference and rally. TV coverage and all. I don't want to keep leaving you like this."

"You must go," she said.

446

He sighed. "I'm worried about you, Izzy."

"Kaito, this crisis is much bigger than us. I'll be just fine."

He shook his head. "You know I'm not much for political speeches. And lately, I kind of mix up my words. Have to speak slowly so as not to slur."

"You'll do fine, just don't make it political. Just speak from your heart. They want to hear it straight from the source." She drew a big breath. "You have many fans and you're a hero once again."

Kaito took it in.

"Look," she continued. "Finding our love for dolphins brought us across the sea to Manami, who gave us the chance to love each other. That's more than I ever thought I'd have. Just knowing I can give what's left of me to you, gives me great comfort."

"That sounds like a version of the Japanese way," he said.

"Well, maybe it is, but there's no dishonor involved. It's all about honoring the best that is in us."

He smiled, taking both her hands. "If you only knew how much I love you, Izzy."

"I'll take that with me," she said. "Now, get ready for your speech and let me rest, okay?"

He called Hoiki.

"Yes, Yamamoto-san?"

"You had asked me what I wanted. Could the dolphin biotelemetry research continue under Dr. Ogawa?"

"I can do that," she answered, "But Yamamoto-san, will you come forward in a press conference?"

"Yes."

Chapter Forty-Four
Shibuya Rail Station

Kaito arrived at the Shibuya rail station for the press conference in a pouring rain. Working his way past the TV broadcasting trucks and the rain-drenched crowd of Hoiki supporters, Greenpeace and Communist party followers, he spotted Kimmi.

His umbrella tangled with that of a young woman who yelled out, "Kaito Yamamoto is here."

The crowd cheered. Kaito bowed. They cleared a path to a makeshift, tarp-covered platform. Bright lights snapped on and reporters rushed in Kaito's direction.

Kimmi scooted under his umbrella and hugged him. "Kaito. So Manami came back to you in the bay?"

"Yes, and she gave me an awfully good answer."

Kimmi guided him past the throng of reporters to the back of the platform where candidate Hoiki was waiting. They bowed and shook hands.

"Thank you for coming, Yamamoto-san," she said. "Are you prepared? There will be major coverage."

He nodded. "Yes. As much as I could be for something like this."

She pointed to the bank of microphones. "I and the citizens of Tokyo really appreciate you coming. I'll make a short introduction."

Cameras flashed as the candidate held up her hand and quieted the applause from the anxious crowd.

"Citizens of Tokyo, Japan, and members of the press, I am honored to introduce Kaito Yamamoto-san, who many of you know from his years at OceanWorld, his advocacy on behalf of wild dolphins and from the recent report from the Bay."

Applause rose up from the crowd. She raised her hand. "Mr. Yamamoto has some very important information to share with you."

Kaito scanned the anxious faces beneath the dripping umbrellas and hoods. He took a deep breath to remind him of the need to speak slowly into the microphone. "Thank you, Madame Hoiki. F-first, I am happy to report, there is no longer a threat of a tsunami."

Cheers and claps followed.

Kaito smiled. "The dolphin warning calls have ended. There is no need to evacuate. We are no longer in danger."

The clapping grew louder, and a man yelled out, "What happened?"

Kaito held up his hand. "Let me explain. Some of you may remember Manami, the dolphin I had trained at OceanWorld."

"We loved her," a woman shouted.

"Yes, and in April of 2010, I was in my boat following her and her pod as they headed north along the coast toward Miyagi. She had been fitted with a recording device on her dorsal so I could monitor her behavior associated with her vocalizations. While feeding there, Manami and her pod mates began some unusual barking and frantic tail-slapping and breaching."

The crowd listened intently.

"Based on my previous research and recordings of her, I realized she was giving out a warning call and it meant dangerous and bad water. The pod left the area in a hurry. A day later a six point four undersea earthquake occurred resulting in a tsunami hitting the coast. I believed then she knew a tsunami was approaching and in dolphin language was giving a warning."

The crowd hung silent on Kaito's words.

"So, when a pod of dolphins showed up barking in Tokyo Bay four days ago, I hurried to determine if it was Manami. It was her, and she made the same unique warning call she did in Miyagi. I recorded it and believed it."

"We believed her too," a woman shouted out, followed by agreement from the crowd.

"Thank you," Kaito said and added, "That's when I tried to get the word out, the Times Herald article ran, and unfortunately, many panicked and worse."

"Mr. Yamamoto," a reporter jumped up. "Katashi Humuri from Nippon TV News. But you said, we no longer have to worry. How can we be sure a tsunami isn't still coming?"

Kaito held up his hand up again. "Yes, let me explain. Only two hours ago, when Manami and her pod reappeared under the Bay Bridge they no longer made that warning call. Actually, the opposite. Her calls indicated all is safe and good."

The crowd muttered and some clapped.

"How can we be sure?" a reporter asked.

Kaito tried to tamp down the rumblings with both hands. "Manami and her pod would *not* have come back into Tokyo Bay if it weren't safe for them. In other words, she must have sensed the earthquake fault movements had subsided, apparently just as fast as they had started, and she came back. So, by returning and *no longer* giving the warning call, I knew we were now safe."

A single muffled clap echoes in the distance. Soon, the clapping of the crowd drowned out the pouring of the rain. Madame Hoiki moved to Kaito's side. "Thank you, Yamamoto-san. Would you be willing to take a few questions?"

Kaito nodded. A woman wearing a bright orange poncho among a bobbing sea of dark umbrellas raised her hand. Hoiki pointed to her.

"Thank you," she responded. "I'm Chiyo Hattori, from *Green Party Quarterly*. Are you saying there's a possibility that, in the future, dolphins could actually help us detect undersea earthquakes days before they happen? Isn't that a big leap for science?"

Kaito nodded again. "Yes, it is a leap, but one that could be made if we had dolphins to help us understand the undersea movements of the earth's crust. With aquatic biotelemetry, we may be able to have much better warnings. This research although new, has great potential to discover and create a warning system that would give us days rather than minutes to evacuate. If I may add…"

He glanced at Madame Hoiki who nodded. "That potential all depends on how each of us regards nature. If you believe…" He ran his hand over the crowd. "Believe that all species are equal, then we can work together to safeguard the planet we all live on."

More cheers, shouts and hands go up.

A reporter wearing a floppy bucket hat waved both his hands. "Madame Hoiki, Haro Hamada from the *International Herald Tribune*. How about that? Would you be in support of looking into these ways of improving our current warning system?"

"Yes, of course." She leaned into the mics. "If I am elected, I will meet with top scientists in our government, including Dr. Isao Ogawa, a leading marine biologist and research colleague of Mr. Yamamoto's, and propose funding for dolphin biotelemetry projects."

Kaito waved to his old colleague Okawa, who saluted him back.

From behind, Kimmi said to Kaito, "Would you have ever imagined that?"

Kaito turned around and smiled at Kimmi, then bowed deeply to Madame Hoiki.

"Where did Manami go, Yamamoto-san?" a man shouted out.

Kaito stepped back again from the mic and looked at Madam Hoiki. She gestured to go ahead.

"Thanks for asking." He drew a long breath. "I trust Manami will be living out her life in her natural home, she's very old now, like me."

"And how about you, Yamamoto-san?" the man asked.

He glanced over to Kimmi. She smiled.

Encouraged, he continued, "Most scientists agree that life on earth began in the depths of the ocean. That is why I believe we are all children of the seas." Kaito turned to the side, quickly swiped his cheeks, and looked back at the crowd. "So, I guess you could say—" he laughed, "I too will be going home to the sea."

Candidate Hoiki faced Kaito and began clapping. The crowd picked up and cheered in unison.

Kimmi gave Kaito a long hug and whispered, "Sounds like you just fulfilled your promise to Elizabeth. How is she doing?"

"Yes, Ogawa and others will now take up the cause. Thank you for helping me, Kimmi. I'll never forget you." He reached into his coat pocket, pulled out a folded sheet of paper, and handed it to Kimmi.

She opened it to reveal Elizabeth's gold charm bracelet and a note. She looked at Kaito, tears starting to form. She read:

Dearest Kimmi,

This bracelet symbolizes everything that was good in my life. Thank you for keeping Elizabeth's spirit and Manami's love alive within me. May you always have a charmed life. Love, Kaito.

Their eyes meet and she whispered, "Thank you."

"Thank you," he said, reaching down, picking up a cardboard box and handing it to her. "And here are Elizabeth's journals. Hopefully you can find the best way to share her, all our stories."

"I will." She set the box down. They hugged.

Wiping her tears and holding the charm to her heart, she said, "You two sparked a mini-cultural revolution in Japan. I and the rest of the world will never forget you two."

"You played a big part in that too, Miss Matsuda."

Chapter Forty-Five

Returning to his apartment, Kaito found Elizabeth was resting well, so he relieved Mrs. Ishihara. Exhausted after many nights of little sleep, he warmed up a sake, undressed and slipped into bed beside Izzy. She had made him promise to give her an update on the press conference when he got home.

She was sleeping on her side of the bed, facing the wall. "Izzy. It's me. Do you want to hear about the press conference?"

She didn't wake or stir.

Afraid to touch and startle her, he got out of bed, went to the other side and put his head up to hers. She was breathing deeply.

He whispered, "Izzy. Izzy, you wanted me to wake you."

She blinked. "Oh, Kaito. I'm sorry. I'm so tired."

"Me too, but you wanted to hear—"

"About the press conference? Yes, please. Turn me over and get in bed. I'll just listen, okay? My throat is sore."

He turned Izzy over with little pain in her body or in his hands. Then, giving her a few sips of water, he crawled under the covers. "It went great, Izzy. It was pouring rain, so the crowd wasn't too large, but the press corps was well represented. Mostly Hoiki's loyal supporters and a large contingent of Greenpeace folks and Communist party fans. Mrs. Odaba was there and Naiko of course, wearing his frumpy Mao cap."

"I spoke pretty well, but only for a short time. I covered what you suggested, the basic facts and Manami's call and what it meant. The crowd was quite happy. Oh, and the press wanted me to come back and answer questions. And it was then that I mentioned your contribution. Naiko and Mrs. Odaba led the cheers."

"How...nice," Izzy said.

"Hoiki was fantastic. She didn't push me to endorse her at all but said my appearance would help in her final day of the campaign. The big news was her statement."

Elizabeth's eyelids started to droop.

"Izzy-chan. Do you want to hear more?"

"Yes, yes. Please."

"Hoiki not only promised to back my and Dr. Ogawa's research, but would you believe she said she'd propose a total government ban on all dolphin and whale hunting?"

Her eyes remained closed and in a soft voice, she asked, "Really?"

"Yes. And she might just win the election to be our first 'green' prime minister. The polls now show her ahead. Wouldn't it be a glorious gift?"

She nodded and smiled.

"That's not the only gift. I spoke to Mother the other day and we both decided to set up a non-profit foundation in your name. The Elizabeth Yamamoto Foundation for Cetacean Research and Protection, and she has donated the first quarter billion yen. And I'm going to ask Kimmi to help set it up."

"Thank you, Kaito," she said amidst a cough. "That means s…so much to me."

"Oh, and I gave Kimmi the bracelet and she was so happy. Told her to carry on in your journalistic tradition." Noticing Izzy's eyes closing again, he added, "I waved to the wet crowd and here I am."

She managed a nod.

"That's enough," he said. "Until morning, that is. We both need our sleep."

She puckered her lips. He kissed them and said, "Goodnight."

Some hours later, Kaito opened his eyes and found her sleeping peacefully with what seemed, as much as he could make out in the dark, like a smile of contentment on her face. He reached over to cuddle closer.

Her body felt cold.

He pulled the covers up and rubbed her upper arm.

She didn't move.

He kissed her cold lips as if to waken her, then held her tight and wept.

#

When Kaito awoke in the morning, he found his pillow soaked from the night's storms of tears. His arm was still around Elizabeth's now stiff body and prickling with the sharp needles of cramped nerves. He had to face the inevitable. As the chief mourner, it was he who had to notify others, make arrangements, push the cremation button and dispense with her ashes. He told himself he had the duty to be strong and stoically execute an appropriate and practical plan.

All cried out, he still felt paralyzed to do any of this, yet he knew he had to at least take a first step. What he feared the most was seeing her beautiful green eyes ashen and lifeless, how that would haunt him. But he got out of bed went to her side and not only found her eyes closed, but that slight smile of happiness was still there. He would build on that premise somehow.

Shinto tradition called for the family to now wash the body, starting with brushing water on her lips. He got on his crutches, dampened a washcloth and gently dabbed her lips. But despite having bathed her many times when she was alive, he couldn't bear doing that now. He then called the funeral home to arrange for transport and cremation the next day. He found some solace realizing that once he learned she didn't have long to live, he arranged to have her name carved in the family gravestone in Wakayama.

Then confusion set in. Because Elizabeth had requested no services be held, he had to honor that, but it left a deep void in his heart. Who could he ask for help? His mother came to mind, and he would call her at some point, but not now. She would surely recommend the traditional Shinto twenty-step program like she did for her husband before they spread his ashes at sea. For the next few hours before the hearse arrived, he wandered in a daze in and out of the bedroom, asking Izzy what to do, trying to remember what she had said to him when she talked about dying.

Feeling full of despair, he flicked on the TV news.

A banner running below the commentator read: Hoiki wins election—Japan's new prime minister.

"Wow," he said to himself.

The talking head was saying, "The polls were tight, but apparently, the public's top of the mind concern about the tsunami threats weighed heavily on the vote. They simply weren't happy with Kobe's handling of it. Apparently, the greenies, the big Communist party regulars, the youth vote, and the intervention of Kaito Yamamoto easing the fear over a tsunami, put her over the top."

The screen turned to her acceptance speech. "I will not only fund Yamamoto's research for a biotelemetry early warning system, but I will press for a permanent ban on all dolphin and whale hunting."

He thought about playing the many phone messages he had but realized most would be from the press and couldn't deal with that now. He knew one or more of the messages would no doubt be from Kimmi, checking up on him and Elizabeth, so he decided to at least call her.

"How's Liz? And how are you doing?" She asked.

"That's why I'm calling." He took a deep breath. "I am and I want to start a foundation in Izzy's honor."

"In her honor?" Kimmi asked.

He paused, his tone becoming somber. "Elizabeth died last night, Kimmi. Peacefully in her sleep."

"Oh, no," she cried. "I am so sorry. How are you managing?"

"Not well up until now."

"This is so sad. How can I help?"

"Can you help set up that foundation? It'll focus on sponsoring research and education for dolphin and whale preservation."

"Oh, how wonderful. But I'm just so sad about her passing. I loved her like she was my sister, and a great teacher with incredible intelligence, skills and a big heart. I will miss her so much. That would be very fitting, and I'd be honored."

"One more thing, if I could, Kimmi?"

"Of course, anything."

"You're such a friend, Kimmi. In going through her things, I found a large box in the closet with dozens of notebooks all marked chronologically from when we first met in Miami. Would you believe she documented our whole relationship and doings for some thirty-five years? In them, she not only described everything in detail but poured her heart out along the way. The words are so beautiful, I think they should be preserved and shared in some way. Can I give them to you?"

"A treasure like that? I'll be more than honored."

"Thanks Kimmi. This has given me a framework for the future. I've got to run. Talk later, okay?"

As soon as he hung up, Elizabeth's words came to him. She had wanted to live with good memories before she died. She wanted to swim with him and Manami. "That' it!" he yelled out again.

After the hearse came and he hired them to prepare the body for the next day's cremation, he got to work on the plan.

He would design a private service that would blend both their beliefs and cultures. A modern Japanese American homage to what they both devoted their lives to—the creatures in nature, specifically dolphins and whales.

Even though neither one of them were particularly religious, both Christianity and Shintoism had similar values and concepts when it came to spirits and the afterlife. To Elizabeth, her soul would be reborn in heaven. Kaito's *kami* spirit would live on in nature—trees, mountains or oceans.

So, like her God the father, Kaito believed that nature is our parent. *Where her one God is all powerful and all knowing, my gods are many and reside in nature and have powers beyond human control or understanding. Both our spirits can meet again in a final happy resting place.*

For the next few days, Kaito readied himself for his journey. He sold all his worldly goods—boat, car, apartment and placed the money in the foundation Kimmi setup. He notified all family and friends on both sides of the Pacific. He met with Dr. Ogawa and handed over all his files and equipment, pleased to see he had made offers to some of the top scientists in the field.

Following the cremation, he purchased a small dolphin-themed cloisonne urn for Elizabeth's ashes. Finally, he purchased a bus ticket for Kada Bay in Wakayama Prefecture and called his mother.

"Hello, Mother."

"Hi, Kaito. How are you doing? So sorry I couldn't get back from Paris to be with you after Elizabeth's death."

"That's okay. As I said on the phone, she didn't want anything special, or any services held for her. Thanks for the large gift you made to the Elizabeth Yamamoto Cetacean Foundation. We have already received and additional over twelve million yen from some twenty-four thousand individual donors and organizations around the world."

"You're certainly welcome and I plan on leaving another quarter billion yen from my estate when I die. But how have you been managing, my son?"

"Fairly well. Just staying focused and busy. Not wanting to feel the hole in my heart."

"What will you be doing then? I saw you and new PM Hoiki on TV. Guess you'll be immersed in the research."

"Actually, the research will mostly be in the hands of Dr. Ogawa and his newly hired young cohorts who will be making the advances in intra-species communication."

"Good then. Some rest for you. At eighty-six, I'll be finally retiring myself this year."

Kaito heard a commotion in his mother's office.

"Hold on a minute, Kaito," his mother asked. Moments later, she said, "Sorry, Kaito."

"It's okay, Mother. Time to go anyway. Thanks for all you have given me in my life and how kind you've been to Elizabeth. I love you."

"Mm, Kaito. What's going on? You seem a little down."

"Didn't mean to concern you, but I am now living with a rare disease called ALS. Had it for some time actually. It's rarely painful."

"Oh, Kaito. Why didn't you tell me. That's incurable, isn't it?"

"Yes, they tell me one to two years at most, maybe less than a year. But death is inevitable and why cause you worry? It's no problem, really. I'm accepting of it. Elizabeth taught me a lot about leaving life to the living."

"So, it's bad then?" she asked in between a sniffle.

"Not bad, Mother. Just what it is. I'm going to make the best of what time I have left. Please don't worry or feel bad. I know where I am going and I am in peace. Thanks, Mother. Goodbye and I love you."

#

Chapter Forty-Six
Kada Bay, Wakayama Prefecture

Kaito stood on the station platform for a long moment and admired how the soft peaks of Mount Koya laced and graced the sky—nothing like the sharp concrete that scraped the skies of Tokyo.

He climbed, with some difficulty, onto the bus that would take him to the thousand-year-old Okunoin cemetery. Placing his small suitcase on the rack, he smiled at his fellow sojourners. They came not to visit the dead, but in the Shinto tradition, to visit spirits that live on in nature.

The sweet scent of gardenias, a flower his mother planted near their front door, lured Kaito off the bus into the nearby flower shop. He chose two flowers—red spider lilies that, tradition says, grow in the place of your last goodbye, and bluebells, which in the Japanese meaning of flowers, signify gratitude.

Walking over the wooden bridge, he entered what seemed to be another world to him. The dense canopy of cedar trees hid the sky above, and below, moss blanketed the ancient gravestones into a ghostly green. He cocked his head and heard the familiar *hooo-hokekyo* song of a bush warbler hidden deep in the shadows. The bird's spirit lifted his.

He stopped for a moment in the mausoleum to gaze upon the vast ceiling of lanterns said to have been lit for hundreds of years. He slowly made his way to the modern portion of the cemetery. The rows of tightly spaced, shiny granite blocks contrasted with the patina of the past. One hundred seventy-six marked the row where the Yamamoto family gravestone was placed upon his father's death.

Reaching the gravestone, he clapped his hands together and bowed as deeply as his stiff body allowed. There, he didn't pray for Elizabeth, but in the Shinto tradition, honored her spirit. He had great respect for her beliefs in another life with her one God, but she loved his belief in her spirit living on in nature and with him.

He placed the red lilies in the center of the built-in granite vase and surrounded them with the blue bells of gratitude. Kneeling, he ran his finger over each carved letter of Elizabeth's name in Japanese. He was pleased he had done this and knew for sure his mother welcomed her as part of the family.

He closed his eyes and pictured her in Miami wearing tennis whites, the moment he first was attracted to her. The sharp, cold relief of the letters belied the once warm yielding of her skin. As he passed over the letters of her name in English, he sensed her American spirit—the force that helped him snap out of his reserved and submissive ways.

Holding dear to her name, the letters spoke to him of her love and how she made him into a much better man—a man who was now honored to be carved below her. His name was dyed in red as was the custom for those still living, but that would soon be taken care of.

With that thought in mind, he struggled to stand up, lost his balance for a moment, then bowed. He picked up his suitcase. Turning, he waved goodbye to her in that American way, which meant, 'see ya around'. He still had a way to go.

When he got off the local train in Kada, the ocean air told him he was getting closer. He would visit the Awashima Shrine, known as a special sanctuary for girls and women with health problems.

He walked carefully along the moss-covered stone path to the shrine and felt his breathing becoming heavier. The fiery-orange gates of the massive shrine were imposing, and today he was welcomed by three rows of tolling bells dangling from the roof. He entered the building and gazed upon the raised loft, which held several rows of porcelain-faced, kimono-clad dolls. To him, they look like a miniature choir. Since the Edo period, the dolls were believed to have souls and powers to influence human life.

He bowed, clapped his hands two times, and asked them to help find and unite him with the spirit of Elizabeth. Then, to protect the lives of Kimmi, his mother, sister, friends and everyone that he ever worked with and knew. He contemplated how important it was to protect our natural world, before each of each of us died and return to the earth, sky and water. For a brief moment, he pondered his own spirit, and wondered how it would go on through others.

He bowed to the dolls, then walked around the grounds to look at the many niches between the rocks and under the trees. He found collections of figurines left by pilgrims, for priests to cleanse their spirits. Passing groups of dragons, toads, rabbits, and kittens, he finally came to a large gathering of little Buddha statues in various poses and expressions.

He opened his suitcase and took out the God of fishermen statue. It was the smiling Buddha holding a rod in one hand and a red fish in the other, the one owned by his family for generations. With a pat on the head, he left it there as an appeasement to his father and to his departed ancestors. It was here where Kaito felt he was living his life in reverse and getting closer.

From the shrine, Kaito walked in the mid-afternoon sun to the nearby Kada Bay. When he reached a small marina, he sat and rested on the edge of a dock. He took off his shoes, rolled up his pant legs, and rubbed his stiff and cramped muscles. Like he did as a child, he kicked his feet in the water and laughed out loud.

Farther up the bay, a fishing boat was unloading the day's catch. He tied his shoes together, put them around his neck, and walked barefoot toward a fishmonger's shop. Near the front of the building, an old wooden *sabani*, a five-meter-long working boat, laid beached in the sand. It had a sharp bow and a high stern ideal for ocean swells. Inside, it was retrofitted with a pair of western style oarlocks and was in a condition and size for a single rower to handle.

He entered the door of the shop, and found a burly, leather apron-wearing proprietor filleting a pile of flounder. Kaito spoke, "Good afternoon, sir, is that your boat out front?"

The man did not look up. "Mister, can't you see I am busy. We don't rent to tourists anymore. The boat hasn't been in the water for over two years."

"I am not a tourist. I am happy to buy it," Kaito offered.

The ruddy-faced fishmonger squinted at Kaito standing with his bare feet holding a suitcase. He grunted. Then, he picked up his knife and jabbed it toward the door. "Mister, the restaurant over there is waiting for this fish."

Kaito bowed. "How much is the boat worth to you?"

"Huh," the man chuckled and wiped his brow. "That scow already had slow leaks before we beached her. The planking is even more cracked and dry now. She ain't seaworthy."

Kaito coughed and shuffled his feet. "I'll take my chances."

The man shook his head and went back to his fish.

Kaito raised his voice. "Look, sir, I am the son of a *ryoshi* fisherman. Fished since I was fourteen. Captained a pilot boat for ten years."

The man stared at Kaito. "Can you do an old man a favor? I just want to take it out for a few hours and relive my youth."

The man stuck his knife in the butcher block, shook his slimy hands, and ambled toward Kaito.

Kaito opened his wallet. "I'll give you a hundred thousand yen for her, if you'll throw in a couple of oars and help me get into the water."

Soon, the man tossed Kaito's suitcase into the boat and shoved him off into the bay. Kaito smiled broadly as the water cradled and gently rocked him. He was finally going home.

Picking up the oars, he pointed the prow toward the mouth of the bay and pulled, strong and steady, ignoring the pain. Any feelings of loss and illness drifted past the boat, formed behind into eddies, and swirled away. Seeing the fishmonger standing at the shore, slowly shaking his head, made him laugh and he felt a childish joy.

When he passed a fisherman scrubbing the saltwater from the deck of his boat, he recalled the drudgery his father always assigned him. In deep respect for his ocean-going brethren, he stood up with the oars, caught his balance, and shouted, *"Hai."* When the man looked up, he bowed to him at the waist.

Approaching the mouth of the bay, the wind tossed Kaito's hair and tickled his ears. The salty air inflated his lungs and braced his breath. His stroke quickened as the ocean waves bounced a welcome.

Passing the turning point between bay and ocean, the color of the water changed. Behind the stern, it was tinted green from blooming algae, but out here, the water became gray from the churning of the deep ocean.

He thought of the changing currents in Elizabeth's eyes. How they pulled him in, talked to him—the varied colors telling him when she was happy, sad or wanting. As the waves crested higher, he raised the oars and watched the droplets of water trickle down the shaft.

Looking up, he saw a herring gull snatch a wiggling fish from the surface. Once again, Kaito felt one with nature. He felt a great happiness surrendering to it. Below, the leak in the boat covered his toes with water. Laughing, he threw his shoes and his phone overboard.

He was coming to join them in the place they both loved. He reached into his suitcase and took out the urn of ashes. He kissed the top of the jar and held it close to his chest in a hug. Feeling her spirit, he began to experience what she finally showed him he could do—cry tears of joy. Tears of thanks for so many things.

"Thank you, Izzy, for everything you gave me. Enhancing my dream. Believing in my courage. Giving me your love. And together, how we showed others that with love, hope and freedom we can always find a better way."

He kissed the urn goodbye and emptied it into the water. Elizabeth was now there with Manami, waiting. *My spirit will live on with theirs and we will swim together forever.*

For now, he would simply row.

The water caressed his ankles.

Soon, the sky would darken and meet the waters.

He would row.

When the stars above faded away, he would be reunited below with his two sea princesses.

Made in United States
North Haven, CT
18 January 2025

64640640R00252